To Phil
Enjoy.
J. Emmy Smith

SEND IN THE
CLOWNS

SEND IN THE
CLOWNS

J. GREGORY SMITH

THOMAS & MERCER

Text copyright © 2013 J. Gregory Smith

Published by Thomas & Mercer
PO Box 400818
Las Vegas, NV 89140

ISBN-13: 9781477805961
ISBN-10: 1477805966
Library of Congress Control Number: 2013901625

To Connie Garcia-Barrio, for

making all my books better.

COUL*RO*PHO*BI*A

Noun

An abnormal fear of clowns.

1

UP AND AWAY

New York City, Manhattan

Laura Stark stole an extra minute under the shower's warm stream after Drew stepped out, savoring the afterglow of their morning "steam session." His pale skin appeared to ripple through the pebbled glass when she watched him disappear into the bedroom.

She didn't exactly regret that they lived apart, but when he was like he'd been this morning...well, it was too bad they couldn't live in bed.

"Want some coffee?" Drew hollered over the whir of the bathroom fan. It was a rhetorical question she usually didn't even bother to answer. She craned her neck to check the digital clock. Crap!

"Better make it to go, hon. Sid will kill me if I'm late."

"Righto."

Laura skipped makeup. They could do it at the station. She didn't give a rip what Sid or the rest of the staff thought about how she looked off camera. She felt she was holding her own for someone in her early thirties—she looked old enough to be taken seriously, but still pretty enough for the camera.

She slipped into her clothes and hurried to the kitchen. With his blond hair, Drew Gantry reminded her of a surfer. And he was irresistible in a T-shirt and boxers.

"Casual day for accountants?" She took the brimming mug and sipped her coffee. OK, he did *two* things great.

"*Forensic* accountant sounds sexier, don't you think?" Drew flexed for her, and she pretended not to notice. "I've got a couple extra minutes. My early meeting got cancelled."

Laura glanced at the kitchen table, then into the living room where a picture window overlooked Central Park several blocks away. That window was where all her money was going. At over two million bucks, the place owned her as much as she owned it, but the easy walk to the station and stunning view made the price tag more bearable.

"Drew, where's the paper?"

"Sorry, babe. I'm a gigolo, not a butler. Probably just full of news, anyway."

She never understood why a smart guy like Drew never showed any interest in world events. Sure, her stories carried a heavy tabloid slant, but still. Though he claimed to watch her show, she'd often wondered if he just said that.

She took another sip of coffee and walked toward the front door. "You don't mind if I take the paper with me?" she called over her shoulder.

"Be my guest. Wait, I'm *your* guest." He took her by the shoulders, careful not to muss her clothes, and gave her a deep kiss that sent a current of heat through her belly.

"Have a great day. I'll lock up when I go."

Laura opened the door and glanced down for the *Times*. Then she saw the balloons.

The sight of the bunch of blue balloons floating above her sucked the air right out of her lungs so that her scream lodged in her throat. Her legs turned to rubber, and she braced herself on the doorknob.

She managed a moan and staggered back. The balloons seemed to follow her. They made a nails-on-chalkboard squeak when they rubbed against the door and each other.

Drew caught her before she fell. Now they looked like a kaleidoscope of blue eyes staring at her.

"You all right? Babe, what is it?"

"It's Max" was all she could squeeze out.

✹ ✹ ✹

"Sit here. Have another sip." Drew held the cup, and Laura took a few gulps of the now tepid coffee. She didn't trust her shaking fingers. It felt like she'd spent half a lifetime sitting on the kitchen chair. The room eventually stopped swimming, but her hands still felt clammy.

"I'm OK." Maybe saying it would make it so.

"You looked better that time you got food poisoning. What makes you think it's him? It's just balloons. Probably a mistake. I'll check for a card." Drew put the coffee down and headed to the front door.

Laura's heart hammered in her chest, and the adrenaline brought her voice back. "It's not a mistake, and they *are* the message."

"They can't hurt you, babe. It'll just take a second."

"Just get rid of them!"

Drew stopped and stared at her like she'd spoken in tongues.

She held his gaze and lowered her voice. Much more yelling and she'd be worthless for the segment she was supposed to tape. "Drew, I won't have those things in my home. Put them down the trash chute, please."

"OK, OK." He continued to stare but started moving toward the door again.

Laura took another sip of coffee and felt the acid churn in her stomach. If she were a smoker, she'd probably have lit two. Did she trust her legs yet?

Muted pops sounded in the hallway, and she screamed. Her spinning mind identified the sound as gunfire. Max had sand-bagged Drew, and she was next...

The pops continued. She realized it was just Drew bursting the goddamned balloons so they would fit into the trash.

Pull it together, lady. Better call Sid and tell him...tell him what? *Hey, Sid, can't make the meeting. I'm having a moment here after my ex came out of nowhere to tell me he's back in my life. What? No, I didn't see him, but he left these balloons, see...No, no note, but I'm sure it was him.* Screw it. She'd tell him in person. If it really *was* Max, Sid had to know.

The front door opened, and she fought a trapped feeling that roiled her guts until she saw Drew appear.

"All gone. No note. Now no balloons. How come you're so sure? When's the last time he contacted you?"

Laura never talked about Max to anyone. She'd mentioned her failed marriage in passing when she and Drew had started dating, but that was it. "Not for years. I heard a rumor he'd started a business here in New York, but he disappeared long before that, back when we were in Georgia. That's where I hit him with the restraining order, and I thought he'd taken the hint."

Drew sat down next to her. "You never told me." He took her hand. "Did...did he hurt you?"

She could tell he wasn't sure how to frame the question. "Not the way I think you mean. He never hit me, but he scared me." She shuddered.

"I can see that. But why would he bother you now?"

"How should I know?" The sharp tone slipped from her mouth despite herself.

Drew didn't take the hint to back off. "I mean, you're on TV every night, and your picture is plastered all over the buses and subways in the station ads. It's not like he wouldn't know you were here."

"What part of 'I don't know' did you miss?" She lowered her head and bit her lip. "I'm sorry; you're only trying to help. I'm just jumpy." She leaned into his side.

Drew put his arm around her. "You got a big scare, but it's over now. Let's talk more tonight. You OK? I should get ready to go." He paused, possibly for effect. "Unless you want me to stay."

"I'm all right. I've got to get to work. Maybe it's this Marchetti interview. It might've gotten to me more than I wanted to admit." *Like hell.* She'd faced tough thugs before—not this tough, but she was tired already.

She excused herself, stood up, and went into the bathroom. While washing her hands, she opened the medicine cabinet without thinking and saw the old bottle of Xanax tucked behind the nail polish remover. The clear liquid magnified Dr. Ruffino's name on the prescription label.

Another blast from the past. She closed the mirror without touching the bottle.

❋ ❋ ❋

Laura headed outside into what should have been ideal late-summer weather. The sun's rays were working their way between the high-rises, and the air felt cool but not chilly, as it would soon enough. She turned up Third Avenue for the four-block walk to the studio.

She nearly collided with a customer coming out of a coffee shop with a tall latte in one hand and a smartphone in the other.

They did an awkward do-si-do around each other and muttered the standard curses that in the Big Apple pass for "Howdy, stranger."

Smartphones, idiot owners. She shook her head and kept walking. Usually her commuting radar steered her automatically around other pedestrians like she was psychic. She was off her game today.

She checked her own phone and scanned down the in-box for anything urgent. A relative term, as nothing short of a fire at the studio would take precedence over her interview with Ray "the Machete" Marchetti.

She'd get only one shot, and she still couldn't believe he'd even bother to show at all. She would have thought that a notorious mobster, accustomed to walking away from countless murder raps, would want a breather from the media.

Well, you flushed him out, didn't you? True, but she hadn't forced the guy's lawyer to suffer an inexplicable attack of conscience. What was she supposed to do when Marchetti's lawyer called her just days from the biggest win of his career?

"Ms. Stark, Daniel Bigelow here." Of course she'd recognized the voice right away. She'd spent enough time in the courtroom covering the case to know his raspy cadence. "Please record what I'm about to say, but I'm warning you, if you put it on the air, I'll deny everything."

She was hooked as soon as the man told her he wouldn't be able to live with himself for helping his client skate for the murder of his wife. Total bullshit, but whatever his motives, what he said next electrified her reporting instincts.

"I have the purse. You make sure Mr. Marchetti hears *that*— and in my voice. He knows what he did. If he doesn't grant you a candid interview, it'll find its way *back* to the evidence locker."

The bloody purse that had vanished from the police property room had triggered a firestorm of controversy and shattered the prosecution's case. Even the obvious corruption, swarms of lies, and blatant cover-up had failed to shake the defense, and the Machete had once again wriggled out of the noose.

Nobody could explain why Bigelow had suddenly grown a conscience, and efforts to reach him for follow-up questions had gone unanswered. Not that she blamed him for lying low.

She didn't know why Marchetti had agreed to the interview either. It wasn't like she'd intimidated him, recording or not. It didn't prove anything. But there it was. Right now, she had to pull herself together to get the scoop of a decade.

A grimy man stumbled in front of her, and she stopped short to pick the best path around him. He stood his ground and held up a bouquet of roses. The perfume from the blood-red blooms mingled with the stench of garbage that clung to the filthy guy. Ugh.

"Flowers for a pretty lady? Only five bucks." His words were so slurred that he sounded like he had only half a tongue.

Five more than the derelict paid, Laura was sure. "Not interested." She cut past him and crossed Third Avenue toward the WBAC studio on Sixty-Seventh Street.

Halfway across the street, she heard the same slurred voice boom over the rush-hour din.

"C'mon, lady. They'll last longer than *balloons*."

She whipped around, but the disheveled figure was nowhere in sight. As horns blared, she scanned the crowd for another instant, then scurried the rest of the way across the street. She leaned against a lamppost to catch her breath, her heart pounding like she'd sprinted all the way to work. "It can't be," she repeated to herself like a mantra until she reached all the way to the entrance to the studio. She looked over her shoulder so many times her neck cramped.

She yanked open the door, whispered under her breath, "You just imagined it," and decided to believe that until the interview was over.

2

BUM'S RUSH

WBAC

Laura backed into the lobby and moved toward the security desk. She scanned the regulars filtering through the glass doors. No sign of a derelict florist.

"Ms. Stark? Anything wrong?"

Leo, the senior member of the security staff, was staring at her. His jovial expression darkened, and he rose out of his chair. His bulk reassured her.

"I'm OK. A street guy gave me a start." *Keep believing it.*

He peered out beyond the glass-walled entrance. "What's he look like?"

Laura gave a weak laugh. "It's easier to describe what he smelled like. But just to be on the safe side, if a weird guy asks for me—"

"It's what I'm here for." Leo smiled, but she saw the steel in his eyes and loved him for it. A big, brown bear of a man, he always made her feel like she'd come home when she walked through the door.

"You're the best."

She heard more of the "Laura Stark at the Anchor Desk" in her voice. Good. She'd need it today.

✳ ✳ ✳

"Sweetheart, you look like you've seen the proverbial ghost. You didn't do the interview without me?" Sid Gold, executive producer and part owner of WBAC—who was usually hunkered down behind his enormous desk in the corner suite at this hour—was waiting for her in the reception area. He didn't need to underscore the importance of the day.

Laura allowed him a quick hug. She had an inch on him, even in flats, and could smell the Vitalis that anchored his wavy black hair. He wore his trademark white, button-down shirt with no tie, and one more button open than she liked, but he was the guy who paid the bills. He'd peddled his "sleazy chic" routine into a small media empire, so why mess with success?

"Marchetti's not due for another hour. You cleared the back entrance with security?" Her head swam with details, and she tried to remember where the hell she'd put her notes.

"You just concentrate on the interview, sweetie. Jeez, you look like hell. No offense. Gracie'll fix you up. You have your approach?"

Gracie, all five feet of her, waved Laura toward the makeup room. Gracie could cover any pallor on her face. Sid followed like a puppy. There was no doubt about his passion for the business; he sure didn't need the money.

"Yes, I've got it." Which was true. Marchetti wasn't about to be tricked. So she'd come at him straight and see where he went.

"Still stuck on the direct run? Sure you don't want me in there with you? We could tag team." Sid bounced on the balls of his feet like he was jogging in place.

"Christ, Sid, we're not going to wrestle the man. He wouldn't have agreed to come in if he didn't have something to say. He'll get to make his points, but this is our house and we'll get our shots in. I know what people want him to say. The question is, will he tell us?"

"Doesn't matter. This is gonna be great TV." Sid reached to hug her again but checked himself. When they arrived at the door to the makeup room, Sid stopped her.

"If it isn't him, what's with you this morning?" Sid reached for her hand. "You're shaking."

Laura pulled her hand back. "Nothing. Well, probably nothing. I got a little scare; it's just nerves." She felt tears start to form and pictured herself under the klieg lights. The image forced her body into a controlled posture and her face into a cool mask.

Not quickly enough to fool Sid. "What?"

She clenched her jaw. "Max."

Sid knew some of her history. "You sure?"

"No. It's all very sneaky, but that would be his style, wouldn't it?" She got a grip. "I might just be imagining things."

Sid took a deep breath. "OK, sweetie. Get through this morning and you can take a few days." He lowered his voice. "And if you need to talk to anybody…" He didn't finish the sentence.

She knew what he meant. A shrink. Like when she'd first come aboard.

But this was different.

"Dr. Ruffino passed away." She still missed him.

"This is New York; there's plenty more where he came from."

Sid's penchant for thinking out loud could be jarring to those who didn't know him. Laura had long since grown accustomed to his style, but still, the remark stung. Laura suspected Ruffino might have been the last shrink she'd ever trust. "Let's talk about it later."

She stepped into the makeup room and plopped down in the padded chair. Gracie pulled on her apron and set to work. "Ms. Stark, you worry too much. It will show on your skin." Her

Filipino accent came out in a soft, cinnamon-scented whisper. When she wasn't talking, her jaws worked her red gum nonstop.

Laura barely registered what Gracie was saying, but the familiar voice soothed her nonetheless. She focused on the task ahead, forcing aside all other thoughts.

Twenty minutes later Sid ducked his head into the makeup room.

"You ready?"

"How many times do I have to tell you? Yes, I'm ready." Her voice snapped like dry twigs.

"Good. 'Cause he's here."

3

DUST IN THE WIND

Newark, Delaware

"Closure." A Western term for a Western craving. Eastern philosophies took a much more elastic view of life. And death. Ever since he could remember, Paul Chang had teetered between Chinese and American cultures. Fluent in both, he'd been embraced by neither. Chang had to admit that he felt a fleeting tug for some sense of resolution. True to form, his mother had passed away without providing any.

Now her body lay in her living room ready for viewing, and he was sure she was looking down on him and taking satisfaction in his confusion.

On her deathbed, this tiny woman, who'd dominated his life as a youth and complicated his struggle to find his place in the world as an adult, had left him with one final puzzle.

In her native Mandarin she'd said good-bye to her longtime caregiver, Shu. "Thank you."

To Chang, however, her last words were in the English she had never grown to love. "You still here."

A statement. Or more? Chang turned it over and over in his mind, not with the patient rigor of a trained detective, but with the perpetual vulnerability an only son has with respect to his mother.

Was she thanking him for remaining loyal? Telling him to live his life on his own terms? Or was it one last sarcastic dig at the fact that he'd shown up?

Knowing her, she'd probably meant all of those things.

But he *was* still here. As were most of the people who mattered to him. Shu, his teacher, friend, and often surrogate father figure. Nelson, who'd been his NYPD partner before joining Chang to form East-West Investigations. Carl Hull, now colonel of the Delaware State Police, had made time to come to the wake. Chang appreciated the effort, as well as the fact that he'd agreed to be one of the pallbearers. Nelson, all 120 pounds of him, had also readily accepted the honor of pallbearer, forgetting that his policing and detective strengths were strictly cerebral, and that he'd have trouble managing the weight of the casket on the traditional wooden carrying pole.

Hull, built like the power-lifter he used to be, would more than take up the slack. Chang didn't worry about Shu, who, despite appearing to be a bald, old man, hid true strength beneath his placid features.

Chang took a final look at his mother's face, far more peaceful now than it had ever been in life, even in deep slumber. Chang had made sure that the attending monk would adhere as closely as possible to tradition. He'd been embarrassed to admit that some of the nuances of the ceremony escaped him and some aspects wouldn't work due to practical considerations. He'd allowed for seven days of prayer (not the forty-nine some practices specified) and agreed to place the body in her home for the wake, which was only fitting. In the end, everyone, including her, had known that the cancer she'd beaten so many times would win the last round. Tai Kai, which meant dragon queen, was a woman who always got her way, and she'd wanted to die at home.

She wore a white silk dress, and the mortician had styled her black hair into a bun. Incense burned, and Chang glanced around to make sure that the collections of priceless jade figures still in view were only animals. Red paper covered all those depicting deities.

Shu had removed all the mirrors, and Chang watched as the monk, a local man he didn't know, inspected the room. It was almost time. Where was Colleen?

As if on cue, the front door opened, and the bright red hair of his ex-wife, Colleen O'Leary, flashed into view. He saw that was the only red on her. She wore respectful black, the same color as his suit, and no jewelry.

If mother's going to haunt the place, this is when she'd do it. Chang didn't dare speak the thought aloud, as he didn't want to give his departed mother any ideas. Colleen had given up trying to be friends with her mother-in-law years before she divorced Chang. His mother had never made any effort at all.

"Sorry I'm late. There was a wreck on I-95 near Philly," she said. As she gripped Chang's arm, the usual electricity surged though him.

"You're just in time. The monk's about to seal the coffin." Colleen stepped forward and bowed. She whispered a few words and lit a stick of incense next to a burning white candle.

When the monk began to speak in Mandarin, everyone turned away from the coffin.

"Why—" Colleen began.

"Bad luck to see it," Chang whispered.

Colleen turned and gently took his left hand. "This OK?"

The monk began to pound nails into the coffin, chanting all the while.

Chang felt a flicker of pain in his reconstructed left hand. It was probably a reflex. He hoped the raised scars that crisscrossed his mangled paw didn't bother her. Multiple surgeries, wires, screws, and endless physical therapy had left his hand functional, but it remained an often excruciating reminder of a difficult chapter in his life. At least Colleen understood. She'd been there when his hand was crushed while rescuing her and his mother from Tong gangsters.

✳ ✳ ✳

Once the coffin was safely in the hearse, Chang and Colleen joined Shu and Nelson, who were waiting by Chang's red, late-model BMW 3 Series sedan. It looked much like the one he'd been forced to sell after a near collapse of his fledgling detective business a couple of years earlier.

He placed a stick of burning incense in the cup holder, wondering how long the stink would last.

"You have enough legroom back there, Nelson?" Chang asked as he started the car. He cranked up the air conditioner but cracked the windows to let the smoke escape. He was already sweating in his dark wool suit. Colleen sat next to him, and he noticed her nose wrinkle at the stench.

"Sorry, it's customary. It won't take long to reach the cemetery."

Shu sat behind Colleen and stared out the window.

"She was." Nelson was folded behind Chang's seat like a middle-aged spider.

"Huh?" Chang always felt like conversations with his friend started in the middle. He didn't have the energy to decipher what he meant right now. He shifted the car into reverse and glanced over his shoulder.

"Your mom. She was proud of you."

Shu nodded like they'd just been chatting about it.

"Not polite to mind-read at a funeral, Nelson." Chang felt embarrassment creep up his neck in a red flush.

He saw Nelson's shrug in the rearview mirror.

"It's coming off you like a shout. There's no shame in wondering. She seemed stingy about complimenting you, but I could see it every time you were together."

Wherever he started conversations, Nelson always came to a point eventually. His ability to read people and absorb the every subtle nuance and subconscious thought made him a peerless interrogator—and poker player. Chang prided himself on his ability to put up an opaque wall that even Nelson couldn't penetrate. But it was hard to maintain, and Nelson never let up if he was interested. Only Shu could block him for any length of time.

"Well, I didn't ask you…but thanks, Nelson, I appreciate it."

"She attack most when she want to feel safe," Shu added.

Colleen joined the nodding chorus. "If that's true, I must have threatened her every time I walked into the room."

Chang thought she had a point. "You didn't have to be in the room, hon. She couldn't help herself. But I doubt she would have been satisfied even if I'd brought home that *nice Chinese girl* she always talked about."

Colleen punched him in the shoulder. "Who was she?"

"Hypothetical." When was that AC going to kick in?

❋ ❋ ❋

The procession drove over a small bridge near the All Souls Cemetery. Chang heard Shu whispering in Mandarin, but he couldn't make out the words.

"Shu?"

Shu ignored him until they were over the bridge, and then he spoke in English. "Mister Paul, I was telling your mother that we were crossing water."

"Why?" Colleen asked.

More long-forgotten traditions gnawed at him. "That's right. The soul of the departed must be informed whenever you bring the body across water, otherwise she might not move on."

※ ※ ※

They reached the entrance to the cemetery minutes later. Chang waved to the trooper who'd stopped traffic for the procession. That must have been Hull's doing, as he was sure he hadn't made any calls for this.

At the grave site, Chang saw a number of unfamiliar faces: Mother's community friends. She'd complained about "those peasants down the street," but he could see now from the turn-out that she'd been much closer to her fellow Chinese immigrants than she let on. He felt a flare of shame that he didn't know their names or more about that part of her life.

Face it, at the end, half the time you tried to stay away—until guilt made you check in.

Chang took a moment to pay his respects to his father, whose headstone flanked the deep rectangular wound in the earth. Chang wasn't sure how his father would feel about the preparations he'd arranged for his mother. Father had always pulled Chang toward perfect assimilation in America, right down to sparing no expense to ensure he spoke flawless English.

Mother would have complained until the last spade of earth was shoveled onto the coffin. But there was no need. Chang could hear her disapproval ringing in his head. He'd never be "Chinese" enough for her. That reminded him. He pulled out an incense holder from his pocket. At the end of the ceremony, after the rest of the party had thrown in a handful of soil, he'd collect some to bring back to her house.

He kept the holder in his right hand. Colleen held his left in a gentle grasp while the monk chanted and some guests wailed on cue to show respect. That was one thing Chang would never allow anyone to see. He'd been a cop for too long. The stoic culture, within both the NYPD and then the Delaware State Police, had its own rules. Tears weren't in the playbook.

The various prayers sounded formal to Chang's ear, and some of the language escaped him. His Mandarin was decent, but conversational rather than formal. His spiritual side remained an "evolutionary journey," to borrow Shu's diplomatic phrasing.

His mind wandered. Was Nelson right? Had Mother really been proud of him? She'd never wanted him to go into law enforcement. His decision had left deep scars on their relationship and left the family's antique dealing business in tatters. His father had tried to make the best of a new career by teaching art history at the University of Delaware.

Chang's many years of public service and numerous commendations had never seemed to move the woman.

But the official reprimands? The mistakes and failures? Those were catalogued in her fierce mind, readily available to be thrown back in his face at every opportunity.

And then there was Colleen.

Petty corners of his heart wanted to blame Mother for their breakup.

Don't dare lie to yourself at her grave site.

Chang gave Colleen's hand a tiny squeeze, which she returned, and the jabs of pain repaid him for the thought. *No, Mother. I can't hang that one on you, much as you would have loved to take credit.*

She left because you nearly strangled her in your bed.

Did the nightmare absolve him? In his dream, he had fought a Tong assassin, only to awaken to a fresh nightmare: the end of his marriage.

His neck itched, and he scratched the thick, corded scar where the real killer had tried to exact revenge. Chang had killed that one, and he thanked any deity who would listen that he hadn't hurt Colleen worse in that horrible instance.

He savored the irony of the fact that the echoes of that last scrape with the Tongs a couple of years earlier had in fact brought them together again.

Sort of back together.

Their rekindled relationship burned only so brightly. What was the expression? Friends with benefits. He enjoyed the "benefits" and held fast to the hope they really were more than friends.

These days, he saw her whenever he was in New York, and she came down to Wilmington to visit. They'd met and married while he was a cop in New York, and he appreciated that she'd left a job with the *New York Times* to follow him down to Delaware. Once their marriage fell apart, there hadn't been much to hold her there, especially when the *Times* took her back.

If she ever needed a fire walked through, he'd be first in line. In the meantime, he accepted the current arrangement.

＊＊＊

When the monk gestured to the gathering, Chang and the rest of the group turned away so that no one would see the coffin being lowered into the ground. When it was down, Chang took his place in line as mourners lined up to pay their last respects by tossing in a handful of dirt. The short, slow shuffling toward the hole with the polished wood casket lid felt interminable.

Chang was last and collected soil for the incense bottle. He dropped a handful of fresh earth on the coffin lid and heard it land with a final thud.

4

READY OR NOT

Chang's Mother's House

"Want to stop in?" Chang was exhausted and couldn't wait to get back to his own house.

"Can't, sweetie. I've got to hit a deadline, and the notes I need for it are back at home."

"I understand. My turn to come to you next time anyway. Under better circumstances."

"It's a date."

He still liked hearing that. It reminded him of the days before they got married. He gave her a kiss and watched her get into her car.

He felt more leaden with each step he took toward his mother's red front door.

※ ※ ※

"How is hand?" Shu actually looked awkward. Chang hadn't thought it possible, but he supposed these were extraordinary times.

Chang flexed the fingers of his left hand. The wires gave off electric tingles that he knew were his own imagination, but the tight tendons and dull ache in his joints were no illusion. "Not too bad, considering."

Shu reached into a cabinet and took out five jars of his home-made salve. It smelled worse than death and worked better than anything on the market.

The simple sight of the jars filled Chang with dread.

You knew this was coming.

It didn't make it easier. There was something about the concrete proof of all that effort, when Shu never normally made more than one batch. "You're really going?"

Shu nodded.

"Job here finished. Good time to think about what is next."

Chang heard Shu's words in a daze. Amid all the madness that swirled around his life, Shu was the rock.

"Where will you go after Chinatown?"

Chang saw a cloud pass over his teacher's eyes. "Not sure. See friends first, maybe travel to China?"

"Yeah? You sneaked out the first time. You might need a passport. And how would you get back?"

"You not only one with tricks."

Chang saw that spark in Shu's eye that was laughter in anyone else. He might pull it off.

But why would he want to?

Why not? Now that your mother's died, he's more or less out of work, right?

"Just come back here before you try something like that. Maybe I can...help."

Chang didn't know all the circumstances of how Shu had come into the country, but he knew that none of them were legal. He suspected that Shu had been fleeing a past. It was a long time ago, but people, places even, could have long memories. If Shu was determined to go through with it, Chang could arrange some paperwork that would give him a good shot at returning without getting entangled with Immigration.

Chang was less concerned about Shu's return to Chinatown. He'd been back several times himself over the last few years, and any of the old enemies who were still alive had either scattered, gone into hiding, or landed in jail.

Shu would have gone back sooner if not for his mother's decline. He'd never left her side at the end.

"I'll keep training." Chang fumbled for words.

"I know."

"Haven't seen the dragon for a long time now. The meditations are working."

Shu gave a little smile.

Chang hoped he wasn't tempting fate, but the dark creature in his heart that craved satisfaction when he was under duress seemed dormant. His hand throbbed the way it often did after a long day. He had to admit that stable corporate clients and a lack of people trying to kill him helped him maintain his serenity. Maybe the dragon had died of boredom.

Part of him missed the adrenaline surge, but other parts welcomed Colleen back in his life.

"You will be fine. I not go forever."

So why did it feel like good-bye and not see you later?

5

MACHETE CUT

WBAC

Laura tried to think of the makeup on her face as armor. She resolved to keep her roiling emotions buried, no matter how long the interview dragged out. The camera forgave nothing, remembered everything.

Marchetti had his reasons for doing the interview.

And she had hers.

Besides, what was the guy going to do? Strangle her on camera with piano wire?

She wanted to chuckle at that but restrained herself.

A pasty intern inclined his head toward the studio door. As soon as she opened it and saw the man getting miked up in the chair across from hers, the jokes evaporated.

Ray Marchetti remained seated while the tech hid the wire on his mike within the folds of his charcoal Zanetti suit. He wore his equally black dyed hair slicked back, and his tan made him look like he'd been on a cruise rather than a monthlong murder trial.

The animal power under the expensive clothes gave him an undercurrent of sex appeal she was ashamed to acknowledge. Maybe she just had a thing for dangerous men. Laura realized the dead wife might have thought the same thing at one time. He turned toward her.

"Laura Stark," he said. "A pleasure to meet you without a bailiff between us."

Laura approached him and shook his large hand, trying for a firm grip. His manicured nails looked odd against his thick, strong fingers and scarred knuckles. His dark eyes were hard and flat.

"Mr. Marchetti. Thanks you for coming in. You understand you are welcome to have an attorney with you off camera."

Jessie plugged in Laura's mike as she sat down. She was already wired up.

"I've got nothing to hide," he said, crossing his legs. "Even the judge agreed."

"Which one?" If only she felt as brave as she sounded. She hoped the camera was rolling.

Marchetti's brilliant white smile morphed into a rolling laugh. "Take your pick. I sit here a free man."

"Let's get started." The lights blazed. "Some of my viewers think justice was perverted and say you may have played a part in suppressing evidence."

Marchetti smirked. "What are you implying? I regained my freedom thanks to skilled representation presenting my innocence, despite a corrupt government case packed with lies."

"That would be your attorney, Daniel Bigelow. We thought he might be here with you today." Laura hoped—for the lawyer's sake—that he was on the other side of the world.

"Haven't seen him lately. Perhaps he's taking a well-earned rest." Marchetti's smile turned predatory. "Besides, I'm innocent." He leaned toward her, and a wave of musky cologne washed over Laura. It smelled cheap and expensive at the same time.

Laura's thoughts raced with her heartbeat. "Then tell us, why did you come in today?" She figured he must want to show off; maybe she could trip him up. He knew the truth was out there. Was he using her to deliver some secret signal to Bigelow?

"You said it yourself. People think I did something wrong."

"It wouldn't be a first."

"I'm a misunderstood businessman." A smug grin tugged at the edges of his full lips.

"Why do you think that is?" Laura saw that the bastard was relishing every moment.

"*I'm* the victim here. The state concocted lie after lie, like they always do. And they put me through hell when I just want to grieve the loss of my wife." Marchetti wore his professed innocence like a shoddy mask.

Laura thought she heard a snort from one of the cameramen. She focused on Marchetti and bore in. "Next you'll tell me the state conjured up the purse."

He leaned back in the chair, and the arrogance poured off him. "They seemed to *un-conjure* it, didn't they? It's not that big a stretch to think they made it up in the first place."

"You deny the existence of the bloodstained purse?"

"Who knows? The prosecution doesn't. Besides, my wife had a lot of stuff, you know? I didn't keep track of it all."

Laura pressed further. "What if that purse turned up?" What was he playing at? Marchetti had listened to the tape from Bigelow. She didn't want to bring it up on the air. He knew that, but still…

"Well, that would be awkward."

"It'd make you a liar, Mr. Marchetti."

"I've been accused of worse." The smug grin vanished, and he leaned toward her like they were alone in the room. She could've

SEND IN THE CLOWNS

sworn the AC kicked into overdrive. "But there's a world of difference between suspecting and proving."

"Indeed there is." Why did she feel like a card player whose
winning hand had just been trumped?

"If you have something you want to say, I'm all ears."

Was he daring her to...*Oh God*. Laura realized Bigelow never
got away. He was dead, and the purse destroyed.

"I'm here to listen, Mr. Marchetti." A minute earlier she'd
been cold. Now she thought she might melt under the lights.

"Then may I ask a question?"

She felt like she was floating above herself and heard herself
say, "Sure."

"Where do I go to get my reputation back?"

6

OFF THE HOOK

Laura sat in her office with the door closed and fumed. The staff left her alone, and she appreciated having five minutes to collect herself. Sid wouldn't be so considerate, and she checked her face one last time just before he reached her door.

At least he knocked.

"Not your best, but we have enough to work with. I'll tweak the lead-in and promo, and we should still kill 'em tonight." Good words, but as he spoke, he was studying her like a coach worried about his star athlete.

"I didn't think he'd confess on the spot, but I thought we had a strong hand, and I guess we know why he came in…" She stopped the hitch in her chest and stuffed enough of her frustration into her emotional "later" basket to continue. "Sid, you know he killed him, right?"

"Who? You mean *her*, the wife?"

"No. Well yes, but the lawyer. It's the only thing that makes sense. Why else would Marchetti come in like he did?"

Sid paused, a rarity for a man who looked like he was running even when he was seated. "Yeah. That sucks, but they couldn't try him again. Double jeopardy and all. Man, I would've *loved* to put that purse on camera. We'd have beat the networks for a week."

"Sid, I think a man is dead."

"Correction. A lawyer."

Her expression must have finally registered.

"Sorry, bad joke. But Bigelow is no prince, and he knew who he was messing with."

Laura sprang from her seat and started pointing in the air. Sid called it her "aha dance," when she was figuring something out. "That's just it. Bigelow knew what he had and its importance. I'm not buying that he grew a conscience. He tried to flush out Marchetti."

"I guess it worked." Sid leaned against her desk.

"Bigelow's no dummy. How could he not expect a reprisal?"

Sid stared at the ceiling. "Maybe he believed his own bullshit, thought Marchetti was a maligned businessman."

They shared a fleeting laugh. But it wasn't funny. "Sleaze or not, he couldn't think Marchetti wouldn't retaliate."

"Suicide by mobster instead of suicide by cop?"

"Extortion? He must've been making a mint off Marchetti in billable hours though. Seems odd to kill the goose."

"And the Machete ain't no fuckin' goose." Sid did a passable imitation of Marchetti. "Kid, you really don't look so hot. I think you have enough on your plate."

She'd actually stopped thinking about Max for a couple of hours. "Marchetti wouldn't come after me." She had her teeth on a thumbnail before she realized what she was doing and stopped just in time.

"I was serious this morning about talking to a professional. It might help and couldn't hurt." Sid leaned back and held up his hands in a nonthreatening gesture. "I know a shrink; I think I have his card in my office, tops in his field."

"I don't need to navel-gaze about Max and why he bothers me. I need to act."

"What are you saying?"

She hadn't known until she opened her mouth. "I'm going to the cops."

Sid stood up. "You sure about that?"

No. "Yes. I'm a taxpayer, damn it. They have to help me." She slammed the desk with her fist and knocked over a cup full of pens. They scattered across the floor, just like her thoughts.

7

COP A FEEL

Nineteenth Precinct Station

Laura checked her purse for her pepper spray before she bolted for the elevator. In the lobby she made for the security desk. Leo was perched on his threadbare stool, and a younger guy she didn't recognize was manning the sign-in book.

"Leo, can I ask a favor?"

"Of course. You feeling better?" He stood up, towering over her.

"Yes." She paused. "Listen, I know you can't leave your spot, but can you keep an eye on me while I go down the street? I want to let the police know about this morning, and I'd feel safer if you could see me across the street."

"My momma raised me better than that. Terry, cover me here for five."

The kid nodded.

Laura wanted to tell him not to bother, but she felt too relieved to speak.

Remember that when you get cold feet at the door, lady.

Leo walked behind her, literally blocking the sun. The shadow he cast made Laura imagine she was being protected by a grizzly bear.

The Nineteenth Precinct sat next to a firehouse, a single block from the studio. She figured her apartment must also fall under its jurisdiction, so it seemed as logical a place as any to start.

The light turned green. Nearby pedestrians gave her a second look, and while she did sometimes get recognized as a local celebrity, she knew it was Leo's presence behind her that was drawing attention.

Maybe when she walked into the station without him she'd be regarded as a run-of-the-mill civilian. However, she wished it would be one of those times when her fame gave her an unfair advantage.

Fat chance.

* * *

Laura gave Leo a wave and pulled open the glass door. She'd sworn never to set foot in a police station ever again. But what choice did she have?

Maybe she could talk to a new detective and…

"May I help you?" A tubby sergeant with iron-gray hair peered at Laura. "Is that Ms. Stark?" He nodded to himself.

She read his nameplate. "That's right, Sergeant Bell. I need to speak to a detective."

Bell's jaw muscles bunched, but Laura thought she saw a trace of a smile. "By all means. Shall I tell him what it's regarding?"

She wanted to say as little as possible in the crowded entryway. Some of the older officers had already begun to inch closer and whisper.

Great.

"Harassment. I guess you could say it's harassment related."

"Take a seat, Ms. Stark, and someone will be right with you." The way Bell pronounced "Ms.," it sounded like he'd just used a week's worth of *z*'s.

* * *

Laura focused on her phone and tried to ignore the whispers and icy stares swirling around her. As she shifted in her seat, she felt the plastic chair rock like one of the bolts had broken.

"Ms. Stark?"

She thought the voice sounded familiar and turned, hoping to find a friendly face.

Oh God.

Before her stood the blocky frame of Ron Sieger. He'd aged since she last saw him, which had been years earlier during the fiasco with his uncle. But a little gray hair wouldn't be enough to make her forget him.

The feeling seemed mutual.

"I understand you wish to file a report." He didn't extend his hand.

"I had no idea you were assigned here. I would have—"

"Would have what? We're all professionals here. And your fame would precede you in any precinct."

"Could we go to your office or somewhere private? I feel like we're putting on a show."

"I would have thought you'd enjoy that. Please, follow me." Sieger walked toward a locked door. He got buzzed in and held the door open for her. Laura walked down the short corridor. The floor felt tacky under her shoes and smelled of pine disinfectant. The fluorescent light tubes hummed, and she could hear raucous laughter from deeper in the station.

She opened the steel door Sieger indicated.

An interview room. Complete with a one-way mirror and bland gray walls. She already felt like a criminal.

"Sit, please." Sieger's tone reminded her of commands given to a dog.

"Is this a waste of time?"

"Ma'am, I haven't heard your complaint yet."

"You know what I mean." Maybe she should just leave.

"Do you mean why did *I* catch your case?"

"Something like that."

"Your lucky day you picked my house, but yeah, Bell asked for me specifically, if that's what you're wondering."

Laura gritted her teeth. "Look, Detective. Are you or anyone in here going to listen to me? I get your grudge. But since you want to put it out there, your uncle wasn't descended from Nazis, true. But his affair wasn't made up by the *Post*, was it?"

Sieger looked like she'd slapped him. "Maybe not, but there's guys here and around town who owe their lives to Uncle Wolf, and they take the fact that he got hounded to death by the media a little personal."

Old pangs of guilt stabbed into Laura, and she fought a craving for a Xanax. "I deserve that, and I'm still sorry about your uncle. I know that won't bring him back, but would you at least give me credit for the fact that I didn't do it on purpose?"

"I give you credit for what happened. You were the top person on the story, so you own it. That's the way I see it, and so does everyone on the force who watched that miserable hatchet job."

"I was off the story by the end. I knew my sources were wrong."

Sieger shook his head. "You media hacks never get it. You put the blood in the water. The rest of the sharks showed up to finish the job, but the first cuts came from you."

He was right. She'd been as eager as anyone to beat out the competition with the scoop that the leading candidate for chief of police was descended from Nazis. It turned out they had the right town in Germany but the wrong Sieger family. But by then the fuse had been lit, despite her later retractions. Who knew the other outlets would stumble across a real affair, or that the man would take it so hard he'd kill himself?

"Fine. Never mind that what the producer told me wasn't true. I should have checked myself. Now I do, on every story I put on the air. You can send someone in to throw coffee on me now."

She saw that that appeared to make an impression. Sieger had never admitted to being responsible for the rash of drinks thrown in her face after Wolf Sieger's suicide. Never by the same person, but she always suspected he'd played a part.

Sieger scowled. "I don't know what you're talking about." His tone indicated otherwise, and he looked like he'd chip a tooth if he ground his teeth any harder.

"I can't change history but wish every day that I could."

"Got it. But moving on and forgetting aren't the same."

Laura snatched up her purse. "I knew this was a mistake."

Sieger seemed to snap out of his anger. But she sensed it boiling just beneath the surface.

"Please sit. I said we were professionals, and I meant it. You blindsided the whole house when you walked in here. It dug up some bad memories." He took out a pad and began scribbling.

Finally.

"I think my ex-husband, Max, is stalking me again."

Sieger stopped writing. "Yeah?"

Laura related her morning, starting with the balloons and continuing with the homeless man.

"That's it?"

"Even coming over here, I felt like he was watching me. He used to do it all the time. That, and a lot of other stuff. I had to get a restraining order on him."

"When? Do you have a copy?"

"Not on me. It was back when I lived in Atlanta. Is there a way to get it renewed or something here in the city?"

Sieger smiled. "It's not a library card. Besides, it was out of state and sounds like a while ago."

"What about now? He's back. Actually, he lives and works here in New York. Has for years. I checked."

"Why come to us now if he's been bothering you all this time?"

"He hasn't. I didn't even know he was around until someone mentioned it to me. He has this entertainment company, called Laughing Matters, and—"

"Slow down. He hasn't bothered you for years, and all of a sudden he leaves you balloons? That's it?"

She knew it sounded weak.

"You don't know Max. That's never *it*. It's his way of saying he's starting all his shit up again."

"What shit is that? Did he ever hurt you or threaten you?"

Her voice was starting to shake as much as her hands. "Don't I look threatened? No, he never hit me, but he found subtle ways to let me know he could do that—and more—anytime he wanted." She accepted a bottle of water from Sieger and struggled with the top. He opened it for her and handed it back.

Way to impress the big, strong man, Laura. She took a drink.

"He's like, I don't know. Is there such thing as a ninja clown?"

Sieger chuckled. "Not that I know of. You don't mean like a Ninja motorcycle stunt rider?"

It took Laura a moment to register what he was talking about. "No. I mean it more literally. Max grew up in a circus. It was a really strange upbringing, but he learned some crazy physical skills. He does trapeze, makeup and disguises, knife throwing."

Sieger looked up from his notepad. "Knives?"

Laura nodded. "I could go on and on. I think his company does acrobatic shows, things like that. But I remember he scared the shit out of some guy at a bar who tried to hustle him in darts."

"This is fascinating stuff, but where does it leave us? Based on what you've told me so far, you can't be sure the balloons were from him."

"And the homeless man?"

"We have a bad homeless problem in the city."

Laura felt her shoulders slump, like a marionette with cut strings.

"Ms. Stark. You're a smart lady. Why would a guy with a good business drop everything, after all this time, to come after you?"

"Maybe not as smart as you think. Don't you think I knew this would be an uphill battle?"

Sieger shrugged. "Do you want to file some sort of statement? I have to tell you that without more to go on, I wouldn't even phone Mr. Stark. You sure you aren't overreacting?"

"I thought this was a police station. Why does everyone want to put me on the couch?" *First Sid, now these bozos.*

Sieger's expression suggested that maybe they should.

Laura knocked over the water bottle and sent it skidding across the metal table when she tried to catch it. "Goddamnit!"

She fought back tears when it hit the floor. What the hell was the matter with her? That's not how she acted in public. Not ever.

Sieger picked up the bottle from the floor and screwed the cap back on what was left. "You sold me."

"Oh?" She felt hope swell in her chest, and her emotions ping-ponged in her head.

"I get that you're scared out of your mind. And in a twisted way, I admire your courage at coming in here. I still can't do much officially, and off the record, you'd be wasting your time trying this at another house. Nobody's going to do you any favors."

"They wouldn't help me because…"

"I didn't say that. I meant right now. If Max shows up and makes a direct threat or tries to get into your place, anything like that, you call 911 and don't worry. But I won't lie and tell you you're not despised."

"But by then he could do anything to me." Laura knew she sounded desperate. Sieger paused for so long that Laura began to wonder whether she should just leave. He reached into his wallet and pulled out a worn card.

"I don't know why I'm doing this. Maybe because up close, you aren't as big a self-serving bitch as I thought. I still don't like you, lady, but take this."

"Your card?" Was he hitting on her?

He shook his head. "Not mine. A friend's. Has a PI shop in Delaware, but he's licensed in New York. He used to work homicide here with me. He and his old partner, both NYPD, were some of the best I ever saw. Still are."

What? "You're shilling for some friends?" But the idea had some merit. "Mr. Sieger, you've given me lots to think about. I may call some investigators in the morning."

"Throw the card in the trash for all I care. But still, off the record, don't bother with any of the good firms in town."

"Why, they all loved your uncle too?" At least anger was a refreshing change from terror.

"Nope. But they do value good working relations with the NYPD." Sieger paused to let that sink in. "And before you misunderstand, that wouldn't be my doing. Lots of folks have long memories and don't follow my example."

❋❋❋

Laura rode her anger across the street and had the entrance to WBAC in sight before she even remembered to look over her shoulder. Nothing unusual. She breezed into the lobby. Leo grinned when he saw her.

"Ms. Stark. You got me. Good one!"

"Sorry?" She was about to thank him for his help.

"Next time won't be so easy." He held up a neatly lettered, white rectangle with a piece of tape on it: KICK ME!

She tried to smile, but her body felt as though it had just been plunged into ice water.

8

CHANGE OF PACE

Wilmington, Delaware, East-West Investigations

"So he's gone?" Nelson leaned back in his chair and stretched. He'd been hunched over his computer screen like a spider, ever since Chang had walked in the door two hours earlier.

It took Nelson that long to bring it up. Though they'd buried only his mother, Chang felt like he'd just lost two people. "Not forever. Shu will be back." Chang said it louder than he intended. "He hasn't had any time off for, let's see…years."

"I'm sure he'll at least say good-bye and let you know where to find him. You OK?"

"Why?"

"You look a little off." Although Nelson was generally quite blunt, he could be diplomatic when he tried.

"Lots on my mind. It still seems surreal." He rubbed his temples. "As big a pain as Mother was, I miss her."

"I can imagine." Nelson, who'd grown up in a New York orphanage, had never known his own mother. He stood up and wandered to the front of the small office, which was slotted in a strip mall in the upscale neighborhood of Greenville. His scrawny body swam inside his blue, button-down shirt.

"You ate the last cookie." Nelson made it sound like Chang had just crashed his car.

"Sorry. Betty will make more, I'm sure…She'll be back in an hour?"

Betty, once a busybody coworker of Nelson's in the IT department back when they all worked for the state police, now helped them out part time, which suited her retired lifestyle. Chang believed it was her full-time mission in life to put weight on Nelson, whose metabolism appeared to speed up with age. Chang by contrast had to watch every calorie. This made him think about his long workouts with Shu and how much he'd miss him.

"Right. She's going to help me with the report for Centennial."

"How'd that go?" Chang forced himself to sound interested. Fat stacks of background investigations meant retainer checks and a business in the black. He took a moment to cast his mind back to when the company nearly closed.

But don't lie. They're boring. Yes, but they keep the divorce case/peeping Tom aspect of the business to a minimum.

"Mostly choirboys, couple boozers, one pothead, and one hothead."

"How so?" The phone rang.

"Bar fights. Guy quit drinking, and I was going to recommend him. Want to double-check for yourself?"

Chang reached for the phone and shook his head. If Nelson met the guy and said he was good, that was enough.

"EWI, Chang speaking."

"You're lucky you still have a head left to speak with, you prick," the voice on the other end growled.

Chang sat up and looked over at the caller ID.

Blank.

He glanced out the window and thought of the .45 he kept locked in his desk. He was getting soft. Nowadays he carried it in the field only if the job might get hairy; otherwise, he didn't even bother. "We're all tough on the phone. Do you have a specific complaint, or are you going to switch to heavy breathing?"

Nelson stopped his work and looked at Chang.

"You still sexy, or is life outside the city getting to you?"

"I don't date women with deeper voices than mine."

He heard muffled laughter. "Damn it, Chang! I had a whole page of insults, and you go and make me laugh."

Wait. "Sieger? Are you playing with city property again?"

More laughter. "How ya doing, buddy? Nelson there?"

"Yeah. He's here." Chang put the call on speaker.

"Hi, Ron." Nelson waved like he could see him.

"Just you guys listening?"

Chang assured him they were alone and thanked him for the recent sympathy card. Sieger hadn't even known his mother, but he'd always been a class act. "What's up?"

❋ ❋ ❋

"I'm throwing you a bone, so you guys owe me one." Ron sounded like he was smiling.

"Depends on the bone." Chang's pulse picked up.

"Quick background. You guys remember Uncle Wolf?"

"Of course." Chang and Nelson spoke together.

"I never got a chance to work with him, but I only heard good things," Chang continued.

"At least on the force," Nelson added.

"You're still sharp, Nelson." Sieger blew out some air, and they waited for him to continue. "Then I guess you remember when he was up for chief, and that whole shit storm blew up over his ancestry?"

Chang did, but the details were fragmented. Nelson spoke up. "There was some scandal over the fact that he was descended from Nazis, right?"

"That was the first part, and it turned out to be bullshit. They got the town where our relatives lived right, but they got the wrong Siegers. That didn't stop the media though. They reveled in it. The *New York Post* ran that big picture with the headline SIEGER HEIL. You like it?"

"Ouch." Chang didn't remember that one.

"There was more." Nelson wasn't asking.

"Yeah. Once the media frenzy was rolling, they kept digging until they found out—surprise—Uncle Wolf wasn't perfect."

"It was stealing...no." Nelson stared into space. Chang pictured him rummaging through his mental filing cabinets. "Cheating. He got caught cheating."

"He's not in front of a computer, is he?" Ron asked.

"Nope," Chang said.

"You're a scary dude, Nelson," Ron said.

"Thanks."

"Anyway, the affair they uncovered was real. He wasn't a Nazi, but he'd blown the Mr. Clean image. It didn't just destroy his chance at chief though. When Aunt Tess left him, it pushed him over the edge."

"Was there more than that? Divorce isn't exactly the end of the world. We survived it."

"Don't know about you; I couldn't get out fast enough. Anyway, Uncle Wolf ended the affair, but he was old school about divorce. Not an option. She was old school too, and affairs weren't gonna fly. I saw the guy go into a tailspin, but I never would have imagined he'd punch out like he did."

Nelson spoke. "His suicide shocked everyone."

"He couldn't bear the shame. I'm pissed he took that way out. But it never would have happened if those vultures hadn't been scrounging for a few ratings points."

Chang leaned back in his chair. "Sounds about right. But why the painful walk down memory lane?"

"I was just getting to that. Remember the specific story that kicked the whole thing off?"

"I don't. Seemed like it all happened fast. Nelson?"

"TV. They scooped the papers." Nelson closed his eyes, and Chang watched his lids moving like a dreamer in REM mode.

Sieger whistled. "You gotta get this guy on a game show. Nelson, for Double Jeopardy, remember the reporter?"

Chang jumped in. He didn't have perfect recall, but he still got paid to figure things out. "Our bone."

"Not in the form of a question." Nelson smiled while he kept his eyes shut. "Got it. Who is Stark?"

"Wow, we have a new champion." Sieger paused. "And yeah, Chang, that's the bone."

✳ ✳ ✳

Chang took notes and Nelson listened while Sieger recounted his meeting with Laura Stark.

"The dropped water bottle wasn't shtick?" Chang asked.

"Broadway-worthy if she was faking it. No, she's spooked all right."

"Wish I could've seen it." Nelson spoke aloud, but Chang thought he was probably saying it to himself.

"You'll have to trust me on that one." Sieger apparently thought that was meant for him.

"*You* believe it. That comes through even over the speaker," Nelson said as he tore open a sugar packet and dumped the crystals onto his desk. He began doodling in the white pile with his fingertip.

As long as he cleans it up later, Chang must have said to himself a thousand times. And Nelson always did.

"So where did you leave it?" Chang knew that hypotheticals could eat up the rest of his day, and he still had bills to pay.

"Ball's in her court, but I wouldn't be surprised if you heard from her. She looked terrified, and from what I saw she's a cool lady. For an unscrupulous bitch, that is."

9

BONE APPÉTIT

"It's her." Nelson held his hand over the phone receiver despite Chang's repeated efforts to convince him that the hold button actually worked.

Chang dried his hands and moved to his desk. Betty was gone for the day, and he covered the phones while in the office to avoid having callers deal with Nelson's unorthodox customer relations skills, which tended to put off prospective clients.

But nature had called before Laura Stark.

Chang took the receiver rather than risk having Nelson drop the call while trying to switch to speaker. "Mr. Chang?"

Smooth, confident, professional voice. Silky where Colleen's voice had a smoky undertone.

"Ms. Stark? Detective Sieger said you might be in touch. I'm glad you called."

"Are you? He must not have told you what he thinks of me."

Here was where Nelson might have been too forthcoming. "We're familiar with your history with the department, but from what he told me, I don't think that has anything to do with your complaint or what they can do."

"I don't want us to waste each other's time. I'm in New York and not sure how you could help..."

Chang could hear a defensive edge in the clipped tone of her voice. "We're in New York all the time. We spent the early part of our careers there, and I was born and raised in Chinatown."

"I know."

Chang sat up. Of course she'd checked them out, but it felt odd all the same. "OK, so you know Detective Sieger didn't foist you off on a couple hayseeds."

"I first thought Sieger had thrown me to his cronies and maybe worked out a kickback in the process. But..."

"But?" Why should he care what she thought?

"I checked out your record and your partner's. Controversial stuff, but I saw a couple unconventional problem solvers. And that's what I need."

He heard her take a sip of something and thought her mouth must be dry. Her cool delivery was an act.

"Ms. Stark, I think we're on the same page. First time since I picked up the phone. How may we help you?"

* * *

With Laura's permission, Nelson joined the call. Chang made sure he understood the need for discretion.

She outlined her recent strange morning, starting with the balloons, through the interview with the mobster Marchetti, all the way to the Kick Me sign. When she finished, she asked them to call her by her first name.

"OK, Laura it is. And call us Paul and Nelson." It was a small step, but he'd take it. He really wanted an excuse to get up to New York. "So you're sure that for whatever reason your ex, Max, is back in the picture. Any idea why?"

"Before this, I hadn't heard from him in years."

Nelson spoke up. "Not alimony, nothing like that?"

"No. I don't need money from him. Nothing else either. He has his own business, so he's OK financially as far as I know."

Chang jotted down a dollar sign with arrows in two directions on a small notepad. "If you hire us, we'll look into that. Maybe this is a prelude to some sort of shakedown."

"He's never been after my money before. Of course when I worked at small-market stations, there wasn't much to go after."

"Any sense that he wants to get back together? Any sign of jealousy? Are you currently in a relationship? And is it new?"

Chang heard the tension spike in her voice.

"Back together?" She laughed, but Chang discerned no humor. "It would never happen. Anyway, yes, I'm in a relationship. I've been dating Drew for a couple years."

"No big announcements?" Nelson asked. "Engagement? Banter about your boyfriend on your show?"

Now some ice.

"I may work for a tabloid network, but I'm a serious journalist. I don't do *Regis and Laura*. I keep my personal life to myself. That includes online. The web's teeming with weirdos."

Chang and Nelson shared a glance.

"That's fine Ms....Laura. We have to start with the most common reasons for domestic disputes and work our way from there."

"OK. I guess I'm more used to asking the questions. Between you and Sieger, I feel like I'm the one under investigation."

"Here's what we'd like to do. We'll do a background investigation on Mr. Stark and see if any red flags pop up. I'll even get a feel for his movements, just to make sure he's going about his business and staying out of yours."

"Max *is* a red flag, but I get your point. That makes as much sense as anything." Laura's laugh sounded more genuine, if a little bitter. "I mean, it's not like I can send you over to rough him up."

"We don't do that." Chang smiled.

"Not as a fee for service." Nelson didn't.

Chang was grateful they weren't on video chat. She seemed to take it as a joke, and Chang decided to let her.

"And understand, you're not to bother Marchetti. I really don't think this is him." Laura spoke fast, and Chang heard a cautious note in her voice that he thought might turn into fear.

Chang agreed but needed to make sure she understood how they worked. "The Kick Me sign isn't a mobster's style. He'd be more direct; and no, we don't want to aggravate him for no reason." Chang paused. She'd just have to get used to certain ideas. "But we have to follow leads wherever they take us."

10

TIPS IN THE NIGHT

Laura's Apartment

"You did what?" Drew looked like he was going to drop the plates he was carrying into the kitchen.

Laura felt her jaw clench. "I didn't just pick them out of the Yellow Pages."

"PIs from Dela-*where*?" Drew could look cute when he was annoyed.

This wasn't one of those times.

"I did background on both of them. They were homicide cops here, and then for the state cops in Delaware. They solved some major cases, not that you'd have heard of them."

"What's that supposed to mean?"

"It means you don't read anything that's not related to sports or new accounting rules published by FASB."

Drew clanked the plates into the dishwasher and glared over his shoulder. "Excuse me for being good at my job."

Laura saw the chances of salvaging the evening vanish, but found she didn't care. "Yeah, well, excuse me for being good at *mine*. I didn't believe Sieger, so I checked them out. They're the real deal. Who cares why they left the city? They're experts at tough cases. Especially the weird ones."

Drew looked confused. "What's weird about your case?" He drained the dregs of a glass of red wine that was on the counter. She wasn't sure whose. "Are you positive you even have a case?"

"What do you care? It's my money. When it comes out of your account, you'll get a say."

He looked like she'd thrown cold water on him, and she wished she'd left that last bit on the editing room floor. "I thought I was entitled to an opinion, but I can keep it to myself." He wiped his hands on a dishtowel and squeezed around her to head into the living room.

Shit.

"Drew."

Her voice slowed but didn't stop his march for the door. He turned. "Obviously this isn't a good time tonight," he said.

"It's not that."

"No?"

"I didn't mean to bite your head off. Not all of it anyway." That got a little smile. "I get that you don't buy the whole *Max is back* thing. Join the club. But even if all of you are right, the peace of mind alone will make it money well spent."

Her cell rang just then, and Drew let himself out. Just as well, but she hoped he wasn't still as pissed as she'd been. She dug out her phone and checked the caller ID. XXX-XXX-XXXX. It was one of her most reliable—and mysterious—tipsters.

Her pulse spiked as she snatched a pen and a sheet of paper that had started out as a grocery list.

"Laura Stark."

"STP here. Do you require verification?"

Her heart pounded. "Yes. What does STP stand for?" The voice was the same cultured accent she always had difficulty placing. Almost Boston Brahmin, but mixed with something else.

"Stop the Presses. Shall I continue? Fine work on the Marchetti interview, by the way."

It was him. "Thanks. Go ahead."

"You'll love this. Have you ever heard of Pietr Orrlov?"

She wasn't up to trivia just now. "The name sounds familiar..."

"Lambs of Strife?"

That was it. "The adoption charity? From Russia?...No, *he's* Russian, and he runs an adoption agency for kids orphaned by fighting in Chechnya?"

"There's a reason I send you my very best."

She felt a strange swell of pride at the virtual stranger's compliment. "What's up?"

"His nonprofit status for one. Listen carefully. Orrlov has two sets of books and has been skimming funds from public and private donors. Who knows how many tykes could have been saved if he wasn't so busy shoveling cash into his pockets, all while playing the big-shot philanthropist."

"How do you know—"

He cut her off. "All you need to know is that I have proof."

She pictured her meeting with Sid. "It's going to have to be good. He's very popular and politically connected, if I remember correctly."

"I have the books. Both sets. Bank accounts, transfer records, everything. Interested?"

"You have to ask? Where can I find the information? The sooner I get it, the quicker we can verify it and put the story on the air if it holds up."

"It'll find you. Can you be in front of your office building in an hour?"

"Do I get to see you again?" She'd forced this man to appear in person the first time he fed her a story. He'd balked so much that she thought she'd have to write him off. But he'd shown up in a trench coat, hat, and glasses no less, all five feet of him. He'd looked like a kid on Halloween, but he'd spoken with that deep, sophisticated voice. The same one as now.

STP laughed. "You get to meet Benny with Kamikaze Kouriers."

She had to ask. "We have the exclusive?"

"If you hurry." He hung up.

* * *

Laura hated to admit that she actually enjoyed the cloak-and-dagger stuff, if it led to a payoff. Plenty of kooks called her unlisted tip line. The number wasn't exactly a secret, and most of her reliable sources had it. But she liked to think that keeping it out of the Yellow Pages reduced the number of crank calls.

Most tips were crap or just a case of dueling grudges where one side or the other tried to use her station for PR.

Not STP. Over the years he'd given her more hot tips than all her other sources combined. After that first time, she'd never seen him in person again, but his leads always panned out.

He must be some well-connected whistle-blower. Whoever he was, he didn't do rumor. He always gave her stories that practically produced themselves. More often than not, he provided hard documentation. How he obtained it she never knew, and Sid insisted she not say or do anything that might get her caught up in anything illegal. STP always gave them accurate info, so she didn't ask questions.

* * *

It may have been the city that never slept, but the relative quiet in front of her office building gave the area a different vibe. The cleaning crews had long since finished, and only a handful of lights dotted the towering building. Overnight crews were busily doing their thing inside. She didn't know the name of the guard at the desk, but while she stood outside, she tried to remain in his line of sight and clutched her pepper spray. She was close enough that she could bang on the glass to get his attention (or wake him up).

Part of her wanted someone with her for protection. But Drew was pouting, and she wasn't inclined to ask him for help. Besides, she liked to keep this aspect of her job under wraps. When the tips led to big stories, they were an ace in the hole that Laura wasn't eager to share. Let them wonder: How does she do that?

Just when her imagination was starting to crowd out her ambition with thoughts that she was being watched, she heard the blast of a car horn and a string of curses down the street. She saw a pair of cars nearly collide as a bicycle shot between them and wove toward her.

The rider darted between two parked cars and executed a perfect hop to clear the curb. He pedaled furiously straight at her, and she knew he was going to crash right into her. His helmet had an open slot cut down the middle to make room for a bright pink Mohawk. She made a break for the street to take shelter between cars. However, before she got to the curb, he reached her and jammed on the brakes. He slid sideways, the rear tire skidding right at her, until the bike came to rest a foot away from her body.

"Stark?"

She nodded. He held up a hand for silence and yanked out a portable radio. "B here. Package delivered. What's the time?"

Laura could hear static hiss, and then a disembodied voice replied that it was 11:23.

"Yes!" As the rider pumped his fist, Laura saw that his knuckles were covered with letters. His right hand said DON'T.

"You're Benny?"

"You know it."

His left hand displayed the word LATE.

"Don't late?"

Benny pulled off his helmet and held his fists up to his temples like two horns. She read left to right and finally understood. An ornate letter *B* was centered on his forehead.

"Don't B Late. Cute. What have you got for me?"

"Contempt. But it ain't personal. Somebody got this for you too."

He took out a thick envelope and handed it to her.

She wasn't sure what to do next. Should she tip this joker? "Thanks, uh…"

He must have been a mind reader. "No tips, lady. Your gratitude is nourishment for my soul."

"What?"

He laughed as fast as he pedaled. "Just playin'. But don't worry about it. Your man hooked me up with a tight bonus if I got here by eleven thirty."

"Good job."

"Always." His body looked like it was made of wire and ink. "You need me again, ask for B."

"B for Benny. Got it."

"B for Benzedrine." He cracked up and sped off on his bike, playing chicken with an oncoming car.

Now Laura felt vulnerable, like a predator who'd just made a kill and wanted to eat it before the scavengers swept in.

The longer she was on the street, the more exposed she felt. She marched down the block to Third Avenue. She was tempted to hail a cab. But she didn't have far to go, and the bright streetlights boosted her confidence. Exhilaration won out over paranoia and spirited her home.

***

When Laura turned the top lock on her door, she felt like she could finally exhale. She tore open the thick envelope and noted at once the tidy way all the information was organized. She set aside the computer CDs and skimmed through the documents. The dual accounting ledgers clearly showed the money trail and even included bank accounts and passwords.

She'd learned long ago to let the legal department worry about staying on the right side of the law. She hadn't done anything criminal to obtain this information.

The information in her hands would enable anyone to access the records and verify the printouts. She knew she wouldn't though, nor would Sid allow anyone in the company to do so. She was sure that that would be breaking the law. But she was equally certain that the ever ambitious attorney general would be able to secure the necessary warrants to confirm the story spread across her dining room table.

Later.

Right now she had the biggest scoop since…well, since the Marchetti interview, but this would keep eyeballs glued to WBAC for a solid couple of weeks. She already had more than enough material to justify asking Mr. Orrlov some pointed questions.

Pointed? Hell. More like skewering.

It was time to wake up Sid.

11

DILIGENCE DUE

Wilmington, Delaware

"What do we have so far?" Chang waved Nelson into the conference room but kept one hand on the doorknob. He didn't want to get his hopes up for an interesting case just to have Nelson's research burst his bubble.

"Betty, can you hold any calls while we're in the conference room?"

Betty looked up from the invoices she was preparing. "Are you sure you don't need me in the room to take notes?"

Chang knew better. She was a great worker and looked out for Nelson, but her sweet tooth for gossip posed a danger to sensitive client relations. And she was no dummy. She sensed that the "little research project" for Laura Stark was going to be more interesting than compiling billable hours.

"This client is pretty twitchy. I think we need to keep things close to the vest until we know what we're dealing with and to earn her confidence." Laura Stark would dump them in a flash if he shared any sensitive information.

He closed the door on his disappointed office assistant and would-be amateur sleuth.

"One of these days, she'll be a big help," Nelson said as he spread out his files on the polished wood table.

"She's a big help where she is. As for any research, we'll see. For now I just want your thoughts."

Nelson yawned and stretched. His thin limbs reminded Chang of a daddy longlegs.

"It took a while to get a handle on Max, but I think I have enough. And we can backfill from Laura if necessary. For now I wanted to get as much as I could without her filter."

"Makes sense." Chang let Nelson get warmed up. Some days the guy barely spoke; others he wouldn't shut up.

"Some of the early stuff came from when Max was in college. Interesting fellow. He was a promising football player on scholarship at the University of Georgia." Nelson slid a blurry photocopy of an old newspaper article toward Chang.

Chang read the title: CIRCUS CATCH.

"His nickname. He played receiver and built his reputation on acrobatic grabs. More importantly, it talks about his upbringing. The guy literally grew up in a traveling carnival."

"Laura mentioned something about that. What does it say?"

"It's a fluff piece, so nothing too juicy. But it talks about how his mom used to be a trapeze artist and fortune-teller, and he learned all sorts of things from his extended 'family.'"

"Sounds like he was pretty good. What happened to his football career?" Chang worked a racquetball in his left hand while he listened. He could tolerate the pain if he started slow and gradually increased the effort. Somewhere in the middle of the exercise, his hand felt almost normal before fatigue began to tease fresh agony from the joints.

Nelson perked up. Chang knew that meant he was about to reveal some important clue. "He got his knee blown out."

Chang felt the ache begin to set into his fingers. "It happens. So he left college?"

"Slow down, that's not what's strange."

Chang waited. Best to let Nelson work at his own pace.

"The opponent who injured Max has a history of his own."

"Who was it?"

"Dave Stonebreaker." Nelson smiled.

Chang knew that Nelson didn't follow professional sports of any kind, so he'd done his homework. "*That* Stonebreaker? The one who played for the Giants?"

Nelson nodded. "Right up until he got tossed out of the league for repeated steroid use."

Chang wasn't much for sports either, but he recalled the headlines because several things about the case had felt wrong. "He died under strange circumstances last year, right?"

"Coroner said a heroin overdose. The weird thing is, all published accounts referenced a history of steroids, but never narcotics."

"Funny habit to jump right into. Not exactly a performance enhancer."

"The official version speculated that he was depressed. Maybe he was. But I agree, it doesn't pass the smell test."

Chang tried to regain the forty-thousand-foot perspective. "So what does that have to do with Max Stark?"

Nelson traced a finger over the white scar along his head, thankfully the only lasting remnant from his brief time in a coma a couple of years earlier. "Probably nothing. Just keep it in the back of your mind. Max's injury wound up costing him his scholarship. The only reference I could find quoted him saying that it was just part of the sport and he'd find another way to stay in school."

"And did he?"

"I know he graduated, and that he met Laura while in school."

"So far that's admirable. Good attitude toward adversity..." But something gnawed at Chang.

Nelson met his gaze, and Chang knew they were thinking along similar lines. He listened closely as Nelson continued.

"It's still a fuzzy picture, but I'm not seeing a lot of evidence of him being a good sport. This is the same man who forced Laura to get a restraining order against him. I'm sure she could furnish us with plenty of examples of his temper. And all the accounts of the injury agree: it was a dirty hit from Stonebreaker."

"He was known for those. What else?"

"Not much until stories started springing up about his company. This'd be after his divorce from Laura."

"Something called Laughing Matters?" Chang tried to remember what else Laura had told him.

"Yes. Their website describes it as a full-service laugh factory."

"Which means what, exactly?"

"Looks like everything from magic shows to full-blown, stunt-filled stage productions. They do conventions and corporate gigs and fill in with smaller parties."

"So his circus background wasn't just hype."

"Doesn't look like it. But like a lot of businesses, they've had a rough go of it lately."

Chang leaned forward. Classic motives got that way for a reason. Money, power, revenge. "How bad?"

Nelson thumbed through a stack of pages. "Based on these tax returns—"

Chang interrupted. "Please tell me you used a dead end to get those."

Chang had a list of dummy accounts he used for sensitive searches and whenever he needed to create "authentic" false IDs. He liked to think of this particular investigative tool as a gray area. His conscience let him live with the fact that they were illegal, since he only used them for good. If his conscience tried to mention slippery slopes, he hummed a few bars from a Chinese opera he disliked to tune it out.

"I didn't think I needed it for a simple business credit report. But I had a hunch it might uncover problems, so I used the dead ender on the top of the list for both. Want me to burn it?"

Chang searched his memory. "That was Rodney Caesar Three, right?"

Nelson nodded.

"Don't burn it yet, but we need to make sure 'Rodney' sticks with this case only."

He hated to lose an ID, but crooks were more sophisticated than the cops these days, and he knew a sharp outfit could trace unwelcome searches back to him, even if he was legally permitted to look. So he did what was needed to do to protect himself and his staff. If that also gave him more latitude when he needed to dig deeper, so be it.

"OK. You'll be glad to know 'Rodney' learned that Laughing Matters has been hemorrhaging cash the last few years. They're still meeting their rent and payroll, but for the life of me, I don't see how. Revenue has plunged."

Chang spoke. "So how's he keeping the lights on? Business loan, lines of credit?"

Nelson looked at him. "Nothing like that on here. And I doubt he's been applying, judging by the lack of credit checks."

"Think he's been hitting up our client already?"

Nelson closed his eyes for a moment. "We've gotta meet her. We could always ask her directly. I'd know then for sure. But it's certainly possible."

"She's had enough, and now we're her way out?"

"Lots of unanswered questions."

"I think we need to take a run up to the city. I want to see this Max in person."

Nelson puffed out his chest. "And I'll see this Laura in person."

12

CHARITY CASE

Manhattan

Laura was glad they'd brought Eddie Tua along as part of their field camera crew. Built like a Pacific island fireplug, he used to play rugby and had seemed immune to pain in the two scuffles she'd seen him in when they faced angry interview subjects.

She had a feeling today might be number three. For a well-regarded charity, Lambs of Strife appeared to take its mission and itself and its security seriously. She knew they were on the right track when their initial interview requests were rebuffed.

Sid's instincts lit up along with hers, and he'd practically pushed her out the door when she suggested a direct, impromptu street interview. Her more uptight colleagues might call it an "ambush."

Laura had given fair warning. And after reading all the documents, she had little sympathy for the great humanitarian Orrlov.

Eddie set the camera along the back path to the parking lot. She had an intern, Tina, an ambitious young woman, sent to the front to smoke them out. The really guilty parties would either hunker down and refuse to come out or bail. Either way, it would make for great footage. The weasel couldn't dodge them forever, and they could document Orrlov's reluctance every night, if necessary. He'd probably get his own graphic intro and ominous theme song.

* * *

"Twenty bucks says he bunkers." Eddie rechecked the lighting for his camera.

"You're on." Laura felt her blood pumping. She could see the appeal of the sensation the so-called trash TV reporters experienced when they caught up to their quarry. She knew some of the network snobs who had driven her away looked at her the same way, but she didn't care a bit. She answered to her own standards, and a scum like Orrlov deserved whatever he got. So what if that called for a little direct action? Unlike those perfumed princesses at the networks, she wasn't afraid to get out of the studio.

* * *

"There he is." Twenty minutes after Tina texted about her first attempt to speak with Orrlov, Laura counted five people, including one perfectly coiffed silver-haired skunk—the man himself— leaving the building.

"Damn, I owe you a Jackson." Eddie followed close behind Laura.

They saw her coming and formed a phalanx around Orrlov.

"Looks like an offensive line." Laura didn't slow down.

"Or a scrum." Eddie went silent after that.

Laura knew he was already rolling with the camera.

"Mr. Orrlov. Laura Stark, WBAC. May I ask you a few questions?"

He hit her with an oily smile meant for the camera and kept walking. "Please, we are late. Another time."

She knew where this was going but fired a few questions at him to get them on camera and on the record. Just like a good attorney, she knew the answers already.

"Mr. Orrlov, how do you respond to allegations that your organization has embezzled up to half the funds earmarked for adoptions?"

"I have no comment," Orrlov replied coolly, cowering behind his wall of protectors. Eddie held the camera up high to get a good shot of the incredible shrinking philanthropist.

"Mr. Orrlov, what do you think auditors will say when they learn about your two vacation properties in the Bahamas? Records indicate the shell company that owns them is tied to you. Any thoughts?"

None in front of Eddie and the unblinking eye over his right shoulder.

Laura saw a scrawny suit whisper first to Orrlov and then to one of his goons. She knew she didn't have much time.

"Mr. Orrlov, any comment ahead of what the attorney general will say?"

"About what?" Orrlov looked genuinely puzzled but turned away when his attorney hissed something at him.

"Stay tuned for his press conference," Laura bluffed. She was fairly certain that after they talked to the AG, he'd initiate an investigation.

One of the bodyguards advanced. He reminded Laura of Dolph Lundgren when he played the intimidating Russian boxer in the Stallone film.

"Interview finished, thank you." He nearly pushed her out of the way.

Laura shouted at Orrlov's retreating back. "Mr. Orrlov, is it true you set up offshore accounts to launder money...two in the Caymans and one in Switzerland?"

Orrlov didn't turn, but Laura's specificity caused his spine to stiffen, and she watched the tension ripple down his back.

"Interview over!" The blond guard tried to swat down Eddie's camera. Eddie, who bragged that he had a black belt in "lens-fu," saw it coming and protected his tool of the trade. The guard bumped into Eddie and said in a loud voice, presumably for the camera, "Don't push me."

"Didn't touch you, man. Hey." Eddie shuffled back while the guard, who towered over Eddie by several inches, made another, more serious attempt to get the camera. All he ended up with was an armful of Eddie, who obliged by grabbing him back. Laura moved in and took the camera, while Eddie kept the guard tied up. She saw from the corner of her eye that Orrlov had made it to the parking lot before any of the other guards noticed the scuffle.

"Let go, man." Eddie had the guard wrapped up in a bear hug so that he couldn't get away or hit Eddie.

At least until reinforcements arrived.

One of the other guards had already doubled back and was headed toward them. He ran fast for such a big fellow, but then he slowed, torn over whom to go for first. Laura aimed the camera to capture the scuffle.

"Gimme the tape."

A local boy. Pure Bronx accent.

"You can't be serious." Laura summoned her most indignant tone.

"I look like I'm kidding? You ain't recording this."

Am too, thought Laura.

Then Eddie and the Russian guy hit the ground, and she heard the expensive fabric of the guard's suit rip.

Time to wrap. The Bronx bomber was closing in, and while she didn't think he'd hit her, she knew that at the very least he'd smash the camera.

"OK. It's off. You made your point."

"Good. Now hand over the tape and get lost."

"Tape? Where have you been? This is all digital. The whole story is already beamed back to the studio. How famous do you want to get today?"

He still looked like he was going to smash the camera.

"They're ten grand and my boss'll sue. Ask anyone."

Laura was relieved to see that Orrlov didn't overpay his hired muscle.

"Fuck it. Break it up, Dimi."

The Russian let go and punched Eddie once in the chest. It sounded like knuckles on a ripe melon.

"*Kefe!*" Eddie spat.

Eddie had taught some of his native language to people at the station, and Laura knew that it meant roughly: "Screw yourself."

"He said sorry about the suit. You guys run a helluva charity." She hoped the guys in the van were ready so that they could make a quick escape.

Eddie stayed between her and the guards all the way back to the street.

※ ※ ※

"You OK?" She saw Eddie check a scrape on his arm. Tina drove while they kept an eye out for any angry pursuit.

"It's cool. You got it?"

"I got it. And your baby is fine." She handed him his camera. Laura knew she was second to his equipment in the pecking order.

"So what do I owe you for running interference?" Despite the trembling, she also felt pumped.

Eddie smiled. "Twenty bucks."

"Sounds fair. And Sid's going to pin another purple camera on you." Sid may have been a cheap bastard when it came to upgrading equipment, but he took care of his people.

13

SPECIAL REPORT

"As you'll see in the following video, we tried to speak with the head of Lambs of Strife to get his side of the story. For now though, his side appears to be a wall of lawyers." Laura maintained eye contact with the camera and read the script she'd polished with Sid a few hours earlier.

As the footage began to roll, she rechecked her notes.

Eddie sat behind one of the cameras and grinned when all the pushing and shoving began. Len, the producer, counted down while the clip neared completion.

"Further efforts to contact Orrlov by phone were unsuccessful, as were additional efforts to speak to him in his multimillion-dollar brownstone.

"The attorney general's office declined to comment, saying in a written statement only that they were aware of the allegations and must review the relevant information."

They cut to commercial. Laura wasn't going to mention that the AG had had plenty to say when they'd brought him the info from STP. She was careful to protect her source, and the AG had had no choice but to conclude that the information looked "troubling." (She *loved* that soft, PC terminology.) AG Trip almost drooled when he saw it.

Best of all, the AG's office could verify everything legally, and then the real fireworks would begin. She and WBAC would have a front-row seat.

Every time she saw the canned footage of the kids the organization was supposedly helping juxtaposed against that smug Orrlov accepting yet another humanitarian award, she was struck by two thoughts. First, how many kids had never made it out of Chechnya thanks to Orrlov's greed?

Second, it couldn't happen to a nicer guy.

14

FIELD TRIP

Manhattan

"Back in the old stomping grounds," Chang said, pulling Nelson's car into the tiny opening of the underground garage near Laura Stark's television station.

"I didn't realize how close the Nineteenth was to here. Now I see why she went over there in the first place." Nelson's head was bobbing, and Chang knew he was trying to get in sync with the city. He wished the guy would carry an iPod or something so he'd at least look like he was listening to music. He thought Shu would probably understand how Nelson felt.

I wonder if he's in Chinatown now. Never mind. Let the man have his time.

Nelson had first linked up with Chang at the NYPD shortly after the little guy'd been assigned to the Nineteenth.

"It's changed a lot." Nelson was taking in his surroundings.

"Shops and things, yes, but otherwise it's the same." He checked his watch. "We have time to drop in on Ron. Laura won't be free for at least an hour."

"I'm rusty."

"You talk to clients all the time." *When necessary*, he failed to add.

"No, for all the energy around the city. Takes practice to block it out."

"Country mouse." Chang wove through the lunchtime crowds crossing Third Avenue. He felt naked walking around town without his weapon.

Nelson seemed to be humming to himself, and Chang hoped he'd finish by the time they got there.

"Haven't been here in ages." Nelson spoke as much to himself as to Chang.

"Miss it?"

"No."

"At least you aren't a possible murder suspect. Can you imagine how strange that felt?" Chang wanted to help Nelson relax, but the memory of sitting in the precinct's interrogation room all but cuffed was still fresh in his mind and made him squirm. Ron had just been doing his job. He hadn't known at the time that Chang had been framed.

Chang didn't hold a grudge, and after Ron had given them such an entertaining case to work on, they had to stop in.

Potentially interesting.

"I can *imagine.* Can you see me as a homicide collar?" Nelson asked and gave a little smile.

"Sure. I know you. You're a dangerous guy." They reached the door. "Ready for some awful coffee?"

✳ ✳ ✳

"Is that...?" Sergeant Bell looked up from a sheet of paper. He'd noticed Chang but was now staring at Nelson. Bell had been a fixture here for almost twenty years. Chang tried to remember how different Nelson must appear to anyone who hadn't seen him in years.

Back in the day, Bell had worn a mullet and bragged endlessly about his hockey skills.

"How ya doing? You need to take a seat? Can I get you anything?"

"I'm fine, Bell. How's the slap shot?" Nelson looked at the floor while he spoke.

"Hey, you remembered. I don't get out there too much anymore, but I coach the young guys some, you know? Hey, Chang."

"Bell." They'd never been close. Chang had never played hockey, but Bell used to try to beat him on the pistol range. It drove him nuts that Chang always outshot him.

"What brings you here?"

"I'm not in trouble again, if that's what you're wondering."

"I never thought that was you last time..."

Liar. "Of course not. It wasn't a good situation for anyone. Glad it's over."

Bell looked at Nelson again, and Chang knew the wheels were grinding in his head when he saw the man turn pale. The gin blossoms on his nose stood out against his pale skin.

In an instant Chang felt like he'd channeled Nelson and knew exactly what Bell was thinking: that Nelson was dying from some wasting disease, and his old partner was taking him around on a farewell tour.

Nelson caught the unspoken exchange. He nodded. "I've dropped some of the flab from when I was on the job, Bell, but I'm OK."

"Sure, right...I didn't..." Bell shook his head. "Sorry. I saw that scar. And the hair."

Nelson used to have jet black hair that looked like a bird's nest, and he'd been merely skinny, not scrawny and graying like he was now. His short hair accentuated the scar that ran across his bulbous head. Chang knew he was proud of his "war wound."

Nelson pointed at it. "This? That wasn't a scalpel. It was a foot. I think. Maybe a bat. Tell the truth, I'm still fuzzy, but whatever it was just shook things up a bit is all."

Chang let Nelson have his fun. At the time, he'd thought his partner was going to die, but Nelson was tougher than he looked.

"Well, good to see you. You work private now, right?"

"In Delaware or wherever business calls." Nelson sounded nonchalant.

"Sieger around?" Chang saw Bell was running low on small talk.

✳ ✳ ✳

"What the hell'd you guys do to Bell?" Sieger asked as he cleared the papers and junk from his desk and set the Styrofoam cups of coffee down on the edge. He lifted a stack of files off a chair and motioned for them both to sit.

"He's trapped in the past." Nelson looked around the room, and Chang knew he was absorbing details like a camera.

"Yeah? Speaking of which, Chang, you should challenge him to a shootout for beer. I'd love to see him freak out about it and then buy our brew."

Chang raised his arms. "I'm clean, boss. You can frisk me like before if you want."

Sieger smiled. "I'll never live that down, will I? Just following orders. You'd have done the same thing."

Chang waved it off. "You're right." He felt a throb of pain in his left hand.

"So how's our girl?"

"We're here to see her. Seems she may be onto something."

Sieger leaned forward. "Yeah?"

Nelson shook his head. "Don't know yet. We do know the ex is a flake and strapped for cash."

"How do you know?"

Chang nudged Nelson's leg with his foot. He half expected Nelson to tell him to stop kicking him.

"Still just a hunch, but if you read the old newspapers, he's a strange character."

Chang put on a poker face to cover his relief. If Nelson got excited, he was as single-minded as a bloodhound on the trail, and he might overlook nuances—like which investigation techniques were strictly legal.

"We're going to get some more background from Laura, and then I may take a walk."

Chang knew Sieger would let that hint go. There was nothing illegal about a private citizen walking the streets to take in the sights. He wouldn't ask more.

Not that it mattered at this point. Chang wasn't convinced that Max was the one doing the harassment or even that he was a grave threat. They needed to learn more.

"Sounds like a plan. And thanks for not spreading the word about why you're up here."

"We don't talk about our clients." Chang felt a bit insulted that Sieger even mentioned it.

Nelson lowered his voice. "About that. I saw the old clippings on what went down with your uncle. I see why everyone's so angry, but the more I looked, the more it sounded like she was only part of the problem. It started with faulty research and snowballed."

"No offense, Nelson, but I don't give a shit how it started. It's how it ended that burns me."

"All right."

"Sorry. Still a sore spot."

Chang looked at his watch for effect. "I'm guessing you won't want to join us, but we should get going."

"Good guess. You guys around for a beer later?"

"I could lay the dust with a frosty," Nelson said.

Chang and Ron stared at him. Nelson rarely drank, and sometimes his efforts at "regular folk" banter still caught Chang off guard.

✳ ✳ ✳

"Ms. Stark is expecting you?" The huge guard at the front desk looked like he could have played football back in the day.

"Right." Chang gave him their names. "We haven't met in person, just over the phone." He was used to people describing the big Chinaman and the scrawny white guy.

The guard nodded and stood to walk over to a phone on the wall. Chang saw the man had a slight limp.

Nelson watched the guard too.

"OK, wait here. She'll be down in a moment to take you up. You'll need these." He handed out temporary passes in laminated plastic cases with metal clips.

Nelson didn't move to sit. He looked at the guard long enough to get the man's attention.

Now what?

"Yes?" The guard smiled, but Chang saw his eyes grow wary.

"How'd you hurt your knee?" Nelson pointed to it.

"That? Just gets stiff when I sit too long. Old ball injury."

"Do you remember the day?"

"It was a long time ago."

"But you remember?" Nelson bore in.

Chang was about to take Nelson by the shoulder when the guard met the little guy's gaze.

"His number was seventy-four, and he got a fifteen-yard penalty while I was out for the rest of the season."

"Sorry."

"We won the game. Why do you want to know?"

"Just wondering."

"He always like that?" The guard spoke to Chang.

"You have no idea."

***

When Laura stepped out of the elevator, Chang recognized her immediately. He noticed that she picked him out of the group milling around the lobby and figured she must have done her homework as well.

He saw her react with a look of surprise when she'd gotten a good look at Nelson. Chang knew that despite his own unusual size, more people got flustered when they first met Nelson.

There was different and there was Nelson. Luckily he didn't seem to care.

Laura seemed to regain her composure in the time it took to reach them and shake their hands.

"Would you be more comfortable if we went for a walk?" Chang knew how fast rumors could circulate in an office.

"No worries. I'm a big shot around here. I've got my own office and everything."

Chang knew she was being tongue in cheek; she was one of the station's biggest draws. He'd bet her office was almost as large as the owner's.

They headed up in the elevator in silence. Then she led them through a maze of cubicles and down a hallway lined with offices.

Sure enough, when they reached the corner, he saw a door with her name on it in gold letters.

"Home sweet home. Feels like it anyway." She plopped down in a big leather chair and indicated the two seats in front of her. "Can I get you guys anything?"

"Just water for me," Chang said.

Nelson was taking in the pictures on the wall and didn't look like he'd heard her.

"Nelson?"

"Sorry. Chai if you have it." Nelson nodded like he expected to hear a selection of flavors.

Chang saw the slightest twitch at the corners of her mouth. He was glad to see that she now appeared more amused than creeped out by Nelson, who often had that effect on people, especially women.

"I'll have an intern grab some. Any type in particular?"

"Oh, I'm easy. Chai of the Tiger."

"Sorry?"

Enough. Chang intervened. "Nelson, I don't think the Tea Hee chain has reached New York, so she has no idea what you're talking about." Chang turned to Laura and whispered, "Local shop in Delaware."

"Water too, then."

Chang tried to relax. Nelson's social awkwardness asserted itself whenever he was confronted with quick choices around strangers. "He's a crack investigator…"

"Yes, I know. You guys left quite a trail here and in Delaware." Laura retrieved a couple of water bottles from a mini fridge next to her desk. She handed one to each of them. "I'll have to add the chai to my next contract rider."

Chang smiled back at her. He was still getting used to having someone trust his skills right off the bat. He usually had to prove himself to new clients too lazy to check his history.

"If you googled us, you saw a bunch of articles. One of the writers—"

"Flannigan. He sure hated you. I know how to read between the lines. Remember, I'm press too."

"We can read too, and I think you got a bum rap. Partly, anyway," Nelson said, trying—and failing—to speak around a sip of water.

Laura waited for him to finish coughing.

"You don't have to flatter me. I already hired you." She stopped, and Chang glanced at Nelson, who wore an expression of pure confusion.

"At the risk of hurting our small business, neither of us is good at sucking up. Nelson has explained to me that there was more to the Wolf Sieger business than what appeared on the news."

"I didn't hire you to clear my name, but thanks for the vote of confidence."

Chang could tell she was offended, but also knew that she hadn't gotten to the top with a thin skin.

Nelson the Clod suddenly turned into Nelson the Investigator like he'd thrown a switch. "I'm not convinced yet. Tell me. Did you work from an original tip from your producer? Was that what started the story?"

"I told you already. Why…"

Nelson stared at her eyes. He didn't even try to be subtle. Chang wondered whether this was a good idea, but at that moment, it was between them.

"I needed to see your face in person. Did you rely on the original source, or did you check it out yourself?"

"Nobody believed me, but I went with what they gave me. I assumed it was true until it was too late." She squirmed in her seat but made no move to leave. Or kick them out.

"Would you take it back if you could?"

"Pointless question."

"But would you?"

"It's my biggest regret, but I can't change it. I own it."

"Ron Sieger hasn't forgiven you. Neither have the cops. Have you forgiven yourself?"

"I had to move on."

Nelson sat back and managed a sip without spilling. "That's the first thing you've said that isn't true. I won't hold it against you."

That last remark seemed to startle Laura out of a trance. "Excuse me?"

Chang jumped in. "He flunked diplomacy. He has a knack for reading people, and that was his clumsy way of saying you earned his trust."

"I was doing fine." Nelson looked hurt.

"That was weird. You'd make a hell of a reporter. Or a trial lawyer."

Nelson shuddered. "No thanks."

Laura picked up a pen. "OK, let's move on to the task at hand. You said you learned some things about Max?"

"Right," Chang said. "We found enough background on Max to support your concern, but what we want to know is, were you aware of his financial situation?"

"What do you mean?"

"His business has been struggling for several years. In fact, he's bleeding cash, yet he's somehow staying afloat."

"Well good for him, I guess."

Chang thought her confusion looked genuine.

"We figure he must be supplementing his income. He hasn't now or ever before approached you for money?"

"No."

"Not in some coercive way? Extortion or..." Chang let the thought dangle.

"If he was, and if it was bad enough that I was paying him, I wouldn't admit it, now would I?"

"You wouldn't have to," Nelson said. He looked at Chang. "He's not getting it from her." Nelson drummed the fingers of his free hand on his thigh, like he was typing.

Laura turned back to Chang. "So how do you know so much about his finances? You didn't send Nelson over to talk to him?" Chang could see she was only half joking.

"I won't get into trade secrets, but don't worry. We have good and discreet sources."

Laura stood up. "Are you sure? Max is smart. Don't take the clown act to heart."

Chang handed her the copies of the tax returns. He let her look through them before taking them back. "We're good at what we do."

"I'm sure. It's just that he's...I want to say sneaky, but that sounds too benevolent." Laura smoothed her skirt.

"We're sneaky too."

Nelson shook his head and pointed at Chang. He was glad Laura looked amused. It wouldn't last long.

"So what's next?" she asked.

"All we know so far is that the guy is unusual, with a threatening past and recent money troubles. Those are red flags but hardly concrete proof of anything. I need to know if he's really coming around here, and if it is to bother you."

"Or worse," Laura said.

Chang nodded. "So here's what's next. I assume you don't have any idea what he drives?"

"Not a clue."

"Didn't think so. I made a reservation for a car rental. Nelson will follow up with any additional questions and let you get back to work. I'll take the rental and swing by Max's warehouse."

"Don't do that." She looked frightened. "You might provoke him. I mean, maybe I'm exaggerating. Maybe he's not shadowing me after all."

"Thanks for the concern, but if I do my job right, he'll never even know I was there. And you're not especially convincing. You just broke into a sweat, and you strike me as a cool lady."

He was gratified that the cheap compliment appeared to work, but he didn't flatter himself. The lady was petrified, and he didn't need to be Nelson to see it.

"What are you going to do?"

He waved her off as he left the room. "I won't bore you with details."

15

A CLOWN GROWS IN BROOKLYN

New York City

Chang left Nelson with Laura and planned to catch up with him later.

Or not, if he could reach Colleen. Nelson would understand. Chang could return the rental back in Delaware just as easily.

Chang wasn't sure what to expect, but he knew that Max's company was located in a warehouse in Brooklyn right by Trinity Cemetery.

He must like quiet neighbors. Nelson had noticed that Max listed the same address for his home. Had that been a fiscal decision, or did he hate long commutes?

Just as well. This way he knew where to find him.

Chang pulled the innocuous silver Chevy out of the rental slot and over the deadly spikes next to the signs warning him not to back up.

"Never retreat."

He headed for the Queensboro Bridge and wondered whether this was going to be a waste of time.

You're getting paid, ergo, not a waste of time.

He didn't know when his subconscious had picked up Latin, but it had a point. And his gut told him something here was way wrong. The guy had Laura terrified.

Sure, Ron Sieger wasn't convinced Laura had a problem, but Chang knew better than to trust his friend's judgment in this case. Ron carried too much emotional baggage to think clearly about this one.

As Chang wove his way through midtown Manhattan, he was flooded with memories from all the years he'd worked here. Here a corner grocery, there a jewelry shop, all of which had been touched by crimes of one kind or another.

He liked to think he'd done more good than harm, but the city churned on in vibrant indifference.

✷✷✷

Chang started looking for parking a couple of blocks out. The neighborhood looked run-down, with trash strewn on the sidewalk nearest the train tracks. He supposed a Realtor would say the neighborhood was well lived in. He couldn't say how well the residents lived, but he did see pockets of care amid the tagged walls.

He'd studied a map and knew that Laughing Matters occupied a large warehouse alongside the train and subway tracks that bordered the cemetery. The street that ran in front of the building was one-way. So he knew that when Max left, he'd have to drive past where Chang had parked, right by a basketball court.

He noted that there was a subway station nearby and bus lines ran like veins through the area. But a business built around entertainment and fancy shows required a truck, and probably vans.

Sure enough, from where he was, he could see the plain brick building sat in sharp contrast to a truck garishly painted with clowns and balloons that was parked in front.

Laughing Matters: Where we take humor seriously.

He already knew the website address and wasn't planning on phoning the toll-free number just yet.

It was clear from the look of the headquarters that they got little to no walk-in traffic. The business must get by on call-ins and referrals, though evidently not many of either lately.

He figured the truck was used for the more elaborate shows. If Max was as low-profile as Laura had implied, Chang doubted he would be driving around in that monstrosity.

He took out his cell phone and pretended to talk on it while he waited. Passing traffic, pedestrian and vehicular alike, seemed to take no notice of him. *Good.* He'd been worried because the next block over was all warehouses, and the workers there would be aware of any strangers. The row houses and basketball court served as decent cover for a random parked car.

After a half hour, he began to think he might be wasting his time. Then he saw a white van turn a corner a block away and stop in front of Laughing Matters.

It was him.

Although he looked older, Chang recognized him immediately from the picture Laura had provided. Chang watched as the tall, lean figure hopped out of the van and headed inside the building through the front entrance.

Chang looked for a limp but didn't see one. The man wore loose, blue work pants and a denim shirt, and from the way he carried himself, he appeared to be fit. Chang was too far away to take a measure of Max's eyes. The face in the picture showed intense dark eyes that betrayed nothing.

With Max inside, Chang was tempted to walk by the front of building but decided it was too risky. Max might come out, and Chang didn't want to make an impression on the workers hanging around the place across the street.

So what? Nobody would expect him to be so bold.

Chang pulled on a baseball cap and took out a small tracker. It was about the size of a deck of cards and would take only a second to attach. He popped open his car door. His muscles creaked after being in the car for so long, and he took a moment to stretch. It wouldn't do to have his back go out on him.

He'd barely walked ten yards when Max emerged from the building and jumped back into the van. Chang saw that he was carrying a leather satchel.

As the van started up and began to back up, Chang hopped back in his car and keyed the ignition. He leaned over and rooted through the glove box as the van passed him and turned at the basketball courts right in front of him.

That had been too close. Chang watched the white van through the chain-link fencing and then started following from as far away as he dared. He hated doing big-city tails with just one car.

Back when he was with the Department, they could coordinate several cars and keep a suspect in sight indefinitely.

Single-car tails were hard to pull off with a leery subject. So far he didn't see any sign that Max knew the heat was on. *What heat?* Chang reminded himself that they didn't know anything yet, other than that he was an unusual guy with a checkered past.

Still, it was fun to be back on a case, and he half hoped this would turn into something interesting. Not just for the money, though it was always nice when the client was able to pay her bills.

"OK, Mr. Clown, where are we going?" Chang followed Max onto the Belt Parkway. He relaxed a bit because he could hang back, and his silver car blended in among the other vehicles. He didn't detect any signs that he'd been made.

He knew it was reckless to be doing a tail this soon, but he needed to get a handle on what they were dealing with.

Max continued for several miles and signaled well before taking the exit toward Coney Island Avenue.

"Playing the boardwalk?" Chang muttered.

Nope.

Max turned off the road near Sheepshead Bay and parked outside a shopping center a block from where the big yachts were docked. Most of them were charter boats used for cruising up and down the bay and around the city. Lined with nice restaurants, boutiques, and small offices, the shopping center looked quite posh. Chang saw a border of trees and upscale homes across the strip of water.

Chang found a spot in the parking lot across the road where he had a view of the van and the bay. He could hear the gulls and smell cooking fish and meat.

He hunched down in his seat and held his phone to his ear. After a couple of minutes, he began to wonder whether Max had slipped out of the van without his noticing. *But how?*

The sliding door on the van finally opened, and Chang thought that Max had brought a passenger with him. This guy wore a painter's cap and had blond hair. He had a bulky gray sweatshirt and...the satchel. Chang peered through the windshield as the guy walked toward the water. He studied the man's gait and estimated his height. The man walked differently, but the height was right...

He took a couple of shots with the camera in his phone. They wouldn't be much good from this distance, but they were better than nothing. His big camera rig would have been way too obvious. He glanced back at the van, half expecting to see the door open and Max emerge.

But there was no sign of anyone else in there.

Chang studied the figure more closely. It had to be Max, didn't it? The guy had reached the Ocean Avenue Footbridge, which crossed over to the other side of the bay.

Beyond the bridge lay a neighborhood lined with stately mansions and beyond that, Manhattan Beach Park.

Why not park over there if that was where he was headed? More important, what was up with the disguise? Chang was tempted to follow on foot, but the bridge gave a perfect view of everything along its entire length and on either side.

As if on cue, the guy stopped and spun around near the half-way point. Chang ducked down in his seat. He was sure there was no way the man could see him in the car.

Then why is your heart pounding?

It was nowhere near as "exhilarating as getting shot at without result," as Churchill once said, but Chang nevertheless felt like he'd just dodged a bullet.

He peeked under the brim of his baseball cap and watched the guy cross to the far side of the bridge. He eyeballed the blond hair until he lost sight of it when the man crossed the street.

He toyed with the idea of following by car, but by the time he worked his way through the lights and traffic, he doubted he'd find him.

Besides, he had his chance, assuming that the van was empty. One way to find out.

∗ ∗ ∗

Chang switched to a baseball cap with Mandarin characters that read "Good Eats!" He added spectacles with clear, round lenses, and a set of headphones, then dug out a stack of bright green flyers from his goody bag. He palmed the tracker in his left hand and held the flyers over it. He ignored the dull pain in his fingers.

The doctors had said he had a good chance of regaining the full use of his hand, but the persistent numb spots made him doubt it. Shu had outlined a training program to take advantage of the deadened areas, and he planned to get right on it as soon as the feeling portions stopped transmitting pain.

Chang put Shu out of his mind and regained his game face. Steady background research work in Delaware had fattened the bottom line but dulled his instincts.

He walked across the street and started on the row of cars where Max had parked the van.

He began to stick the neon green flyers under the cars' windshield wipers. They advertised "Wing Chow's Authentic Chinese Food from China!!!" The address and phone number were for a real place in Chinatown, but it was a handbag shop run by a nemesis from Chang's childhood. Eddie Chow would forever be a young tormentor in Chang's mind. Eddie had always led the pack when it came time to single Chang out for "chase the water buffalo."

Chang gave Eddie's number out whenever he needed a quick bogus reference.

The largest establishment on the edge of the parking lot was a steakhouse. Chang wasn't surprised that by the time he reached the van, someone had bolted out the door and started yelling at him.

Continuing to pretend to bob his head to the music, Chang glanced through the windshield. The driver and passenger seats were empty, and behind them all he saw was the darkened back of the van; there was no sign of anyone inside.

"Hey asshole, I'm talking to you!"

Chang let out a squawk and dropped his stack of papers next to the van. "You scare me." He laid the accent on thick.

"This is a restaurant. Get the fuck out of here with that." The burly staffer began to snatch the sheets off the windshields.

As Chang squatted down to pick up his papers, he reached under the van to attach the magnetic tracker. He stood and tried to straighten the flyers into a neat stack.

He saw the staffer pulling off the last flyer.

"You try? Is good."

The guy looked at Chang like he was garbage. Just what he wanted.

"You got to be shitting me." He jerked his thumb toward the steakhouse. "I eat here for free." He squared off on Chang. "Who said you could be here?"

"Boss say OK. So no problem."

"OK, bullshit. You ever come back here, I'll kick your ass all the way back to Chinatown. Got me?"

"Thank you." Chang felt the dragon in his chest stir from its deep slumber. He took a step back and it was gone.

The man peered at the flyer. "Who's your boss?"

Chang dialed back the accent to make sure he was clear. "Mr. Edward Chow. He not scared of you."

"He's gonna hear from me."

16

UNRESTRAINED

WBAC

"He'll be careful?" Laura still felt uncomfortable talking to this odd man. But she'd done her homework, and Nelson really *had* been a cop.

Despite the surgical way his gaze could cut through her, the man didn't appear to judge her—unlike the rest of the police force.

Nelson wriggled in his seat like a little kid. Counterintuitively, she took that to mean he felt more relaxed. "Sure. He misses being in the field. It's been slow for that kind of work lately."

"Not all car chases and guns, huh?"

He touched his scar. "Those can be hard on the body. I'll take boring."

"Now that you mention it, so would I." She checked herself. "At least in this case. I have plenty of excitement with my job, but they don't come after me."

"Not even Marchetti?" Nelson spoke without hesitation.

"He might if there was a reason. I think he used me for his own purposes."

"Some might say the station used him back."

Laura smiled. The guy had a blunt style, yet he didn't make her feel like he was trying to score points. "We benefited. No doubt. That's how a lot of the leaks work. I try not to flatter myself that people come out of the woodwork and feed me tips just because they respect my journalism."

"No?" There were those eyes again.

"OK, I do a little. I make sure that my sources and the stories get a fair shake. I owe them and my viewers that."

"And yourself?"

"Are you sure you aren't a shrink?"

"I saw plenty of them when I went away. None of them looked like me."

"Your breakdown?" She was surprised he'd be so upfront about it. He'd gone to pieces after his and Chang's last case as NYPD officers. If she remembered correctly, only Chang had rebuilt his career as a cop in Delaware. Nelson had gone into computers or something.

"Yup."

"You're a trip. While you're here, what else do you need from me?"

"I wanted to get a sense of Max."

"You guys did a good job of that. Hell, you know more about his business and finances than I did."

"Not today-Max. The one that first scared you to death."

✳ ✳ ✳

"I met him in college and got swept away by how mysterious he was. It definitely wasn't his jock side that drew me in." Laura hadn't felt so put on the couch since she'd actually last spoken to a shrink. "He did all these little things, like find me in the library and do a magic trick to conjure flowers just when I needed a laugh the most. It's hard to explain."

"Try."

"Maybe it'd be easier if you knew what it was like going out with frat boys."

"Can't help you there," Nelson deadpanned.

"One big goof after another, all hormones."

"Not Max?"

"He was different. It was like he was dialed into me. Every time we talked, he listened, and I could tell he really heard what I was saying. You'd be surprised how rare that is."

"That I get."

"Later that intensity took on an edge, and it became less charming and more..."

"Frightening?"

Laura nodded. "Eventually. At first I thought it was just the way he was coping with stress, like his feelings for me were filling holes in his life. I don't know."

"You're doing fine." Nelson watched her with an intent expression, his eyes seeming to pull the words out of her.

"I had the sense that he'd overcome so much. I lost my parents when I was young, so I respected that. He was so secretive about where he came from." She gripped the side of her desk like it could help her stay anchored in the present.

"Circus catch?" Nelson held up the article.

"The backstory he gave out was like a polished press release. He'd tell anyone who would listen about being raised with the circus and all the interesting people he grew up around, but it was all pretty thin if you looked hard. He kept the dark stuff to himself."

"Like what?"

"Something big happened with his mother. I mean she drank, that was clear. He was embarrassed and didn't want me to meet her. After he got his knee blown out..." Laura felt the years slip away like a silk-lined coat.

"Yes?"

"He changed. After the injury, he lost the scholarship and thought he'd have to leave school."

"I was wondering about that."

"Keep wondering. Somehow his mother got him the money. It was a touchy subject. He must have learned something around the time we graduated because, suddenly, that was it between him and his mother. She even skipped our wedding. She never once called, never tried making any contact until she died."

"What happened then?"

She hoped Nelson could see in her eyes that she wasn't making any of this up, even though she still had difficulty believing it herself.

"The funeral was surreal. When we got the news, Max said right away he wasn't going." Laura stared at the floor while she pulled the details from the depths of her mind. "I wasn't surprised, I guess, but then he got a certified letter." She remembered she'd been home sick from work and had to sign for it. The thick white envelope had sat on their mail table until Max got home that evening.

"I remember hearing Max say, 'It's from her,' and then go down to the basement with it clutched to his chest. He didn't come up for hours. When he finally did, he looked so pale…" Laura felt her fingers tremble and pressed them into her leg.

"Did you ever see it?" Nelson asked.

Laura noticed the nuanced phrasing. Not "Did he show it you?" It left open the possibility that she might have sneaked a peek. "No. I think he must have burned it because he smelled like smoke when he came upstairs. Wait, I just remembered, the smoke detector chirped while he was down there, and he had a battery in his hand. God, I haven't thought about that in years…" She shook her head. "Anyway, all he said was that he'd changed his mind and that we would attend the funeral after all."

"How'd you feel about that?"

"I didn't know her at all. I just saw her through her effect on Max. Obviously there was lots of anger, but there he was, ready to wade in."

"He didn't say why?"

"He said maybe it would give him closure or something like that. It sounded like BS psych-speak. I knew he didn't mean it, but that was the only answer I'd get."

"Was he always that private about his past?"

"Always. Aside from the happy-face version he gave the public, he was a vault." That wasn't quite true.

"Except...this was weird. He got excited when he told me about some of the people he thought might be there. I recognized a few names from the wedding, but I was just hearing about others for the first time. I took it that it was his carnival family on parade in a strange way."

"So what was so unbelievable?"

Laura swallowed hard. *Get it out, lady.*

"Esther Stark had insisted on a closed casket. We'd heard she died from cancer, and I suppose she looked pretty bad at the end. But that wasn't the reason."

"Why then?"

"We were in the middle of the ceremony, and I swear, I thought I heard a thump from inside the coffin."

Nelson stared.

"I figured it had to be my imagination. But sure enough, a few seconds later, I heard another, and then others started to look around, including the preacher."

Laura dug her nails into her palms. "Just when it got to the point where I was sure something had gotten in there, we all heard a voice start to yell."

"From inside?"

Laura nodded. "Clear as day. I'll never forget it. 'Hey, what's going on? Where am I?' Max staggered, and one of the ladies screamed. I got a look at everyone else, and they all seemed to recognize the voice."

"Esther? Max's mother?"

"Apparently. Max seemed frozen to his seat, and one of his friends rushed forward right when the voice started hollering, 'Let me out, let me out!'" Laura paused. "Then his friend opened the casket, and damned if there wasn't a tape recorder. A goddamned tape recorder sitting on this dead woman's chest."

"That's new." Nelson had his eyes closed.

"And right before he could shut it off, she let out the loudest cackling laugh." She felt tears try to come and focused on her anger toward Max instead of her sympathy from the past. "Max darted forward and smashed the recorder, then slammed the lid back down. He didn't say a word. Christ, what was there to say?"

"How did it happen?"

"That's what everyone wanted to know. Max went from being like a zombie to a frenzied lunatic. Two of the carnival guys had to hold him back after he decked the mortician. It turns out he put the recorder in there after some lawyer threatened him to make sure he honored the deceased's last request. The lawyer lied and told him the message would bring comfort to the mourners. Sick bitch."

"Who was the lawyer?"

"Some hick shyster Esther paid off. Guy named Sam Trawler."

Nelson wrote the name down. "Did Max punch him out too?"

"He never found him."

"Never?"

That one simple question sent an icy shiver down her back. In all these years, she'd never even looked the guy up. All those memories lived in a dusty trunk in her mind, and she'd worked hard to block them out. Nelson's question stabbed through the dark. "I don't know." Laura paused and decided Nelson should know the rest. "Before you ask, I never looked into it."

"Why not?"

"Maybe I didn't want to know." She took a deep breath. "One of the older friends told me, while Max was out of earshot, that Esther started doing more than just reading fortunes for men right about the time Max lost his scholarship."

"Was she turning tricks?" Nelson asked.

Laura nodded. "And not the kind that involve rabbits out of a hat."

"Max never knew until that letter, did he?" Nelson spoke in a soft voice.

"Like I said, sick bitch."

***

Laura felt wiped out, like she'd been on a run around Central Park. "So that was the beginning of the end. After the funeral, Max wasn't just withdrawn. He became a totally different person."

"How so?"

"He'd fly off the handle at the smallest things. We'd always had disagreements, but after the funeral, he always escalated any contention between us. When I didn't back down, I began to worry that he might get physical."

"How'd he hold himself back? What did he say and do exactly?" Nelson closed his eyes.

"I think he didn't actually stop himself. He just didn't take it out on me."

Nelson peeked at her with one eye.

"One time he stood there glaring, and he kept closing his hands into fists and then opening them again." Laura could still picture it so clearly that the room seemed to dim around her. Then she noticed that Nelson, whose eyes had closed again, was balling his own hands in slow motion. She wondered if he was aware that he was doing it. "He stood there like that, for what felt like forever, then he stormed out without saying a word."

"But he came back?"

If she'd been home, she would have excused herself, gone straight to the medicine cabinet, ripped open the old bottle of Xanax, and taken two. Instead she clung to the desk like it was a life raft. "A couple hours later. He still didn't want to talk, but I saw a bruise on his cheek, and the knuckles on one hand were cut."

Nelson opened his eyes and looked at her.

She let go of the desk and wrapped her arms around her body. "That scene played out a few more times, except that he looked less banged up and more relaxed each time he came back. That should have been comforting, but it frightened me even more."

"Why?" But Nelson nodded a bit like he agreed with her.

"Don't ask how I knew, but I think he was getting better at picking and winning fights—and that he enjoyed them. And all because I made him angry."

Nelson looked surprised. "You *made* him? That's not the Laura I met talking."

She shivered. "I haven't thought of it like that in ages. You're right. Victim-speak 101. But at the time, he made me feel like the fates of strangers were in my hands, and if I pushed his buttons, someone else was going to pay for it."

"Didn't you think it was only a matter of time until he cut out the middleman?" Nelson spoke neither down nor up to her. Laura found it refreshing.

"Yes. I'd even started working on an escape plan because I was sure he'd eventually get around to me. But then he changed again. All of a sudden, there were no more fights, with me or anyone else as far as I could tell."

"In what way?" Nelson sat still as a sphinx, absorbing Laura's words.

"I don't know if you saw in your research that Max worked in insurance sales. Sounds boring, considering his upbringing, but he was great at it." Laura remembered the crystal awards that used to dot their mantle. "I was so caught up with my own job at the time that I didn't see how bad he was getting at work until it was too late."

"He was losing sales?" Nelson doodled on a writing pad he pulled from his back pocket.

"No. Pranks."

Nelson's pen stopped in midscribble. "How's that?"

"Practical jokes. Max was playing tricks on his customers, and they finally caught up to him. He was selling more than ever, but he finally pushed it too far."

"What did he do?"

"Stupid stuff. Short-sheeting beds, mustaches on family pictures. The last straw came when he glued an old lady's dentures to a door handle. I remember he said he'd told his boss that he'd done her a favor since 'she hadn't had her teeth around some nice knob in decades.' Can you believe it?" She still couldn't, even as the words came out of her mouth.

"He told you that?"

"He even sounded proud of himself. He'd found a new way to vent his rage. After that, things went downhill fast between us. Just when my career was taking off, he derailed, professionally and personally."

"Did Max try to get help?"

Laura shook her head. "He wouldn't even admit anything was wrong. He kept going on about how he wasn't going by the rubes' rules anymore. I suppose I was one of *them* before long because he tuned me out completely. I did try, but the Max I'd known was gone, and the new version seemed to like it that way."

Laura felt the loss tear into her chest. She'd second-guessed herself for years, before ultimately moving on. "It's funny. When I got a job offer in Miami, I accepted the position and started making arrangements in my head before I even thought of telling Max. Sounds cold, I know, but that's how far apart we'd grown."

"I believe you."

"When I finally told him I was going—without him—I actually thought he'd be fine with it. Talk about young and stupid."

"What was his exact reaction?" Nelson leaned forward, and Laura felt the intensity in his gaze.

"He was cold to my face. Yes or no answers, otherwise the silent treatment. I wasn't supposed to leave for Miami for a few months, but I was so uncomfortable I got a temporary apartment."

"He wouldn't leave?"

"Wouldn't hear of it. After I moved out, I started to get the strangest calls. Not the usual oddball fan. More specific, and invariably really dirty. When I finally engaged one of these weirdos in conversation, I found out Max was leaving my number in men's bathrooms."

"Was that it?"

"You know better. You can't get a restraining order for something so trivial." It hadn't felt trivial though. It was like the perverts could see her when they muttered their filth.

"He followed me. All over town. The one time I tried to confront him, he looked at me with these dead eyes. I'll never forget it. I was able to get a restraining order in record time. It helps to know the right people, but I wasn't sure how getting served would affect him. I was pretty naive back then, but I still didn't put all my faith in a piece of paper as a shield."

"What about after you got down to Florida?"

"The order must have been more effective than I thought. It wouldn't have much effect out of state, but the fact that I'd fought back must have counted for something. I didn't hear from him again after that."

"And you came straight up here from Miami?"

"Right. And nary a peep from Max. I didn't even know he worked in the city until recently."

"But he knew about you."

"With all the ads and controversies and being on TV, I would think so."

"Why now?"

"That's your job, isn't it?"

"Fair enough." Nelson put his pad away.

Laura felt exhausted. She definitely needed a serious caffeine boost. "You should think about becoming a therapist, Nelson."

He blushed. "My hourly rate is lower. And I haven't gotten you any answers yet."

Laura smiled at him. "So now what?"

Nelson checked his phone and scrolled through his text messages. "Now I drive home alone. Paul's got a date with his ex-wife."

Laura had heard about her. "She's a pretty good reporter for the *Times*. Metro section, right?"

"Yup."

"Dating your ex? No thanks." Laura shivered at the thought.

"That's why I like to play the field. I'm in no rush to get pinned down."

She didn't know the guy well enough to tell if he was joking, but she could swear she saw a hint of a smile.

He continued. "But I need to button up a couple things and talk to Paul. We'll call you with an update soon. In the meantime, stay alert, and if you feel you're in any danger, call the police."

17

ALL ACCOUNTED FOR

Manhattan

Drew stared at the old photos. One guy looked like a scarecrow, the other like a sumo wrestler in a good suit. These guys were the cavalry that Laura felt so good about?

Sure, maybe they'd been hot shit once, but that was years ago. They'd solved some crime in Delaware. Big deal. As if a serial killer, or whoever it was, wouldn't stand out like a neon sign in that sleepy state.

Whatever. He was pissed that Laura hadn't shown more faith in him to deal with the situation.

OK, so maybe he hadn't been convinced there was anything to worry about, but like he always told his clients during a forensic audit, show me *all* the information, and then I'll let you know if you have a problem.

Once Laura had shared the tax returns with him, he knew two things. First, this Max character's business, Laughing Matters, was pissing out cash, and the man had either found another way to cover his bills or would need to soon. Second, these so-called detectives were scamming Laura. They couldn't have accessed those tax returns legally. So their ethics were shit. Who knew what "facts" they'd turn up to tap poor Laura, all in the name of "security"?

Not if he had anything to say about it. This guy Max thought he'd push his girl around to squeeze her for cash? Drew had grown up in Brooklyn, put himself through school, and clawed his way into a good position with a top-notch firm. Plus, he'd been a decent amateur boxer.

If this clown...Drew sat at his desk and laughed out loud. That's *exactly* what the guy was. If he wanted a fight, that red nose sure would make a good target.

He doubted it'd come to that. The dude slunk around like a coward. Call his bluff, and the cockroach would surely scurry back out of their lives, and all this crap would blow over. No more trouble, no more expensive detectives.

He double-checked the number and picked up the phone. This was going to be fun.

※ ※ ※

"Yes, I'll hold." Drew gripped the phone and made sure nobody was hovering around his desk. All clear.

"Max Stark speaking. How may I amuse you today?"

Seriously?

"You can start by laying off Laura, for one." Drew thought he heard a sharp intake of breath, but when the man spoke he was cool.

"And who are you, Magoo?"

Who talked like that? "Trouble, if you don't back off. I have your number."

"We're in the Yellow Pages. Glad you called, but I don't catch your drift."

Drew had expected that. Not just because he was coming at the guy out of the blue, but because he could be recording the conversation. Now he wished he was.

"Take your money problems and personal hang-ups somewhere else. She's with me now, and even if she weren't, you're the last person she wants to hear from. Or do you need a restraining order in New York to get the hint?"

"I think I follow you." Max's tone didn't change a whit. "Touching protective instincts. It's good to know you're looking after her. Gotta tell you though, you're auditing the wrong set of books. I haven't seen Laura in years, as long as billboards don't count."

Drew didn't believe him, despite his convincing tone.

"So you didn't leave balloons at her door?"

"I don't even know where her door is. My turn. Why do you think my business isn't solvent? You seem so sure."

Drew didn't feel quite so sure now. Was this all a big mistake? He wasn't about to admit to hacking into Max's tax files, especially when he wasn't the one who'd done it. Besides, Laughing Matters might be recording the call, for "quality control purposes" or some such thing.

"Lucky guess. But if you aren't reaching out to her, you have nothing to fear from me." He wished he'd put more bass in his voice.

"*That's* a relief."

Sarcastic prick.

Drew held the dead phone in his hand and tried to reconcile the feeling in the pit of his stomach with what should have been the thrill of victory.

18

DIG IN

Wilmington, Delaware, East-West Investigations

Chang turned off Route 52 and into the parking lot for EWI, and spotted Nelson's car.

Good, they could start their meeting on time.

Betty sat up front by the phone and was hard at work on a stack of background investigation candidates. She seemed to like the tedious, basic verifications. If anything didn't check out, she'd pass the file to Nelson. Her beehive hair swayed back and forth as her head moved between the pages and the computer screen like a metronome.

"Betty, how's it going?"

"Afternoon, Mr. Chang."

He'd given up asking her to call him by his first name. Must be some rule she had about not getting too close to someone who had killed people. At least she no longer flinched when he spoke to her.

Still, she kept the office running smoothly, especially when he and Nelson weren't around, and they'd been able to add another retainer client for backgrounders, thanks to her assistance. He just needed to be careful not to share any sensitive information because she found such confidences too juicy not to blurt out.

He'd learned to let her natural curiosity (Nelson's term) work for him with routine verifications.

"Meeting with Nelson?"

"Yep. Just us, thanks," Chang said, determined to head off her interest. He was happy to see she had plenty to do.

Nelson strolled into the conference room and settled into a chair. He placed a small stack of papers in front of him. "How's Colleen?"

Chang let the memories of his particularly energetic date the previous night flow through his mind. He'd been tired that morning, but every morning he could wake up next to her was worth the early alarm and groggy drive back to Delaware.

"Good. She said to say hello." Chang poured himself a cup of coffee and took a sip.

"I told you it was me she was thinking about…"

Chang nearly sprayed his coffee all over his shirt. "Does your sense of humor always have to kick in right when I'm in the middle of drinking something?"

"Can't predict the weather." Nelson still seemed pleased that he and Colleen were friends now. Back when he and Chang had been cops together, she'd never trusted him.

"So what have you got?"

Nelson recapped what Laura had told him. Chang leaned back in his chair and tried to picture the guy he saw sneaking around the footbridge. "I'm inclined to think she's not exaggerating."

"Me too. While we were talking, her pupils dilated like she was on drugs. Nothing phony about her fear."

"We can help her. The question is, is the guy a threat to her now?" Chang explained how he'd placed the tracker on the van. He glanced up to confirm that Betty was still at her desk. Then he logged into the tracking program on his laptop and turned the screen to show Nelson. "OK, there's the van, and over here"—he tabbed over on the program—"we can see where it's been." Chang saw the red dots indicating several locations.

"Cool."

High praise from Nelson.

"Of course we'll know more over time, but so far I don't see anything odd, aside from whatever he was up to in Brooklyn. Otherwise, the van spent most of its time at Laughing Matters or what looks like errands to places you might expect, like a supply house and other quick stops."

"Not near Laura's place or the TV station?"

Chang shook his head. "But we'll see." He switched back to real time and saw that the van was sitting in front of the Laughing Matters warehouse.

"What was so strange about the stop in Brooklyn?"

Chang described Max's furtive behavior. "What sealed it for me was the way he turned around suddenly in the middle of that bridge. He'd have made me if I was on an active tail."

"For a clown he acts more like an operator."

"If he was up to something. But if it was legit business, why go through all the costumes and long walks? Why not just pull up to a place and go right in?"

"Sounds like you answered your own question. Do you think you could tail him now if he goes there again?"

"Now that I have a better idea what I'm up against. Sure."

"Then you'll find this interesting." Nelson picked up some papers and recounted Laura's story about Max's mother's funeral.

Chang couldn't help but think of his own mother's service. The contrast jarred him. "I guess we know where he got the bizarre genes."

"More than quirky." Nelson held up a page. "The lawyer that set up the theatrics at the funeral."

"Trawler."

"Yes. Sam Trawler. Laura never followed up, but it turns out he disappeared soon after."

Chang met Nelson's gaze. "And?"

"He was found in a graveyard on the other side of Georgia."

"I take it you mean not in a coffin?"

"Trawler was in a coffin all right, but the grave was from the recent funeral of a young girl."

Chang closed the laptop and stared at his partner. "I'm not following you."

"From what I could piece together, someone entered a cemetery outside of Valdosta, Georgia, and dug up a fresh grave," Nelson said.

"Grave robbery gone wrong or something?"

"An anonymous tipster said he saw a thief. When the cops came to check it out, they could see footprints and shovel marks. So, they got the OK to dig up the grave."

"And?"

"They were almost in time."

"He was…"

"Trawler was alive when he got put in with the fresh corpse of a young lady and buried. He suffocated while waiting for the cops to dig him up."

Chang rubbed his aching hand and remembered his own desperation when he'd had to fight for air while trapped underwater. He took a deep breath, as though it could help Trawler. "Any arrests?"

Nelson put the paper back on the table. "Long story short, no. Unsolved. I can call around if you like, but this is ancient history. I'm sure they have their suspicions though."

"You too?" Chang began to see Max with different eyes.

"Yes. But there might not be proof, even with today's technology, if the killer was careful. It happened more than fifteen years ago."

"OK. Well, we can't assume it was him, but the buried alive theme can't be a coincidence with that bit his mother pulled at her funeral."

"Do we tell Laura?" Nelson asked.

"She doesn't need to be any more frightened than she already is. And we don't know for a fact that it's true. But I think between that and everything else, we ought to operate on the premise that this guy isn't just weird, but dangerous."

"And smart."

"You think?" Chang wondered. Murderers could be slippery without being brilliant.

"He seems to enjoy a performance. That kill had real flair."

"Maybe. For now it's safe to say we can't send Laura a final bill. Maybe he slips up, and we can get Ron in on the picture." Chang looked at the tracker program again.

His quarry sat.

No. His quarry's *van* sat.

19

BUT IS IT ART?

Laura's Apartment, One Week Later

"No, I wasn't drunk." Drew's defensive tone was starting to grate on Laura.

She struggled to remain civil. "Drew, I don't think you heard me. I'm waiting for a call back from my best source. I've already got half my team dropping their plans tonight in case this lead, whatever the hell it is, pans out." She glanced at her smartphone again, even though she'd barely taken her eyes off it for the last hour.

STP had been cryptic when he'd called earlier. "Biggest story yet. By far. Get your people ready for an Emmy chase. Call you later." And with that he was out.

Then Drew had shown up.

"I don't think *you've* been listening. My car—"

"Damn it, Drew. All you've done is complain since you walked in the door. I would have told you I was busy if you'd bothered to call."

"You've been busy all week."

"It happens." *When did he get so clingy?*

"Whatever the fuck is going on with *me* this week doesn't just *happen.*"

Laura tore her gaze from the phone and looked at Drew. Sort of felt like the first time since he'd barnstormed his way in the door. "Honey, you don't look so hot."

"Just listen to me for one minute. I get the *Laura Stark, on the case* bit. I do. But pretend I'm a source for a second."

"OK." She forced herself to listen. He never got like this. Which was precisely part of his charm, she'd always thought.

"Remember your guess that my car got swiped by a thief who lived nearby or something, since it wound up across the street?"

"Kids? Out for a joyride?"

"I thought about that. But get this. You know how I am about checking the mileage?"

She decided this was not the moment to needle him about the little logbook he kept in the glove box. "Yeah."

"Same mileage."

"Really?"

Drew nodded like his head was going to pop off. "The thief took my car, drove across the street, and parked it."

An icy finger traced a shiver down her back. "Tell me the other stuff again." *So I can actually listen this time*, she omitted.

Drew ticked off the offenses with his fingers. "One. My newspaper was canceled, but I didn't do it. I still like the sports section. The guy at the subscription department said he spoke to me personally and that I cursed him out. Said he recognized my voice and everything. Prick. Two, I get to work and they've shifted my appointments because I supposedly called in sick."

"You don't think it was a mistake?"

"Do you know me to be a scatterbrain?"

"No." He was the most organized man she'd ever met. The room suddenly felt chilly. "What else?"

Drew's face flushed red.

Laura thought he was going to blow a gasket, but then she saw that it wasn't rage, at least not all of it. "What?"

"You're going to be pissed."

"Probably. Spill."

His shoulders sagged. "I wanted to help."

She stared. "How?" Time felt like it was slowing down.

"I called Max."

"Shit. What did you say?"

"I told him to back off."

No.

Drew continued. "He sounded like a wuss. I figured a little scare would make him back off, and life could get back to normal for us."

"How's that working out?" Laura regretted the sarcasm immediately. This might be serious.

"Would you believe the cops think I'm nuts? I called them about the car to get them to dust for prints. The jackass on the line said if nothing was missing, there wasn't much of a case. No proof the car was stolen. Can you believe that?"

"I can." Laura probably wouldn't have gotten even that much courtesy. "So they refused to come out?"

"Pretty much. If I wanted to take the day off, they could send someone by to take a report. I finally just hung up."

"So what do you want to do?"

"Kick the weirdo's ass."

Laura's gut clenched. She didn't want to inadvertently stir up Drew's pride, but she knew that Max could handle himself. "Don't..."

"I won't hit him or anything. This isn't the playground and neither of us is a child, even though it seems like he hasn't noticed that. Other than the car, he's pulled only kid stuff." Drew paused.

"Chickenshit kid stuff. So I'm going to go into his backyard and embarrass him a little."

"You shouldn't—" Laura's phone chirped. She looked at the ID: XXX-XXX-XXXX.

"Laura Stark."

"STP. Ready?"

She looked at Drew and pointed at the phone; then she grabbed a pen. Drew gave her a silent wave and slipped out the door.

❋ ❋ ❋

"I hope you have your team ready."

"Yup." Her heart was pounding.

STP gave a short laugh. "I guess my credibility is high. OK, things are going to move fast, so listen close."

"I know shorthand. Go." Laura scribbled on the paper to make sure the ink was flowing.

"Don't interrupt with how I know what I know. There's proof for all of it."

"I'm listening."

"New York Attorney General Bennett Trip just got the same package that's on its way to you now. He's a hack and a fool, and if I'm right, he's burning up the phone lines violating his oath of office." STP exhaled like he'd just taken a drag on a cigarette.

"OK." Laura wanted STP to know she was keeping up on her notes.

"You know Griffon Lewis?"

"The billionaire? Insurance empire and philanthropist. Art collector. Need more?" Where was this going?

"No, *you* do. He's also asshole buddies with His Honor the mayor."

"And?"

"And Griffon is as big a collector of *stolen* art as legit. He's got a world-class secret collection."

"How do you—"

"Ah, ah. You promised. I'm sending you detailed pictures and some friendly advice."

"What's that?" Her pulse raced. The pen tip flew across the notepad like it was possessed.

"Thanks to me, the AG knows all this. He *should* launch a raid to catch the bastard red-handed."

"You're sure he won't?"

"He said it might take time to evaluate the evidence, get a warrant, you know the drill."

She did. The AG could get a warrant any time of the day or night. "He's going to tip him off."

"So true. He's going to protect the mayor's buddy. By the time he gets around to serving any warrants, where do you think the evidence might be?"

"Switzerland?" *Damn.* "He'll serve that warrant; I'll make sure the pressure is on from the public. But better still to catch Lewis in the act. When is the earliest he'd get the tip?"

"That's why you're my favorite." STP almost purred into the phone. "A courier, same fellow as last time, is on his way to your office as we speak. Included in the files might be the location where Lewis keeps his stash. A film of him rushing things into a van or truck might make for compelling viewing."

Laura thought about how long it would take her to reach the office. She debated for a split second about giving out her home address. "Wait. Can you redirect the courier?"

20

MAN ON THE STREET

Manhattan

Laura sat fidgeting in the van outside the San Remo apartment building with Eddie Tua. The licorice stench from his incessant chewing of "stakeout food" overwhelmed the cramped space.

She didn't care. If Lewis was going to panic, he was too old to move all of his artwork out on his own. But since he probably traveled with a bodyguard, he'd have some muscle to help him lift heavier pieces.

"You sure about this?" Eddie chomped away and checked the time on his phone.

Laura flipped through the folder of pictures, keeping watch on the building's side door where deliveries were made.

She was sure the doormen had spotted the vehicle, but in this case that probably didn't matter. Given the number of celebrities who lived in the famous building, this was practically a paparazzi parking zone. They almost blended in.

Tonight their target was more used to operating behind the scenes. And he might be counting on his comparatively lower profile to cover his tail.

"This source hasn't missed yet. Look at this, Eddie." She spun her laptop around to show him some notable heisted masterpieces and then held up the digital pictures STP had sent to her.

"Damn. He's bold. That's a Picasso. Don't know this one."

"Vermeer. This is huge." Laura pointed to another. "Van Gogh. A couple of them." Although most of the items were paintings, she wondered how he'd get the sculptures out.

"I've got something." She saw a couple of San Remo uniformed staffers helping a silver-haired man in a raincoat and fedora with a hand truck and steamer trunk. He directed them toward a black Range Rover that had just pulled up. Laura saw a thick-necked driver and noted that the vehicle's backseats were down to allow for more cargo.

"That's him." They both leapt out of the van, and Eddie flipped on the camera light.

"Mr. Lewis? Griffon Lewis? Laura Stark, from WBAC. We're doing a story on stolen art and smuggling. Mind if we ask you some questions?"

The driver moved fast to get out of the SUV, but not in time to prevent Eddie from capturing the look of pure horror on Lewis's face.

Shock gave way to fury. "Why are you bothering me? I'm busy. You want an interview, call my secretary."

"Not your attorney?" She moved away from the driver, who slowed down only long enough to look to his boss for guidance.

Laura held up some pictures of the stolen pieces. The shots were close up enough to provide detail but also wide enough to show the interior of Lewis's inner sanctum.

Viewers wouldn't know anything about that. But Lewis clearly did, and his mask slipped again.

"What...what are you talking about? Get out of here. This is harassment."

The driver moved in. His suit did little to hide his muscular bulk, and he probably outweighed Eddie, who didn't flinch.

"What's in the trunk?" Laura added for effect. She knew the old bastard wouldn't slip again tonight. She looked at the driver.

"OK, we're leaving." They backed away, but Eddie never dropped the camera. Lewis never dropped the trunk either. They loaded it into the SUV and sped off with their unknown treasures.

Their little stunt may have not done much to help the prosecution in a legal case—if there ever was one.

But it would be TV magic.

＊＊＊

"Slow down." Sid Gold's sleepy voice came over the line.

Laura gave him a moment to wake up. She hated to call him past midnight like this. Usually. But this time she didn't care what time it was.

"Ready?" She took his grunt as a yes. She filled him in on what STP had given her and their little chat with Griffon Lewis.

"And you can actually see the old guy's jaw drop?" Sid was awake now, and his excitement came through the phone.

"In living color. Eddie is helping me cut up the promo pieces now." Laura loved the discretion Sid gave her when she had a hot lead, and so far she'd never given him a reason to regret it. She waved at Eddie, who had just emerged from the editing room for more coffee, and gave him a "me too" gesture.

"He's pretty versatile for a camera guy," Sid muttered. "Don't tell him I said that. He'll want a raise."

"I won't," she lied.

"I'll be there in an hour," Sid said. "We're gonna make some friends with this one."

＊＊＊

Laura, Sid, and Eddie shared an impromptu breakfast scavenged from the nearest all-night coffee shop.

"Boss, I'm gonna crash on the cot for a few if that's OK," Eddie said as he stretched. Laura could see dark circles around his strong round eyes.

"Please. We're fine here. Good work, Eddie." Sid smiled.

"You bet." As Eddie left the room, Laura saw that the rare compliment put a bounce in his step.

Sid checked his watch. "Think seven thirty is too early to beat Bennett Trip to the punch?"

"I doubt Lewis got much more sleep than we did. I'd guess he melted his cell phone, and at least one of his calls might have been to the AG to try to get ahead of this. I'm sure they know each other."

"But you don't know if they're friends?"

Laura shook her head. "STP mentioned the mayor, so I figure the AG would at least want to be on Lewis's good side."

"Maybe not anymore." Sid pointed to the spread of photos from the package STP had sent. "You're sure your guy said the AG got the same thing?"

"He assured me. We'll find out."

Sid took another bite out of his bagel and wiped a few crumbs off his white, open-collar shirt. Laura wondered if he slept in his gold chains and decided she didn't want to know.

"Let's give him until eight o'clock. Public servants need their beauty sleep," Sid said.

Sid didn't get a chance to finish his bagel.

21

FRIENDS IN HIGH PLACES

WBAC

"Put it through," Sid said to Mary at the switchboard. He gestured for Laura to sit down, then hit the button for speakerphone. "Sid Gold. How may I help you, Mr. Trip?"

"You can take me off the goddamned speaker for starters." Bennett Trip's voice carried a rasp Laura hadn't heard before during press conferences.

Sid tossed Laura an earpiece to allow her to listen in on the conversation without being able to talk. It was a neat gadget, and this way, she didn't have to worry about Trip overhearing her breathing. "That better?"

"Look, you can't run this story you're working on today." The man sounded winded.

"Can you be more specific? We're a news outfit, and we've got our fingers in a lot of pies."

"Cut the crap. You know the one. The art smuggling story? That's an ongoing case. I only just opened the investigation, and you go all cowboy and pounce on the man on the pretense of rumors."

"Rumors? We got the same package you did. Those shots are plenty clear and look to me like they are from a private residence. Our source says it was Lewis, and based on how he acted, I'd say that's fairly compelling."

"Damn it, do you have any idea how sensitive this is?"

"You're giving me a good idea, Mr. Trip."

Laura could see that Sid wasn't doing this just to support her. He lived for this.

"Well, then I'm sure, given the stakes, that you can see fit to hold off just a day or two while my office does the hard part and verifies whether there's any fire to go with the smoke." Trip started to sound like a guy used to getting his way.

"So you just want to make sure everything checks out, is that it?"

"Right."

"You're not running interference for anyone, are you?"

"I'm not sure I care for your tone, Gold."

"You're saying Griffon Lewis didn't call you to try to bury it?"

"Of course not. I resent the implication."

"Nothing personal, Trip." Sid grinned and leaned back in his chair. "Since you aren't trying to tell an organ of the press how to cover a story, or when, for that matter, I won't point out that the evidence dropped in our laps will likely disappear while you do your *proceed with caution* bit."

"You're right."

"I am?"

"Yeah, you're not going to tell me how to do my fucking job!"

Laura pulled out the earpiece. Trip was gone. "That went well."

"His constituent outreach needs work." Sid checked a list of the promo pieces they'd pulled together overnight. He took out a pen and circled several numbers. "Run these outside and tell Jerry they start with the nine o'clock news. Heavy rotation. If he needs to bump Credit-Mendit, that's fine. They're slow payers anyway."

Such guts! "I love you, Sid."

Sid spread his arms to show his hairy chest, fake tan, and gold chains. "What's not to love?"

***

Laura walked back toward Sid's office after making sure Jerry had the promo spots in order. The instant the first one ran, they'd make a permanent enemy of the state's AG. Sid's army of lawyers would build a wall around the station, but she prayed his finances were in order. Assuming they were, they could respond with daily coverage of the AG's abuse of power. She'd lead the charge.

***

Laura's contacts felt like sand in her eyes, so she ducked into her office to find her eyedrops.

"Damn," she said as the tiny bottle wheezed out a feeble hint of mist. She flung it in the trash and remembered the backup bottle in her desk drawer. Rummaging through the top drawer, she found the glasses case with her spare pair. She snapped open the case and found the little bottle. The cool drops soothed her eyes in no time.

"What the hell is this?" As she was putting the bottle back in the case, she noticed that something was on the lenses of her glasses. She took them out, looked at them, and then dropped into her chair with a moan. The lenses had clown faces drawn on them with a black felt-tip marker.

She threw the glasses down like they were smeared with a virus.

Laura whipped her head around and even peeked at the space under her desk. Her heart was thudding in her chest, and she forced herself to breathe slowly. She tried to remember the last time she'd seen her glasses. Not the case, but the glasses themselves. It had to have been weeks, maybe more.

She took another deep breath and tried to push the fear out with the air. "He could have done this a while ago. A long time ago. It doesn't mean he's here now."

She bit back a scream when a head popped into her doorway.

Sid waved at her. "Hurry," he hissed. "C'mon! What's the matter with you?"

"Coming." She spoke automatically and kept telling herself the drawing was an old trick and to get back in the game.

❊❊❊

She'd just about convinced herself by the time they reached Sid's office. The first promo spot was twenty minutes out.

Inside Sid's office he handed her the earpiece.

"Trip again? Do you want to tape his rant this time?" she asked.

Sid frowned. "You ever tried jail food? Hell no. And it isn't Trip. Actually, he told me the truth. It wasn't him that Lewis called."

Laura cast her memory back to STP's call, which in her current sleep-deprived state felt like it had been a month ago. Fatigue dragged on her thoughts. "Wait. The—"

Sid's intercom buzzed. It was Mary. "Line one, Sid."

Sid signaled for quiet, and Laura shoved in the earpiece.

"Mr. Mayor."

Laura's fatigue vanished. Malcolm Glacier was not only mayor of New York City but also—just as STP had warned her—a patron of the arts, legit or stolen, it seemed.

"Mr. Gold, sorry to bother you this morning."

"I'm honored, Your Honor."

"Yes. I understand you had an unpleasant discussion with my hotheaded AG."

Laura tried to read between the smooth words and measured tones. No luck. Glacier was a lifelong pro and did little to quell rumors he might someday make a run for the White House.

"No problem, sir. It comes with the territory."

"I'm sure. The reason for my call is to ask your forbearance in this matter."

"Sir, with all due respect, we covered this with Mr. Trip." Sid glanced at his watch and showed Laura. Fifteen minutes until the first spot aired.

C'mon Sid. Don't cave...

"Yes, well, there is more at stake here than you know. I'm afraid I can't be terribly forthcoming. But what if I gave you my personal guarantee that AG Trip will hand down indictments, and you'll get the first interviews with him and myself, if you like." The smooth voice never wavered, but Laura sensed the tension underneath. Whatever was going on, it had to be huge for the mayor to volunteer to toss his supposed friend and fund-raiser under the bus.

Sid grabbed a pen, and Laura did the same. "That's certainly generous, but you must realize that we have a mountain of credible evidence on Mr. Lewis. And while I'm sure you had no idea about his illegal activities, this represents a perishable opportunity."

"I understand—"

Sid interrupted. "Perhaps if you gave me a clearer idea of what you are referring to, I could give your request the proper consideration."

Laura loved the way Sid's manner of speech began to match Glacier's diplomatic phrasing.

There was a long pause. Again Laura couldn't tell whether the mayor was stumped or if it was merely for dramatic effect.

"This is completely off the record, but before I say any-thing—and it won't be much—you need to understand that any irresponsible treatment of this information could result in thousands of deaths."

He hadn't even disclosed anything yet, but he certainly had their undivided attention.

Glacier continued. "Mr. Lewis is involved, as am I, in some negotiations that are at a fragile stage. Any disruption, including your unfortunate discovery, might jeopardize the progress we've made to date and put countless innocents at grave risk."

Laura scribbled furiously and held up a note to Sid, who nodded. He spoke. "Unfortunate? Are you saying you knew about Lewis's illegal art collection?"

"Of course not. I meant unfortunate with regard to the timing only. Rest assured. He'll be dealt with appropriately at the right time."

Now the slick voice was glossy with arrogance.

"Mr. Mayor, that sounds intriguing, but I would have to have more than vague references and assurances to bury this story."

"Do you doubt my word?" Indignation on tap, the lifeblood of a good politician, but the wrong approach with Sid, Laura knew.

"Do you doubt mine?"

"I've said more than I should."

Sid made a circle of his fingers and began to make crude jerk-off motions in the air in front of him. "It appears we're at an impasse, sir, and I must be candid. The clock is running. We're about to tease the story at the top of the next hour."

Another pause, this one not for effect, Laura was certain.

When Glacier finally spoke, his tone matched his name. "Very well. I shall make other arrangements. Assuming you follow through on your threat, I will be making an announcement soon after."

"Fine. We'll send a crew over."

22

SWING TOWN

Brooklyn

Drew sat in his car near the warehouse and drummed his fingers on the steering wheel. He looked again for any telltale marks around his ignition switch but could see no sign that his car had been hot-wired. He was past hoping that the cops would be any help at all, but he had no doubt about what had been done.

He used to think Laura was paranoid, both because of the grudge the police held against her and because of what a head case her ex was. Not anymore. Now he wondered if the cops were punishing him because they were dating.

Nah, they were just douche bags.

Speaking of which. This Max character thought his crap would work on Drew like it did on Laura. Drew Gantry didn't run from a fight. Max wanted to play games?

"You're about to find out just what a prick I can be, clownie." Drew opened the car door.

* * *

Drew walked toward the entrance. Shitty neighborhood, but this wasn't a walk-in kind of a business. He saw the panel truck with the Laughing Matters logo emblazoned on the side, and the sign on the door, so he knew he had the right place.

He'd debated what to wear. His power suit didn't seem right. Besides, if this guy wanted to tangle, the last thing he wanted was clown blood on his Armani. The thought made him smile. He'd opted for loose jeans and a sweatshirt, which gave him room to move if Max wanted to get cute.

But Drew doubted he would. He figured the guy would pipe down, especially when he saw that two could play the "I know where you live" game.

The glass door, set in a white wall with peeling paint, was locked. Drew leaned on the buzzer.

Nothing.

He pressed it again—for longer than he considered polite.

"Whataya want?" came from a dented gray speaker next to the button. He didn't recognize the voice, but the sound quality was drive-through buzzy.

"Max? Max Stark?"

Pause.

"He expecting you?"

The hired help. "No, but tell him it's Laura's boyfriend."

Longer pause. "Yer funeral, pal."

The door lock buzzed. Drew pulled open the door before he could change his mind.

In what could loosely be described as the lobby, he saw circus posters and photos—presumably of the elaborate shows they'd staged—on the walls. On one side there was a counter and on the other a couple of desks with computers on them, but there was nobody in sight.

"Hello?" Drew peered around the counter and saw a glass-walled office in back with rectangular windows inside. It was too dark to make out much more.

He jumped at the screech of a door opening farther along the wall to the left. A short man with receding red hair and freckles approached him. "You're the boyfriend?"

Drew recognized the rough voice from the speaker and wondered for an instant if this could be Max, but then he remembered that Laura had said he was tall. And this guy was nobody's idea of good-looking. His nose looked like it'd been broken sideways with a pool cue and left to heal on its own. It reminded Drew of the V-shape of a "greater than" symbol. He wore coveralls, and his fingers were embedded with dirt, like he'd washed them right after being booked by the police.

Maybe he had. "Where's Max?"

He held out a grimy paw. "Marty Potempkin."

Drew shook it out of reflex and was surprised by the grip; maybe the guy was like the roadie for the outfit. He thought he caught a hint of an eastern European accent, but—like the rest of the guy—it sounded dim.

"Is he here?"

Marty hooked a thumb toward the wall. "Max is in Swing Town."

Drew felt deflated. "He's not here? Why didn't you just tell me that in the first place?"

Marty smiled. "That's our training area. He's practicing. Said to send you back."

"I'm not here for the tour."

Marty held a door open. It looked black inside. "That's what you think."

✳ ✳ ✳

Drew ignored the hammering in his chest. He stepped through and felt cool air. The echoes made him think he was in a large open space, but the windows, if there were any, were blacked out, and his eyes needed time to adjust to the darkness.

Slam!

All he could hear after the door banged shut was an intermittent squeak. Now it was nearly pitch black inside. He felt for the door. As he expected, it was locked.

"People know I'm here. They're going to wonder if I don't come back..." *Stop babbling. They want to scare you, is all.* Served him right for showing up without a plan.

He heard thumps on the wall above his head, and the squeaks sped up.

He took out his cell phone to use as a makeshift flashlight. The light wiped out whatever night vision he'd started to get, but he could finally see what had made the thumps by his head.

Three gleaming spikes were embedded in the wall not six inches from where his head had been.

Throwing knives?

A bright flash appeared to his right, and when he turned to look, he saw an inverted white skull with flaming orange hair streaking toward him in midair.

"Yahhhhhhhh!" the skull screamed as it flashed by. Drew dropped his phone.

His mind took in images faster than his body could respond. He felt something hit him on the shoulder, and dust exploded around him. He watched a body arc upward to the left and realized that it was a man with a flashlight hanging upside down on a trapeze.

The skull appeared to tumble and then soar back up again, and Drew realized it had to be several trapezes.

"Get down here, you chickenshit!" Shame and fury flooded Drew's body. He'd give this guy something to remember. What the fuck had he thrown on him?

The light was suddenly extinguished, and all Drew could hear was the slowing squeak of the trapezes.

Then he heard faint music coming from across the room. A calliope?

"Really?" He shouted into the darkness.

He squatted to pick up his phone and, staying low, made his way across the room. His eyes scanned for movement and—even more attentively—for a door or window so that he could get out of this funhouse.

"You done yet?" Drew called out.

A spotlight shone on him from behind, and he saw a white-headed figure crouched in front of him. He nearly launched himself at it but then realized he was looking at himself. Goddamned mirror.

He took a moment to look at what was all over him. His entire head and shoulders were covered in white powder. His blond hair appeared ancient. Wait a minute...

Drew touched a finger to the powder and tasted it.

Flour.

What was it the kids called it? *Oh yeah.*

"You *antiqued* me? Are you nuts?"

The spotlight went out, and Drew stood in the dark for a moment as the stupid carny music rolled in the background. Then the guy—it had to be Max—flashed the light onto his skull mask, pointed at Drew, and laughed loud and deep.

He was at ground level now.

"Son of a bitch..." Drew sprinted forward.

Just before he reached the guy, Drew's foot snagged on some sort of cable, and he fell flat on his face. He turned his head at the last instant and managed to avoid a broken nose, but his phone smashed on the concrete floor.

More raucous laughter as Max darted through a doorway. Drew regained his footing and raced to reach the door before it shut. There were no more trip wires, and he shot through the opening and into daylight.

He found himself on a shabby patch of grass between the back of the building and the fence line that guarded the train tracks beyond.

He'd made it out the door only a few seconds after Max. He should have seen him running away.

Drew looked up. A glittering, blue sphere filled his vision and drenched him when it burst on him.

Rubber fragments hit the ground—all that was left of a water balloon.

Drew saw his chance with the fire escape but, despite the rage that fueled his legs, couldn't get within six inches of the bottom rung.

"Get down here, motherfucker!"

Drew ran around to the front of the building. The doors were locked, and he saw no lights on inside.

He looked up at the roofline from the street. He paced back and forth a few times but saw no sign of Max or Marty or anyone at all.

Drew considered calling the cops before he remembered that his phone was inside and probably no longer worked anyway. He hurried back to his car. He pulled off his sweatshirt, which was now encrusted with a doughy mixture of flour and water that smelled like library paste.

As he started the car, he saw his reflection in the rearview mirror. He looked like he'd been in a fight with a baker.

And lost.

23

STAKEOUT

Colleen's Apartment

Chang sat on the couch in front of the TV at Colleen's place in the Bronx and listened to Colleen rattling plates in the kitchen. She'd already declined his offer to help, and he was content to sit quietly and enjoy a peaceful moment. He wondered if she liked these casual moments as much as he did. Even more than their renewed sex life, he liked these domestic snapshots that reminded him of when they were still married.

Colleen came out of the kitchen carrying a plate of cheese and crackers in one hand and a glass of white wine in the other. He forgot what kind, though she'd told him.

Some detective.

But he was off duty.

"Did I miss the opener?" Colleen sat close and took a sip. "Need a refill?"

"No thanks. They're just about to go to the top story." Chang took a fast gulp of his wine and noted it was getting warm. It didn't matter. He'd never been much of a drinker, and even with the dragon in hibernation, he wasn't interested in tempting fate. Especially not around Colleen.

"Laura didn't fill you in much, did she?" Colleen bit into a cracker.

"I barely got a chance to talk to her. She's like you when she's on a big story. A real pit bull."

"You sure do know how to sweep a gal off her feet."

"I try. This bombshell must be big. She wouldn't even listen to my update. But I guess that means there haven't been any new incidents."

He'd told Colleen about Max and what they'd found out so far.

"You think he's dangerous, not just hung up on her?"

Chang craned his neck to glance at his laptop. The pulsing red dot of the tracker program showed that the van hadn't moved. "He's a wacko of some sort. Very strange background, and yes, I think he might be."

"What does Nelson think?"

"He wants to look Max in the eye, but he's even more convinced than me that the guy's a time bomb." Back when they were married, Colleen never mentioned Nelson, even when he was Chang's partner. He'd won her over by risking his life to defend her. Chang still felt a pang of guilt that he couldn't have been there, but the ache in his hand reminded him that they'd all gotten to play the hero that day—and pay the price.

Colleen shivered and leaned into him.

The commercials ended, and Chang watched Laura Stark appear on the screen in all her klieg-lit glory.

"Good evening. We open today with the shocking details of highly regarded philanthropist Griffon Lewis, who has apparently been supporting the underground trade of high-profile, stolen art treasures. WBAC has learned through confidential sources that the following priceless works of art were, at least until a few days ago, located in the private residence of Mr. Lewis."

The camera cut to a rolling series of shots depicting a posh apartment interior and various paintings that Chang didn't recognize. His area of expertise, acquired from his uncle and father, was limited to Asian jade and Chinese dynastic artwork. The video captioned each piece and where it had been stolen.

Colleen whistled. "Some list."

"You know Lewis?"

"I met him once or twice when I covered charity functions. Typical patrician power guy. He always seemed to be in a good mood, but he was probably half in the bag after a night of half the city telling him how great he was."

"That'll do it." Chang piped down when Laura started speaking again. The video switched to an ambush-style camera shot of Lewis outside his apartment building.

"When we caught up with Mr. Lewis, he was less than cooperative, and we can only speculate about what he was doing at that hour with a steamer trunk." Laura voiced-over the clip.

During his tenure as an NYPD detective, he'd always resented the media's interference, particularly in high-profile cases.

"That was a cheap shot," Chang said. Still, he had to admit that Lewis looked guilty as hell of something.

Colleen shrugged. "She's known for pushing the envelope. But the guy had a chance to tell his side."

Laura continued, on camera. "The attorney general's office refused to comment, but we understand a search warrant might be forthcoming at some point."

Laura's sarcasm came through despite her dry delivery.

Laura nodded at something that Chang figured came in over her IFB earpiece. "We're breaking away to go to field reporter Kevin Little at the office of Mayor Malcolm Glacier, who we understand has a statement related to this report."

The shot flipped to a forest of microphones clustered on a podium decorated with the New York City seal. Cameras whirred and bulbs flashed as the mayor strode to the podium.

Chang didn't know Mayor Glacier personally. He'd left the city by the time Glacier took office.

Glacier was tall and thin with chiseled facial features, high cheekbones, and gleaming eyes that reminded Chang of a raptor. He had iron-gray hair that spoke to vigor and experience in equal measure. Perfect white teeth, a deep tan, and a handmade suit completed the effect.

Glacier looked every inch the career politician, which was all Chang needed to see to know that he probably wouldn't have much use for the guy.

He concentrated on the mayor's eyes. Despite his practiced ease at the podium, Chang detected stress in the way the man gripped the stand.

"Good evening. We learned this afternoon about the breaking report you're seeing now. From the outset I want to make clear that everything alleged is hearsay, until such time as these allegations can be investigated by the attorney general's office and such other departments as deemed necessary by the governor's office as well as my own."

Glacier looked up from his notes, and Chang saw the pain on the mayor's face. He knew the stress was real, but the mayor looked like he could conceal the reasons with the best of them.

"I wish Nelson could see this."

"Why?"

"The guy looks like a squirrel."

"Shh."

Glacier continued. "That said, we want to address even the appearance of impropriety. As it concerns a close friend of this administration and myself, I wanted to say a few things."

"Why? Nobody said he stole art."

Colleen leaned forward as if to hear better. "He might be president one day. Damage control."

"Griffon Lewis has been a valuable ally and close friend for many years. He's supported this administration and done great things for the city of New York. All the while he's asked for little in return. Over the years we've seen him gather numerous humanitarian awards as well as one of the finest private collections of art the world has ever known."

Now Glacier looked nearly distraught. Chang wasn't buying it.

"But as we all are human, we can fall victim to our passions, even when they lift us up. Griffon Lewis cared, above all, for the genius captured in art. Did his passions drive him to pursue such objects regardless of where they came from or how they were obtained?"

"What's he doing?" Colleen asked.

Chang knew this game. "Throwing his *good* friend under the bus."

"Time will tell. But I stand before you to say that never once did I, or anyone in my office, either in our personal or professional dealings, have any knowledge of Griffon Lewis trafficking in stolen treasures. On the contrary, we stand foursquare in seeing to it that any recovered works of art will be returned as soon as possible to the rightful owners. Furthermore, let me say that the actions of one man—again, if true—must not be permitted to stand in the way of the important work we have done and will do."

"Damn. He sure is." Colleen shook her head. "Did you know that Lewis was one of Glacier's largest fund-raisers? They call him Kingmaker, and he was always mentioned whenever anyone speculated that Glacier might someday seek higher office."

"I think there might be an opening for a bigwig sponsor. Tells me something though."

"What's that?"

"He must know Lewis is guilty. Glacier just branded the guy radioactive."

✳ ✳ ✳

After dinner Chang stared at the computer and the obstinate red dot. He knew he was probably wasting time waiting for Max to make a move. In the van, that is.

"Do you need to try Laura again? Feel free to use my phone."

"No point today. I'm sure she's stirred up a huge firestorm and will be busy with that." Chang stretched. "Thanks for letting me do my virtual stakeout here."

"Nice to have company on a school night." Colleen rubbed his shoulders and leaned into him. "It gets lonely on stakeouts, doesn't it?"

"Yes ma'am, it certainly can." He turned and kissed her.

"Think you can tear yourself away from that screen for a few minutes?"

"Maybe more than a few." He picked her up and carried her into the bedroom.

Don't throw out your back, Tarzan.

Everything held up just fine.

❋ ❋ ❋

Chang lifted Colleen's arm off him and crept into the bathroom without waking her. It took a moment before he realized that he hadn't dozed off for only a few minutes, he'd slept for several hours.

Falling asleep next to Colleen used to terrify him because he feared that he'd have a recurrence of the nightmare. The fact that she no longer dwelled on his sleepwalking attack showed her unspoken confidence that he wouldn't wake up trying to hurt her while battling phantom assassins from the past.

He'd have to remember, whenever he was tempted to complain about boring backgrounder contracts, that there seemed to be a real link between sleeping well at night and an absence of people trying to kill him.

He saw that Colleen would need to be up soon, so he went into the kitchen to make coffee.

While it percolated, he climbed back into the bed and hugged her naked body. He couldn't get enough of the feel of her skin and wondered if he was trying to make up for all the years they were apart.

"Mmm. I've gotta go to work."

"They called. The building is closed with a bomb scare."

"Yeah?"

"Could run into lunchtime. Can't be too careful."

"You don't say." She pressed against him and kissed his chest.

She was the only woman he'd ever known who made his scars feel sexy.

He heard a shrill beep that he thought might be the coffee maker. Then he realized it was his laptop in the other room.

"The tracker."

"What, now? It's five thirty."

"He never moves this early..."

Colleen reached for him. "Catch up with him later."

Chang wanted nothing more than to stay right where he was. But Max had already established something of a pattern and hadn't gone near that waterfront site since the time he followed him.

Now he was breaking his pattern. Chang couldn't be sure that's where Max was headed, but his instincts screamed at him that this was a crucial opportunity.

Realizing how far Colleen's place was from the waterfront spot where he'd planted the tracker, he knew he'd have to hurry if he was going to beat Max there. If it turned out Max wasn't headed there, Chang would be in a far better position to follow him than from clear across town.

"Babe, I swear I'll make this one up to you..."

He climbed out of the bed, and Colleen laughed at his aroused state. "You're in no condition to go chasing clowns. You'll get sued."

Chang pulled on clothes and tried not to think of what he was missing. He managed one out of two.

24

TRACK STAR

Brooklyn

Chang trundled down the stairs and out to the parking lot. Colleen might be right about the false alarm. Max might just be running errands for his business. Chang couldn't shake the guilt he felt at leaving, but at the same time he'd never forgive himself if he screwed up this chance to learn more about Max.

Chang needed forty minutes. Max would take twenty if he drove straight there without any stops. If so, Chang was going to find himself hanging out and staring at yachts all day for nothing.

✻ ✻ ✻

Chang parked on Shore Boulevard on the other side of the walking bridge Max had used the other day. He had a fine view of the multimillion-dollar yachts across Sheepshead Bay. He checked his laptop and saw that Max was still trolling around near the warehouse in Brooklyn.

He pulled out a painting kit and a half-finished canvas with boat sketches on it. Betty had done it for him two days earlier, when he'd given her a photo to copy. She'd offered him a beret to complete the look, but he thought that might be a bit much.

Might all be too much if the guy never shows.

Chang had to trust his instincts though. He left the artist disguise on the seat beside him and watched the laptop. The red dot stopped at the warehouse.

His heart sank. He needed a new plan.

He reviewed the tracking history, which mostly followed a local pattern in the vicinity of the warehouse. He'd need to replace the tracker's battery soon if this kept up.

Hang on. Movement.

Chang stared transfixed as the red dot crept closer. His pulse matched the tracker's rate until he saw Max take the Coney Island exit off Belt Parkway.

He climbed out of the car and set up his painting easel so that he had a view of the walking bridge. He wanted to make sure he could see whether Max crossed it, but not be so close that the guy would walk right by him. Fifty yards ought to be enough.

✳ ✳ ✳

Chang battled the dual temptations to head back to his car to check the laptop and grab his binoculars from the trunk. That kind of move would be too obvious even for an amateur. Besides, this guy had shown him something the first time he'd followed him. He just needed to be patient.

Let your hunch play out.

He reminded himself to focus on height. If Max had used a disguise the first time, Chang should expect him to do so again— and he knew better than to look for the same thing.

Although the bridge wasn't clogged with people at rush hour on a weekday, a steady stream of joggers and women pushing strollers was crossing in both directions.

The ebb and flow of people started to lull him into a less vigilant state. To rouse himself, he stepped close to the railing and stretched, then took in the light dancing off the water and the hypnotic bob of boats docked across the bay.

At one point, he had to shoo away some nosy art critic who started in on his "brushstrokes." Chang spoke in Mandarin and told her to mind her own business, smiling all the while. She eventually concluded that he couldn't understand her and gave up.

Then Chang noticed a tall guy with long hair and a bohemian-style backpack. Although it was the man's height that initially drew his attention, he then noticed the way the guy stopped in the middle of the bridge as though to take a camera-phone picture. Chang saw him turn his head to look back the way he'd come.

Chang made sure his baseball hat was on low. He put on his sunglasses and made full use of the tiny mirrors inside the frames to keep an eye on the end of the bridge while he pretended to work on his masterpiece.

The hippie continued across the bridge toward Chang's side of the bay. Chang watched him cross Shore Boulevard and head down Exeter, a narrow, tree-lined one-way street with large houses and small front yards. Not much room to hide. Chang packed his picture up and crossed the street on the other side. He avoided his own car and was grateful that his picture was small and easy to carry. It would have looked peculiar to be walking around with a huge canvas under his arm.

Manhattan Beach. Big houses, punctuated by even bigger homes. This was a high-end neighborhood known for Italian, Jewish, and Russian ethnicities.

Chang kept a long half block between himself and his mark. Hippie/Max walked with an unhurried stride.

He planned to stroll by, once Max got wherever he was going. There were more drivers than pedestrians along this street, but a few nannies and dog walkers provided movement. There was nothing worse than getting caught out as the only other person on the street.

Where was he going? Max paused at the corner of Exeter and Hampton Avenue and took out his phone. Chang slowed down but tried not to be obvious.

Max turned right on Hampton, heading east. Chang sped up while Max was out of sight. When he had about a quarter of the block left ahead of him, the hippie reappeared. Max had doubled back, crossed Exeter to Chang's side of the block, and was now heading west on Hampton.

Damn.

Chang broke into a cold sweat and fought to appear calm. He couldn't change his direction or pace now, but Max had walked within thirty feet of him. There was no way he hadn't seen Chang.

When Chang reached the corner himself, he turned left to head west as well, but by then Max had vanished.

Chang fought the urge to swivel his head and scan the street blatantly. He had no choice now but to continue in the same direction Max had gone.

He felt like he'd just stepped into a static electricity field the way the hair rose all over his body. He was being watched. He didn't break stride but knew this was worse than being made. Max was hidden and locked onto him.

Chang kept walking and cursed himself for such sloppy field craft. There was nothing left to do but bluff it out. He decided to walk toward Manhattan Beach Park, a plausible destination for someone who didn't look rich enough to live in one of these houses, and one that would also provide cover.

When he reached Ocean Avenue, the next possible right, he took it. The tingle on his body began to fade, and he was tempted to double back, if only to try to get a glimpse of his target.

He glanced over his shoulder.

Standing on the corner he'd just come from was the hippie. He was staring right at him. Even at that distance, the eyes didn't lie. Those dark pellets drilled into him. Max.

Chang stopped and faced him. Now what?

Chang felt like they stood there staring at each other for an eternity. It was probably only a few seconds, but then Max, headband, long hair, and all, raised his right hand in a two-fingered peace sign.

So much for subtlety. Chang began to walk toward Max, who continued to hold up his hand with the two-fingered sign.

Chang was about to speak when Max raised his other arm and gave Chang the double peace sign. Max waggled his face so that his jowls shook in a passable impression of Nixon.

Then he took off.

Chang bolted into a sprint and yelled, "Wait!"

By the time he reached the corner, Max was gone. Chang tried to calm his breathing and focus his attention. The dragon could sharpen his senses, but on this summer morning it was nowhere to be found. He strained his ears for pounding footfalls, but the ambient noise, even in this relatively quiet neighborhood, made it impossible for him to detect the sound of steps.

The laughter he heard was his imagination, but he knew he'd earned it all the same.

25

WINS AND LOSSES

Laura's Apartment

Chang sat across from Drew at the dining room table. The guy looked like he hadn't gotten much sleep. The late afternoon sun highlighted the dark circles under Drew's eyes.

"Thanks again for letting me in."

Drew cracked his knuckles. "No problem. Laura should be here any minute. I'm glad she could break away at all with all the hornet nests she's kicked over lately."

Chang took in the tremendous view of the trees in Central Park. "Sounds like you kicked one over yourself."

"Speaking of which, I may owe you an apology."

Chang could see those didn't come readily to the guy. He was out of his element for sure. Something had knocked out the cocky attitude that infused all the photos of him around Laura's place. "For what?"

"To be honest, I thought you were part of a scam to milk cash from Laura."

"What changed your mind?" Funny, Chang was sure Laura had thought the same thing at first.

"Since she's not here, I'll admit I wasn't sold on how dangerous her ex was, or that he was even the one bothering her."

"You are now?" Chang sensed the guy was dying to talk to someone.

Drew summarized his recent experiences, culminating in his visit to Laughing Matters.

"Laura knows all this?" Now Chang really wished Nelson were here. If what Drew had just told him was true, Max was out of his mind.

Drew nodded. "She didn't want me to go near him, but I figured the guy was a pussy. I hadn't planned to punch him out, unless he started it."

Chang thought the guy looked like he could handle a bar fight, but this Max was one big X factor. "Not my job to lecture you, but that was stupid."

"I had no idea what a freak he is. I'd press charges if the fucking cops weren't such douche bags." Drew paused. "Uh, sorry. I forgot you were a cop too."

"Card-carrying d-bag for more than twenty years and in two states no less." Chang did a mock bow from his seat. "I'm aware of the history between Laura and them, but you'll have to take my word for it that they'd be professional. I'll add that I'd have trouble making a case without any evidence. You didn't get a picture of yourself covered in flour?"

Drew shook his head. "My camera was in my phone and that's gone. I tried to call it but no luck. I just wanted to get that crap off me. It probably would've ended up online anyway."

"It could have been worse."

"How?"

"Those knives could have hit you."

✳✳✳

"I don't have much time." Laura slammed the front door behind her. She sounded winded but looked great. She wore just the right amount of makeup, and Chang saw her eyes dance. She was in the right job. "Drew, you told Paul what happened?"

"He did. Now that you're here, is it OK to share with Drew my encounter yesterday?" Chang kept in mind who his client was.

Laura didn't hesitate. "Yes, tell him. This is good progress. I feel like people finally believe me here."

"I don't know about progress, but you do have a problem on your hands, and I think it *is* Max." Chang was stunned by the look of relief on Laura's face. He hadn't realized until that moment how much his doubt must have shown on his face. He'd understood that her ex-husband was more than a little strange. But when an attractive, famous woman lives in a big city and is on TV every night, he knew that whack-jobs came with the territory.

He described the tail and warned Drew not to discuss the details outside the room.

"Long story short, he made me, he ditched me, and wherever he was going had to be nearby because he wouldn't have known I was following until after he'd crossed the bridge at the earliest. Does that neighborhood mean anything to either of you?"

They both shook their heads. "There are some gorgeous mansions there. But I haven't done any stories or anything around there that I can remember…"

Chang thought about her recent stories. "What about Marchetti? Do you know if he lives there? Any chance Max could know him?"

Laura frowned, deep in thought. "No, we did some live shots out in front of his place on Mulberry. The place used to be a parking garage, and they turned it into a huge house."

"Just a thought. He may own property all over town. I'll have Nelson run that down." Chang made a note.

"And I have no idea who Max knows."

Drew squirmed in his seat like a little kid. Chang was tempted to ask if he needed to use the bathroom.

Laura noticed as well. "Go ahead, Drew."

Drew ran both hands through his blond hair. "I feel like crap about this, but I have to fly out of town in the morning for a work trip I can't cancel. But I feel like I'm running away."

"From what?"

"From Max, I guess. I feel like I should stay here and protect Laura."

Aha. Ego massage time. "Well, I can't stay here as bodyguard if that's what you mean."

"No," they both agreed.

"I wanted to get your thoughts on how safe it is for Laura to stay here on her own. Should she move out for a while?" Drew looked like the thought had just popped into his mind.

Laura's expression confirmed what Chang was thinking.

"No again. Drew, this is my home, and I don't want to run away either. Max wants to play games, and that's why Paul and his friend are here and why I told the cops in the first place. But for all that, he hasn't actually threatened me."

"No?" Drew's flushed face indicated to Chang just how much she'd embarrassed him. He didn't think she even realized it.

"Well, he hasn't physically threatened me." Laura paused, and Chang guessed she was thinking about everything that had happened recently. "I'm way too busy to take off right now. That's a nonstarter. But on the plus side, that means I'll be at work most of the time, and I should be safe surrounded by everyone there."

"Makes sense," Chang agreed.

"But when you're home?" Drew pressed.

"If you want, after your trip, you can be here when I get home," Laura said.

Drew perked up. "In the meantime, we can make sure the doorman is extra vigilant. Paul, is there anything you can do with the police?"

"Not explicitly. But I get your point. I can talk to Ron…"

"That prick…" Drew said.

"…happens to be a friend. He'll listen to my professional judgment. If it looks like we have hard evidence that Max poses an imminent threat, we may be able to take some action."

Drew laughed. "Maybe Sieger'll take a pie in the face. That ought to be good for some time in the pokey."

Chang smiled at the image of Ron covered in custard. "We'll keep an eye on Max the best we can, and I'll try to stay in the area as much as possible." Chang turned to Laura. "Then we can move on him if he does try something. You don't need me on retainer."

"He picked a hell of week to start this shit again."

26

BAGGAGE

Colleen's Apartment

That night Chang dreamed of Colleen in her younger days, when he'd brought her to meet his mother. The introduction had been more stressful than getting shot at, but he needn't have worried. His mother had hated her, just as he'd expected.

In this dream they sat at the table and Shu brought platter after platter of steaming dishes. With each course his mother smiled more and more.

After what must have been hours, his mother left the table and said in clear, unaccented English, "Remember, don't try to go swimming..."

The scene shifted, and Chang realized he was underwater, trapped and chained to the bottom of a pool. Colleen was across from him and looking at him with all the faith in the world. She didn't appear to register that she was underwater and likewise chained to the bottom. Between them was a huge butcher knife.

Chang reached for the knife, and Colleen began to let out shrill screams that sounded more like beeps. *Beeps...*

Chang woke up with his face turned into the pillow and a stuffy nose. His left hand ached under his body, and he didn't even try to move his fingers. The sound jarred his brain into wakefulness. The laptop.

He looked over at Colleen, who merely stirred at the sound, and got out of bed, but not before checking to see that she had both her hands and there was no sign of blood.

The wall clock showed that it was barely four a.m. He stumbled out into the hallway, stubbing his toe on the chair next to the table where he'd left the computer. He tilted up the screen and saw that the red dot was moving. He rubbed his eyes and stared at the screen. Max was moving uptown, along Park Avenue. Every couple of minutes he'd stop, then continue straight ahead.

That was new.

Chang grabbed his clothes.

※ ※ ※

Drew came back into the bedroom and kissed Laura on the head. She opened her eyes, and he moved to her mouth. "I'll miss you," she said.

"I'll call when I get there. Please be careful."

"I'll be on the phone at the station most of the time. You can catch the show online."

He loved how she looked without makeup and all sleepy. "OK." He glanced at the clock. "I gotta scoot. They won't hold the plane." He grabbed his suitcase, glad he'd decided to pack the night before so that he could stay over with Laura.

When he reached the door, he saw that the door chain was unlatched. The rest of the door was locked. He almost said something, but it was too early to scold her about security. He'd mention it later. They had talked about it and agreed: the more security, the better.

He was careful to lock and test the door when he slipped out.

※ ※ ※

The tracker showed that the van was making its way up Park Avenue at a leisurely pace, so Chang plotted an intercepting route. He shot down the Major Deegan Expressway and took the exit for the Third Avenue Bridge. Thanks to the early hour, he made it into Manhattan in no time.

Chang drove down Lexington, racking his brain to think of what Max might be doing that far north at this hour. Clown wake-up calls? The Harlem Circus Clowns and Psycho Ex-Husbands Club?

When he reached Ninety-Seventh Street, he turned off Lexington and pulled over so that he could watch traffic heading up Park toward Harlem.

He watched the red dot on his laptop creep steadily closer. The program updated frequently, so he could mark the van's progress with accuracy. He kept an eye out for the white van. He also had his camera ready. He still felt naked without a weapon, but he had a few odds and ends in the car that would serve in a pinch, and wouldn't get him tossed in jail if he got busted.

He shifted his gaze between the computer and the street. *Shouldn't be long now...*

As the dot entered the map intersection on his computer, he looked up but didn't see the van. Maybe the delivery truck that was in the street was blocking his view. He looked down and saw the dot turn left onto his street one block ahead. It was still dark, but how could he have missed it in these well-lit streets?

The street was narrow here, and he started to pull forward to follow. But the damn newspaper delivery truck was in the way. That guy had to be climbing up Max's rear from what the tracker showed. Was Max looking for an address? Chang swept his gaze right and left. Nope.

He finally got a chance to pass a block later at Madison. He tried not to be too showy with his driving or Max might notice him again. As soon as he cleared the delivery truck, he scanned the street for the van but saw only open road ahead of him. His stomach dropped. He pulled into the first available spot and saw that the red dot was now behind him and slowly catching up. A glance in the mirror confirmed that the delivery truck was the only vehicle moving toward him. He got a look at the driver.

A black man. It didn't look like a disguise. Chang pulled in behind the truck at its next stop.

*** *** ***

Drew checked e-mail on his phone while the line of sleepy business travelers wound through the cattle chutes at JFK International Airport, waiting to be devoured by the electromagnetic maw of the TSA checkpoint.

Moo.

It was still early, but he figured Laura was up and at 'em already. He barely saw her when she was on one of these hard-breaking stories. For once he was glad because Sid and the crew probably wouldn't give her a moment's peace. Max wouldn't try anything then.

Drew felt a stab of rage he had no way to express. The humiliation Max had subjected him to stuck in his craw like nothing since high school. He wanted to apply the same remedy too. Ryan Billip had had a lot less to say after Drew broke his nose with a perfect jab.

What he'd give for the chance to demonstrate on Max.

"Sir, please step forward." A heavyset woman in a TSA uniform motioned him ahead.

Drew waved a fast apology to the line behind him and plopped his shoes into the bin. He hauled his bag onto the conveyor belt. His phone and the junk from his pockets went into the plastic rectangle, the great equalizer of airport society.

He padded through the metal detector and reached for the bin to reassemble his stuff. Was his bag still in there?

The guy craned forward and stared at the screen, then got on the radio.

Great. Now they're going to rummage through my bag. I had everything folded just right.

Right on cue. More TSA. Wait, those were cops. "What seems to be—"

Drew didn't get to finish. What felt like a truck suddenly hit him from behind, and his body slammed to the hard floor before his mind could catch up. It knocked the air out of him, and when he tried to speak, he couldn't utter a word.

As his arms were yanked behind his back, he finally pulled some air into his lungs. The guy who'd hit him looked like an NFL linebacker.

"What the hell?" Drew felt handcuffs being cinched around his wrists.

"Sir, is this your bag?"

"You want to search it, all you had do was ask." He shut up. These guys weren't smiling. At all.

"Yes or no? Is it your bag?" another cop asked. He was short with a cheesy mustache.

"Yeah, it's my bag." Drew's head swirled.

Mustache cop began to read him his rights.

"Wait, what am I…?"

The guy continued without pausing. "Do you understand these rights?"

"How about my right to know what the hell is going on?"

"Sir. Do you understand these rights, or do you need them read to you in Spanish?"

"Yes, I understand." Drew fought to stay cool. He was far from it, but he didn't want to give them reason to slam him to the ground again.

The big cop hauled him to his feet. They frisked him by hand, then used the hand wand. Then radio chatter. Drew felt every pair of eyes on him in the security line and finally felt compelled to yell out, "It's a mistake!"

"Quiet, sir."

❋ ❋ ❋

Chang got out of the car and called out to the driver. "Excuse me." He held out his PI license.

"I'm busy here. Can it wait?" As the man loaded a newspaper machine, he looked at the ID. "You some kinda cop?"

"Not anymore. Ex-NYPD." He hoped that carried more weight. He was itching for an answer.

"OK. What is it?"

Chang waved his hands palm down. "Nothing to do with you, but can I take a quick look under your truck?"

"Why?"

Up close, Chang was sure this was no disguise. The height was wrong. This guy was stocky and short. "You're not gonna believe this, but my assistant, trying to break her in"—he shot the guy a leer and saw the man's imagination fill in the gaps—"she's got skills, but let's just say her spy work has room for improvement."

"Man, I gotta keep my schedule..." He looked ready to scram.

"Got it. See, she put a tracking device on the wrong truck, and now I'm following you all over town when I'm supposed to be... well, I can't say. But it sure doesn't have anything to do with you or your truck."

"For real?"

Chang had gotten him curious. There was no harm in closing the deal. "Yup. Take a look." He pulled out his laptop. "See? That's us. If you move, it'll follow you on the map."

The guy nudged Chang's shoulder. "James Bond shit!"

"Well, the Bond girls didn't make James look like a jackass. So can I take a look? I know it's here somewhere."

"Go ahead." The guy laughed, which suggested that he'd give Chang enough time to find it if it wasn't too well hidden.

It wasn't. He saw that Max wanted to be sure he found it right away. When he yanked the magnetic unit off the car, he heard something metallic drop to the pavement. He picked it up.

A peace symbol.

❋ ❋ ❋

"You expect us to believe you know nothing about it?" The little weasel-looking cop leaned in.

Did they issue bad-breath gum to the cops just for talking to suspects?

Drew knew his sweating made him look guilty, but he couldn't help it. He tried to keep his voice down, but he wasn't doing so hot on that front either.

"It's not my fucking gun!" He forced a pause. "Look. I don't own a gun. I don't like guns, and the absolute last thing I'd ever do is bring a gun to the goddamned airport. I actually wanted to get where I'm going, see..."

"I think you're officially delayed, pard."

"I figured that one out already." Drew pressed his shackled hands down into the table.

"Maybe you just forgot it was in there. It happens." The linebacker-size cop appeared to have drawn the "good cop" straw. After nearly caving in his rib cage, that is.

Drew read the name tag. "Officer Powell, did you see how neatly my bag was packed? Does it seem likely I'd toss in a weapon by mistake?"

"Which leaves very few possibilities," Russell the Weasel said.

Drew's head reeled, and he forced himself to think. He knew he didn't have to talk to them. Very likely he was hurting himself by doing so, but he knew he was innocent. At the same time, whether he spoke up or not, they had his suitcase, and there was a loaded 9mm pistol he'd never seen before, right under his silk hankies.

"I know how it looks. But I know you must have checked my records by now. They're clean. I'm an accountant."

"Always the quiet ones..." Russell muttered.

He's just trying to be an asshole.

"And whoever that gun is registered to, it isn't me."

"It came back stolen. You into drugs, Mr. Gantry?" Russell kept poking.

"No. And I packed my bag last night. It was in my sight the entire time until I took it to my girlfriend's." He left out her name, though he knew they'd find out eventually.

"You two have a fight?"

"No, why?"

"Hell of a trick to play, if that's what you're implying."

This was going nowhere. He was going to trap himself if he kept..."What did you say?" All of a sudden, Drew understood. *Shit.*

"You saying your girlfriend planted a weapon?"

"No. But I think I know who did. Damn." The cops leaned back, and Drew knew he was being taped. "Sorry, guys. I'm done talking until my lawyer gets here."

27

EXTERMINATOR

Laura's Apartment

Chang sat on the couch and watched Laura pace back and forth. "Tell me everything." He glanced at the tracker on the coffee table. He wanted to talk, but he could tell she would burst if she didn't get to update him first.

She saw the tracker, but it barely fazed her. She related the details of Drew's arrest.

Chang took notes so that he didn't miss any details. Nelson wouldn't be here for another couple of hours, and he knew that his partner would grill him. Laura would be off to do the news at that point. He didn't like it, but everything seemed to be breaking at once.

Seemed like old times.

"Back up. When's the last time you or he saw the suitcase open?" He wished he could ask Drew himself, but after posting bail, Drew had boarded a later flight.

"Let's see. Nearest I can figure, right before bed, when he dug out his toothbrush and something to wear in the morning."

"So you're sure the weapon couldn't have been there before then."

She shook her head like a terrier. "No way. You haven't seen the man pack. His suitcase practically comes with a table of contents."

Chang could relate, but he didn't think it would advance the conversation any to say so.

"And Drew said he had the case in his possession the whole time, from when he left in the morning until the time he reached the security line?"

"That's what he said. He insisted that was the case."

Chang thought for a moment. He didn't want to scare Laura, but weren't they beyond that point? "Assuming that's true, you know what it means?"

Laura had been bouncing around so much the last few days that Chang had barely been able to reach her, but now he appeared to grab her full attention. She stopped pacing and stared at Chang.

He watched the color drain from her face and thought he might need to catch her, but she stayed on her feet.

"He was in here, wasn't he? But the doors were locked."

Chang had brought a briefcase that contained some of his best detective goodies, including his lock pick set and fingerprint kit.

"It's a little late, but don't touch anything just now." Chang walked to the front door. The doorknob would be a waste of time, but he took out a magnifying glass and studied the lock on the outside of the door.

"What?" Laura walked over, steady on her feet. That was good. Chang could tell she was tough.

He peered at each lock. They all had typical usage scratches from keys. He took out a penlight, gripped it in his teeth, and leaned closer to give his aging eyes a chance.

"Come here. See this? There. Shiny fresh scratches, narrower than a key would make." He pointed out the same marks on each lock. He noted that there were quite a few of them. Maybe Max wasn't all that skilled or was just learning. *Interesting.*

"He picked them?" She looked at the door like it had something foul on it.

Chang held up one of his own picks. "See how small they are? They work, but they can leave those little marks. You wouldn't notice them if you weren't looking for them."

"But I had the chain drawn. Drew's always getting on me about it."

"If Max can take these on, he can handle a simple chain. You guys heard nothing?"

"No," Laura whispered. Chang thought she might break down.

"Are you all right? He's gone now."

"For how long? He really came in, didn't he?"

"Looks like *someone* did. That's all we could prove, and it really only looks suspicious. It'd be tough to prove the timing. I could dust for prints..." He really wasn't sure there was any point. Anyone this careful would have worn gloves, wouldn't he? But it never hurt to try.

Laura began to tremble, and Chang guided her inside. He made sure she heard him relock the doors.

"That suitcase was in our bedroom." Laura spoke almost to herself. "While we were sleeping. He came into my bedroom with a loaded gun while I was lying there helpless." Now her voice rose, but Chang heard anger and steel mixed with her justifiable fear.

He nodded. "We can't prove it, though I'll look for clues. You never know. But I think you're right." Chang paused, then continued, "There is one bit of good news."

"He took a piss and remembered to put down the seat?" Laura wiped her eyes.

Chang smiled. "You're here. Whatever the reason, he's still playing games. He could have hurt you, but he didn't."

"That's the message, isn't it? I can get you anytime?"

She'd told him about the trick with her glasses at work. "Sounds about right." Something was still bothering Chang though.

Laura went into the bedroom, and Chang could hear her rummaging around. He was about to ask her to leave everything alone but decided not to bother. He had enough to tell Ron about the case, and given that it would be coming from a friend and former colleague, Chang knew that what he said would carry weight. But beyond saying "I believe you," Chang knew there wasn't much they could use to get Max locked up.

Besides, what would be the point? He'd get out soon enough, and who knows what he'd do after that?

Chang had just realized what was bothering him when Laura rushed out of the bedroom.

"It's gone."

"What?" Chang asked.

"I'm sure of it. I never wear it, but..."

"Laura, what?"

She looked at him like he'd interrupted a conversation with herself.

"Oh. A locket. I put it away in my jewelry box because I wanted to reuse the gold chain but never got around to it."

"So there's jewelry missing?"

"Just the locket. I wanted to check in case it really was someone else. What's the first thing a thief, even a sneaky one, will grab?"

"Cash and jewels," Chang agreed.

"Right. But my old engagement ring and some other pieces I really should put in a safe-deposit box were still there. Even my antique emerald ring is just lying there."

Chang grabbed his fingerprint kit. "Don't touch it anymore. Maybe we'll get lucky."

He found some prints on the jewelry box and lifted them. "We can get these checked. When you talk to Drew, let him know I might need a set of his. I doubt the Feds will be eager to share."

"If I wasn't sure before, I am now." Laura stood in the doorway.

"What's special about that locket?"

"It had a picture of Max and me when we were in college."

"You kept it?"

Laura shrugged. "Just because I *wish* we'd never gotten married doesn't mean I deny it happened."

Chang thought of all the pictures of himself and Colleen from better days that he'd kept. And that she still had around her place. Of course *they* were getting along well these days.

"Fair enough. Don't get your hopes up on the prints though. I'm doing this more for our own knowledge. I doubt they would stand up in court. This crime scene isn't exactly clean."

"That's the first time I've heard my housekeeping skills described that way."

"I didn't mean it like that…" Chang stopped when Laura gave a small laugh.

"A joke, Detective."

Chang chased the elusive thought in his brain.

"Paul?"

He held up his hand. Something felt very wrong.

"Who did you tell about Drew's business trip?"

"Me? Nobody. It's been so busy at work that it's all shoptalk when I'm there."

"How about Drew?" Chang was close but not quite there.

"Everybody he worked with, I suppose. It's a big firm. Why?"

Chang paused again. "Right. But who knew Drew would be here the night before his trip?"

"Again, I try to keep my private life exactly that. Drew, I don't know. But what difference does it make? I thought you were sure it was Max."

That was it. "Hey, I'm dying of thirst. Can I get some water in the kitchen?" He put his fingers to his lips and gestured for her to follow him.

In the small kitchen, Chang turned on the water full blast and kept his head near the spray. He crooked his finger, and Laura leaned in.

Chang whispered, "I couldn't figure out how Max could have known exactly when to come to your place. How would he know Drew would be here?"

"But Drew's here a lot."

"With a suitcase?"

Laura, no dummy, pointed to the rest of the place. "You think he can hear us?"

Chang nodded. "Keep it light and follow my lead."

Chang stood up and said in a normal voice.

"I'm gonna step out and grab a smoke."

"Take your time. I'll see if anything else is missing." Laura knew he didn't smoke. She caught on fast.

Outside the apartment, Chang called Nelson.

※ ※ ※

Chang waved to Laura when the cab picked her up. She'd tried to insist she could walk but relented when he explained he'd have to escort her the entire way. He also made her agree to text him that she got to her office safely.

Funny, she hadn't trusted him at all when they'd first met. Now he had full access to her apartment and even her computer.

He'd need it.

The doorman, a decent enough guy named Quincy, let Chang back in. Laura had cleared Chang and Nelson to enter but insisted that they show Quincy their IDs. Quincy was an older man who spoke with a slight French-Canadian accent. Chang thought he was sharp enough, but real security wasn't his job.

He didn't know how Max had entered the building, but that wasn't Chang's biggest concern. He would start with Laura's apartment and work from there.

He had just planted several telltales. If Max showed during this window, Chang wanted to know.

As the elevator climbed to the seventeenth floor, Chang considered that the apartment's position made a cat-burglar entry unlikely. He made a mental note to ask Quincy about the window-cleaning schedule.

He didn't want to tell Laura too much, but he realized that the number of scratches around the lock might not actually mean that Max was an amateur lock picker. He now suspected that Max was very good at picking locks—and that the number of scratches in fact indicated that he'd entered the apartment on numerous occasions.

No more. He'd make sure of that. Once Nelson arrived, he'd take care of things, and they would see to it that their client had a safe place to sleep.

Chang used the key that Laura had given him and saw that the telltales were all intact. The tiny threads and scraps of paper he'd wedged around the doors were a simple trick but hard to detect or defeat. He cleared the rest of the apartment—more for practice than with any real expectation of finding Max—and sat down to wait for Nelson.

* * *

A couple of hours later, Chang got a call from Quincy that a Mr. Nelson Rogers had arrived and should he send him up? His ID checked out. Chang agreed and smiled at the man's efforts to sound official. Sometimes respect came from unlikely places, but apparently Quincy was impressed that he and Nelson were ex-NYPD.

There was a timid knock on the door, which sounded just like Nelson. Chang peered through the peephole and saw Nelson wearing an exterminator's cap on his huge head. Chang laughed at the gold, embroidered bug corpse and opened the door. "You made good time."

Nelson pointed to his cap. "You have a choice in pest control, and we thank you for choosing us." The heavy case in Nelson's hand was dragging one shoulder down. Probably would have killed him if he'd taken the stairs.

Chang gestured to the room and put his fingers to his lips.

Nelson lugged in the case and put it on the floor. Chang locked the door and opened up the case. He took out a couple of electronic units, each of which was roughly the size of a cigarette pack. Chang gave one to Nelson and then turned off his cell phone. Nelson followed suit, and they split up.

Chang got a signal immediately and pinned down the area of greatest strength in the living room.

Laura's desktop computer was in the corner. She'd told Chang that she used this one mainly for surfing the web and shopping, and that she did most of her more secure work on her laptop.

Chang noted the dust in the chair and figured she hadn't spent much time on it lately.

But the device really lit up near it. Chang waved it around and got the strongest signal by the mouse. He picked it up and took it apart. Yup. A commercial-grade wireless transmitter made to look like and function as a wireless mouse. "Nelson."

Nelson came in like an awkward mime. One arm was covered in dust, but he grinned and held up a thumb-size transmitter. He mouthed "Bedroom, headboard." Chang nodded and waggled the mouse. Nelson took a look and gave a thumbs-up.

Nelson was still getting up to speed on high-tech weapons and spy gear, but the guy's background with computers, particularly all the work he'd done for the state police in Delaware, gave him deep computer skills that put Chang to shame.

Nelson could spot a mouse from a mile away. Chang pointed to the computer and handed Nelson the password access codes Laura had given him.

Chang went to the kitchen, but the signals there were faint. He plugged up the sink and began to fill it with water. While the water flowed, he resumed his search. One signal led him to the bathroom. He half expected to find a camera. Nope. But he did find another transmitter attached under the sink.

The last thing Chang found was a phone tap. He pulled the tiny unit off and rechecked the phone. Clean. Like the rest of the place.

He turned off the water in the kitchen and got Nelson's attention. "OK?" he asked silently.

Nelson frowned with concentration and pawed around the back of the computer. He tossed Chang a tiny object that he caught in the air. A keystroke counter.

Chang took all the transmitters and dropped them into the filled sink. "There." Nelson peeked into the kitchen. "Spy soup?"

"Cook until done." Chang pointed to the computer in the living room. How are we doing over there?

"Good, I think. The counter was the last thing I found. I'll get the cover off and check for anything else, but nothing is transmitting. Then I'll run exhaustive virus and malware checks."

"I think we're clean."

"Those were all battery?"

"Aside from the key counter and phone tap, that's right," Chang said.

"You know what that means."

Chang did, but he liked to hear the way Nelson was thinking. "Go."

"He has to change the units or batteries, which means he's come in here more than once. Wouldn't surprise me if he came up with reasons to come back."

Chang was glad he'd asked. "I hadn't thought of it that way."

"C'mon, sure you did."

"No, I knew he came back. The lock scratches tipped me off, but not the part about the excuses. That explains why he planted so many different bugs. Some of it's overkill, and some, like the keystroke counter or the tap on the landline, are unnecessary. Don't you think? Laura uses a cell and her laptop most of the time."

"Add to that the fact he could have hurt her. Anytime, for years probably—but that he didn't tells us a lot." Nelson checked the computer. "Looks OK. I think we got it."

Chang hooked a thumb toward the kitchen. "He's gonna know the game is up."

"I'm sure he expected that. So far he's been consistent."

"How so?"

"A step ahead of us the whole way."

28

OUT OF HAND

WBAC

"Keep trying." Laura ran her hands through her hair. So far she'd had no luck reaching Griffon Lewis, and not even the courtesy of a "no comment" from his lawyer.

The AG had pulled a complete reversal: after initially stone-walling the case, he'd just had a press conference announcing a full-bore investigation. He'd even outlined his intention to empanel a grand jury and seek indictments for Lewis on all manner of felony charges stemming from stolen art trafficking.

They had good footage of the cops raiding his house and removing boxes. Predictably, Lewis had ducked the press and refused to comment.

Meanwhile, Mayor Glacier seemed determined to outdo even the attorney general in the total discrediting of Lewis, offering the full cooperation of his office, including candid access to information he'd be under no obligation to reveal, according to legal experts Laura consulted.

No longer the lone wolf on the case, Laura had to work hard just to keep up with the swell of coverage now that the full power of the press had been unleashed. Lewis was fast running out of friends, which was nothing short of amazing considering the billions at his disposal.

"Something's going on." Laura plopped into a chair in Sid's office. Sid looked as exhausted as she felt, but the spark in his eye said he was having a ball. The news operation was humming, and all from a story *they* had broken. For Sid it didn't get much better than that unless, of course, it was a chance to do it again.

"Still no answer from the AG or the mayor either? Lemme try. They're so mad at me, they'll take the call just to cuss me out." He winked at Laura. "Sit tight." Sid picked up the phone and put it on speaker.

"Angie, sweetheart! Sid Gold from WBAC."

"We're really busy here, Mr. Gold. I'll have to take a message."

"What? You say the mayor has a bastard kid and wants me to give him an internship?"

"Mr. Gold."

"Hey, I need two minutes, Angie." Sid laid the obnoxious voice on thick.

"It's Angela or Ms. Hart...never mind. We don't have any time for games."

"Your boss always says that if we don't have the facts we just make them up. Tell him we're going to live up to that standard, and it'll make my example look tame."

"Are you trying to blackmail him?"

"Ms. Angie, I resent your tone. Obviously you're stressed out because Glacier won't stop hitting on you. Don't worry, you won't be named."

"I'm not worried. You haven't gotten my name right yet." Her tone dropped to a near whisper. "I can't talk here."

Damn, he was good.

"Tell the mayor I'll hold off until I can confirm a second source, but *some*one had better call me soon at this number." He gave her a private cell number.

Sid hung up. "I hate throwing my weight around like that."

"Obviously." Laura took a deep breath. "Whatever's happening, they're on lockdown, and the AG's office is worse. But I know they're going to have some sort of announcement soon."

"As soon as they can figure out what to say," Sid agreed.

"She wanted to talk."

Sid grinned. "She just needed a sympathetic ear. You and Eddie stand by. She's gonna say something good, on confidential background of course, but that's OK. We don't want the heat for leaking it to fall on her. She has a crush on me."

"Who doesn't?"

＊＊＊

Laura hated the wait. A storm cloud of news was about to burst, but there wasn't anything they could do but monitor all their sources. Once it broke, the story would be everywhere. She checked in with Chang, who confirmed that new locks were in place. He assured her they were pickproof, and underscored the fact that if she lost her keys, she would need to replace the whole lock assembly.

She shuddered at the thought of all the bugs in her place, but it certainly explained how Max knew that Drew was about to take a trip. She'd had only a moment to call him to let him know, and it had been hard to read his mood. He was swamped with his project in San Diego, and the arrest had shaken him up.

She wished there was something she could do for him, but at the moment the roller coaster just kept rolling along at a breakneck pace. It didn't leave much time to hold his hand.

In some ways, she was glad he wasn't around for Max to target, but the question of who might be next sprang into her head.

She didn't have long to ponder it though. Sid burst out of his office, yelling, "Laura! Eddie!" Eddie raced from the break room like a running back on a dash for the end zone. Laura jogged over to Sid.

Sid looked flushed, so she knew it must be big. "Take the police and emergency scanner, and jam over to Lewis's place."

"But we already have…" Laura began.

Sid cut her off. "You two are the ambulance chasers. The team that's in place will stay with the Lewis entourage."

"Ambulance?"

Sid sounded out of breath. "Our secret source just told me the cone of silence is because everyone is trying to figure out how to spin the news that Griffon Lewis is dead."

"Whoa." Eddie shouldered his camera bag.

"How? And why hasn't this already broken?" Laura asked.

"Same answer covers both questions."

"Sid…tick-tock…" Laura didn't have time for Sid's dramatic windups.

"Yeah, sure. Get this." He lowered his voice to a whisper. "Right now they want to say *accident* and leave it at that, but they haven't even called the ambulance yet because of the way the body was found."

"Murder?"

"Oh, way, way better."

"Sid!"

"Autoerotic asphyxiation."

✳ ✳ ✳

Eddie managed not to crash on the way to Lewis's place, but Laura had to endure an endless stream of off-color comments. "Will it say 'Death by monkey spank' on the coroner's report?"

She tried hard to ignore the juvenile prattle that the whole city would be indulging in soon enough. It wasn't just bizarre; it also raised so many questions.

"I mean, maybe it's me, but if I had a billion dollars I wouldn't do *anything* by myself. You know what I mean?"

"Yeah, Eddie, I think I got the idea for the last fifty blocks. All right?" Laura didn't mean to tear his head off. "I just need to think."

Eddie took the hint.

Sid, good as his word, was right. When they pulled up, Laura could hear a siren getting closer. Big city or not, she knew it was coming there.

She tried to imagine how long Lewis must have been... what...? Was he hanging by an alligator-skin belt in a cedar closet full of furs? She fought off a wave of giggles.

Eddie caught it. "See? Better get it out now so you don't do that shit on camera."

Laura embarrassed herself by bursting out laughing. She wanted to say it was just a release of all the recent stress. If asked, that was her story and she'd stick to it.

❋ ❋ ❋

The horde of reporters staking out the San Remo didn't know the nature of the ambulance call, but everyone pounced, in the likely case it involved someone famous. The body came out the side door on a gurney, covered by a sheet.

Eddie bulled his way through and made sure to get the shot.

The instant several members of Lewis's inner circle emerged, the reporters went wild. Now they had a good idea of who was under there. They descended on Lewis's attorney, a guy named Braverman, who looked like he was bracing himself to wade into a school of piranhas.

"Can you confirm that's Griffon Lewis?"

"Did he kill himself?"

"Was he shot?"

The questions overlapped but hewed to a similar theme. Laura waited for her chance.

Braverman held up his hands. "We'll have a statement shortly. Please give us the opportunity to reach all the members of his family…"

"Is it him? Is it Lewis?"

Braverman paused for what seemed to be an excruciating length of time. While he was bathed in a sea of flashes from the cameras, the lawyer in him was struggling to cover up what was obvious. He nodded. "The city has lost an exceptional citizen and world-class philanthropist. His great works will only be tarnished by the fact that he couldn't live to see his good name restored after these unfounded claims are proven false."

The reporters buzzed again with questions.

Braverman puffed out his chest. "Can't you allow a good man a moment of dignity before you start spreading lies about his life?" He glanced at Laura, and she figured this remark was intended primarily for her, since she had been the one to break the original story.

The sanctimony gave Laura the strength she needed to fill the momentary lull. "Mr. Braverman, can you comment on information we have that the body was found hours ago in a less than dignified position?"

Braverman blanched. She saw she'd hit a nerve.

She finished before the pandemonium erupted. "Do you deny that Lewis was found hanging in his closet, nude from the waist down? Is that why everyone waited? And could he have been saved?"

She might as well have tossed a grenade.

The news of Lewis's death would have already led every news outlet in the city.

Now it would lead nationally. And everyone knew where to go for more details.

❋❋❋

Eddie leaned on the horn and nudged the van through the group of reporters surrounding it. This wasn't a scoop; it was the bombshell of the year.

Laura would have been terrified she was getting it wrong if she didn't trust Sid as much as he trusted her.

Braverman's expression had given her and everyone else enough to run with, and now that the genie was out of the bottle, it would dominate the next few news cycles.

Now they had to get back to the station and air it. Maybe Sid had more to go on; if not, she was going to get sued.

The adrenaline began to wear off on the way back, and she could see Eddie hadn't been immune to it either. They rode in silence until he broke it.

"Hey, did it look like that sheet was sticking up when they wheeled him out?"

29

PALM READING

Laura's Apartment

Chang and Nelson sat at Laura's dining room table as Chang sorted through a stack of newspapers.

All of them featured what was being called "the shot heard round New York," which consisted of a blurred photo of Lewis, in all his half-nude glory, dangling in his closet. Chang's personal favorite was the *New York Post*'s, whose caption read "Performance art."

Laura wore a blue dress and camera-ready stage makeup. She'd popped back home between segments. Chang knew she must be exhausted under all the pancake. Laura may have been paying them, but he felt like he needed to schedule appointments just to brief her on her own case.

"Thanks for staying in town last night, Nelson. You too, Paul."

The selfish part of him loved the chance to work in New York because it meant he could spend more time with Colleen. Times like this, they almost felt like a normal couple.

"Thanks for covering the cost of the hotel," Nelson said as he looked at the shots and held a couple of the newspapers next to each other. Chang could see that they all featured the identical leaked photo. The source remained a secret, but it had hit all the networks and print outlets about the same time.

"All part of the 'plus expenses' part, right?" Laura cracked a smile. "But while we're on the topic, we need to figure out what to do about Max."

Chang admired her ability to compartmentalize.

"I don't do bodyguard work anymore," Nelson said. He couldn't take his eyes off the pictures.

Laura cocked her head, as though trying to figure out if Nelson was serious.

"He's an acquired taste," Chang said. "But he's right. We do want to ensure your safety, but you didn't hire us to become a security team."

"You don't think this Max thing is going to go away on its own?" Laura's tone made her question more of a statement.

"It's going to get worse, and then resolve itself one way or another." Nelson didn't even glance up.

Laura looked like she'd bitten into a lemon.

Chang checked his irritation at Nelson's bluntness. "Nelson flunked bedside manner at the academy."

"Resolve itself how?" Laura had already moved past the remark.

Nelson fired up his laptop.

"If Max wanted you dead, you wouldn't have gotten a chance to hire us in the first place." Nelson glanced at Laura briefly, then back at the picture. He scratched his scalp near the scar on the side of his head.

"So if it isn't to hurt me, what? Just to scare me? It's working."

"There are stranger motives." Nelson looked up while his laptop finished booting up. "I didn't say he couldn't or wouldn't hurt you, but he isn't ready to try yet. I'm not sure exactly what makes him tick."

"So what are you suggesting we do now?'

Chang cut in. "We started off wondering if you were just imagining Max was stalking you."

"But now you're fully on board." Laura made clear it wasn't a question, but Chang answered anyway by holding up the RF detector he used every time he reentered Laura's place. So far, no new bugs.

"We know you're being stalked and that our number-one suspect is not only behaving suspiciously, but that he's more than likely going after Drew."

"Likely?"

"I know, but I'm speaking about what we can prove," Chang said.

"All right." Laura listened.

"Nelson, tell her what you learned about the gun in Drew's bag."

Nelson was clicking away on the laptop like he was in another universe, but he spoke without missing a beat. "It turned out it was stolen from a security firm owner who's legally licensed to carry in New York. It was reported stolen along with cash, cameras, and other valuables."

"Including surveillance equipment. Bold crime." Chang felt his normal paranoia level spike. He made a note to call Betty and ask her to change the alarm codes at their office as well as activate the hidden surveillance camera when they weren't there. "Sound like someone we know?"

Laura seemed to grasp the next step. "So you think we have enough to go back to the cops? I don't think they ever started loving me."

"Not any cops, but yeah, I do think it's time to have a sit-down with Ron Sieger."

"But he—"

"Hates you. I know." Chang spoke in a gentle voice. "But we trust each other, and, while we have nothing close to a legal case, Ron needs to hear what we've got and what I think."

"What good will that do?" Laura looked frustrated.

"We upped the ante with Max, and he knows we're onto him, at least as far as his stalking you. But I can't babysit you forever, waiting for him to make a move. We need to cast the net wider, and Ron, believe it or not, may have some way to help." Chang turned to Nelson for support and saw that his friend was deep inside himself. "Nelson?"

Nelson was rocking back and forth, and his fingers were flying over the keyboard. Photos flickered on the screen. Chang heard Nelson whispering, "Come out, come out, wherever you are."

"Is he OK?"

Chang shook his head, but said, "He's fine. Right, Nelson?"

Nelson hissed. "That's it! OK, now..." His fingers began flying over the keyboard again.

Nelson looked flushed, but Chang saw a look of serenity suddenly cross his face. "Laura, do you plan to run another segment on Lewis committing suicide?" Nelson asked.

"Nobody is calling this a suicide. It was an accident. A really strange one, but—"

"It's wrong."

She stiffened. "Nelson, the whole city is exploding with this story. The last thing I need is a morality lecture."

Chang interrupted. "That's not what he meant. What are you saying, Nelson?"

Nelson looked at them both. "See for yourself." He pointed at the computer. "Griffon Lewis was murdered."

30

CLOSE UP

"Catch us up, Nelson." Laura stood behind the two men so they could all see the screen. "You learned something about Lewis?"

"No. And I don't know anything about his personal life that isn't already public knowledge. But look at this picture." Nelson pointed to the unblurred, graphic image that was all over the Internet.

"We've all seen it. Could hardly miss it," Chang said.

"But you're not looking." Nelson sounded impatient.

"I think it's clear what he was doing—or at least trying to do. People die from it sometimes by accident. It happens," Chang said.

Nelson shook his head vigorously. "I *know* what it's supposed to look like." He was blushing. "But I'm telling you, the body is posed."

"How do you know?" Laura was paying close attention.

Nelson turned beet red, but he didn't waver. "Look at his hands. He's holding himself with his right hand."

Chang saw just that. Lewis was perched with his butt on the edge of a footstool leaning forward, and held up by the rope around his neck. "Presumably he thought he'd be able to tip backward and sit up enough to reopen his airway. Except it didn't work out that way. That's the point, isn't it?"

"Paul, don't be dense. I get that. But Griffon Lewis is left-handed."

"How do you know?" Laura asked.

"I didn't." Nelson caught himself. "Maybe I did, way in back." He pointed to his head. "But that was what bothered me about the picture, something seemed wrong."

"You mean aside from a risky habit of pleasuring himself in his closet?"

Nelson ignored Chang's sarcasm. "Some of the regular shots of the guy must have stuck in my mind, but I didn't know what it was until I started studying some pictures online. Look." He pointed to several publicity shots taken at various events.

"Holy crap." Laura leaned in to get a closer look at the screen.

Here was one of Lewis signing a giant check, with his left hand. Another of him playing tennis, lefty again.

"But that doesn't prove anything." Laura sounded like she was trying to convince herself.

Chang knew better than to doubt Nelson. "True. But the medical examiner could probably determine if he..." Chang wanted to phrase things delicately.

"Indulged in an ambidextrous manner?" Laura supplied.

"Well put, yes," Chang said.

"Professional broadcaster," she added with a little smile.

"Do you know who released the picture?" Nelson asked Laura.

"No. As far as I know, it showed up online and the tipster was anonymous. Once it got out, of course it spread like wildfire," she said.

"The medical examiner's office is going to be embarrassed." Chang rubbed his chin.

"That's the funny thing. They deny it was them. Nobody believes them, but they're having a fit. They insist it isn't their picture." Laura started to pace.

"They took photos though, right?" Chang knew any scene of that kind would require such documentation.

Laura nodded. "That's one of the things we're meeting about. It's a side story, but if what you say is right, Nelson, it changes everything."

"The AG must be freaking out. If they prove the picture wasn't taken or released by the medical examiner, they'll know this whole thing wasn't an accident," Chang said.

"We think they *are* freaking, but they're doing it behind the curtain. We just assumed it was because it all looks so weird that they needed some time to figure out how to spin it," Laura said.

"If Nelson's right, it could be for much bigger reasons. But if it wasn't the ME's photo, who took it?" Chang stood up. "We were talking about next steps, and this is all the more reason to get together with Ron. Maybe he can keep an ear to the ground for us."

"You won't need me for that." Laura looked at her phone. "Only twenty messages. I'd better run. Call me later. Don't forget to lock up." She caught herself. "Sorry, reflex. I always say that to Drew."

※ ※ ※

Nineteenth Precinct Station

"Too early to knock off for beers. Will you guys settle for lousy coffee, or do you want to go out for something decent?"

"I could use a chai," Nelson said.

Ron made a face. "I only drink those after I get a pedicure."

"I think I neglect my feet," Nelson said, with such a straight face that Chang couldn't tell if he was serious or not.

"C'mon, let's go out." Chang didn't want to risk being overheard.

Ron took the hint.

The prelunch crowds were spilling into the street as the trio walked down the block. Chang kept an eye out for anything unusual but reminded himself that his filter that detected the slightest offbeat person in Delaware was overwhelmed in the city.

They stopped at a coffee place called Sacred Grounds.

"I think they sell that granola-flavored coffee here." Ron held open the door for Nelson. "Don't say 'narc.' The place will clear out, and we'll never get served."

"OK." Nelson strode in and stopped at the board, which was crowded with offerings rendered in different colored chalks.

Chang walked to the line. "I'll handle the orders." It'd be dark before Nelson figured out what he wanted.

They sat down at a small table, and Ron looked ready to listen. "Our girl's sure been busy lately."

"That's one of the reasons we need to talk. She's right about the ex-husband."

"Yeah?"

"We might need your help."

"Anything for Laura Stark."

Chang didn't take the bait. Ron could rehash his beef with Laura later. He gave Ron a quick rundown of what they'd discovered and told him they were sure Max's actions were escalating, especially because he'd involved Drew. Chang left out the part about the tracker—no need to bog the man down with details, especially if they were illegal—but did describe how Max had given him the slip.

"If she came to me with this, I'd think she was crazy. And after I tried to prove it, I'd know she was. But you're not kidding?"

Chang didn't need to answer that, and Nelson was too busy nursing a burned tongue. Happened every time.

"Never seen anything like it," Chang said. "You can talk to the boyfriend. He thought Laura was paranoid too; you could tell. Not anymore."

"And you believe what this boyfriend had to say about what happened at the warehouse?"

Chang nodded. "At first Drew thought *we* were a couple crooks. By the time he left town, on bail now, he trusted us to keep Laura safe."

Ron sat still. He took a deep breath and blew it out toward the ceiling. "OK. Sounds like we have a first-rate whack-job for the husband. Any point in dusting for prints at her place?"

"I already did and have some latents if you want them, but the scene was tainted by the time I got there. By now all we'd learn for sure is whether or not he'd been there, and the bugs tell me he was. Would we find enough to hold up in court? I doubt it."

"Stay on this, and tell me about anything we can make stick. We'll pick him up. It won't be a permanent solution, but maybe this is a case where the little stuff adds up, and we can get him some lockup time," Ron said.

"Thanks, and if I need a plate run or some other info…"

Ron held up a hand. "Let's take it on a case-by-case basis."

Chang took that as a yes. Ron just didn't want to give away the store. If he needed to bend the rules, he reserved the right to say no.

"So Nelson, you had something else?"

Nelson was staring at the people coming and going and looked lost in his own world. Without even turning toward Ron, he said, "Oh yeah. Griffon Lewis was murdered."

Ron abruptly stopped sipping his coffee. Chang thought he'd do a Hollywood-style spit-take and spray coffee across the table, but he kept his cool.

"Just like that?"

"I'm sure the body was posed. And Laura said she heard the medical examiners are claiming the picture isn't theirs. That's easy enough to prove, and if true, then the million-dollar question is, who took the picture and then decided to leak it?"

Nelson showed Ron the pictures and explained his theory.

"Holy shit." As Ron leaned back, Chang heard his chair squeak.

He thought it might break under the big guy's weight. Between himself and Ron, they weighed more than half the skinny kids in the place put together.

"Ron, you OK?" Chang saw that the man had gone pale. It took a lot to faze him.

Ron gave a furtive look around and leaned in as he whispered, "This stays between us, clear?"

The men nodded. Nelson was looking straight at Ron now.

"A buddy with the FBI told me that Lewis wanted to talk deal. He wouldn't talk with the AG because he's in the mayor's pocket. He insisted that the Feds be the ones to cut a deal."

"All for art theft charges?" Maybe. They were felonies after all.

"Only partly. Lewis saw they were throwing him to the wolves, and he said he knew about more than just art. He said the scandal was much, much bigger, and it involved national security at the highest levels."

"What?" Chang didn't bother to hide his confusion.

"I know. Maybe the guy just snapped under the pressure. Looks like he was into some weird stuff."

"Or not," Nelson piped in.

Ron glanced once more at the shots on the computer and lowered the screen. "Let's say that's right. So Lewis wants to talk to the Feds, and then he's suddenly murdered. The timing's certainly suspicious."

"For who?"

"That's why we make the big money," Ron said. "Start with who gains by his death."

"His heirs." Nelson almost sounded like he was joking.

"We can set his family aside for the moment," Chang said.

Ron spoke. "Lewis was the mayor's go-to guy on the social and fund-raising fronts. I think he was a low-key power-behind-the-throne guy. I know if Lewis wanted a project to move forward, it stood a good chance; and if he didn't, it stood none."

"After Laura broke the story on Lewis, the mayor ditched him like he was a child molester, and the AG fast-tracked a case against him. Why?"

"Money? Politics? How or why I don't know, but those are probably our best places to start."

"Just business, nothing personal?" Nelson spoke up. "If Griffon Lewis wasn't into the autoerotic scene, then someone went far out of their way to humiliate him."

Ron twirled a butter knife in his fingers. "You're right. Lots of ways to stage an accident. I'm going to talk to my FBI pal and the guys I trust in my house. We don't have enough to open a murder investigation for now."

"No?" Nelson's insights usually outpaced the legal system.

"With the players we have here? You worked in this town." Ron shrugged. "But it's early days still. Without your observation, we might never have even started looking."

Chang cut in. "The key, if it was murder, is who or what did Lewis threaten by what he might expose? Think you can get more out of your friend?"

Ron smiled. "Well, it's not like I ever saved his life, but I bet if I can bring him fresh intel, he'll horse-trade." He turned serious. "But this is the big leagues. If I stick my nose into this and it touches either the AG or the mayor, I'm through in this city. I might get blackballed even if there are charges that stick."

"It's not so bad." Chang half joked. Chang and Nelson hadn't been run out of town on the proverbial rail, but they'd certainly worn out their welcome with the NYPD brass.

Nelson pointed to the latticework of scars on Chang's hand and his own head. "See what you've been missing?"

"If you can make it in Delaware, you can hack it anywhere, huh?" Ron drained his coffee. "You've given me a lot to chew on here. Lemme talk to some people, on the down low, and see what else shakes loose. And remember, *I* might believe you, Nelson, but it won't be my call." Ron stood.

"I appreciate that." Chang and Nelson stood. Nelson ended up tipping over his chair. It drew a few looks, and Chang saw a look of pity from a girl in Birkenstocks. He thought he overheard the word *hydrocephalus*.

Nelson looked over. Apparently his ears still worked fine. "Nope. It's all me. I think it might have been too many crossword puzzles as a kid."

The girl stared at her phone and blushed.

Nelson started toward the door.

Ron stared. "I'd forgotten."

"Smooth with the ladies like always," Chang said.

31

ONE EVERY MINUTE

WBAC

"Laura, I love you to death, and you've been a gold mine lately, but you're going to have to give me more before we mess around with a rumor like that." Sid shook his head, but he was bouncing on his toes after Laura told him about Nelson's discovery.

"We might be the first to make the connection, but we won't be the last. We might want to be prepared." Laura figured it stood to reason that others would eventually see what seemed obvious now.

Yes, but no one else, including you, noticed, did they?

Nelson was one of the strangest characters she'd ever run across, but she knew his record. It was something else to see Nelson and Chang at work though. Nelson acted like he was half cop and half Ouija board, and Chang was a hell of a lot smarter than she'd thought he was when she first met them. Her background research had painted Nelson as the brains and Chang as the brawn of the operation, but it wasn't like that.

"Hear me out. You have to admit, it's strange, right? And have you ever heard of Lewis being kinky?"

"I never heard of him being involved with art smuggling either, but when you came to me with that, what was I supposed to do? You dropped all the photos, details, right in my lap. Hell, the stories wrote themselves, and all with the lovely bonus of being true. Same with the charity piece. Airtight."

"I know, but could we at least look into…"

Sid waved her off. "We're flat out as it is. And the whole city is wild for the story. Don't get me wrong, if you get more manna that proves your point, we'll be all over it."

Laura got an idea. "What if you hired Chang and Nelson to investigate it?"

"I have an investigation team on payroll already. I'm looking at one of them." Sid pointed at her. "And aren't your guys busy, or did that get straightened out?"

If it had been anyone else, Laura would have told him to butt out of her personal business, but she knew Sid really cared and wasn't trying to pry. Still, she didn't want to share everything with him. "No, they're still on it, and it's going to keep them up here for a while longer."

How much longer? She wished she knew.

She tried to switch her focus back to the Lewis story.

Sid didn't push it. "Let them do their job. While we're on the subject, if you need any help, just let me know."

"Thanks, Sid. Really."

"So do you think you could reach out to your source, STP, maybe ask if he knows anything about the sex stuff?"

Laura folded her arms. "It doesn't work that way." She knew he wasn't asking her who her source was or for a chance to talk to him himself, though she could tell he was jealous at times—especially during a breaking story, when he looked and acted more like a reporter and less like the station's producer and owner. "He calls me. Always. And on a different phone every time, so there wouldn't even be a point calling back." She'd tried that once years before and it had just rung. Now she knew better. The little man insisted on his privacy.

Her cell phone pulsed. She saw it was Drew. "Mind if I take this?" Sid nodded and left her office.

"Morning." She hoped her enthusiasm didn't sound as forced as it felt.

"Hey." He sounded exhausted. "I see you're keeping busy."

Was that a dig? She'd tried to check in when she could, but they were both swamped with work. "You know how it goes. The hits keep coming. How are you doing?"

"Also busy. The audit here is dragging on. But the client has been understanding."

She couldn't imagine how awkward it must have been for Drew to miss the first meeting due to being arrested. She knew he'd done all he could to downplay it as a huge misunderstanding.

That wasn't quite the word, was it?

"I don't want to get into it over the phone, but we may be on the right track with what happened regarding your case."

"Yeah?" It was the first time he'd sounded upbeat in a while.

"Working on proof, but we have some great leads."

"You sure you can't give me a hint?"

"Not here. I'm at work." She lowered her voice even though she had privacy in her office. The truth was that she didn't want to bring up all the bugs and the danger Max posed while Drew was away. She knew he wanted to be back here to help, but in some ways she was more worried about him than about herself. Max seemed to be taking particular delight in tormenting him. What else might he try?

"Call me later at the hotel, OK? I want to hear about it."

"All right. I'm late for a meeting. Catch you later." She just wished he'd stay away until this was over.

But when will it be over?

***

Laura was about to head to the bathroom when her cell rang again. She thought it was Drew again and was about to let it roll to voice mail, but then peeked at the ID just in case. XXX XXX-XXXX.

STP.

"Laura Stark."

"Getting any sleep?" STP's Brahmin voice sounded smug.

"Not thanks to your latest. This one has legs."

"You have no idea."

What was that supposed to mean? She grabbed a pad. "You're spoiling me."

"Nothing more than you deserve."

"You didn't call to chat, but can I ask a question?"

"You can ask." STP sounded excited, which was unusual for him.

"Was Griffon Lewis really into that autoerotic stuff?"

"I didn't know the man. Certainly not in that way. Why?"

She hesitated to say anything more. She didn't know STP, but the guy had been feeding her stories for years, all of them rock solid. She used to try to figure out who could be so well connected as to have access to such a range of information. Cops might, but the guy she'd met was too short and frail to be a cop. That made her think of Nelson, who was nobody's idea of a lawman.

"I have another source that thinks Lewis might not have died by accident."

"Are you trying to make me jealous?"

Weird. He wasn't usually so—what was the right word?—flirtatious.

She decided to play along. "You know I'm not a one-source gal."

"As long as I'm your most trusted."

"No question." *C'mon, man, what are you playing at?*

"I don't bring you speculation. You know that. But since you asked, I don't know for sure, but it wouldn't surprise me a bit if Lewis didn't die by accident."

"Why is that?"

"You'll see." STP sounded like he was going to burst.

"So are you going to tell me, or is it going to be a surprise?" Laura didn't mean to push, but he really sounded odd.

"Oh, I'm sure you're going to be surprised."

"I'm listening."

"All the stories I've given you will pale next to this one. You think you're famous now? You're going to be a star."

She had a hard time imagining something that could outdo STP's latest bombshell. "You're setting the bar high."

"I'll call you back with the story. Until then, two things."

She knew better than to make demands. He'd tell her when he was ready. "Go ahead."

"I've never lied to you, and I won't start now." STP spoke with a fierce intensity.

"I never said…"

"We looked so young in that picture, don't you think?"

"What picture?" Laura thought of all the stories she'd ever gotten from him and whether or not there had been some grip and grin in the aftermath. All the short men from her past flashed through her mind.

The voice roughened, transforming over the line, and she suddenly felt paralyzed with fear. "Pocket, rocket. Me and you in a locket."

"No." Laura knew the voice. She used to hear it in her nightmares. It was Max's voice for his Highpockets the Clown character.

"I promised to take care of you." Max laughed, raspy and raucous. "I've missed you since your buddies took my toys."

Hot anger mingled with icy fear like two sink taps on full blast. She screamed into the phone. "Max, stay out of my life, you crazy son of a bitch!"

"I remember *that* voice." Max laughed again.

"You're going to go to jail." Laura tried to focus on her breathing and slow the rush of thoughts. "What did you do with the real STP? How did you know he called himself that, anyway?"

"Don't be a rube. Every story was my gift to you."

"I met him…"

"Snap out of it, babe. You met an actor with a distinctive voice. A one-time gig 'cause I knew you'd insist on a meet."

"If that's true, where is he? I want to see him again. Prove—"

Max cut her off. "He retired from earth soon after his work with me was done. That's a dead end, and you're beginning to tick me off. STP was so you'd listen. If you're smart, you'll listen now."

"I'm not scared of you." Laura clung to her anger like a life raft.

"I don't want you to be scared. I want you to hang on my every word. Remember, when I call you back, you're getting a shot at the story of a lifetime."

"You took the pictures. You're the one who broke into Lewis's place." Laura's mind spun.

"Decent security, but I've seen better. You need to use more imagination, Laura." Now Laura heard a dead-on imitation of Marchetti's lawyer. "Ms. Stark, Daniel Bigelow here. I think I may have made a terrible mistake making a guy like Marchetti think I was going to rat him out. It's dark in here, but I do believe I'm head first in a landfill." Max laughed into the phone and hung up.

Laura's breakfast pushed hard up her throat.

She reached a trash can just in time.

32

STARK CHOICES

Chang and Nelson entered the building in the late afternoon when most people were streaming out. Laura was standing by the security guard and some slick-looking guy with gold chains and hair plugs. He looked like a midlife crisis from the 1970s, but Chang understood that it was Sid Gold, the owner of the station.

Laura spotted him and waved him over. Chang acted like a blocker for Nelson, who strolled behind him in his usual self-contained fog. Chang kept an eye out for Max, but he really just tried to check out anyone who matched his approximate height and build. He smoldered with anger.

"Thanks for meeting me here," Laura said.

Chang thought she'd seemed scared before. Now she looked like she was caught inside a waking nightmare.

The short guy snatched up Chang's hand. "Sid Gold. Heard a lot about you, Detective." He looked past Chang. "And you must be Mr. Rogers. You two were some kind of hot story back in the day."

"Good to meet you." Chang tried to shoehorn his remark. "Some of that was exaggerated."

"Great copy," Sid said to them, simultaneously waving to people he recognized, which seemed to include just about everyone. They walked toward the bank of elevators.

"You have some metabolism, Mr. Gold," Nelson said, looking at him.

That actually slowed Sid down a step. He looked back. "Thanks, I guess."

"The energy comes off you in big waves. Like a generator in a small frame." Nelson appeared fascinated and then turned to Laura. "When we can talk in private, I want to hear everything."

"How about upstairs?" Laura said.

Chang answered. "Nothing about the case until I sweep the room."

Sid led them to a private elevator, using a key to call it. As soon as they stepped inside the gleaming brass-and-mirror enclosure, Chang pulled the RF detector out of his pocket. "It's clean." He shook his head. "I should have assumed he would plant bugs at work. If he could—" Chang stopped himself.

Sid caught the pause and glanced at him. Laura spoke. "It's OK, Paul. I'm bringing Sid all the way in. I trust him, and I think we need as many eyes looking out for Max as possible."

"Your call." Chang looked at Sid. "Nothing personal, Mr. Gold."

Sid smiled. "Gotta have a thick skin in this business."

"If he could get to you in your apartment, I should have figured he could also get into the office," Chang finished.

The elevator stopped, and they stepped out near Sid's office. Chang went directly to Laura's first. The RF detector flashed and beeped like his grip on it was causing it pain. He found a bug in the lamp and a tap on her office phone. Nelson swept a conference room and found one there.

They checked Sid's office last. Clean.

❄ ❄ ❄

Chang listened as Laura recapped her conversation with Max. Nelson sat transfixed, like he was recording every word. Actually he was. Every detail would help Nelson paint a detailed portrait in his head; before long he'd know Max better than Laura herself did.

Sid sat and tried to take it all in. The man probably didn't experience this state of stunned disbelief very often in his jaded world. "You're telling me that all these years your STP scoops came from your ex-husband?"

"I'm having a hard time believing it myself, but that's exactly what I'm saying." Laura gripped a pen until her fingers turned white. "All this time I thought he was through bothering me, and now I discover he's been watching me every second, planting stories, shaping my career, for Christ's sake."

"But the stories were real?" Chang had seen his share of stalkers, but this was new.

"I checked and rechecked the info, and his tips always panned out." She dabbed her eyes.

Chang could see it just about killed her to display this much emotion at work. Not that anyone blamed her.

"Why wouldn't they? He either caused them or dug the scoop up himself," she continued, blowing her nose.

Nelson spoke up. "You think he posed as Marchetti's lawyer while you set up that interview?"

"He must have. God, I'm so stupid. Why would Bigelow go and provoke a thug like Marchetti when he knew exactly what kind of man he was?"

Nelson closed his eyes. "Marchetti was supposed to be all worried about that key piece of evidence. The purse, right?"

Laura nodded. "Yes, the one we're sure was stolen from the police evidence locker." Sid watched Nelson, fascinated.

"So, assuming Marchetti orchestrated the removal of the purse, he should know where it was or if it still existed. He'd know it was with Bigelow. I can't think of a reason at that point that they would want such an incriminating item around. Why not destroy it?"

Chang spoke. "Maybe until Laura contacted him, Marchetti believed the purse was gone. I can imagine he'd rather keep his own hands clean. Which meant he trusted Bigelow."

Nelson opened his eyes. "Right. Bigelow, the real one, must have had the purse in his possession. For whatever reason. Perhaps as an insurance policy of sorts?"

"All Max had to do was add a credible threat that Bigelow'd betray him," Chang said.

Sid cut in. "How would Max have any idea? Are you saying Max worked for Marchetti?"

"He didn't." Laura looked like she might shake apart. "He must have spied on the lawyer after he saw me covering the case so closely."

Nelson closed his eyes again. "That fits. He went fishing. He searched the lawyer's place and hit the jackpot. Max knew from following the case how important the purse was and decided to trick Laura in order to flush out Marchetti." Nelson swallowed and continued. "Cold. Max had to know how a guy like Marchetti would respond. The real Bigelow must have never seen it coming. Marchetti got tricked the same as Laura by Max's imitation of his own lawyer. After that, Marchetti took matters into his own hands."

"That's why Marchetti agreed to the interview," Laura said. "He wanted to rub it in my face. He knew he was home free once he'd removed the purse—and Bigelow. After that he wanted to get in his victory dance." Laura stared down at the table and clasped her hands.

Sid looked unconvinced. "If you're so sure Max isn't working for Marchetti, why'd he serve up the lawyer like that?"

Laura glanced at him. "Sid, don't you get it? Max has followed my career, and every chance he got, he inserted himself into the story, digging up dirt or whatever, just so he could feed it to me."

"Like a rogue detective agency," Nelson said. Chang gave him a sharp look. They might cross a few lines now and then, but nothing like this and only to help.

"He got this man killed for me..."

Chang took her by the wrist, gently. "You can't do this. Not to yourself or anyone else. We need you to help us stop this man. He did what he did for himself. Never forget that."

"I wish it were that simple. I was more than happy to get the stories, and I took the Emmys that went with them."

Sid smacked his palm on the huge, polished oak table. "Don't beat yourself up. You have Emmys Max had nothing to do with. He took advantage of your skills as a reporter. Whatever his crazy reasons. But you're still the best I've ever seen."

Laura thanked him, but Chang saw that she was reliving all the stories and estimating the damage she could blame herself for causing.

"Laura, he's that good at imitation?" Chang asked.

"I married him, and he's fooled me over and over. Yes. If he hears a voice he can nail the impression. It's scary."

"How do you catch a guy like that? I'm ready to go the cops. Nobody bugs my place," Sid said. "What can we charge him with?"

"He's careful enough to make it hard to prove," Chang replied. "But I'm not worried about that right now. He's raised the stakes. So will we. I think Drew had the right idea."

"How's that?"

"The direct approach." Chang stood. "I've got a few things to do, but I'll make sure you get home safe. I'll pick you up out front when you're finished with the evening broadcast. If you don't get a call from my cell with my caller ID, don't trust my voice. Just in case, confirm it is me."

"How?" Laura looked confused but seemed to take comfort in the fact that he was watching out for her.

"Ask me the color of my shirt."

"But he might be watching you and…"

"I know. The correct answer is thirty-five forty-four." Chang's old badge number. "He says 'blue,' it isn't me."

"Got it."

"The less you know, the better. But with any luck, this gets sorted out in the morning." Chang didn't add that he'd never had much success with luck, but he planned to straighten Max out. Screw the law.

33

KNOCK KNOCK

Manhattan

The next morning Chang met Nelson in front of his hotel. He wondered if he should use a different car from his own red Bimmer but decided the delay wasn't worth it. Besides, stealth wasn't the point today, was it?

"Why don't you want to call in Ron?" Even as Nelson asked, Chang sensed that his partner knew the answer.

Chang waited until he was in the car. "Want me to say it out loud?"

"I guess so."

"I'm raising the cost of doing business for this piece of garbage." Chang lifted his sweatshirt and exposed his Kimber Compact .45.

"It's not going to look good if you gun the man down."

"I might disagree, but the law would share your view, including Ron. You heard what happened to Drew. Let's just say I'm prepared to defend myself."

"I plan to let my fists do the talking."

Chang laughed at the image. "Partner, you get to watch my back and yell 'look out.' After that, just duck."

Chang would have preferred a tough, seasoned cop like Ron to have his back, but he didn't expect an ambush. Not exactly.

He was tired of playing the game by Max's rules. Ron might help later, but Chang didn't want to waste a favor, and until they could serve a warrant, Ron risked trouble if he were discovered freelancing with Chang.

They drove to Brooklyn, and Chang parked near the Laughing Matters warehouse. They could see that the building across the street from it was already buzzing with activity. Although both the large truck and the white van were parked there, he couldn't detect any sign of movement in or around Max's warehouse.

"He should be open for business."

"Want to stake it out until he appears?" Nelson looked worried. "Not sure that's the best use of our time."

"Nope. It would be a bonus to see him, but I'm happy to call him out in front of his employees. We don't need to protect his reputation. He'll hear about it even if he isn't around."

Chang picked up a prepaid cell phone and dialed the toll-free number on the side of the truck.

"Laughing Matters, where we take our humor seriously. This is Kelsey. How may I direct your call?"

"Just checking your business hours."

"The showroom is open from ten to four. Do you need directions?"

It was ten fifteen. "I think I can find it, thanks."

***

"So what is it you want me to do?" Nelson asked as he walked toward the warehouse with Chang. They saw workers across the street at Painter's Ice Company. The front of Laughing Matters looked quiet.

"If we see him, I want you to look him in the eye and work your magic. Get a read on him, and we might pry more out of him than if I was alone."

"And what are you going to do?"

"One way or another, he's going to change his attitude."

When they reached the front door, they saw that the reception area was dark and the door was locked. Through the glass, Chang could see what the secretary he had just spoken with called a showroom, and there were various pictures on the wall of what looked like an office area. All dark. He saw a pair of signs on the inside of the front door. The first said "Guard Clowns on Duty: No Trespassing" and was accompanied by a traffic-sign-style graphic of a stick figure getting a pie in the face. The other was a hand-lettered sign that simply read "Gone Fishing."

"Cute." Chang remembered Drew and looked up, just in case. He called the number again and reached Kelsey once more.

"Are you in back or something? I'm at the front door of your showroom and it's locked."

"I'm sorry, sir. We're an answering service, but I can take a message. Is there a number where they can call you back?"

"Thanks, Kelsey. He'll be able to find me."

He hung up. Dead end. He thought about going around to the back and practicing his lock picking. The back faced train tracks and a cemetery, which made it tempting.

He turned to find Nelson strolling across the street toward some burly workers.

They looked at him with some amusement. Chang decided to hang back. He caught that they were speaking Spanish. His was pretty bad—other than knowing when he was being cursed at—but Nelson was fluent.

When they looked done chatting, Chang saw Nelson reach into his pocket. He held out a stick of gum. The big guy shook his head, and the group laughed.

Nelson headed back over. While he waited, Chang listened for any movement inside. He went to the big truck and felt the hood. Cold. Same with the van. Odd.

"Partner, I think they were looking for something a bit more spendable than gum."

"Oh." Nelson's gaps in social nuance still surprised Chang even after all these years.

"What did they say?"

"I asked them what was going on across the street, and they told me it's been dead quiet for a couple days. They said it's slowed down a lot lately, but they haven't seen the tall guy at all for days."

"Really?" Now he was itching to get inside.

Chang started across the street.

"Where you going?"

"C'mon."

The men looked more apprehensive at the sight of Chang. He wasn't surprised.

The oldest one approached him. "*Policía?*"

"Ex-*policía*." Chang hoped it translated. He pressed a couple of twenties into the man's hand. "*Gracias.*"

"*De nada.*"

The men returned to work. Chang was pretty sure they didn't have to worry about interference now.

❋ ❋ ❋

"Holler if you see anyone coming," Chang told Nelson. There was an open patch of grass between the fence line dividing the train tracks and the back door. He couldn't pass up the chance to work the door unobserved, but he knew the two twenties would be poor insurance if he took too long or walked out with anything.

He might have time only for a quick look around, but he hoped it would tell him something.

He went to work on the lock, a decent but pickable unit, while Nelson stood lookout. If he'd been in shabby clothes, Nelson could easily have passed for a crazy living under a bridge.

Got it. "If anybody arrives, you flash your detective ID. It'll slow them down, and I'll be right there."

"All right, but hurry."

Chang checked the door for alarm strips or sensors. He was surprised to see none. It was pitch-dark inside, but he had a penlight to use if necessary. He didn't want to give up his advantage by advertising his position, but by coming in the door, that was moot. The light from outside might as well have been a flare. He wanted to draw his gun, but he was the intruder here, and he hated to admit he felt jumpy.

He strained his ears for any alarm sounds, which he suspected would come from the front where a box would chime briefly if a legitimate person were about to key in a code.

Nothing. But the skin on his neck tightened, and his sense of danger went on high alert. He scanned the floor right by the door. Something.

Infrared motion detectors would have picked him up already, and that wouldn't alert him no matter how keyed up he was. Every instinct told him not to step inside. But now that the door was open he had to get in, even if only for a moment.

For the first time in at least a year, he felt the real dragon stir in his chest. Not the raging beast that threatened to take control of his body when he let it give him strength and speed in a fight. This was the cunning side of the beast, the side that sharpened his senses and boosted his reflexes. It surfaced whenever he felt threatened. He let his hearing stretch across the dark room. Creaks and breezes gave him the impression of a vast space.

Something dripped in the far corner. A power box gave off a faint hum. His eyes began to adjust to the darkness.

He looked down again, and this time he saw it.

Barely thicker than a hair, a near-invisible thread stretched across the doorway. He bent down and felt it, his touch softer than a caress. It was stronger than it appeared. Fishing line. He took a slow step over it and then stepped over with his other foot so that he was standing clear of the thread.

"Nelson, keep the door open, but don't come in. Booby trap." He spoke in a loud whisper.

"This is a bad idea."

Probably. But he was inside now. He returned his full focus to the interior. His senses expanded, but the dragon remained in check. Shu had taught him how to control it better than he used to, but he hadn't put it to the test in a long time.

Chang followed the string and saw the first pulley. He followed it with his gaze and, once his eyes had adjusted, saw the bag perched over the door.

Flour. He recalled Drew's experience.

Stay cool. It could be a grenade or a sword or who knew what next time.

Chang moved into the space and saw trapezes and scaffolding. Training area. Made sense.

Chang moved more slowly than he liked, but he stopped every few feet to feel for other trip wires. He saw mirrors and felt Plexiglas walls. He could see why this had felt like such a fun house to Drew.

Chang retreated to a back wall and worked his way along it until he felt an interior door. He estimated his position inside the building and guessed he must be close to where the office portion was on the other side. Was this the door Drew had come through from the office?

He swept his fingertips along the wall, above and around the door frame. He felt something like a slit on the smooth surface and two more next to the first. He wanted to look with the light but didn't dare. He still heard nothing, but his unease had magnified as he'd advanced farther into the room.

He remembered what Drew told him about the knives. Could those be the holes? Yes.

Chang tried the latch for the door and discovered that it wasn't locked. He suddenly felt an electric tingle that made his skin crawl. He pulled the gun out and wrapped a finger around the trigger guard. He crouched and used his left hand to turn the knob. The whole hand ached with the effort, and the muscles threatened to cramp, but he managed to open the door. He squinted at the relatively bright light but heard nothing close by. He felt for trip wires, found none, and stepped through the door.

Chang found himself standing in the showroom and saw the front door on the other side of a counter. He could see across the street; the workers were no longer outside.

He was thinking about walking out the front door, if it was easy to unlock, when he heard a thump. It was back near the office area and sounded like it had come from above.

Max lived here. Was there a loft?

Adrenaline washed the pain out of his hand as he rushed into the office. An open door on the other side led to a staircase. He noticed a desk and more pictures, but there was no time to take it all in. He smelled something. Smoke?

Yes. He heard running footsteps above, charged up the stairs, and shouldered through a wooden door. That's when he smelled the gasoline.

Oh no.

In the center of the sparse loft bedroom was a large bucket. A plastic lid sat nearby. The stench of gasoline mixed with the distinct odor of a burning cigar, which dangled by a thread over the bucket.

Chang reacted without thinking. The burning tip of the stogie was nearing the thread, which was tied to the ceiling. He heard more thumps above. The roof? No time now. Chang raced forward, batted the cigar aside, and stomped it out. Then he saw the unlatched window.

Next to the window a hand-lettered sign read "Close, but no…"

Nelson!

Chang decided against climbing out the window and ran back downstairs. The front door lock had a simple deadbolt knob on the inside, so he unlocked it and flew out the door. He looked left and right. No one. He held the gun at his side and sprinted around the corner. As he turned the next corner, he dreaded what he might see.

Once around it, he raised his weapon, but Nelson was right where he'd left him. Nelson must have heard something, though, because he looked like he was yelling into the warehouse.

"Don't go in there!" Chang shouted. Nelson jumped like he'd been hit.

Chang calmed his imagination and saw that Nelson was only startled.

"I heard running on the roof."

"Did you see anything?"

"No."

"He was going to torch the place," Chang said.

"Let's beat it," Nelson said. "If he rigged anything else, it could go anytime."

"All right. Probably don't need to get charged with arson. Let's get back to the car. I'll call the fire department and tell them I smell smoke."

Nelson smiled. "That's good. They'll have to go in and investigate."

"Yup, and I'll let Ron know what's up. Maybe they can gather some info." They made it back to the street. Chang holstered his gun but scanned the street. The ice company guys were gone, probably off on a delivery. Other civilians were going about their business. Just like that, everything seemed normal.

Chang saw no signs of smoke when he looked back at the warehouse, but he'd still call it in. He knew he'd left traces that he had been in the building, but it wasn't a murder scene, so he wasn't worried.

A block away from the car, he saw something on his windshield. He left Nelson behind and raced up to his car. A folded piece of paper was tucked under his windshield wiper.

Nelson caught up, sounding way out of breath. "Wait, fingerprints."

"That'd prove what?" Chang snatched the paper. The note was written in the same handwriting as the sign in the warehouse.

Chang read aloud: "Run, run, as fast as you can. You can't catch me, I'm the gingerbread man."

34

IN THE WIND

Nineteenth Precinct Station

Chang and Nelson waited for Ron to meet them outside. Chang had called the fire department anonymously. Though the Laughing Matters warehouse wasn't in Ron's jurisdiction, Chang wasn't comfortable confiding in anyone else at this point.

Chang had warned the firefighters about the open gasoline container and what he described as attempted arson. He'd refused to give his name and had disguised his voice, knowing the call would be recorded. He'd also warned of potential booby traps. Then he'd thrown out the disposable phone.

Ron came out of the station wearing an NYPD jogging suit. "Let's walk and talk." They headed toward Fifth Avenue and Central Park, about three blocks away.

"I wish you hadn't screwed around with the fire department. Puts me in an awkward position."

"It wasn't me; I just overheard some stuff." Chang regretted pressing his friend. "Besides, what's better, do nothing and let the place burn down, or get what we can, now that some officials can get a look inside?"

"Congratulations. You got the attention of the fire marshal, and now they want to talk to Max. I did some digging to see what they might have discovered in the warehouse. They want to know who you are, but I think I convinced them to trust me on this one and to focus on what they found."

Chang added another favor he owed Ron to his growing tab. "That's good, but I got the distinct impression that Max's office hours are canceled indefinitely."

As they crossed Fifth Avenue and entered the park, Nelson explained what the men from the ice company had told him.

Ron stopped on the sidewalk. "So they'll put you guys at the scene?"

Chang shrugged. "If they do, they do, but I think some of them aren't legal, so my guess is that could be the last of it."

Ron sat down on the wall next to the statue of the 127th Infantry. "All right, never mind that for now. You believe Laura Stark's claim that Max has been one of her secret sources all this time?"

Nelson spoke. "He knew too many details about the Lewis case and several others she broke recently for it not to be true."

Ron took a minute to absorb the flood of information that represented. "Either of you ever see Max in person? Ever talk to him?"

"Aside from a glance outside his warehouse and when he pulled his Nixon impression the day he lost me, no," Chang said.

"That's not much. You think he's capable of killing Lewis? And if so, why in such a strange way? Did he know the guy?"

"You're asking the right questions. I wish we had all the answers," Nelson said. "But if you want to know if we think he's capable of killing in general, then I'd say yes."

Chang knew Ron respected Nelson's talent enough to give his opinion extra weight.

Nelson told the story of the lawyer who'd ended up buried alive following Max's mother's death. "Now Laura says Max did a perfect imitation of Machete Marchetti's lawyer, good enough to fool her and, we think, Marchetti himself."

"But no proof." Ron didn't phrase it as a question.

"No. But now that we know where and how Laura's story on Lewis broke, Max would have to be a prime suspect for the murder, right?"

"It isn't classified as a murder at this point, but you've sure got me curious. I'll label Max a person of interest, at the very least."

"Will the captain open it up to a murder investigation?" Chang asked.

"Tracey? Normally he might give me the leeway to get the ball rolling. Then if it went south, you know who'd be left holding the bag," Ron said, smiling.

"Sounds familiar."

"Yeah, but in this case we'll need more. Lewis is dynamite, and given his connections, that theory touches the mayor's office." Ron scanned the street around them. "I spoke to my guy who's with the Feds. He was interested in what you guys discovered. And he said to say nice work on the Lewis photo, Nelson."

Nelson nodded at the compliment.

"Anyway, he told me the art stuff was a surprise, but that Lewis was involved in some highly classified negotiations that affected national security. He hasn't been more specific, but he warned me to be super careful around the mayor because it looks like he's right in the middle of it."

Chang's curiosity spiked, but he knew that information would come in discrete pieces while everyone looked to protect their turf, not to mention backsides. "I'm not sure what any of that would have to do with a stalker like Max. Then again, what would a love-struck clown whack-job want with a guy like Griffon Lewis in the first place?"

Ron shook his head. "You said he told her he was feeding her juicy stories."

Nelson sat and absorbed the conversation.

Chang responded, "Right. If we accept that at face value, then why would he pick a big shot like Lewis? I mean, if he just broke into people's houses looking for dirt, he could find easier targets."

Nelson scratched his head. "I don't know what the connection is yet, but there's a link. I can feel it."

"This will all be easier when we get our hands on the man of the hour."

"Easier said than done," Chang said.

"Why? He's got a business and ties to the community. We'll find him."

"No," Nelson said. "I think he's in the wind."

❋ ❋ ❋

"You gonna make it, kid?" Sid was sitting with Laura in her office. She wanted to blame the frantic pace of the last few days for her sudden lassitude but knew it was much more than that.

"Sure." She spoke without thinking but was glad he'd broken the ice. "It's just that it feels like my whole career here has been a lie."

"You know that isn't true. Remember when you first came here? You were in rough shape after CBS canned you and the cops all blamed you."

"How I contributed to a good man's death and wanted to quit the business? Now that you bring it up, I guess it rings a bell." She'd come to terms with but never fully gotten over Sieger's suicide.

"You know better than to own the whole thing. Ultimately it was the real flaws in the 'good man' that got exposed and pushed him to do what he chose to do, not you." Sid paused. "But that wasn't my point. You changed the way you worked and vowed never to air another story that you couldn't confirm for yourself."

"True."

"Well, you said yourself that the stories Max fed you as STP panned out."

"Of course they did. He *caused* most of them!"

"I suppose. But did you tell him to do it?"

"Come on, Sid."

"See? You're too quick to shoulder all the blame. It's noble, but I'll let you in on a little industry secret." Sid leaned in and spoke in a conspiratorial whisper. "Nobility is bullshit in this business. There's credibility and there's ratings, and you have both. Between you and me, don't ask what I'd take if I had to pick just one."

"Was that a compliment buried in there?" Laura smiled despite herself.

"Something else before you go all hara-kiri on me. And I mean this. Max may well be some sort of loon, but he's a pretty good field reporter if you don't concern yourself with ethics and laws and things like that."

"What?"

"Hear me out. Marchetti did what he did, and we all know it wasn't the first time. Did the lawyer have the evidence for real? Or did Max only believe he did?"

"I don't know."

"Me either, but Marchetti sure seemed cocky and relaxed when he came in here. He must have known something for sure, and I'd guess it was more than knocking off a loose end like Bigelow. I think he found the purse itself and got rid of two problems with one stone."

"That's cold, Sid."

"What do you want? Bigelow danced with the devil. I wouldn't want to know the things he must have known about Marchetti. Maybe he was looking for some extra leverage. Then along came Max, who, for his own screwed up reasons, upset the applecart."

Laura hadn't thought of it quite like that. "Maybe."

"Exactly. Maybe. We don't know, but we don't have any control over that. What we do control is how we present the news—and to get it as right as we can while beating the pants off the competition."

"But if Max is doing all this to get to me..."

"Stop. You can't control that either. Max will get caught. But like I was saying, he didn't *turn* Orrlov into a scumbag crook so he could give you a scoop. Ditto Griffon Lewis."

"But he might have killed Lewis." Laura felt the shivers creeping back.

"Your guys gave the cops a head start on that one. They had it as an accident. I think that weird guy is onto something." Sid smiled. "Too bad he'd scare viewers away. He'd make in interesting field correspondent."

Laura laughed and felt bad about it. Nelson couldn't help how he looked, and his awkwardness had a certain charm.

"The point is that he said he's got another bombshell. What are we going to do with it?"

"Share it with the cops," she said without hesitation.

Sid nodded. "Of course. Look, your safety is the most important thing, but if he hands us a story that the rest of the wolves are going to pounce on anyway, don't you think we should run it? *And* try to get him put away?"

"Sure, Sid."

"If people are going to hear about it anyway, they should be ogling you on our station while they do. I didn't hire you just for your brains, you know." He stood up. "End of pep talk. You gonna get some work done?"

"Of course." She did feel some strength coming back. "And thanks."

"Half my job is coddling the high-price talent."

35

BOMBS AWAY

WBAC

Laura made a mental note to push Sid to give Gracie in the makeup room a raise. When Laura checked out her face in the mirror in her office, she found she looked vibrant, fresh, and pretty—the opposite of how she felt. But she had to admit that Sid had made sense earlier, and she'd turned in a solid performance. They had field reports on the aftermath of the Lewis case, and there was plenty of gossip about who would attend the funeral. The biggest rumor was that the mayor planned to speak at the event.

Funny, though—he had been quick to throw his old buddy under the bus when the art scandal broke, he had done a one-eighty since then, going out of his way to praise this man who was so plagued by demons and highlighting the good he had done in his life. She was sure the mayor would give him a soaring send-off and figured she'd be assigned to cover it.

Maybe it was a result of her well-earned cynicism, but she suspected that Mayor Glacier wasn't acting strictly out of compassion—it was more likely that he saw it as a great opportunity to grandstand before an attentive media.

Eddie Tua ducked his head into her office. "Good job today, boss. Is Chang taking you home tonight, or do you need a ride?"

"It's Chang tonight, Eddie, but thanks." Laura felt a wave of gratitude surge in her chest and tears that she'd never allow to surface. Eddie had been watching out for her more than ever, even in the office. Word had got out about the bugs, and Chang now swept the office daily. It was such a strange way to live, and yet she caught herself almost getting used to the routine.

This couldn't last. And of course it wouldn't. If Max was smart, he'd run and keep running. If he continued to involve himself in her life, he'd eventually get caught.

She'd had added security once or twice when stalkers got too pushy, but they were often warped enough to make the cops' job easy.

She knew that Max was different, but she'd never had such skilled backup before.

Still, she couldn't wait for everyone—even those trying their best to protect her—to leave her alone and let her return to a normal life. Drew should be home soon. His project was winding down, and he needed to get back into town to meet with his attorneys to fight the gun charges. She missed him. She looked at the clock. Chang would be by in about half an hour. She decided to try to catch Drew while she waited.

Her phone rang before she could dial. Speak of the devil? She looked at the caller ID, and her heart catapulted into her throat. It read Max Max-Maxx.

* * *

She wanted to call for Sid, but she wasn't sure where he was. Her pulse was pounding, and she could hear the blood rush in her ears. She remembered the rig Chang had set up for her and activated the Parrotech unit to record the call. She cleared her throat and picked up.

"Yes?" She was proud of how steady she sounded.

"So glad to reach you. I thought it would roll over to the voice mail. Do you need a moment?"

"For what?" If was strange to hear Max in his normal speaking voice.

"To set up the recorder, of course."

"Why would I—"

"Dear, dear Laura. You hurt my feelings when you treat me like a rube."

That was always one of Max's strongest epithets. "Fine. Go ahead. It's working."

"Excellent. This is gold, and I don't want you to miss a bit of it. And hello to the hired and professional help."

"It's just me, Max." She tried to channel her anger but also concentrated on not losing control.

"Alone at last."

"Where are you?" Worth a shot.

"Round and about. I seem to be at a crossroads careerwise, and I'm, shall we say, outdoors?"

"Are you asking for a place to stay?"

"We both know better. Besides, you changed the locks. My keys won't work."

Her courage wavered. The thought of him coming and going in and out of her place when she was asleep, for who knew how long, wrenched her gut. She fought through it.

"Want to come out of the cold and talk about it?"

"In time. As a matter of fact, I was coming to the purpose of the call. Would this be easier if I spoke to you as STP?"

"Now you're insulting *me*, Max. What do you want?"

"Sorry, dear." He sounded sincere and—what was the word? *Entitled*. Rage coursed through her body.

"You lost the right to call me that a long time ago. Now tell me what you want, because I'm done playing your fucking games, got it? I don't need anything from you but to hear you're in prison or dead."

"Always a lady…Good things come to those who wait. Here's the scoop, and you can do with it what you like."

"Fine. What do you have?"

Now Max was all business. "In a couple weeks, Mayor Glacier is going to announce a major peace accord between the Russians and the Muslim separatists in Chechnya."

"Huh?"

"Stay with me. Glacier is supposed to be the great peace broker who will bring the two sides together to sign the treaty at an event here in the Big Apple. Representatives from the Chechen rebels and the Russian government all plan to attend an extravaganza with lots of press and a gala celebration."

"How do you know—"

"Laura. You, of all people, should respect sources. Just remember, I told you I never lied to you, and I'm not now."

"Why are you telling me? I'll probably get invited to cover it."

"I insist."

"So what's this got to do with you?"

"I want you to have a front-row seat when it all goes wrong."

Her gut clenched. "What are you going to do?"

"And spoil the surprise? It's going to be huge."

She pictured mass casualties. "I won't go. Don't do it to try to impress me."

"It's not all about you, Ms. Stark. The show must go on."

"They'll stop you. I'll do anything to help them."

"They'll try." Max switched to his STP voice. "It's a pleasure doing business with you again. You always were my favorite."

Gone.

36

PARTIAL OBSERVER

"So you all believe him?" Ron Sieger sat on the edge of his chair after the group finished listening to the tape of Laura's conversation with Max for the third time.

Chang sat in the conference room with Laura, Nelson, Sid, and Ron. Despite his chilly relations with Laura in the past, Ron had agreed to come in. The new tape hadn't given him much choice.

"I guess we should defer to Laura, who knows the man, but I think we're crazy not to take him seriously," Chang said, running his fingertips over the back of his scarred left hand.

"Unless the peace accord is a fantasy," Nelson said.

All heads turned to Ron, who sat in silence until the others began to squirm. Finally he spoke. "This hits the news, and I'll find a reason to make some arrests. We're talking about lives at stake."

Sid gave a "Who, me?" look and nodded in agreement when Ron glared at him.

"This will come out soon. It *is* real. I don't know how he found out, though the mayor's office is getting leaky as hell. They're giddy about this, and it's obvious he's trying to get a huge PR push, especially given the tight time frame," Ron explained to them, looking worried.

"Why is the mayor of New York in the middle of an international relations deal that doesn't even directly involve the US?" Chang asked.

"One of the many good questions I asked. I only got a few answers—and not all of them came from the mayor's office, I can tell you." Ron cracked his knuckles. "It's no secret that the mayor views this job as a stepping-stone to higher office."

"Like the presidency," Laura said.

"Yeah. Exactly like that. The political junkies I asked tell me that the mayor needs to burnish his foreign policy credentials." Ron made air quotes with his fingers.

Sid began to move around the room. "So voilà, he gets to look like a big shot peace broker with this deal, and he wants to play it up with a flashy shindig here in the city."

"You're smarter than you look." Ron hadn't even shaken Sid's hand on the way in.

Chang took the insult as progress.

"I get that a lot." Sid smirked at him.

"But how does a guy in Glacier's position get involved with such an opportunity in the first place?" Laura asked.

"None of my business, according to the mayor's office. That was the most polite way they put it." Ron gnawed at a thumbnail. "In fact, they made it clear that if I kept it up, they'd yank me from the special detail."

"How'd you get it in the first place?" Chang asked.

"I have some friends over there. But based on this latest news, they're going to need someone to talk some sense into them. So far all they're worried about is who can hand out the media passes and manage crowd control."

"What are they doing about security?" Sid asked.

Ron gave him a cold look. "Maybe I'm here and we smoked the peace pipe, but I plan to keep some things to myself. I need your side to assess what I should recommend to the lieutenant."

"That's the question, isn't it?" Chang said. He still couldn't believe how the game had changed. This had started out as a simple stalker case and had now become an international fiasco in the making. "Laura, let's assume Max was telling you the truth, and also that he's willing to do anything, up to and including killing others. Any way to narrow down the possibilities?"

"He's changed. It's him, but he wasn't like this when we were married. And I never knew him to be political in any way. He never cared about that stuff."

"So what? We're talking assassination? Terrorist attack? Aside from having an impact, what's his point?"

Laura shook her head. "I wish I knew. He mentioned the mayor, but there will be plenty of other dignitaries involved. There'll be the Russians and Chechens of course, but the crowd will also have more than its share of big shots."

"He's been targeting rich people connected with the levers of power," Nelson said. "No strictly political types yet, right?"

"I guess Lewis is the closest. And he may have gone all the way and killed him," Laura said.

"So he's progressing?" Ron asked.

"Could be."

"And you say he can look or sound like anyone?" Ron asked.

"Within certain body types, but yes." Chang wondered if he was putting too much faith in the tall, slim body type he'd trained himself to spot.

"That's a security nightmare." Ron rubbed his face. "That's if I can even convince them there's a special threat. The basic security is good, and the foreign agents aren't bad, but they'll mostly be relying on us."

"And where will the blame lie if there's a breach?"

"All over, but I'll get my share."

"There's a solution," Nelson said.

"Yeah?"

"Catch him first."

* * *

The room now reminded Chang of one of those task forces they set up when planning to take down a high-profile target. Ron had asked Sid to step out for the time being, but he wanted Laura to stay as long as she was willing to help.

Now that they had a common goal, Ron's attitude took a backseat.

Ron seemed to read Chang's mind. "To start with, until we get more concrete evidence, there's only so much we can do with official assistance. I have enough information to try to get extra assets in place, but that's for the event itself. As far as an APB manhunt goes, we're going to have to improvise." He gave a little smile. "But that also works to our advantage. You guys," he said, pointing to Chang and Nelson, "can use tactics that aren't exactly by the book, and what I don't know won't hurt me."

Chang didn't need to hear more to understand that they were being granted permission to do whatever they needed to find Max—as long as they didn't get caught.

He could work with that.

Ron continued. "We're keeping an eye on the warehouse, but that isn't to say we have the place under constant surveillance. You say he's a professional sneak, and that's his home turf."

"Maybe he could slip in and out, but as far as his business goes, there's been no activity?" Chang asked.

Ron nodded. "Right. I had to pull rank on the answering service, but even they confirm the messages they are taking aren't getting picked up."

"He's changed careers. He said so himself," Chang said. "We need to figure out if there's a common thread to all the stories he gave Laura as STP."

"But we know the stories were legit." Laura sounded almost defensive.

"I'm not worried about the stories themselves, but rather, who are these people?"

Nelson stood up. "I'll work backward from Griffon Lewis. He was into art, legitimate and illegal; he was rich and well connected. Before that we had Orrlov, another philanthropist who was well loved in the city and prominent on the charity circuit. Then we have the case of Marchetti."

Laura spoke up. "But he never spoke to me as STP in that one. If he hadn't said anything in Mr. Bigelow's voice," she continued, shuddering, "I might never have known."

"But you were already covering that case, right?" Chang asked.

"Which time?" Laura shook her head. "Marchetti is a one-man news industry. I covered his trials a bunch of times over the years."

"That's an established story, then. Which stories would you never have heard of if not for STP?"

Laura thought hard for a few seconds. "Well, in addition to the last two big ones, he was good for a couple breaks a year."

"Try to think about what might connect the different stories," Nelson urged.

"Tell you what. Let me gather my notes and make a list, OK? I'm so wound up right now, I'm sure I'll miss something."

"That's fine," Chang said. "What about Max's accounts?"

"I think I hear my phone ringing," Ron said, and Chang nodded. He waited for Ron to leave the room. Without warrants, Ron knew they might drift into questionable legal tactics.

He was right, of course.

"Laura, if I stumbled across some relevant financial data, do you think Drew would be willing to look over my shoulder when he gets back?" Chang spoke in a deadpan.

She took the hint.

"After what Max did to him, I think he'd help you hold him down if you wanted to go after him with a rubber hose."

"I'll keep that in mind. In the meantime we can use his Social to see if he's opened any new bank accounts or changed mailing addresses, things like that."

Something Chang said seemed to jump-start Laura. "I just thought of something. Max used a bicycle courier to deliver a package of information to me a couple times. Really crazy guy with a pink Mohawk."

Interesting. "What company?"

"His name was Benny, short for Benzedrine, and he had these distinctive tattoos. I'm trying to remember the company. He rode his bike like a maniac, but...got it. Kamikaze Kouriers, spelled with a *K*."

"Excellent. Good job, Laura." Chang loved how fast her mind worked.

"Max probably wore a disguise. Benny said he paid well, and he wasn't into asking too many questions. I'm sure he covered his tracks." Laura sounded suddenly deflated.

Nelson spoke to Laura. "But he may have made a mistake. And if he did, we'll find it. This guy Benny may not know things, but he won't be able to lie to me."

Chang was proud of Nelson. He looked frail and off-kilter, but he was one of the most determined investigators he'd ever met. And if he could have a look at the courier's eyes and body language, they might get a great deal of information.

"Tell me something," Laura said in a grim voice.

"Sure," Chang said.

"What'll you do if you catch up to him?"

"Try to talk sense into him." Chang could see she didn't understand. "Sometimes it takes more than one language to be persuasive."

"He can be dangerous." Laura suddenly sounded frightened again.

"So can I."

37

BENNY AND THE JETS

The Bronx

"You shouldn't have told the dispatcher you were NYPD." Nelson was in some sort of cranky mood Chang didn't have time for.

They took the stairs to the sixth floor. Chang welcomed the exercise and again realized how much he missed training with Shu.

"I didn't lie. I was, and so were you."

"Just because people don't question your current status is no reason to claim it. You're going to land us in trouble."

"Every chance I get." Chang had been surprised that the dispatcher at Kamikaze Kouriers furnished the address. He wasn't sure if the guy was used to being hassled by cops, or if this Benny character attracted the frequent attention of his brothers in blue.

The building's bare lightbulbs and dingy carpet confirmed what they already knew: this wasn't the high-rent district. The smell of cooked cabbage wafted from one apartment. The various stains on the painted brown walls looked like Rorschach blots.

Chang was glad he'd kept his pistol, though he worried he might forget that he wasn't actually licensed to carry it in the city.

He could hear Nelson panting along behind him. He'd have left him downstairs, but there was no one better to look a perp in the eye and ferret out the truth.

And to be fair, this guy wasn't a suspect at all. They finally reached the sixth floor and headed down the hall to apartment 612.

"You should try knocking before I kick it down."

Now Nelson was making jokes. Sometimes the guy's mood was like a weather vane. Maybe he was just happy they weren't climbing the stairs anymore.

Chang rapped on the door, then stood to the side out of habit.

He knocked again and heard something or someone hit the floor, followed by a burst of cursing.

He knocked a third time.

"Just a second," came from inside.

Chang heard flushing and realized the place must be small. Finally he saw the peephole darken. He was sure he heard another curse.

Chang maintained the impassive expression of a man bored by his work. Inside he keyed up all his senses to detect any signs of danger. Often cops learned more from people's reaction to questioning than from the answers themselves.

Ah. He heard the locks being unbolted, and the door opened a crack. The chain, the last line of defense, was still in place.

The guy on the other side peeked out. "What do you want, cop?"

"Who said I was a cop?" Chang spoke in a calm voice.

The whole way up, Chang had wondered whether or not the dispatcher would have tipped him off. Nelson had bet him he wouldn't.

It seemed as though they had woken the guy up. Parts of his pink Mohawk stuck out in opposite directions. Bedhead, punker style.

"You saying you're not?" The guy squinted at the two of them.

"You're not the target, but can we ask you a few questions about a case we're working on?" Chang maintained his level tone.

"You swear I'm not going to get busted? I been good. My PO was late the last meeting. You can ask him."

"I said we're not interested in you. Can we come in?" Chang let an edge creep into his voice.

"I'm not straightened up for company. I'll talk to you out here."

He was shirtless, and Chang saw enough tattoos to make the guy a candidate for the yakuza if he'd been Japanese. His body art consisted of a mishmash of Asian symbols, Celtic crosses, and cartoon characters. Here a Goofy, there a Donald Duck—and a decent dragon in flight.

"So you're Benny?" Chang asked.

"In the flesh."

"And ink." Nelson was fascinated.

"Whoa. You're no cop. You collecting strays?"

"I used to be a stray, when I was in the orphanage. But that was a long time ago. Who did all your work?" Nelson seemed to take no offense.

"I like to spread the wealth, you know? I tried a lot of cats. Some better than others."

Chang pointed to the dragon on Benny's chest. "That's high-end work."

"Good eye. My pride and joy. Got it in Chinatown. You got one too?"

"Just on the inside." *And you don't want to see it*, Chang didn't add.

"Hey, this is fun and all, but uh…what the fuck do you want?"

"You delivered a couple times to a reporter, late at night, a special bonus?" Chang asked.

"I keep real busy. Not much room for whos. I'm all about the where and when."

"You know Laura Stark? You met her twice, once recently in front of WBAC, and the second time you were redirected from there…"

Benny nodded, and Chang pictured his pink hair as the bristles of a broom.

"To an apartment building. Over on Third Ave." Benny talked fast.

"That's it." Chang felt a glimmer of hope for this flake.

"What about it?"

"I'm interested in the guy who hired you."

Blank stare.

"The one who paid the bonus…" Chang prompted.

"I got my assignments from the dispatcher. You know, same place that gave away my address, am I right?" Benny nodded like he knew the answer already.

Nelson shook his head.

Chang looked from Nelson back to Benny. "Strike one. This guy deals directly with you, doesn't he?"

"Nope." Benny folded his arms across his dragon like he was trying to keep it warm.

Nelson stared at him and glanced at Chang. "Yup."

"Dude, what is your deal?"

Nelson perked up. "I've got several deals. I happen to be one of the best poker players you'll ever meet."

Chang suppressed a smile. He didn't want to kill their momentum. Nelson barely knew the rules to poker, but he was telling the truth. Nobody could ever bluff him.

"Ain't got time for cards, stickman. And I don't talk about clients. Not good for business."

"Make an exception. He'll never know it was us," Chang said.

"Let's search the place; there might be clues inside." Nelson sounded downright assertive. For Nelson.

"You and what army, bro?"

The hall was empty, but they didn't need to do this out here. Chang shoved Benny back with one hand and nudged the door open with the other. Benny stumbled into what looked like the living room.

"Thanks, we'd love to come in." He and Nelson slipped inside the door. Chang lifted his shirt to expose the butt of his pistol, as Benny recovered his balance and reached for an aluminum baseball bat.

The dragon—Chang's, not Benny's—never stirred, and Chang could see the guy's heart wasn't in the fight. He was rattled. Just where they wanted him.

"No thanks, we can't stay for tea. We have to go in a minute." Chang lowered his voice. "Totally unnecessary and very unwise. We just have a couple questions about the guy, and we'll go."

"This is bullshit. You need a warrant."

"Cops need a warrant, and we're not cops. We are, however, trying to find the guy who hired you. In case you care, he may be dangerous." Chang struggled for patience.

"Then I really want to piss him off, don't I?" Benny's voice rose.

Chang wished he could take that one back. "Did you ever see him?"

"That's just it, man. He'd call and give me a drop-off, and tell me where I could pick up the stuff. If I did the drop he'd leave a bunch of extra cash."

"He'd leave the money where anyone could find it?" Chang asked.

"That was another weird thing. One time it was right outside the building in an envelope. And you've seen this hood. I wouldn't leave anything around that wasn't nailed down or—"

"Guarded," Nelson said.

"You're no dummy."

Chang could see that Benny was cooperating. Which wasn't good because it meant he couldn't give them much. Then he saw a shadow flicker across Nelson's face. "What?"

Nelson spoke to Benny. "You're holding something back."

They stared at each other for a tense moment, and Chang thought he might need to stoke the pressure, but Benny just sagged.

"All right. The last time he really put me on the clock. He'd left the package by my place, and I had to ride it all the way into the city. Then he made me change directions like you said."

Chang nodded encouragement. "Go on."

"Well, after I delivered the package and called the number to confirm, the guy said to come back home and look in the same spot where he dropped off his stuff, and there'd be a big bonus. I didn't waste any time. I got here, and a guy from the hood, big dude everyone calls Oso—you know, 'Bear'?"

"I know the word," Chang said.

"Anyway, he's hanging around outside. I'm ready to jump him if he sees and takes my stuff. Probably a bad idea, but I took some, uh, vitamins for the trip, so I was feeling bold."

Chang understood and didn't care if the guy had been amped up, as long as he told a straight story. "Got it."

"Yeah, well, I didn't need to worry. Right when Oso notices the envelope and reaches under the bush for *my* payday, something hits him."

"What was it?" Chang asked.

"You won't believe me."

"Try us," Nelson said.

"Pie."

"What?" Chang tried to picture it.

"I told you."

"You mean like pie you eat?" Chang asked.

"White custardy shit. And all I see is this dude in the shadows. But it nailed Oso, and then I hear this really rough voice say, 'Hands off, rube!'" Benny held his hand up like he was about to say, "Scout's honor."

"Then what?" Chang said.

"Then all I hear is Oso cussing in English and Spanish, and he takes off after the shadow man. Chased him around the corner."

"What did you do?" Nelson asked.

"Me? I ran over, grabbed the envelope, hauled me and my bike up here, and went to bed."

Chang didn't even need to ask Nelson if Benny was telling the truth. Nelson asked, "Did Oso ever confront you?"

"He never saw me that night. Good thing too, 'cause he's still looking to kick somebody's ass."

"Why?" Chang said.

"Last time I saw him his whole face was bruised up, and he looked like he was limping."

※ ※ ※

Chang and Nelson stood outside the building, picturing the scene had Benny described.

"Now what?" Nelson asked.

"Sounds like our guy. Think he'll use Benny again?"

"Not if he knows we were sniffing around."

They walked to Chang's car. "I can't see the point of trying to stake it out here anyway. Max could be anywhere, and he could set up a delivery remotely. We could watch Benny, but we'd still only be reacting to what Max does."

"We still have no idea what he's going to do."

"Right." It was frustrating. "He likes to call the shots and is daring us to stop him."

"He's a show-off, and he thinks he's smarter than everyone so he can afford to play with us."

"Seen any sign he's wrong?" Chang didn't mean to sound so negative. He knew breaks came big and small. The key was to be smart and more determined than the opposition.

"At least we know the when, and Ron's going to tell us the where." Chang checked his watch. "We'd better hustle if we're going to make our meeting."

Ron had set up a meeting place back in Central Park so they could learn the latest without getting him in trouble.

❋ ❋ ❋

From across the street, Chang saw Ron waiting by the sculpture and could tell, even from a distance, that he wasn't his usual laid-back self. He looked jumpy and was glancing around so much that if he'd been doing undercover work, Chang would have yanked him off the scene.

"Decaf is your friend." Chang didn't want to startle him, so he spoke from a distance. Ron got up and walked into the park without so much as a hello.

"I'm guessing we won't be bored," Nelson deadpanned.

They followed Ron to a nearby gazebo. Chang was surprised to see him shoo away an older man who was sitting there. The guy looked annoyed, but Ron had flashed the tin, so at least he wouldn't go to the cops. Ron waved them over.

"I gather you've got more to tell us than 'They're holding the ceremony at an Elks Lodge,'" Chang offered, trying and failing to lift his friend's mood. Not a good sign.

"Hilarious. Yeah, I'll cover the location in a second. That secret won't hold with all the prep on such short notice; there's no way. Not that the stupid pricks give a shit about security anyway."

Whoa. "Where's all this coming from?"

Ron took a deep breath and pulled out a photo. He handed it to Chang, who let Nelson look over his shoulder. It showed a military-looking truck with four huge tubes running the length of what would be the cargo area on a tractor trailer. The entire rig was painted in camouflage.

"I assume this isn't the new and improved Hummer?"

Ron's expression told Chang to stow the jokes.

"I'm not up on military stuff. Is it a fuel truck, chemical weapons?" Chang continued.

"That, my friend, is a Russian S-400 SAM launcher," Ron said.

"You're worried, so I'm worried. Tell me why?"

"I have it on very deep background from my sources that this, or one just like it, is the reason the Russians have finally agreed to come to the table to talk peace with the Chechen Muslims."

Chang stared at the picture. "OK. Where's this going?"

"Word is, one of these trucks went missing recently. It's their latest technology, and more importantly this one was loaded with the longest-range 40N6s."

"How long?" Chang said.

"It can hit airborne targets up to two hundred and fifty miles away. And it's outfitted with the latest gear to defeat countermeasures," Ron said.

"You know my expertise is confined to the weapons I can carry. What's the upshot of all this?"

"As you can see, it's a large truck and doesn't exactly blend in. However, Russia is an awfully big place, and so is Chechnya if you're trying to hide one vehicle."

Chang thought he was beginning to understand. "So they think the rebels scored one of these somehow. But now what? Are they worried the rebels will sell it off to the Chinese? One truck isn't that big a threat, considering the size of Russia's military."

Nelson nodded. "It is to whoever it's pointed at."

Ron smiled, but he didn't look amused. "Kewpie doll for the little guy. The Russians aren't admitting it, but my contacts said it's clear the Russian president is afraid it'll be used on his jet to take him out. A perfect terror move for the Chechens."

"That would be pretty bold."

Ron shook his head. "You don't think it's past them? The biggest of the Muslim separatist groups is an outfit called the Sword of Jihad. They've hit some huge targets before, and they aren't afraid of spilling lakes of blood. Their leader is sending a representative to set the peace deal."

"Doesn't the fact that the Russians are prepared to talk peace telegraph to the Chechens—and the rest of the world—that they're scared?" Chang asked. "They hate looking weak."

"Maybe that's why they're doing this," Nelson said.

"You lost me," Chang admitted.

Nelson continued. "Ron, the missile launcher is still a secret, right?"

"That it's missing? To the general public, yes."

"That's what I mean. Well, how will it look if the Russian president suddenly stops making his big, bold appearances in Chechnya? As a show of strength, he lands by helicopter on bases that sometimes get attacked, doesn't he?"

Ron smiled with more warmth. "Someone here watches the news. Yeah. He even parachuted in one time. He's ex-military, so he loves those showy photo ops, and the public eats it up."

"With one of these launchers tucked away in some cave or even in the middle of the city, he'd be crazy to come in on a chopper."

"He wouldn't stand a chance. It's always somewhat dangerous to visit a forward base, which is why he gets to look brave when he drops into 'war zones.' Only in this case, the Sword of Jihad would have the advantage," Ron said.

A gorgeous blonde with shoulder-length hair and a tight, white tank top jogged by. Chang and Ron stole glances at her and shared a brief smile.

Nelson never missed a beat. "But if it isn't public knowledge, can't they have a peace treaty and still maintain his dignity?"

Ron returned to the business at hand. "Never that simple. What would you do if your enemy had that weapon and you were losing face?"

Chang thought for a minute. "I'd turn every man and woman under my command out to find the thing and either retrieve it or destroy it."

Ron nodded. "Well done. I'm not sure what the Russian word for it is, but my guy says their GRU, the intelligence arm of their military, is going ape shit looking for this thing."

Nelson said, "They're buying time."

"Exactly," Ron agreed.

"But if the Sword of Jihad has the weapon system, why bother coming to the table?" Chang asked.

"We still have lots more questions than answers, but this is an interesting piece of the puzzle, wouldn't you say?"

"That's a sophisticated piece of equipment," Nelson said. "It may not last indefinitely without expertise. Maybe they're getting a better deal if they agree to give it up. Do they admit they have it?"

"I've been flying above my pay grade most of this conversation," Ron said. "So I don't know. It's anyone's guess why the players are doing what they're doing."

"But you figured out what this has to do with Max, right?" Chang could dream, couldn't he?

"Oh sure. I thought that was obvious." Ron chuckled, then turned grim. "It says this much: Whatever his reasons and however he learned about the peace talks, if he succeeds in taking out a key player or otherwise ruining the event, these two sides will have every reason to go right back at each other. Maybe harder than ever. Both sides have been quiet for a while, but from what I hear, they've been preparing for a major escalation."

"Any good news?" Chang said.

"I don't know. But I can tell you, the event itself is going to be held at Empire Hall," Ron said.

Chang knew the place. "Over on Sixth Avenue," he said to Nelson.

"I know." Nelson looked insulted. "That's a big space."

"Room for everybody who's anybody. Going to be a gangbusters shindig to create maximum exposure for Hizzoner the Mayor." Ron made no attempt to hide his disgust.

"I didn't hear you use the word *discretion*."

"Or *security nightmare*," Ron grimaced. "We can barely keep track of all the press passes, and that's just coming out of Glacier's office. Then we'll have the Russians and the Chechen contingent."

"We'll just have to catch Max before then so you can take it easy."

"Would you mind?" Ron's voice dripped sarcasm.

"If we see a Russian missile truck rolling down Broadway, we'll let you know."

Ron saluted. "You're both great Americans."

38

ODD COUPLE

Laura's Apartment

Laura lit another candle and glanced at the clock. Traffic should be light this time of night. She hadn't gotten any more texts from Drew, but it was good to know his flight had landed on time.

She jumped a little at the buzz from downstairs. "Yes, Quincy?"

"Mr. Gantry to see you?"

"Send him up." She was still getting used to the deluxe treatment from the doorman. Most of the time, tenants simply buzzed friends in, and he'd wave them up, assuming it was OK and not wanting to appear to pry—though everyone knew he watched over the place like he owned it.

Five minutes later she heard the knock at the door and peeked out the peephole. Blond, tanned, and tired, her boyfriend was back. She fumbled with the locks.

"Hey, baby." He handed her a bunch of blood-red roses and put his suitcase down.

She put the flowers on the mail table and seized him in a bear hug. She kissed him hard before he could say anything else.

"Wow."

"I'm sorry about everything," she started.

"Me too. Getting away for a little helped give me perspective. You didn't ask for this."

"No, but neither did you."

"True."

"Hey!" She punched him in the chest and took a deep whiff of his cologne—traces of melon and jasmine, faint after the flight from California, but still there.

"We're in this together." He kissed her back. "Like it or not, am I right?"

"I don't know, honey. If you walked away you might be safe."

"But you wouldn't."

She wanted to tell him she'd be fine; she had all the help she needed. But she couldn't seem to let go of him.

＊＊＊

"He's the funny-looking one?" Drew handed a mug of coffee to Laura.

Neither had gotten much sleep the night before, but she felt better than she had in weeks. "Be nice. But yes. Nelson'll be here later, and you two can go through some records. If you're still up for it."

"Too tired to do anything else right now." Drew grinned at her. "But that's a big 'Hell yeah.' Anything I can do to track the mother down works for me."

"You do know, though, we don't exactly have permission…"

"Can't hear you, I have flour paste in my ear. I didn't give permission for that either."

"I know, but…"

"But nothing." He pulled her in close and planted a gentle kiss on her forehead. "At this point I regard everything we do as self-defense."

* * *

The buzzer sounded, and Laura hit the button.

Quincy spoke. "Mr. Rogers here."

"He knows the way. Thanks."

When Nelson arrived, she didn't even have to use the peep-hole because she recognized his timid tap, tap, tap. She looked out just to get in the habit and saw his salt-and-pepper hair and huge head perched on his body.

"Hi, Nelson."

He glanced all around the room before looking her in the eye, then dropped his gaze to the floor. "How are you doing?"

"Better now that Drew is back." She watched Drew enter the room. He wore jeans with a hole in one knee and a green, cotton T-shirt, tight enough to show his muscles. Nelson had on a baggy, blue button-down that failed to conceal his thin frame.

"Detective." Drew shook Nelson's hand. "We can set up over here." He pointed to the dining room table.

"I'll leave you kids to play. Half a day is all I get for vacation." She'd practically threatened to quit on Sid, but he wouldn't be Sid if he didn't give her a hard time about taking a break.

"Lock up behind me, and help yourself to whatever looks good in the fridge."

She already knew that Drew would. It was all she could do not to badger Nelson to "Eat, eat, eat!"

* * *

"Where's Chang?" Drew slid the laptop around so that both he and Nelson could see the screen.

"He's with Officer Sieger checking out the layout at Empire Hall, where the peace event is scheduled to take place."

Drew recoiled at the name. That guy had put Laura through the wringer. "You sure he's the best guy to coordinate with?" He wasn't sure how much Nelson knew.

"He's about the only one we've got on the inside; and yes, he's very good."

"You're not just sticking up for one of your own?"

"My own?" Nelson looked at him and got what Drew meant. "Oh. I never really felt like *them*, even when I carried a shield. I was more of a truffle pig."

"Huh?"

"No disrespect to the profession. I found things they couldn't. The rest of the stuff wasn't really me."

"That I can believe," Drew said. Then he added, "And no insult to you either." He wondered where Nelson would ever feel comfortable.

"I have a thicker skin than you think," Nelson said, turning to Drew. "You're smarter than you appear. Does it ever bother you to be judged on your looks?"

Drew sat up straighter. He hadn't seen that one coming. "I guess it depends on who's doing the judging. If it's a gorgeous woman, it's OK." He remembered where he was and—even though Laura wasn't there—felt compelled to add, "Not that I'd do anything about it."

Nelson met his gaze and turned back to the computer. "I can see that. No worries. Everyone likes to be ogled once in a while. As long as they know we have minds too, you know?"

Drew honestly couldn't tell if the guy was serious or not. "I'm curious, and let me know if it's too personal, but where *do* you feel comfortable?"

Nelson paused, and Drew thought he'd hurt the guy's feelings.

"On a case, but not this one, not yet. Eventually the clues build up, and I can see through the mist until I can put on the perp's skin and look through his eyes. It's scary and exciting, but I feel like I can almost make him come to me, and that brings him to justice."

Drew knew how many killers Nelson had helped put away. "But that can't be it. Otherwise you'd almost want to have a killer around so you could wake up to catch him."

Drew saw Nelson start a bit and regretted saying anything.

Nelson's whisper was almost inaudible. "Definitely smarter than you look." He spoke up. "Not as bad as all that. I'm comfortable in front of one of these. We have that in common."

Nelson's fingers flew across the keyboard. "Hand me those receipts. Ready to go clown hunting?"

39

GILDED CAGE

Empire Hall

Chang paid the cab driver and climbed out in front of a building with soaring marble columns. Standing less than ten stories high, the building was dwarfed by the surrounding skyscrapers. He tried to imagine that the taxi was a limo and that cameras and fans were swarming around watching the entrance.

Instead of a throng of admirers and paparazzi, Chang was greeted by Ron Sieger, who was flanked by a couple of guys he didn't know. Their suits were too nice for them to be cops.

"Thanks for coming." Ron shook his hand, then introduced Chang to the other two.

"Paul Chang, former NYPD and a security consultant for this event, meet Chris Tyler and Dillon Prager. They're with the mayor's advance team." Ron spoke fast, and Chang could tell these kids were already stressing him out. Both were in their late twenties, and from their slicked-back hair and cuff links, he could see they thought they knew everything.

"Gentlemen."

They looked at him like he was an odor they couldn't place. "I wasn't aware the NYPD required consultants, especially not freelancers." Prager spoke.

The bureaucratic nightmares of his former life came rushing back to him in a rancid wave of anti-nostalgia. Chang took a deep breath and pictured a calm lake as he spoke. "I'm working pro bono to supplement the department. I have a unique insight into what I think may be a specific and credible threat."

The well-coiffed twins shared a look, and then Tyler spoke. "Yes, we've heard. The great clown conspiracy."

Ron grimaced and shot Chang a nothing-I-can-do-about-it look.

Chang understood. He knew right away that these fools would be useless.

He tried another approach. "Have you had a look inside? Quite a place, isn't it?"

Prager snorted. "Only three weddings, including one last year where I was best man."

They walked through a set of heavy brass doors and into a massive ballroom covered with polished marble and gilt walls. An intricate domed ceiling of stone capped with glass soared a full seven stories above them in the center of the room, and a massive chandelier hung from the ceiling.

"I take it the Sistine Chapel was booked?" Chang thought it might help to loosen these stiffs up.

"So was this place. Glacier got a wedding bumped. This hall books years in advance."

Chang had wondered about that. "I imagine that ruffled some well-heeled feathers."

"You don't know the half of it," Tyler said. "We made it right though. I think we landed on our feet quite nicely."

Tyler and Prager shared a laugh.

Chang saw the room could hold hundreds of people and knew that it probably would. "The stage will go over there?"

"For the ceremony? Yes." Prager pointed to the far end of the room.

Chang pictured the room full of people and lights and flash-bulbs and shook his head. He looked around. "I see six emergency exits. Is that it?"

Ron spoke. "Yes. That's one bit of good news. We can cover those, and barring an emergency, we can control the flow of the crowd through the main door."

"What is good is also bad, because that means fewer ways to get out in a hurry."

"We can't live in a bubble," Tyler said.

"What about the roof?" Chang asked.

Ron spoke. "There is some access for maintenance. Best option is to put a guy on the roof and maybe sweep the maintenance area."

Tyler and Prager both shook their heads. Prager spoke. "Listen, I know you have a job to do, and we certainly appreciate everything you're doing to keep us safe. But Mayor Glacier sent us with very specific instructions. This is a sensitive act of diplomacy, and tensions will be running high. The evening must run smoothly, and if we scare the guests or spook the principals, we could have a major incident. The mayor wants everyone to be relaxed and to have a good time."

"And preventing an attack gets in the way how?" Ron looked like he was about to lose his patience.

"Detective. The mayor has his detail, and you know the people are good because they are *your* people," Prager said.

Chang couldn't help picturing the police as some sort of tribe.

"And the Russian team will have some security, and of course that means we had to allow the Chechen representative a guard or two, but we know you'll be keeping an eye on *them*."

Chang began to think of Prager as an international incident waiting to happen. "Personally, I think it's a mistake to allow either visiting team weapons. But maybe it'll be fine. They once let Arafat wear a pistol into the UN." Chang tried to sound conciliatory.

"Huh?" Tyler scrunched his face and dismissed Chang. He turned to Ron. "Just make sure the security is in place but not overly visible."

"Does the mayor not understand the potential danger—"

Prager cut Ron off. "Detective. These people have no reason to double-cross each other, believe me. I can't go into the details, but I promise you, they will be all smiles. Your job is just to make sure the guests are well behaved."

Chang couldn't believe the patronizing tone from these kids. Wait, yes he could.

"It's the uninvited guests we're concerned about," Chang said.

"That's your *job*." Tyler corrected himself. "I mean his." He jerked a thumb at Ron, who looked like he wanted to bite it off.

"If you'll let us do it," Ron said, his voice taking on an edge like a growl.

"There will be federal assistance too, since this is an international affair. This place will be crawling with security," Prager said.

"Look. So far the biggest threat has been homegrown, and we don't know what he might try. But he's got a dangerous mix of skills," Chang said.

Tyler snickered—it was the first word that came to Chang's mind when he heard that condescending laugh. "The clown again? Don't worry, I can guarantee clowns."

"What's that supposed to mean?" Chang asked.

"Remember I told you we had to bump a wedding? Well, part of the agreement was that we had to honor the entertainment they hired. Rather than compensate them for cancelling, the mayor insisted they go through with the performance. The guests will love it."

Chang felt a horrible sinking sensation and saw that Ron did too. "What entertainment?"

Prager clapped his hands like a little kid. "The Solara Circus."

No.

"Why don't you just issue our suspect media credentials and be done with it?" Ron said.

"I knew you'd be like that." Tyler waved Ron off. "Listen. Your team will get every name and ID for the necessary background checks. They're used to dealing with security, so it should all be very smooth."

Some of the building's catering staff waved to Tyler and Prager. "Excuse us."

"All the principals may get taken out, but the cakes are going to be perfect," Chang said, rubbing his eyes with the heels of his palms.

"Better get this guy first, Paul," Ron said.

40

CLOWN IN A HAYSTACK

Laura's Apartment

"Where'd you get these?" Drew held up a sheaf of bank statements.

"You never know what you might find in the trash, especially after the fire marshal searches a place for fire hazards." Nelson never took his eyes off the screen as he zipped from site to site, searching for signs of activity from Max or his company.

"It doesn't sound like standard protocol, but if it's accurate, we should be thankful for what we've got."

"That's a good attitude." Nelson spoke in a detached monotone.

He'd told Drew about their visit to Max's place.

"You're lucky he didn't throw anything on you."

"I think we surprised him—a little anyway. He was busy clearing out, but he improvised that gas trap fast."

"No sign of him since?"

"Not at his place. I'm hoping the scraps we found might be enough to track him down."

Drew thumbed through the pages. "Any luck on these accounts?"

"All cleared out or inactive, so far."

All the Laughing Matters business accounts had gone dormant. The people at the answering service sounded puzzled, despite their professional bluster.

The company website still promised thrills and laughs, but all the phone numbers rolled to the service.

"We ready to quit?" Drew stood and stretched.

Nelson looked at him, and Drew could swear he saw an expression of disappointment. "Why? Can't you smell it?"

"Smell?"

"You look for irregularities. They're here, I know it."

"That's the problem. The whole thing's irregular. The business dropped off the face of the earth, and all the accounts flatlined. He scrammed." Drew didn't mean to yell, but the apartment was starting to feel small, and he wanted to go for a run to clear his head.

"Now you know what to look for." Nelson seemed pleased.

"How's that?"

"You said it. If this is all irregular, then look for a regularity to stand out."

* * *

Drew's eyes had that sandy feeling they got whenever he spent too many hours in a row poring over papers. Nelson had printed account activity from every link he could associate with Max Stark's Social Security number. They started with recent accounts and worked through to older statements.

"Hey, what's this one?" Nelson handed Drew a bank statement for which Max was a coholder.

Drew looked at the sheets. "I know this name. Martin Potempkin. That's Marty, the toxic gnome who let me into the fun house with Max." Drew felt a surge of anger.

"He's one of the employees, but nobody else who works there shared an account with the owner. It isn't his regular bank either."

Drew scanned the list of deposits and withdrawals. Most of the withdrawals were at an ATM—and always the same address in midtown. "Wait. The activity stopped a couple weeks ago. Then look here. It starts back up with another withdrawal, this one for the maximum five hundred dollars allowed. Same thing over the past three days. There's still a couple thousand in there."

Nelson looked electrified. "Where? Where's the ATM?"

"That's new. From the same bank, but this ATM is located in Brooklyn."

"Same one every time?"

"Yeah. And always near evening." Drew saw Nelson's eyes blaze. Damn, he did look more alive.

He couldn't lie. This was a lot more exciting than flagging an embezzler. "He's draining the account, but he doesn't want to go to the bank."

"He's staying near his stomping grounds. This might be the mistake we're looking for."

Nelson grabbed the phone.

✳ ✳ ✳

Chang listened while Nelson broke down what they had found.

"How many days until the account's empty?" Chang asked.

"Looks like two." Nelson ran a finger down the printout. "And that's if he drops it all the way down. He wants the cash because he's underground, but he may not be greedy."

Chang saw they had a window, if they hurried. "I'll brief Ron. He may need to be the guy to get close, if I can sell him. Max knows me, and your time in the forty isn't what it used to be, partner." Chang noticed Nelson didn't bother pretending to be insulted. They knew Max was slippery, and this might be their only shot at him.

Chang continued. "Tell you what. You and Drew meet us near P.S. 319. That's about five blocks from that ATM. We'll rally there and set up our next move."

Nelson wasn't a tactical guy, and Chang didn't like the idea of involving Drew, but they might need another set of eyes.

Chang called Ron and briefed him. "We have to move fast."

"This is a long shot. You sure?" Ron asked.

"First whiff in a week from this nut. What backup can you bring us?"

"Couple choppers and two SWAT teams, plus some K-9 and…"

"I don't have time for this." Chang checked his temper.

"Seriously? You know the official line? Max is a footnote in the marshal's report and a curiosity. Captain Tracey won't touch anything risky, and that goes ten times where this guy and the mayor are concerned. He's not buying our theory, and the last thing he'd do is send the cavalry on a speculation."

"No dogs?"

"You get me, and I'm clocking it as personal time." Ron dropped the sarcasm.

"I'll stop complaining long enough to say thanks. And I'll pick you up."

41

TAKEOUT STAKEOUT

Brooklyn

"What do I do?" Drew reminded Chang of a rookie, fresh from the academy but without any of the useful training. He already regretted allowing him to come.

"Not a damn thing." Ron's irritation told Chang that he took Max seriously.

"I wish we had *some* backup." Chang knew this was literally Max's backyard, and if he was as smart as they knew he was, the guy would have a slew of escape routes up his sleeve. He'd also probably put up a fight if cornered.

"That makes two of us," Ron said. "I won't check you for anything you aren't licensed to carry."

"Probably a good idea." Chang knew that Ron understood he was armed but wouldn't draw unless necessary.

"It's a dangerous neighborhood. You never know what you might find lying around," Ron added.

Chang tried to imagine Ron using that line on Captain Tracey.

***

Chang and Nelson and Drew watched the entrance to the Grand Street Grocery from a Chinese takeout place across the street.

Chang poked at his food as he kept an eye on the after-work crowd filtering in and out of the store. He hoped the bribe he'd given the owner would keep him quiet while they lingered.

Chang had a radio, and Ron sat in his car nearby. The plan was for Chang to call Ron in with a quick description of what Max was wearing so Ron could pick him up fast.

Once they had him, they wouldn't have much reason to hold him, but if he resisted maybe they could hang onto him for a while.

"Nelson, watch the eyes. You need the picture?"

"No need to insult me in front of people. I'll know what he looks like no matter what he's wearing." Nelson picked up an egg roll and gave it a sniff.

Chang tried to use the chopsticks with his left hand. It hurt just to hold them, but Shu had suggested it for therapy. The nerve damage in some places made manipulating the sticks almost impossible. But six months earlier he'd barely been able to hold a pencil, so it was progress. The sharp and dull pains from the effort played a concert inside the hand but helped him stay focused.

"How'd you hurt your hand?" Drew pointed to the lattice-work of scars.

"It's a long story," Chang said. It wasn't that he minded the question, but even if he told Drew the truth, the guy would never believe him. "But it got crushed. I think the rehab and surgeries hurt worst of all."

"Really?"

"No." He tried to think of something else. Rainy days were agonizing, so he was grateful the skies were clear.

*** *** ***

When they'd been at their seats long enough to test the "hungry again after an hour" theory, Drew startled Chang and Nelson.

"There he is!"

Nelson's head popped up and he peered through the window. "Where?"

"Short guy in the coveralls. See?"

"The target's not short. We're looking—"

"Not Max. The other one. Marty. He just went inside."

"Coholder of the account? Interesting." Chang radioed Ron and relayed the ID in a quiet voice. "How do you want to play it?"

"He's not wanted at all, unless your buddy wants to file a complaint, but we could follow him in case he meets up with Max."

Chang thought about it. "Nelson, did you get an address list for the employees?"

Nelson nodded.

"Ron, let's snag him when he comes out. You're the only car, and he's on foot. If he bails, it's going to take us a minute to get over there. He knows Drew, but not me—at least that I know of."

"Any sign of Max?" Ron asked.

"No. I think we may have to play the hand we've got."

"OK. Let me know who to grab."

Marty stepped out into the late-day sun and squinted. He carried a soda in one hand and a sandwich wrapped in paper in the other.

Chang got up, and the others followed. He waved to the owner, who pretended not to see anything. Chang should have known better. The guy didn't want to get involved.

"Ron, the short guy, redhead, looks like he got hit hard in the face with a crowbar. Walking west on Grand Street."

"Got him."

"We'll have Drew hang back. I'll work behind him, and you can pull ahead and make the stop. I'll go concerned citizen if he rabbits back our way."

"Light touch, huh?" Ron meant no weapon, Chang knew.

"It's me." Chang knew that wouldn't reassure his friend.

"I can catch this guy for you," Drew said, apparently eager to prove himself. The last thing they needed.

"Stay back, out of our way. You mess this up and I'll make you sorry." Chang had no time to be diplomatic. Marty walked off with a sense of purpose.

Nelson hadn't memorized where he lived, but if Marty had just bought dinner, Chang figured it must be nearby. With a face like that, a hot date was unlikely.

Chang would never have said that out loud around Nelson.

"Drew, stay out of sight, like around the corner. He knows what you look like." That seemed to sink in, and Drew hung back.

One less headache. Chang made sure he could clear his gun if necessary. He didn't know much about this guy, and the last thing he wanted was for him to hurt anyone in some desperate act.

Marty walked toward the end of the block. Chang was glad that the buildings were close together and even flush with each other in some cases. Less room for the quarry to maneuver.

Chang walked fast, his long legs covering ground more quickly than Marty's. The man was looking straight ahead. That was fine. "Take him, Ron," Chang whispered into the radio. "Don't let him reach the corner."

"No problem."

Chang could hear the engine on his BMW rev up as Ron shot down the street.

He pulled up with a dramatic screech that made Chang wince. He was clearly used to cruiser brakes that weren't as responsive as the Bimmer's.

Marty reacted instantly. By the time Ron popped out of the car, Marty had dropped his food and started sprinting back in Chang's direction.

Chang decided to let him get close before tackling him rather than charge and make him bolt into the street. He looked faster than he'd let on.

"Stop. NYPD!" Ron's voice boomed down the block. Bystanders scurried out of the way or otherwise took cover. Maybe they expected a firefight to erupt. Chang saw no sign of a gun, so he acted like a confused civilian. Just a few more seconds…

Twenty yards before he got to Chang, Marty veered toward a building and leaped. He caught the bottom rung of a fire escape.

Damn.

Marty scurried up the ladder and was near the roof by the time Ron reached Chang.

"Didn't see that coming."

Chang wanted to kick himself. "Circus people. Sorry. Can you circle in the car? I'll see if I can find a way to the interior of the block."

Chang doubted he could duplicate the jump, and by now Marty would be running across the roof. Better to try to meet him on the other side. He ran back toward the store, which would have a back door.

"We'll go around the block and look for him," Nelson said. He and Drew ran off, and Chang didn't have time to argue.

He pulled out his pistol and raced through the store yelling: "Police business."

The owner looked frightened but not I'm-about-to-be-robbed scared, so Chang must have looked convincing.

"Back door?" Chang said and gestured.

The owner looked all too happy to have the big armed man out of his store, so he worked the locks and let Chang into the back.

The area consisted mostly of the back walls of apartment buildings, but in between, narrow pathways formed a strange maze, something like the slit canyons in Utah.

Chang scrambled down a path and climbed over several gates that turned the back area into an obstacle course. Each one reminded him of his bulk, and he struggled to make it over with his bad hand, which was unable to support any weight. He was forced to reholster his pistol, and he'd have to hope Marty wasn't willing to take things to a lethal level. No matter what, the guy had to come through the interior of the block.

After tearing his pants and a chunk of his leg on a spiked fence top, he emerged into a more open area composed of all the backyards of the buildings on the block.

He could hear a commotion bouncing around the walls, but it was impossible to determine where it came from. It sounded like shouting and the screech of tires. He worked his way through the fences and gates, grateful when they weren't locked. He hoped Marty was having an equally difficult time. Dogs barked from several homes, adding to the din.

He came around the back of a house and saw a larger yard with an aboveground pool and a break in the wall of homes. It wasn't much, but it was wide enough for a trash can and easily a person.

He saw movement and a shadow and reached for his pistol.
Careful. Civilians everywhere.

He kept his hand on the gun, but left it holstered. A large figure bounded into view. Ron.

"Did you see him?" Ron sounded winded, and Chang felt exhausted.

"No."

"You sure? I pulled around the corner and flushed him back in here. He was just coming out."

"Where're Drew and Nelson?"

"Saw Drew coming this way from the corner. Don't know about Nelson."

Chang spun around trying to spot any easy avenues of escape. The walls were tight, outside the slot Ron had come through. The only other way out was to climb back to the roof or come through Chang and the gates.

He should have seen Marty climbing back up to the roof. So where was he? There were plenty of doors, but nobody in the city was dumb enough to leave them unlocked, were they? He didn't see a light on at the house with the pool, so he figured it was safe to try the door to check. It was locked. The yard contained a kid's slide and some baseball gear. The pool had a cover and a hose dangling off the side.

"I don't hear screaming, so he didn't go into an occupied house," Ron said, frustration playing across his face.

They both heard footsteps in the nearby slot, and Chang turned to find Drew creeping through.

"Where's Nelson?"

"Did you get him?" Drew had a wild look in his eyes.

"Does it look like it? Where—"

"He's watching the street. I left him at the corner to cover two sides. But I saw the guy run back this way." Drew's disappointment dulled his expression.

"Where could he have gone? Jeez, he was quick." Ron shook his head.

"We could use one of those dogs about now," Chang said to Ron.

Chang tried to calm his thoughts and do what Nelson would do: think like the quarry. Running in the wrong direction wouldn't help. He pictured himself panicked and racing through here.

He caught a tiny movement in the corner of his eye. At first he thought it was a trick of the light, but he stared at the pool and the area beyond it. Then he realized what it was.

He gestured to Ron and especially Drew to be quiet. Fortunately the guy saw he meant it and didn't blather on with questions. Chang pointed and crept close to the edge of the pool. He jammed his thumb into the end of the hose hanging over the edge of the pool.

First it twitched like a piece of fishing line, then more energetically. Finally they heard a splash and up came Marty, sputtering and gasping for air.

Ron pulled the cover back and grabbed Marty by the scruff of the neck. Chang reached in with his good hand and helped yank him out of the pool. He checked the guy's hands for weapons, but he was clean.

"So you can't fly." Chang stared at the scarred face and disjointed nose.

"You're under arrest." Ron cuffed Marty and radioed for backup.

"For what? Carrying a sandwich?"

"When a cop tells you to stop, you stop. Now you're charged with evading." Ron Mirandized him.

Smart. Not only would that make the arrest official, but it would explain the disturbance and the 911 calls that would undoubtedly have been phoned in from neighbors. Chang thought he'd better hide his gun in the car before the other officers asked too many questions. He didn't think Marty had seen it.

"Prick!" Drew yelled, running up to Marty. Chang thought he was going to take a free shot and was just getting ready to grab him when Drew stopped short. "Your buddy is next."

Marty grinned like they'd just announced a surprise party. "Hey, it's the flour child! How you doing?"

Now Drew did haul back, and Chang caught the guy's arm at the elbow to prevent him from throwing the punch. "You'll get locked up for assault if he presses charges."

Marty laughed like it was the funniest thing he'd ever heard. "And I would too. My face is my life." He turned to Drew. "You should learn how to take a joke."

"C'mon, Drew, help me get my car." Chang almost had to drag Drew away. He looked like he was going to rupture something.

"You're telling me you've never smacked a suspect?"

"I'm not telling *you* a thing." Chang respected Drew's courage, but his impulse control needed work. Chang understood that combination all too well, but Drew hadn't even been on the job.

OK, Chang had once been a poster boy for impulsive, but that was beside the point.

Once inside the car he scanned up and down the block. Ron brought a soaked but otherwise cheerful Marty through the slot. Chang could hear sirens. The cavalry would arrive in a minute.

"Drew, where'd you say you left Nelson?" The guy should have gotten curious by now. Maybe the sounds of the commotion were better masked than he realized.

"He was right over there." Drew pointed to the top of the block.

Chang pulled the car to the side, climbed out, and walked up the block. He wished they'd given Nelson a radio, but the whole thing had been thrown together in a hurry.

Chang rounded the corner expecting to find Nelson peering down the street. Nope. Lots of civilians walking along, but no Nelson.

His anxiety level kicked up a notch. He resisted the urge to jog to the next corner. When he got there he was right by the grocery store. He saw the owner point to him and speak quickly. Chang gave him a little wave and the "OK" sign, and hoped the guy would pipe down.

He went back to the other corner, where he could see Drew and his car. Marty sat on the sidewalk and looked like he was the guest of honor at a surprise party. Drew looked Chang's way, and Chang gave him an exaggerated shrug as if to say "He's not here." Drew pointed to the other corner and jogged off.

Chang reached for his gun when a trash can near him fell over. He turned and found Nelson lying in an alcove among the trash and recycling barrels.

"He's here!" Chang shouted, but he didn't wait to confirm if anyone heard. Nelson was thrashing around, and Chang thought he saw blood on his face. He reached his friend and sat him up.

Nelson was awake, but he had a red rubber ball in his mouth with clear strapping tape holding it in place. He was hog-tied with the same tape, and someone had drawn a wide, red mouth out of lipstick on Nelson's face. A red line was drawn across Nelson's throat, and a purse hung around his neck.

Chang drew his gun and kept it down by his side.

"Is he still here?"

Nelson, still gagged, shook his head, then shrugged. Chang took it to mean not that he knew, but he might be.

Chang ignored the protest from the fingers on his bad hand as he used them to pull off the tape while keeping his weapon in his right hand. He wasn't getting jumped.

He got enough tape off for Nelson to spit the ball out. For a moment he thought that Max (who else could it be?) had painted Nelson's cheeks scarlet, but then he realized it was fury.

"I was watching for Marty, and he grabbed me from behind." Nelson sounded embarrassed as well as livid.

Chang untied him. "He had to be watching the whole time. What's he wearing?"

"Denim shirt, blue pants, pancake makeup, and a white wig that makes him look like Andy Warhol."

"Probably looks like Dalí by now, but I'll let everyone know."

"He's fast and strong."

"Did he say anything?"

"Yeah. He said, 'You guys took my lunch money. Now see what I have to stoop to?' Then he hung that purse on me."

Chang hunted through it and found a wallet with no cash. He checked the ID. "Bet she's somewhere nearby. Think it was her lipstick?"

Nelson rubbed his sleeve against his face, only smearing the lipstick, but Chang didn't interrupt him. "I'm sure. He made a mistake. He was mad, and this was impulsive. Did you catch Marty?"

"We got him. He looks like he's familiar with the arrest process, but he ran for some reason. You OK?" Chang eyed the red line on Nelson's throat.

"Yeah. Just angry. I thought this"—Nelson touched the line on his neck—"was for real at first. He touched something cold and sharp to my neck, then must have switched to the lipstick."

"Sorry. We ran a sloppy operation, and he caught us napping."

"He does that a lot, but I think he's getting overconfident."

"Why do you say that?"

"He said one more thing before he took off." Nelson kept rubbing his face so that Chang couldn't tell where the color left off and the chafing began. He grabbed Nelson's arm to get him to stop.

"What did he say?"

"He said, 'Tell your pal the show must go on.'"

42

COMING IN FIFTH

Chang let Ron do the talking when the patrol car arrived. Ron explained the circumstances, and the officers had to accept the fact that he'd needed to act fast and there'd been no time to get them involved. It helped that he was giving them the lead on the collar.

Not that it was much of an arrest. The owner of the house with the pool took an unhelpful don't-want-to-get-involved stance once she learned nothing was damaged or missing from her place.

They followed the squad car to the nearby Ninetieth Precinct over on Union Avenue.

Officially Marty could be charged only with minor evading and resisting arrest.

Chang had hoped they'd turn up a weapon, but no such luck. They only found the cash from the account with his name on it. Of course he'd had more than enough time to ditch anything else.

Ron came into the interrogation room where Chang, Nelson, and Drew were writing up their statements. On the way to the station, they'd explained to Drew that he needed to minimize his role in all this. At least Chang and Nelson were licensed investigators working on an active case.

"Nobody behind the mirror," Ron said to indicate that they could speak freely. "I think you should add the Max attack."

"Why?" Nelson's ego had suffered the worst bruising, but Max had sent the unmistakable message that he could get to them if he wanted.

"It may not burnish your tough-guy street cred, but it might add weight when we make our pitch to Captain Tracey and the mayor."

Nelson considered it. "On one condition."

"Yeah?"

"If we can't catch Max first, then I want to be at the door, where I can look at everyone coming in. I've been close enough to Max to smell his breath. I don't care what he's wearing or how he disguises himself. I'll know him if he walks by."

Ron nodded. "I'll do what I can."

Chang wondered what Drew must be making of this glimpse into the internal politics of police departments. Not to mention the politics of politics. Mayor Glacier put that before all else, including his own stupid skin.

"So what do we have?" Chang asked. Now that Marty had been arrested, Chang couldn't go near him.

Ron's face said it all. He plopped into a chair. "Didn't take him long to lawyer up."

"Did he say anything at all?" Nelson asked.

"We asked him basic stuff, and he gave us 'tude the whole time."

"Like how?"

"Like we asked if he worked with Max, and he said, 'Not anymore,' which makes sense if Max has abandoned his business."

"Not quite the same as not working with him though, is it?" Chang said.

"Yeah. When I mentioned the joint account, all he said was 'Severance pay.'"

"Did you ask if he was supposed to meet Max or if he knew where to find him?"

Ron shrugged. "Sure. That was the end of our productive conversation."

"So is he getting a public defender?" Chang asked. He didn't figure a guy like Marty had a lot saved up for a rainy day.

"That's where it gets interesting, if frustrating," Ron said.

"Yeah?" Chang perked up.

"Marty has an extensive rap sheet. He's done time for burglary, robbery, and a variety of property crimes. He's on parole, which we thought might mean he was in for a longer stay as our guest." Ron slid a folder over to Nelson, who began poring over it.

"Wow," Nelson said within a minute. "A recruit."

Ron pointed. "See that?"

"Yes. Paul, Max took Marty under his wing after he got out of prison. If I remember right, he was one of Laughing Matters' first employees."

Chang couldn't recall a time when Nelson's memory had failed him. "So he's been dirty for a while?"

"The dirtiest. Some of the other performers came from sketchy backgrounds, but nothing like Marty."

Ron looked interested. Drew sat, fascinated. He'd ditched the bravado by now. He'd seen the red mark on Nelson's neck, and Chang believed Drew's story about throwing knives.

"Nelson, did any other employees share an account with Max?"

Nelson shook his head. "No. Drew will back me here. Max was very secretive about his accounts, and his personal finances were totally separate from the company assets."

Drew spoke up. "Lots of times with small sole proprietorships we see the owners put everything in their own name for simplicity's sake. It isn't the smartest move, but we see it more than you'd think."

"So that means Marty and Max are tight. Might be tied together in other things?"

Ron spoke. "I don't know that, but I can tell you that when he was busted early on, it was for doing work for the Russian mob. Petty stuff as far as we know, but he was caught stealing for them."

"You sure?"

"That's what I started to say when I came in. Marty's lawyer is Sergey Grinko."

"I've been out of town for a while," Chang said, hoping that covered his ignorance of the players.

"Gotcha. Straight mob lawyer for the Russian crew out of Brighton Beach."

Chang felt a spark. "Max made me when he was in a Brighton Beach neighborhood."

"So Marty used his job with Max as his legitimate employment. But I wonder if he kept up his mob association on the side," Nelson said.

"If he did, he got a whole lot better at his work because we never caught him again until now."

Chang said, "Maybe he had a better teacher. Ron, do you know where the Russians hang out?"

"They don't share their plans with us, but I can tell you where one of the bosses lives. He doesn't try to hide it."

"Yeah?"

"Local head is a guy named Viktor Markov. He lives near Brighton Beach. Same neighborhood where Max lost you."

"That's a lot of coincidences," Nelson said.

"But that still could be all they are." Though Ron was playing devil's advocate, Chang saw he was hooked.

Chang got an idea. "Ron, has the lawyer shown up yet?"

"Grinko? Not yet, but it shouldn't be long now. Why?"

"Marty may not be speaking, but that doesn't mean he has nothing to say."

Ron gave a puzzled look. "I'm not following you."

"I am," Nelson said. "I'm willing to try if you say it's OK."

"Try what?"

✳ ✳ ✳

Chang hadn't spoken to Deputy Inspector Brennan in more than twenty years, but he remembered him as one of the few good guys who hadn't turned his back on Chang by the time he and Nelson were "encouraged" to seek greener pastures.

Now that Brennan ran the Ninetieth, Ron figured that the best and fastest chance for their idea's success was to get his blessing. Usually Chang was more of an ask-for-forgiveness-rather-than-permission guy, but Ron didn't have much pull here, and Chang and Nelson had none. They sent Drew back to Laura to avoid complicating the process with Inspector Brennan.

"Chang. Good to see you again. Maybe later we can find time to catch up, but Detective Sieger briefed me in, and I understand we're under the gun."

"Yes, sir." Chang tried to be polite.

"Don't think I've gotten to be a soft touch. I always did like seeing you and Rogers operate. I don't know what you think you can learn, but I, for one, would like to see you guys at work." They hurried into the observation room.

They lowered their voices to whispers, well aware that the soundproofing was sketchy in these rooms.

"You'll probably see us lay an egg, but we may never get another shot here."

"Understood." Brennan took a seat. "And if I don't like where it's going, I'll pull the plug."

"Understood," Chang mimicked.

Nelson sat closest to the one-way mirror. From there he'd have a perfect view of Marty, who sat at the gray table in the gray room, his head bobbing like he was listening to music.

He looked up when Ron opened the door.

"Grinko's here?"

"Not yet."

Marty folded his arms and closed his mouth, leaving only a little smirk.

Ron sat down across from him. "I thought you might enjoy some company."

"You got a whore in lockup?"

"Answer some questions and I'll see what I can do."

Brennan shifted in his seat. Chang wished he had a way to communicate with Ron, but they'd quickly rejected the idea of a wire. Marty wasn't dumb, and an earpiece would have been obvious with Ron's short hair.

They'd just have to trust Ron and get what they got.

Marty smirked again.

"That's OK. We just wondered why you'd want to go and mess up your parole for a broken-down, failed businessman like Max Stark."

Chang could see a ripple of tension surface in Marty, but his expression held.

"You got a deal with him? He got some side projects?"

Marty sat still, without speaking. But not still enough.

Nelson scribbled on a notepad and whispered, "No."

"Do you even know where he is?"

Nelson tilted his head like a puppy. "Not sure here. But he knows more."

"I mean, after that account is depleted, you might never see the guy again. I don't understand why you'd want to protect him."

Chang wished he could remind Ron to ask yes or no questions. But that was easy to say here. Ron had said he wanted to create a bit of banter, however one-sided, and slip in his questions casually.

"Are you still working with Max?"

Marty pretended to yawn.

"How about the Brighton Beach crew? Seen Viktor Markov lately?"

Nelson's head snapped straight. "Yes."

"Oh, but that would be a violation of your parole. That's OK. Between Markov and Max Stark you have plenty of practice taking the fall for someone else."

Chang heard a commotion coming from the hall. "Party's about over, sounds like," Chang whispered.

"Maybe that's not all you get from Max. I can see why you want to protect him. If I was married, I'd never turn on my wife." Ron put a condescending tone in his voice.

Marty stood up, and his chair tipped over. "You want to back that shit up?"

The door opened, and an intense-looking man in a gray silk suit and blue tie pushed into the room. The cop at the door, a kid Chang didn't know, was about to grab him when Ron help up his hand. "It's OK."

"No it is not *OK*," Sergey Grinko said, pulling himself up to his full five eight and smoothing his thin brown hair. He was graying at the temples, and his eyes showed intelligence beneath all his noise and bluster. "You can expect a complaint to your supervisor."

"I like getting mail," Ron said.

"My client asked for representation."

"Looks like he'll have to settle for you." Ron seemed to be enjoying himself.

Grinko gave him a hard look despite the fact that Ron towered over him. "You have a bright future as a comedian, especially if police work no longer suits you. You are new to this precinct?"

Ron's light banter vanished, and it was clear from his expression that he got the threat loud and clear. Chang knew that Ron would like to smack the guy but would never rise to such bait.

"Marty's not the only one who doesn't have to answer questions."

"On the stand then. It is all the same to me."

"Who's paying your retainer? We didn't find that much on him."

Again with the piercing gaze. "And you are privy to my client's finances how?"

Careful, Ron, Chang thought. This guy was a shark's shark, and he was already keeping score.

"Just judging the man by his clothes. Yours are very nice, indeed. Not the results of pro bono work, I'm guessing."

"And I know your interrogation violated my client's rights."

"I was just talking to him. He didn't have to say anything." Ron smiled, but his eyes grew hard.

"Don't worry, Mr. Grinko. I didn't tell them anything," Marty said, looking almost frightened.

Nelson whispered behind the glass. "Yes he did."

43

TANGLED WEB

"That was fast," Ron said. He was sitting with Nelson and Chang the next morning at their usual meeting spot in Central Park.

"He's out?" Chang didn't really need to ask the question.

"Grinko is good. They posted bail and left together in his Benz."

"Think it's worth tailing him?"

"Marty? Not only am I specifically barred from it, I'm here to ask you guys not to mess with him either."

"Why?" This was new. Ron had been letting them take up the slack and also take more of the risks since they weren't bound by police hierarchy.

"A bunch of reasons, some of which I even agree with." Ron let out a long breath. "Pressure's building, and this Max thing is starting to grind the gears over at the station and with the brass."

Chang and Nelson sat back and surveyed the open area around the gazebo. Chang didn't see anything suspicious but decided they should meet somewhere else from then on.

"Grinko is the real deal. He'll hammer me for provoking his client, and even if I get cleared, it'll still stain my record." Ron picked at the wood on the railing. "I can take that. Thing is, this guy that Grinko *really* works for is also the real deal. Markov is connected all the way back to Moscow."

"So that should make it all the more worthwhile to watch Marty. At least we have a fixed address for him. Max might turn up." Chang could see he was grasping at straws.

"That's one of the things. The gap between what we suspect and what we can prove is getting too big for Captain Tracey to ignore."

"And he was giving it his level best." Tracey had always struck Chang as a coward.

"Maybe not," Ron agreed. "But he still gives me my marching orders, and he says leave Marty alone. He's scared of Grinko. And while it's fun to bandy around terms like 'Russian mob,' Markov has never been nabbed for anything major."

"Maybe his luck's running out," Chang offered.

"Not so far. We haven't been able to touch him."

"Much as I'd like to help on that front, I started this ride trying to figure out Max Stark. I'm still in the dark, but I know we've got a dangerous character on our hands. And a hell of a smart one." Chang thought of all the things they suspected Max of, and the image of Nelson rolling around in that alcove ignited like a bonfire in his chest.

"Looks like Max's business went under, but if what Drew and you saw with his finances is right, he's been doing something to keep it afloat for a while," Ron said.

"Right. Let's assume something illegal."

"I'm good with that," Ron agreed.

Nelson sat and absorbed the conversation with an expression that Chang had dubbed "sponge face."

"Crime plus finances says theft or work for hire," Chang continued.

"I can tell you do this for a living," Ron said.

Chang ignored that. "So Max may be a thief from way back even if we don't have the proof or criminal history. I believe he's good enough to have avoided getting caught."

"He may be good as a lone wolf, but we have at least one other known crook in the mix."

"Right. Max may or may not need Marty's help. But did Marty need him?"

"Laughing Matters was either Marty's livelihood or an important cover. Marty might also turn to what he knows in order to help a friend."

"Even if they're not as close as I suggested to Marty," Ron said, smiling.

Nelson spoke up. "It's a shame the lawyer showed up. He was ready to spill. He was *raw.*"

"Yeah. So fine, we get why Max would steal, pretty much for the same reasons anyone does. But why involve mobsters? That still doesn't make sense to me." Ron paced the gazebo.

"Laura," Nelson said.

"What does Laura have to do with mobsters?"

"You said you think Max is crazy. I don't know if he is or not, but his motives aren't strictly financial," Nelson continued.

"What does that have to do with the mob?" Ron stopped pacing.

"Think about what he's been doing for years. STP? He's found stories, each one bigger than the last, and leaked them anonymously to Laura. When they pan out, her credibility grows and he gains her trust."

"OK, so clowns don't live by bread alone." Ron grinned at Chang.

"Go on." Chang wanted to hear where Nelson was going.

"Laura covered Marchetti, wall to wall, and the public ate up those stories."

"Yeah?" Ron looked impatient.

"Now we know that STP, or Max, gave her more Marchetti, and that last scoop was created for her."

"So why not keep giving her the Marchetti stuff? Like the location of the lawyer's body?"

"He may not know. I think he got what he wanted setting Marchetti off to take action against Bigelow once it turned out that the lawyer really was hiding evidence. It wouldn't have been hard to guess Marchetti's reaction to the betrayal."

Chang thought back to what Laura had told them. "Max mentioned a landfill."

"Could be just a guess on his part. But I might be wrong."

"Still, Laura wasn't covering any mobsters other than Marchetti, and he's Italian."

Chang turned to Ron. "Anything cooking between the Italians and the Russians?"

"Not that I know of," Ron said.

"You're pulling on the wrong threads."

Chang waited. Nelson often talked in zigzags before he reached his point.

"First, you were focused on the money, then the mob, but the common thread is the big story. At least it is for Max." Nelson paused. "And, as it turns out, for Laura."

Chang could sense answers in the fog. "So if we look at Max's motive as wanting to feed Laura bigger stories, we should look at what he came up with as his alter ego STP."

"Exactly."

Ron looked like he was catching up. "After Marchetti you've got Orrlov, a charity that turns out to be corrupt. You think Max tapped the accounts when he exposed the books?" Ron gripped the gazebo frame over his head like he was going to start swinging from it.

"You're stuck on money. He may have stolen something, but think bigger picture," Nelson said.

Chang was amused to see Ron, big as he was, looking like a reprimanded student.

"Go to the next one. Lewis. Lots of curveballs there."

"I still see money. He's not messing with anyone poor. If that's not the link, what is?"

"Russians," Nelson said.

"Huh? Orrlov is Russian, but not Lewis." Ron shook his head.

"Just?" Nelson interrupted again.

"What do you mean, 'just'?"

"When you said Moscow, I thought of the Russians who are part of the treaty triangle we're about to see."

Ron nodded. "Triangle, that's good."

"Is Markov tied to the Russian government as well?"

"That I don't know, but it's a good question for my Fed friend. Let's say yes for now."

"All right. If that's true, then what do the Russians want with Orrlov or Lewis?"

Nelson's fingers traced some initials carved in the wood of the bench. "Lots of unknowns. Let's assume for the moment that Max's reasons for going after Orrlov were Russian based and not personal."

"So Max is doing this for hire?" Ron said.

"Why not? It's a win-win for Max. He gets to make money, and he has a juicy story to feed to Laura."

"And Lewis?"

"That's harder to figure out." Nelson pointed to Ron. "Your guy said Lewis was talking deal, and that he had something big to expose, outside his black market art collection. This treaty sure sounds big."

Chang jumped in. "Since we're putting the Russians under the microscope, what would be their reason for knocking off Lewis?"

"Lewis was going to screw up the deal?" Ron said.

"Maybe. That could also be the motive for the mayor."

"You suspect the mayor of having someone killed? His own friend?" Ron started to shout and caught himself.

"I'm just trying to look at this from every possible angle," Nelson said.

Chang began to feel the first threads of a headache. "This doesn't make sense. If we think Lewis was killed, and I'm willing to believe he was, then how can the reason for his death be to protect the treaty?"

Ron seemed puzzled for a moment. "Both sides are coming to the table for a reason. What we know so far makes a shooting war stakes worth killing over."

"I agree. So why would a guy they hired, namely Max, suddenly advertise to Laura that he's going to do something major to disrupt it?" Chang felt the headache drill into his skull.

44

MOTIVATIONAL SPEAKER

After a trip to a hot dog cart, the three men returned to the gazebo. It felt good to stretch his legs, but Chang wanted to go somewhere else. He felt it was a mistake to be predictable.

On the other hand, Chang liked the sight lines from the gazebo. Nobody could approach them unseen.

"Can't get dogs like these in Delaware." Nelson returned to his usual spot.

Chang took a seat while Ron remained standing. "So we seem to have a contradiction in our theories. Anyone have any ideas on how to reconcile?"

"Astronomy," Nelson said.

"How's that?" Ron looked exhausted.

"I was thinking about how some of the planets in our solar system were discovered."

"By disrupted peace treaties or assassinations?" Ron asked.

The sarcasm rolled off Nelson. "Nope. Neptune wasn't observed directly. It was predicted, based on the behavior of other planets."

"I mean no disrespect, but what the fuck are you talking about?"

"There's a big unknown that's affecting all the actions we've observed. We don't know what it is yet, but we can work on suppositions."

"Such as?"

"Well, we know Max has ties of some kind to the Russians. We know he had inside information about this treaty. He had to get it from someone or learn about it while breaking in someplace."

"OK." Ron folded his arms across his chest.

"Given the Russian connection in the other leaks, I think whoever set him on those victims also gave him the treaty info."

"Or he snooped it from the same place," Chang said.

"Good point," Nelson said.

"So where does that leave us? We know Max said he intends to disrupt the event."

"In a big way," Ron said.

"Right. Though we don't quite know what that means, it's safe to assume that it would hurt the treaty."

"So why would the Russians want to send their guy to screw up a deal, especially if they just got through preventing Lewis from doing the same thing?" Ron asked.

"Maybe they haven't." Nelson stared at the wood floor.

"But you just pointed out the ties between Max and the Russians," Ron said.

"Connections, not ties. An important distinction," Chang said. He thought he saw what Nelson meant.

"Yes. What if Max has gone renegade?" Nelson said.

"But why?" Ron looked confused. "What does he care about a treaty between people halfway around the world?"

"He doesn't." Chang suddenly felt cold. "Think of the threads we're following. This would be a big story for Laura. He helps her make worldwide news. Or there's another possibility."

"What's that?" Ron reached up to one of the roof braces again and stretched his back.

Chang should have thought of it earlier. "Laura is the target, and she has been the whole time."

"But he could have destroyed her anytime he wanted. Why go to so much trouble?" Ron let go of the beam.

"It's in front of the whole world," Chang said.

"What's that?" Nelson pointed at the beam where Ron had just put his hands.

Ron checked his palms and saw they were covered in white powder. "What the fuck?"

"That string wasn't there before." Chang grasped it and pulled gently. A small object dropped down. A tiny gingerbread man hung from the beam, the string tied in a hangman's noose.

❋ ❋ ❋

Chang scanned the area for any sign that someone was watching them. It was too hard to tell in a park like this, where the guy could look like anyone. Nelson went with Ron to find a restroom to clean his hands.

Against Chang's advice, Ron had sniffed the powder, arguing that he'd already been exposed.

Chang understood. Sometimes the not knowing was the worst part. It smelled like flour, and that certainly fit the message, he supposed, but he wasn't willing to put anything past Max at this point.

He couldn't be certain that Max was watching him now, but the skin on the back of his neck crawled. Max had obviously been here, which meant that the guy had followed them or Ron to Central Park. Chang looked around for any sign of an electronic bug and vowed never to be without his detector again while on this case.

He didn't see any bug, but this gazebo, which looked like the house made of sticks from the three little pigs story, could easily have been hiding something.

What would Max learn?

That they weren't any closer to catching him.

❋ ❋ ❋

"I'm fine," Ron said, chafing at Chang's persistent questions. "It was flour. I didn't find anything on the wood."

Chang wasn't surprised. Wood wasn't the greatest surface for prints, and he was certain Max would have been careful. Like it mattered. They knew it was him, which was what he wanted.

"We know something." Nelson stared at the gazebo while Ron put his dusting kit away.

"He's a cocky bastard." Ron's mood had continued to deteriorate.

"Certainly that. But he just lent more credence to our theory."

"What's that?" Ron asked.

"Max is a renegade." Nelson pointed to Chang and Ron. "You two understand the tactical side better than me."

Nelson had a gift for understatement.

"And?" Ron asked, seething.

"If you were planning a covert operation, would you waste time and risk detection by harassing your opposition?"

"Not unless it made tactical sense to piss the opponent off so he couldn't think clearly." Ron leaned against the side of the gazebo.

"Interesting," Chang said. "He's done a good job of making us mad. I hope not ruining our focus." Chang saw that sunk in with Ron. "But I'm not sure his strategy is as subtle as that."

"No?" Ron asked. "You've already convinced me he's clever."

"He is. And arrogant. It adds up. But I think he's messing with us for just one reason," Chang said.

"Because he can," Nelson said. "This is fun for him."

45

DOMESTIC DISTURBANCE

Colleen's Apartment

"If this goes on much longer, you're going to have to start kicking in for the rent." While Colleen cleared the dishes, Chang looked for the remote to catch Laura's evening news broadcast. The speed with which he'd settled into a comfortable pattern with Colleen surprised him. He hesitated to think of it as a routine that had an air of permanence.

"The client's obligated to cover for a hotel, so that's no problem."

Colleen wore her red hair in a ponytail and looked every bit the natural beauty she'd been when he married her. She had on a baggy sweatshirt designed for comfort, but he knew the curves underneath. That she could be so relaxed around him was the greatest gift she could ever give him.

"Yeah? How many stars does this place rate?"

"The food's a three, but the personal service is off the charts." He ducked a fluffy missile. "So *that's* why they're called throw pillows."

"Don't make me get Dad's gun."

The old apartment came with mixed emotions, in large part because it had belonged to her father before he died. The old man had shared a connection with Chang, as he too had been a police officer. But the hard-drinking Irishman had never quite accepted that his only daughter married a Chinese man.

He and Chang had eventually reached an uneasy truce. By the time he and Colleen split, her dad was well past his prime and in his cups.

Colleen settled down on the couch and leaned against him. An ad for antacids faded out, and Laura appeared on the screen.

"How's she holding up?" Colleen asked.

"Surprisingly well." Chang was amazed at the difference between the poised professional and the woman who let some of her fear and doubt show though. Still, on or off camera, Chang admired her strength. She shared that trait with Colleen, and he wondered whether the two of them would hit it off—or if their strong personalities would strike sparks. "All of us think this will come to an end in less than two weeks when the big event kicks off. If we can't catch Max before that." Chang shut up as Laura led with the big news.

"Good evening, I'm Laura Stark. Our top story tonight is the surprise announcement from the mayor's office that the city will host the signing of an historic peace accord between the Russian Federation and the Chechen-based separatist group known as the Sword of Jihad."

"Unreal," Colleen said.

"Maybe," Chang couldn't help adding.

The screen cut to a shot of Mayor Glacier standing at a podium. Laura provided the voice-over. "Earlier today we caught up with the mayor." The shot cut to a close-up of Mayor Glacier, who Chang thought looked beatific under the lights.

Laura stood below the man while he held court. "Mr. Mayor, why are these opposition groups getting together, and why here in New York? What is your involvement?"

"I'm not at liberty to disclose the details of the inner workings of these delicate negotiations, but I can say that we're honored to play any role, however minor, in facilitating the reconciliation of these two parties. If we, as a city, can provide the backdrop to a lasting peace, we'll be truly humbled and will welcome a halt to the bloodshed."

"Humble my ass," Colleen snorted. "He's the most self-aggrandizing egomaniac I've ever seen."

"Coming from a jaded journalist, that's saying something. You should show some respect. I hear he may run for president."

Colleen shrugged. "You could be right. I think he's started right here, don't you?"

"Unfortunately."

"I'm surprised you care that much."

"You know me better than that. We both spell *politician* with four letters," Chang said. "I'm thinking of security. Glacier's priorities are skewed. You should see Ron. He's on board with the Max threat, but he's having a hard time selling his bosses."

"Why?"

Chang pointed to the screen. "Nobody wants to rock the boat. And as far as this guy is concerned, he *is* the boat."

"I haven't covered anything quite like this, but I've been pulled in to a few of the big fund-raisers. There was a ton of security."

"And since 9/11, that's only increased. But now it's like alphabet soup. They'll have the NYPD, the ATF, the FBI, and Homeland Security, possibly others, not to mention the security details for the Russians and the Chechen representative's personal bodyguards."

"Sounds safe." Colleen faced Chang. "Maybe even like overkill."

"That's just it. More isn't necessarily better if it's applied to the wrong places. But that isn't the worst of it."

"No?"

"Complexity. All these agencies dance to their own tune. And if the commanders want to get in a pissing contest about rank and jurisdiction, that makes it even more fun." Chang dreaded the upcoming meeting with the mayor's people to try to get them to take the Max threat more seriously.

Speaking of which…

"What if you catch Max first?"

Chang took a deep breath. "I hope we do, and we're really trying. But he's slippery." Chang outlined some of Max's recent tricks. He owed her that much.

"So you're saying he's following you now?"

"I don't know if it's me or where we meet or what, but I can't afford to underestimate this guy. I've never run across anyone like him."

Chang saw the wall go up with Colleen. His heart sank.

"You have to be shitting me. I thought we were done with all that. What, are you about to suggest I go hide until this blows over?"

"No." He saw what he'd get if he even mentioned the idea. "Look, all I'm saying is be careful. And when I'm not in the field, I can stick with you, just like I have been."

"I'm a city mouse. I'm always careful."

She didn't understand, and he didn't want to go overboard and scare her needlessly. But if something happened to her because of him, he knew he wouldn't be able to live with himself. "I know I sound like a worried parent, but be extra cautious dealing with anyone you don't know." He explained how Max liked to use disguises.

"Got it. No candy from strangers." He thought nothing he'd just said had sunk in, but then she added, "I'll move Dad's gun to the bedroom. You'd better whistle before you come in. I'm a good shot now."

She was. He'd had her bring the old revolver down to Delaware a few times so she could practice on a range. She was a natural. The gun had been her father's backup weapon. A .38 Special—no cannon, but it got the job done and had saved her life once.

She had no permit or registration in gun-strict New York, but he didn't think she'd want to carry it anyway.

That was his job.

46

JUST DO IT

Laura's Apartment

Chang saw the peephole darken, and then Drew opened the door. The doorman had announced Chang, but he was glad they were being vigilant. "Morning."

"The changing of the guard. Any news?" Drew looked like he was enjoying "being involved," as he put it. Chang didn't mind, as long he avoided getting underfoot. He had to admit that Drew was more than a bystander at this point. How much of an asset he was remained an open question.

But this morning he needed him gone. "Not really, Drew. But good job keeping alert."

Chang began the bug-sweeping ritual, allowing Drew to tag along. Chang knew he was waiting for Laura to come out of the bedroom so he could say good-bye.

"They have me on desk duty while my case gets sorted out." Drew looked over Chang's shoulder. "Isn't that what they call it when you guys are involved in a shooting?"

Chang braced himself for the questions. Civilians couldn't help themselves. Always so earnest and sincere. "Ever pull your gun? Ever shoot anyone?" All the way to "What's it like to take a life?" or some such thing, if they were poor at reading body language.

"That's what they call it. At least when I worked for them. They may have changed the official terminology." The apartment was clear of transmitters so far.

Drew opened his mouth but then stopped. Chang wondered if his own expression had cut him off. He was relieved, but scolded himself for being "scrutable." Shu would not have approved.

Later today Chang would slather Shu's herbal paste on his hand. The stuff worked wonders, but carried the pungent stench that reminded Chang of all the old man did for him.

"Hopefully it'll get cleared up soon. But they don't want me traveling for the time being, and I'm sure TSA has me on every friggin' list now. Probably strip-search me for fun."

Chang smiled to be polite but thought about how Max's tricks left lasting marks on people.

Laura opened the door. In a blue pantsuit and white blouse, she looked ready for work. "Hi, Detective." She gestured to indicate the apartment. "How are we doing today?"

"So far, so good. He walked into the bedroom and noted the humidity from the shower and the scent of lilac coming from the bathroom. He could hear murmuring and then the sound of the door. He finished sweeping the bug detector and emerged from the bedroom. "All set."

As Laura sipped her coffee, Chang noticed how carefully she drank it to protect her outfit.

"Drew took off?"

Laura nodded. "He said to call if anything happened or if you needed backup."

"He said that?"

"Those very words." Laura gave a quick wink, and then all the humor left her face. "We should go soon. Sid'll think I got kidnapped."

Neither laughed.

"What I have to say won't take long."

"What? You found something?" The hope that lit Laura's face, which she kept hidden beneath a severe mask most of the time, told Chang this was a risk worth taking.

"I'm going to be as honest as I can with you, and then you're going to have to trust me."

Now her face betrayed a palette of emotions dominated by fear.

"No promises." She set her feet like Chang was going to turn into a wind that might knock her over.

"We have less than two weeks until the treaty event. Max hasn't contacted you at all since he dropped his bombshell, right?"

"He seems to be having more fun tweaking you lately," Laura replied.

Chang's gut rolled, and he thought of Colleen. "True. But the good news is that he can't follow us all at the same time. The other news is that we think it means that regardless of how he got into this to begin with, he's now operating to serve his own interests."

"He always does. What do you mean, exactly?" Laura rinsed her mug out and put it in the sink drainer to dry.

Chang took a deep breath. He was at peace with his own personal ethics. When he'd worked for the NYPD and Delaware, he'd followed his instincts, the rule book be damned if that's what it took. He didn't want to drag Laura into this decision, but she wasn't only his client. This man, however crazy and dangerous, had once been someone she loved.

"Max is out there somewhere on his own. He might evade us before the event, but I have an idea for a way to use Max's tendency against him."

"Good. Whatever it takes."

"That's easy to say, believe me."

Go on, you started this.

"What?"

"It might stop whatever he has planned before the event takes place."

"Great. What's the problem?"

"It might get Max killed. You need to know that."

"What would you do?"

Chang shook his head. "The less you know, the better."

Laura's face turned to stone. He saw the anger in her eyes only.

"Bullshit. That's not my style. And last time I checked, you work for me."

Chang admired her guts. "Fair enough." He told her his plan.

When he'd finished, she paused for a long time. He saw her chin tremble, and she picked at nonexistent lint on her pants. But when she looked up, he saw steel in her gaze.

"Do it."

47

WORD ON THE STREET

Manhattan Beach

Chang was in uncharted waters here and guessed at the best approach. He didn't mind working alone. Back when the dragon used to demand to play and he had roamed the most dangerous neighborhoods of Wilmington welcoming any trouble, he *needed* to be alone.

But today he wasn't trying to pick a fight.

No, but you are trying to start *one for someone else.*

That was a fact. Ron had said as much when he gave Chang the address. And Chang didn't need his friend to tell him the department couldn't come within a mile of this gambit.

Chang parked his car on Oriental Boulevard and smiled to himself. Seemed appropriate. He didn't want to scare the guy by pulling up right in front of his house. The man's defenses would go up as soon as his security saw him.

So he would do the rest on foot. After all, it wasn't "drive" into the lion's den.

Before he got out of the car, he battled his instincts and left his .45 under the front seat.

***

With each step on Coleridge Street, his senses expanded. If this had been the first time he'd experienced the sensation, he'd have wondered if someone had slipped drugs into his coffee.

It was the dragon, not the raging beast of the past, but awake and alert as it hadn't been in years. He felt as though eyes were watching him from every window and passing cars were beaming reports to masters in dark rooms. The tires hissed over the pavement.

Careful. He trusted the hyperalertness, but the dragon's more common fury was expressing itself in a sensory paranoia that threatened to distort genuine sights and sounds.

The dragon was coming up with more subtle ways to take the lead in his own body.

Chang paused and pretended to check a message on his phone. The digits swam in his vision, and he forced himself to count them, first forward, then backward, while he controlled his breathing. Slowly the street returned to focus, and he saw minivans carrying mothers and kids. Cars honked and rolled by. Windows stopped staring at him, and a light breeze wicked away the sheen of perspiration that had broken out over his body.

He'd yanked the leash on the dragon.

You're out of practice.

No time to meditate on it. He had a job to do. Half a block to go.

He felt the windows staring again, but this time he knew it wasn't a mental trick. The huge house, just another mansion on a block lined with them, was flanked with tall columns. A grand staircase led to a double front door.

Chang stopped right in front of the place and stretched his arms high over his head. He felt his spine crackle, and the dragon sent a dose of adrenaline through him that helped loosen his muscles.

He hoped that anyone watching would note that he'd exposed no weapons around his waist.

He flexed his hands. His right felt like it could crush stones; the left ached less than usual. He turned and started up the steps.

The door popped open, and a large man in a cheap jacket stood in the doorway.

"You lost?"

"No, sir." Chang showed his open hands.

The guy had all the finesse of a bouncer. Chang knew better than to stereotype him though. He saw a glint in the man's eye, and reminded himself there was probably a reason he was the front line of defense.

The guy's hair was dark brown, too short to comb but longer than a crew cut. From the man's bulk, Chang gathered that he was plenty strong and that the jacket was an obvious cover for a gun, especially given the summer heat. The scarred knuckles and knots on his skull suggested that the guy would be quick to throw a punch. The bruiser glanced around and could see Chang was alone.

"What do you want?"

"My name is Chang…"

"Didn't ask you that, cop."

Fishing.

So give him some line. "I'm not a cop." Chang took a couple of steps closer to the door.

"That's far enough. You look like a cop."

"I'm on my own now." Chang took another step, and he could feel the man's uncertainty switch to hostility. He wondered if the guy would try to kick him down the steps.

"Congratulations. Now answer my question."

"I need to talk to your boss."

"Who's that?"

"Markov. You going to tell me this is the Red Cross?"

"What do you want with him?"

"Can we do this inside? It's important." Chang might as well have tried to walk past a junkyard dog.

"One more step and you're gonna get crowned."

He wasn't a native New Yorker. Chang detected a trace accent. He thought Russian or some other Slavic tongue, but maybe he was just listening for it.

"Take it easy. I'm here to help your boss. There's something he needs to know."

"Does he know *you*?"

"He's never met me or heard of me, I expect. But we have a mutual acquaintance. Sorry I don't know the right word in Russian." Chang wanted to see if it got a reaction.

It appeared to piss the guy off, but since he hadn't even gotten as far as "hello," Chang didn't make much of it.

"What's the message?"

Chang shook his head. "I don't work with the help."

Chang saw the man's body stiffen, but he backed up the steps. "Wait here."

The guard stepped inside, and Chang heard the lock click. Sounded electronic. He was sure there were cameras on him, but he had no way of knowing if he'd gotten Markov's attention.

A couple of minutes passed. He began to feel stupid and more than a little exposed. He had just started to wonder if they planned to ignore him until he left, when the door opened and the guard stuck out his head. "Mr. Chang? Please come in."

Just like that? Maybe Markov was more on edge than he realized. He hadn't even thought the guard was paying attention when he said his name. And he hadn't even mentioned Max yet.

Chang felt imaginary scales erupt down his back as the dragon asserted itself. He tried hard not to shudder as he willed it to remain in check while still taking advantage of the expanded senses it gave him. It was always a delicate and difficult balance. He sensed danger, and the response to threat urged Chang to react fast.

As he stepped into the marble foyer, he noted the exquisite inlaid patterns. His feet registered the reduced traction. At the top of a set of stone spiral steps stood a man gazing down at him without expression.

Two more men, patrons of the same menswear thrift shop, stood inside the entry hall while the first man continued to hold the door open. Chang noticed that the door itself was metal and that there were reinforcing bolts along the frame. A typical police ram would be no more than a loud knocker on such a portal.

He'd come to the right place.

The door slammed shut like the door of a prison cell.

One of the goons nodded, and Chang figured him to be the next link up the chain of command. "Search."

"No need. Like I said, I'm..."

The first guy moved to grab Chang. With his enhanced awareness, he assessed the man's speed and knew that this was not going to be a gentle frisk.

In one fluid motion, he gripped Chang by the upper arm, spun him around to face the door, and shoved him face-first toward the steel.

The dragon inside Chang surfaced and took control when the goon touched him. Chang went with the forward momentum but used his free arm to deflect and roll his body to the side, avoiding a hard impact with the door. At the same time, because of the goon's firm grip on Chang, the guy was yanked ahead and off balance. Chang continued the motion so that his body rotated around and behind the guy.

He finished the move by slamming the man into the very spot that had been intended for him. It turned out heads made decent door knockers. The guy slid face-first down the steel, leaving a bloody streak.

Now he was a doorstop.

No time to think now. The other two closed in, and Chang saw them come at him as though in slow motion. The younger one threw a looping punch that looked like it would take a minute to reach Chang's head. The leader pulled out a blackjack.

Chang ducked the clumsy punch and used his left arm to hook the guy's punching arm and yank him down. From a squatting position, he redirected the man's forward momentum and executed a hip throw into the leader.

Both men went down like bowling pins. Chang stood and snapped a kick to the puncher's head while he was still on all fours. He crumpled, stunned, as the leader regained his feet, blackjack in hand.

Then Chang heard the unmistakable sound of a rifle's charging handle being yanked back and released. Someone shouted "*Stoi!*" and it echoed off the stone and marble surfaces. He glanced up and saw the muzzle of an AK-47 aimed straight at him.

The dragon was reckless, but not stupid.

Chang raised his hands. "Got a permit for that?"

"*Yob tovoyu mat!*"

Something in Russian about his mother and taboo relations. "I'll have to give you an IOU for that one." Chang saw the leader step forward and swing his arm. The guy was quick when he wasn't off-balance. Chang had time to duck, but he knew if he took the guy out, he'd get shot. So he rolled his head just enough to take a deflected blow from the lead-filled sap.

Even so, the man hit hard, and Chang buckled to his knees. The dragon took a standing eight count too. Before he knew it, the leader had punched him in the nose, and he was on the ground.

Fury filled his body as blood ran down the back of his throat. His legs were still wobbly, and then the guy he had kicked returned the favor. All Chang could do was cover up. Most of the blows that ensued were confined to his body and away from his head, enabling him to clear the cobwebs in his mind.

Between the dragon and the thrashing, he forgot why he was there. All he could think about was whether they meant to kill him. If so, he was going to take down whoever he could.

He concentrated on the image of the dragon's cage swinging wide open. He wasn't bulletproof, but he refused to die on his knees.

The one he'd kicked was in a kind of frenzy. None of the kicks he delivered to Chang's frame were especially hard, but he appeared intent on keeping it up until he got tired or Chang died. Rage flooded Chang's muscles, and the only thing he felt was where the guy's feet were when he kicked him.

Chang shot out his good hand and caught one leg at the ankle. He yanked hard, and the guy went down. He felt something strapped around it…a knife. Chang pulled it out and sensed the leader moving in. The guy at the top of the stairs was screaming in Russian.

Chang didn't worry about him. He'd shoot or he wouldn't, but right now the blackjack was coming toward his head again.

Chang let the dragon take over. Like a bystander, he saw a streak of silver arc through the man's sleeve and felt the blade hit bone.

The blackjack flew out of the leader's hand as he bellowed in pain. Chang had a thought as clear as if it had been beamed into his head that he would be shot through the skull in the next second.

He forced his legs to piston out and leaped toward the recoiling leader. Already the arm was soaked through with blood from the slash wound.

Chang held onto the leader's body to make it risky to shoot at him. The two fell to the floor, but he knew this couldn't last because the kicker was getting up.

Chang rolled under the leader and used his left arm in a choke hold that protected his bad hand. With his right hand, he rested the knifepoint just under his own left arm so he could plunge it into the man's throat. He made sure the man felt it.

"Back off," Chang yelled. How had this happened?

"Put it down. You can't get out." The leader was flustered but kept his wits about him. Blood began to spatter onto the floor from his arm, and Chang wondered if he'd cut into an artery.

The guy with the rifle was screaming nonstop in Russian, but he held his fire. Chang heard lots of commotion in the house.

"I just wanted to talk." Chang wondered if he'd get the chance before they killed him. Had this really been his idea?

Doors opened on the ground floor, and several more men appeared, each of them carrying a pistol. At the top of the stairs, a man in an expensive jogging suit appeared. He had graying temples, and Chang would have known he was the boss even if he hadn't seen his picture before.

Markov.

"What the fuck is this? Who let this rabid yellow bear in here?" Markov barked a few orders in Russian, then switched back to English. "Turn my man loose before he bleeds to death. They won't shoot. Not yet. Who are you?"

Chang didn't see that he had much choice. He decided to say his piece and take his chances. When Chang released the man, he expected him to turn and take a swing at him. But Chang saw the guy get shaky when he saw the mess on the floor. The kicker helped him up, and they shambled out of the room.

Chang tossed down the knife, which bounced on the marble floor. The blade made a metallic ring off the stone.

Four pistols and an assault rifle were aimed at him. He stood and put his hands up.

Markov headed down the stairs, pausing at the halfway point. "There are easier ways to commit suicide. What is this about?"

"I'll tell you, but it should be in private." Chang realized how foolish this sounded, and Markov's laughter confirmed it.

"Perhaps you'd like a drink? Make yourself at home?" Markov shook his head. "I'm busy, and my curiosity has its limits. We're justified acting in self-defense." Markov whispered to the man with the rifle.

"Max Stark," Chang stated. He saw the change in the man's expression, but the guy covered his reaction well.

"You have five minutes. Tie him up."

✳ ✳ ✳

Chang sat in a large leather chair facing Markov, who sat behind his desk. Chang's arms were bound tight, and his legs were taped together below the knee.

Markov kept a pistol on the desk with the muzzle aimed in his direction. Apparently it made him feel safe enough because he sent his guard outside. Not far, Chang was certain.

"You are lucky my wife and children are not home." Markov's dark eyes glittered.

"I just need to tell you something, and then I'll leave."

"You may yet leave in pieces. I want to know who you are and what you think you were doing today."

"I'm a private detective." Chang watched Markov thumb through his wallet where he'd left his real ID. He needed the man's trust if this was going to work.

"So this says. Get to your point. Ex-cop, you said."

"Ex-NYPD and Delaware State."

Markov made a face. "And now private detective. What is next, garbage man?"

"I hadn't thought of it that way. You never know, I guess." Chang reminded himself not to make the man any angrier than he already was. "I was involved in the Topper case years ago, and the troubles with the Chinatown Tongs ran through Delaware recently."

That struck a chord. "They are scattered right now. An interesting situation."

"I hear your Italian counterparts and perhaps even your own associates would like to exploit the vacuum."

Markov feigned confusion. "No matter how long I am in this country, I still find my English is inadequate."

"Never mind. That wasn't why I came."

"We are through with the foreplay, yes?"

"Yes. I'm working for Laura Stark, Max Stark's ex-wife." Chang wasn't Nelson, but he saw enough of a spark of interest to know that Markov would listen to the rest of what he had to say.

"So?"

"I won't bore you with the details of how he has stalked her, other than to say he's behaving irrationally and unprofessionally."

"Why tell me? Take it up with him."

"You know as well as I do. He's gone underground. We can't find him."

"Why don't you do more investigating? This has nothing to do with me."

"I told you my interest. My job is to look after Laura's safety. In the course of our work, we've discovered Max's dealings with others, including a connection to yourself."

"And what is that?" Markov sounded nonchalant but leaned forward.

"An employee of yours named Martin Potempkin."

"He no longer works for me. He hasn't for years."

"Of course. It's funny. Though he worked for Max, when the cops picked Marty up recently, he got your lawyer. Around the same time, we discovered that Mr. Stark is tied to incidents with high-profile Russians. Would you know anything about those?"

"You would make a more impressive interrogator if you weren't bound up in my home."

Chang took that as a yes, but he wasn't here looking for answers, just solutions.

"Good point. Tell you what, I'll stop asking questions and just tell you what we think we know."

"Is that supposed to frighten me?" Markov looked like he was ready to fight.

"Yes, but not the way you think." Chang knew he'd better get to the point quickly, but he wanted to establish his credibility first. "Max has been loose with the things he knows or has discovered. He may have released information through some arrangements with you. That's not why I'm here."

"No?"

"Your associates have a great deal invested in the successful outcome of the upcoming treaty."

"I have seen it on the news." Chang saw what he needed to in Markov's eyes. That hungry look. And no denial of the connection between Markov and the Russian government. Interesting.

"You should know Max leaked word about the event before it went public. Everything he said turned out to be true."

"A little late to worry about that now."

Chang shook his head. "No. He's promised to disrupt the proceedings."

"How so?" Markov didn't even feign disinterest.

"We don't know, but he said it would be dramatic."

"And why haven't you been in touch with your old friends at the NYPD?" Markov pronounced the letters like a curse.

"I have. Do you think I'm working here alone?"

"I haven't seen any surveillance outside."

"They're good at what they do."

"So are we. Don't insult me."

No fool. "If I don't come out of here in one piece, you'll be blamed. Believe that."

"Now the NYPD is sending you on an errand? To get me to do what exactly?"

"Up to you. They didn't send me. The right people know. That's enough for you. I came to inform you that one of your...freelancers has gone renegade and is probably mentally unstable."

"Why not take this information to the official channels?"

"I suspect they'll find out. But I thought I might have more credibility with you, considering I was chasing your ex-employee all over town until he got away."

Markov sat still and stared at Chang. Finally he spoke. "If this Max person never turns up and the event runs smoothly, will you and your friends wonder why?"

An olive branch of sorts? "As a lawman with decades of experience, I'm not in the habit of pursuing things that *don't* happen."

Markov nodded. He reached into a drawer and flicked open a short, cruel-looking blade. Chang saw right away that the man knew how to handle it.

He stood and walked over to Chang. He squatted in front of him and cut the tape around his legs. "Get up."

Chang stood.

"Turn around." Chang obeyed.

Markov cut his bonds, and Chang rubbed his wrists. He could feel all the weak spots in his left hand as the blood returned to his fingers.

"Next time send a letter. But you may go."

"Thank you," Chang said.

Markov led Chang out of his office and back into the foyer. Servants had already cleaned the blood off the floor. Two guards followed nearby, carrying pistols.

Markov walked Chang to the front door. The other guy he'd knocked out was gone, and the bloody streak polished away.

"One more thing." Markov's voice came out a low growl. "If I lose my man as a result of what you did, we will find you."

Chang pulled down the collar of his shirt to show the thick cord of scar tissue that ran down his neck. "You wouldn't be the first."

48

ON THE CARPET

Colleen's Apartment

Chang moved fast after Ron's call woke him up. He struggled into the one suit he'd brought and left at Colleen's place. It looked strange hanging next to the one other piece of male clothing in her closet, her father's old police uniform tucked inside a zippered cover.

"That's good, right? They're taking the threat seriously?" Colleen sipped coffee in her bathrobe. She'd let him shower first.

"That's the problem. Ron said the mayor's office just called him, and he was ordered to bring me with him. It's not like this was scheduled."

"But you've been trying to get a meeting."

"Ever since Max dropped his bomb. But they barely responded. We don't know what caused the sudden change, but since when have these kinds of surprises ever been good?"

"You've got a point."

Chang felt the trousers tight against his waist. He hadn't put on the suit in a while, but he knew he'd better get back to his workout regimen soon. He also knew that wasn't going to happen until this case was solved.

The good news was that the "historic" peace accord was only a week out now. Whatever happened, Chang was certain that it would bring the case to a head; he was less certain that it wouldn't end in disaster.

"Wish me luck."

"You'll make your own luck, sweetie." She gave him a kiss.

He stepped through the door. "But which kind?"

✳ ✳ ✳

"I wish you didn't look like you'd gotten worked over by a couple leg breakers." Ron, wearing his dress uniform, met Chang in front of the Nineteenth Precinct.

They'd ride together to city hall.

"At least they won't make me take my shirt off. Colleen said those goons stomped actual footprints on my back."

"I'm really sorry. I should have gone with you."

"Don't make me wreck those dress blues after you cleaned up so nice. I told you to let it go. It was my own stupid fault. I'm just lucky they didn't kill me."

"I'm still wondering why they didn't."

"I hope it was gratitude or whatever passes for it." Chang held back a smile. It made his cut lip hurt. "But I think it was using your name in vain." The urge to smile dried up. "I don't know why I went off like that."

"You said one of the guys was trying to ram you into the wall."

"That's true, but I could have let him think he was scaring me without actually getting hurt. I just reacted, I guess." Though Chang didn't talk about the dragon—and few knew that side of him—Ron and several others had seen some of the results afterward.

"No point second-guessing now. You're here, and he got the message."

"For what it's worth."

They rode in silence until they reached the iron-gated entrance to city hall, right off Broadway. A uniformed officer checked Ron's ID, then Chang's. He waved them in, and Ron pulled the car into a visitor spot. They got out of the car, and Chang stretched.

Chang always marveled at the building's ornate columns and stonework. He wondered if the majesty of a building was always in inverse proportion to the weasels it housed.

"This sure takes me back," Chang said.

"Good times?" Ron smirked.

"Oh, sure." Chang and Nelson had gotten hauled up there— in front of a different mayor, in a different era—to get reamed out for their performance on the Topper kidnapping case.

"Key to the city, right?"

"More like a one-way ticket out of town." Which was about right, now that he thought about it.

"This time it'll be different." Ron plastered a smile on his face that Chang knew didn't reflect how either of them really felt.

* * *

"You're late."

Chang recognized one of the mayor's arrogant twerp aides as he rushed down the stairs, perfect crease in his pants: Dillon Prager. Not that the other one, something Tyler, wouldn't be impeccably dressed as well.

"It's eight fifteen." Ron looked annoyed already. "You said eight thirty."

Prager shook his head and used a tone of voice normally reserved for children. "The mayor's rule is that 'on time' means thirty minutes early. You should know that."

Prager walked away before Ron could react. Chang jabbed him in the ribs. He didn't feel so jocular but thought it might distract him from how much he hated this place.

Apparently they were supposed to follow. He spoke to Prager's back. "Isn't the mayor's office upstairs?"

Prager spun around. "Didn't they tell you anything?"

Both men shook their heads.

"Typical. We're going to be in the situation room."

Chang's interest perked up. He'd never been down there, and he knew that it had been upgraded after 9/11.

Prager continued, "At least you wore a suit,"—he looked at Chang—"sort of. Come on, it's down here."

✳ ✳ ✳

After a second security check, Prager led them down to a basement room. The rectangular space had a wall of monitors on one side and a large, wooden, oval table in the center. Behind the table another desk and monitors served as a control room.

"Have a seat, and the mayor and deputy commissioner will be right with you."

Prager left the room.

"Bet you could get every game in here on Sundays."

"I'm sure." Chang caught the banal patter's subtext. The room was likely monitored.

A few minutes later, the door opened, and along with Prager, Chang recognized Mayor Glacier, who entered with a man he knew only by reputation, Deputy Commissioner Esteban, who spoke first.

"Officer Sieger, good to see you again." The man shook Ron's hand, and Chang gathered right away that they weren't close.

"Mr. Chang. We've never met, but I followed your career while I was coming up."

He never indicated whether this was positive or negative. Chang could see why the man got along well with politicians. "I've heard about you as well."

Right back at you.

"Very good. Let's get started, shall we?"

"Yes, sir. But I confess you've caught us unawares. We only learned about the meeting earlier this morning."

Glacier smiled with a practiced flash of his teeth. Chang focused on the ice-cold blue eyes. "Glad some secrets can still be kept around here. But while we're speaking of surprises, I got a disturbing call late last night."

"Sir?" Ron spoke. Chang was happy to remain silent until they asked him a direct question.

"Did you send this man on some sort of kamikaze mission to harass Viktor Markov?" Glacier was known for getting to the point.

"No, sir." Ron stopped, and Chang felt the tension build like thunderheads.

"Damn it, son. You're not under oath. What the hell were you thinking?"

"Sir, I didn't send Detective Chang to speak to Viktor Markov." Ron spoke as if he were standing at attention.

"Are you going to tell me you didn't know about it?"

Ron's pause was infinitesimal, but Chang caught it and knew the man was considering lying. He didn't get a chance to weigh in.

"I knew, sir."

Chang saw in Glacier's eyes that that was the right answer.

"I'll tell you both right now, there is a whole lot you don't know going on behind the scenes. The last thing we, or for that

matter this country, need is for the Russians to get aggravated."
Glacier's face flushed while he spoke. "And the Russian I spoke
with last night was most certainly aggravated. He wanted you
arrested"—he pointed at Chang—"and you kicked off the force."
Glacier indicated Ron.

"Why?" Chang asked, primarily concerned about Ron.

"I'm looking at your face, Chang, and wondering how you
can possibly ask that question. I understand some of Markov's
men had to get medical treatment."

"They'll be all right. Besides, they started it." Chang wished
he'd chosen words that didn't make him sound like a child. This
whole discussion felt surreal. "What I mean is, they got rough
with me before I had a chance to warn them."

"Now they've had have a chance to warn me. They
reminded me that the deal isn't done until the final agreement
is signed. They warned me the deal could collapse at any time,
and even if it doesn't, they might decide to hold the event in
Russia instead."

And that was what he was the most worried about, Chang
thought. The only one who might not have heard the naked
ambition in the mayor's voice was Glacier himself.

"Sir, we have a theory that Max Stark was working with
the Russians as some sort of freelancer." Chang decided that it
was time to share his ideas. He knew he had to be careful not
to reveal anything they'd learned through Ron's contact at the
FBI.

Prager interrupted. "Not the Russians; you mean Markov."
Condescension dripped from his voice.

"I didn't mean to imply that he was hired out of the consul-
ate," Chang continued, speaking in measured tones. "But your
office appears to merge their interests, so I thought I'd skip the
distinction that Markov is part of the Russian mob."

Esteban spoke up. "We're well aware of Markov's reputation. I must remind you that suspicions are one thing, conviction and the public record are another."

The mayor resumed, "And touchy international relations and negotiations are yet another. And, if I may be blunt, way above either of your pay grades. I'll thank you not to second-guess our judgment in this matter." Glacier still looked angry, but he'd regained control of his emotions. "We are well aware of who Markov is. But for these purposes, we've found he can facilitate some parts of the dialogue in ways our Russian friends find helpful."

"And if they find it helpful, you find it helpful." Chang couldn't stop himself; Ron had a pension to protect. And Chang saw some sympathy in Esteban's face, but he also lacked the courage to stand up to the mayor. Figured.

"I was beginning to wonder if I needed to lock you up until after the event, but I see you understand, even if you don't approve. About which I couldn't care less."

"Last time I checked, I still needed to be charged with something before being detained." Chang tried to rein in his temper.

"Be grateful that Markov prefers to avoid official scrutiny or there would be a laundry list of charges. And if you become an impediment to the process, Chang, make no mistake about it, we'll come up with enough to hold you for weeks."

Esteban squirmed, and Prager practically beamed. Chang made a mental note to be sure he was registered so he could vote against this egomaniac if he ever won the nomination for president.

Ron sat stone-faced.

Glacier looked down at his notes. When his head came up, it was like a different person had jumped into his skin. He smiled a sparkling politician's grin, and a cheery mask replaced the dark, threatening countenance of a moment before. Chang wished Nelson could have seen it.

"Enough of the unpleasantries. We're on the verge of a great new era in Russia and the birth of a fulfillment of a lifetime dream of lasting peace." Glacier gazed over their heads. "Leave the Russians alone. I'll keep them in line, and they can manage their own web of alliances."

Prager chimed in. "In other words, don't screw this up, and you still get a seat at the table." Glacier shot him a look. Prager corrected himself. "The kids' table, anyway." Prager waved his hands. "Never mind the metaphor. If you'll behave, we have plans for you."

"Plans?" Ron spoke. Chang had never seen him look so uncomfortable. He wondered if he'd see the man sweat through his thick tunic.

The mayor nodded. "We are taking this Max Stark threat very seriously. We just want to keep it in perspective. Commissioner?"

Estaban cleared his throat. "Detective Sieger, I've read your report. You've done some good work here. You too, Mr. Chang."

"Thank you, sir." Chang noted the civilian title. Everything was a turf war with these guys.

"Your theory that Stark played some part in leaking rumors on the Lewis investigation goes further than we're prepared to endorse at this point."

Chang saw a cloud pass over Glacier's face at the mention of his friend. "Griffon Lewis was more troubled than any of us realized. I'm embarrassed that somehow those sordid details leaked, but making the leap that he was somehow murdered is irresponsible."

"We have other examples where Stark has shown himself to be dangerous." Chang could tell that the Lewis idea was closed to discussion and decided it made no sense to try. They acknowledged Max was a threat, which at least gave them a voice in shaping the security plan.

"Leave my friend out of it, and I already said we accept the fact that the man is unstable."

Something was rotten here, but he tried to concentrate on the matter at hand.

"Yes, sir." Chang turned to Esteban. "Our being able to tie Stark to a number of news leaks demonstrates his capacity to use sophisticated deception to gain access to his targets."

"That and his knowledge of the event itself have convinced us that he can deliver on his threat," Ron added.

Esteban spoke. "And what do you think that is? This report is vague on that point."

Ron continued. "We don't know. He claims to want to give Laura Stark something dramatic to cover. Given the high-profile stories he's tipped her to recently, we've got good reason to be alarmed. Not to mention the fact that he's proven he's capable of violence. We have to be ready for just about anything."

Prager rolled his eyes. "Sounds like a cop-out, no pun intended."

"He surprised us and put a knife to my partner's throat. For fun." Chang knew they had something in mind, so best get on with it. "Aside from shadowing his friend to collect money, we think he operated alone. That's good and bad. Good in that it may affect the scope of his efforts, but bad because he can rely on just himself and it's harder to intercept a lone operator if he's skilled."

"Which means…?" Prager shifted in his seat.

"He might target one of the participants, including you, Mr. Mayor, or one of the Russians, or the representative for Sword of Jihad. But those are only a few of the obvious possibilities."

Esteban produced a folder. "We were thinking along the same lines, and it all boils down to making sure Max Stark never gets into the event."

Chang spoke. "Given his talent for disguise and stealth, that's problematic."

Glacier's arrogant grin returned. "That's where you come in."

* * *

Chang and Ron sat and listened to Esteban lay out the various agencies involved in securing the facility. If the show was intended to placate them into silence, it failed.

"Sir, I haven't been out of uniform for so long that I've forgotten the advantages of a layered defense. But it's also true that with layers comes a greater chance for confusion. The kind of confusion a man like Max Stark could exploit."

Prager made a dismissive snorting noise that made Chang wonder what sound he'd make if he were punched in the gut.

"You have been away a while. We've gotten good at this sort of thing with all the terrorism threats."

Chang almost asked Prager where he'd trained, but realized there wasn't time to spar with this idiot. "I have no doubt. But Max is not a radical ideologue or political extremist, nor a religious fanatic. He's the biggest outlier I've ever run across."

"I was just going to get to that," Glacier said. "If he's so obsessed with Laura Stark, why not let it be known that she won't attend?"

"Great idea, sir." Prager looked like he was going to applaud.

Chang wanted to ask him what Glacier's shoes tasted like.

Chang and Ron shared a look. They'd been worried this might come up.

Ron spoke first. "Sir, we strongly advise against that."

"Why?" Glacier looked amused.

"He's said in no uncertain terms to Laura, when she suggested the same thing, that not only would he still go, he'd make it worse."

"How?"

"He wouldn't be specific," Ron said.

"We know Max could reach out and hurt Laura easily, even with us watching her. If all he wanted to do was hurt or kill her, we don't have the manpower to prevent it."

"But manpower isn't the issue here. You said so yourself."

"It depends on how the manpower is used. But for the sake of argument, we know and he will know that you are well guarded," Chang said.

"But as good as he is, he won't hurt Laura?"

"No sir, he won't." Of that Chang was certain.

Glacier gave that predatory smile again. "Then it's settled. She'll sit next to me as a guest of honor. I'll give her the first interview, and she'll be front and center to witness the historic event."

"That sounds like you want to take her hostage." Chang heard the words come out of his mouth before he could stop them.

To his surprise the mayor laughed. "She can always say no. Are you a betting man?"

Chang shook his head. Though he wasn't optimistic, there wouldn't be a better time to try his appeal. "May I make a request?"

"Why not?"

"Cancel the Solara Circus. The flow of civilians and equipment represents a rich opportunity for infiltration, especially for a person like Max who has a similar background."

Prager responded. "A week before the event? You've *got* to be kidding! The Russian envoy, Arkady Romanovich, is a huge fan of this circus. That couldn't have worked out better if we'd planned it."

Chang said, "Sir, I'm sure Max must be thinking the same thing."

"Esteban will outline what we have in mind for you. That is, if you agree to behave yourselves and be team players."

"Of course." Chang figured that left room for interpretation.

The mayor stood up and grinned. "Excellent. The show must go on, as they say."

"That's funny," Chang said. And Prager and Glacier looked at him.

"How's that?"

"Those were Max's exact words to Laura and to Nelson."

49

PLACES, EVERYONE

Laura's Apartment

Chang, Ron, and Drew sat at the dining room table. Nelson leaned against the wall and stared out at Central Park. He'd just arrived, and Laura was on her way.

Chang fought the urge to ask Drew to stop tapping his foot against the table leg; he understood his nervousness.

"Can you get me a special permit to carry?" Drew asked Ron, who was doing his best to tolerate him. Chang was beginning to like the guy even if he'd never make it as an operator. He had guts and wanted to protect his girl, and Chang could certainly respect the sentiment.

"Carry what?" Ron's temper grew shorter with each day closer to the event. It was only three days out now, and he looked ready to burst.

"A weapon. If I'm going to be next to Laura, I may need to act fast."

"You gotta be kidding." Ron didn't try to disguise his irritation.

Chang saw the guy was serious.

"If *he's* packing, I want a Desert Eagle," Nelson chimed in.

He wasn't serious, and Chang smiled at the image of frail Nelson with one of those oversize hand cannons.

"Drew, *I* can't be armed, and I know how to handle a weapon," Chang said. He still wasn't happy about it.

"You won't have a gun on you?" They'd waited until that day to reveal the details of their roles in the event, both because they'd promised Esteban and because it made sense for operational security. It was basically an elegant way to keep Drew in the dark because they worried he might shoot off his mouth.

"No. We'll get into it once Laura shows."

A minute later the intercom buzzer rang.

Chang answered it. It was Quincy. "Mr. Chang? Ms. Laura is here, and…" Chang heard Laura in the background. The second-rate speaker couldn't garble the tension in her voice.

"Chang? Where's Drew?" she asked.

"He went to the bathroom." The guy drank so much iced tea, Chang had begun to wonder where he put it all.

After an awkward pause she spoke again. "What are you wearing?"

Huh? "We're all dressed here, why…" Chang suddenly remembered his earlier precaution that he should give his old badge number instead. "Wait, I get it. Thirty-five forty-four."

"Jesus, don't scare me like that."

They were all about to snap.

"Nelson is here too. The place is clean."

"Be right there." The lift in her voice was amazing.

***

She opened the door, and Drew went and hugged her. He followed her into the dining room where the others were waiting.

Ron had been ready to do his briefing for a while, and his antsy behavior was contagious.

"Good to see you, Nelson," Laura said.

"Ma'am." Nelson tipped an imaginary hat to her.

She cracked a smile and sat down. "I'd be lying if I said I wasn't nervous. What's the deal?"

Chang felt bad that they hadn't been able to say anything earlier, but the mayor—or his ridiculous assistants—had seemed like they were looking for any excuse to toss them out of the process. The approach of the event, coupled with the ongoing silence from Max, had given the mayor's office false confidence.

Chang took the opposite view. The fact that Max had stopped playing games suggested that the guy was deadly serious about going through with whatever he had planned.

Chang resisted the urge to sweep the room again for bugs. He'd just checked it. *Settle down and let Ron talk.* Chang sat where he could observe Laura and Drew. Drew was a potential wild card, and they had to ensure that his well-intentioned but clumsy efforts to help didn't get anyone killed.

Ron stood at the head of the table. "First off, Laura, you don't have to say yes to this."

"Thanks for the disclaimer." Laura spoke with an edge in her voice.

"Everyone, and I think that includes you"—Ron gestured to Laura—"believes Max will somehow punish us if you aren't in attendance."

"I got that impression. In some weird way, whatever he has in mind is for me—whether I want it or not."

"Sounds right. The mayor decided to play along and came up with the idea of seating you next to him for the ceremony. Front and center."

"And I can talk to him?"

Chang noted that the journalist in her surged to the fore.

"Yes. On the record and everything. I'd advise against an ambush-style interview, however."

"Max has that covered." Her attempt at a laugh came out as a screech.

"Where do I sit?" Drew interrupted.

Ron had seen it coming. "We got a VIP spot for you a couple rows back."

"No way. I'm right next to her or no deal." Drew folded his arms across his chest. Nelson stared at him. Chang couldn't tell if he was curious or amused.

Ron snapped his head around and glared at Drew. "What deal? You don't get a deal. You're lucky to get a ticket at all to this shindig. I had to personally calm Homeland Security down to even let you anywhere near the mayor and the other dignitaries, Mr. No-Fly List."

"I was set up."

"I told them that. So now it's on me. You're welcome. May I continue?"

Drew nodded, and Chang was glad to see that some of that had actually sunk in.

"Off the record, I'd ask him anything you want since he's using you as a human shield."

"The guy may be a chickenshit, but he's not dumb," Laura said. "Whatever Max is going to do, I don't think he'd hurt me. Not physically." She whispered the last.

Her remark hung in the air for a moment, and then Ron continued. "The order of the day for the security plan is by the numbers and no surprises."

"We're here because we expect something unconventional to happen," Nelson said.

Ron shrugged. "Yup. That's why we're doing this here. They can't be bothered. I've never briefed civilians like this before."

Chang felt like he was watching the proceedings from outside himself. "Has the system gotten stupider since I left?"

"It's always been full of arrogance and misplaced priorities. Glacier just wants a smooth show so he can bask in the limelight."

"Speaking of which, any movement on canceling the circus?" Chang almost knew better than to ask.

"No way. The Russian envoy, Romanovich, just *loves* the circus," Ron said, imitating Prager's voice. "Couple that with the embarrassment Glacier would face having to admit a security concern, and it's a nonstarter."

"A perfect storm for a clown," Nelson said.

Chang spoke. "You said standard security, but they didn't have much time to pull this together. How's that going to work?"

"Like a Chinese fire drill." Ron smirked at Chang, then turned serious. "Some elements are boilerplate; the rest, I'm afraid, is more security theater than anything else."

"Such as?"

"NYPD's doing the exterior and pre-event sweeps; the other guys are more concerned with the inside once things are set. The room, you'll recall, isn't too bad for crowd control. We'll keep the fire exit doors closed and guarded. Something happens, they open, no sweat, but otherwise we'll keep a tight rein on the entrances."

Chang pictured the various ways in and who would be entering and leaving the room. "Metal detectors at the entrance?"

Ron nodded. "Of course, and you'll love this. Given the fact that the glitterati suck at taking directions and they'll have more metal crap on than a rap star, the mayor came up with the brilliant idea of putting a team of diplomatic Miss Manners types in place to make sure nobody gets their nose job out of joint when they get stopped."

Chang felt his gut twist. "Civilians? I could get an elephant gun in under those rules."

Ron held up his hands. "Calm down. We kicked up a fuss about police union rules, and *that*, not the safety factor, forced a compromise. Now we'll do the checks while the diplo-dorks explain the *process* to the guests." Ron smiled. "That's not the really good part."

"Yeah?"

"In addition to the metal detector, we've negotiated a 'Max-detector.'" Ron pointed to Nelson.

Nelson perked up. "Me?"

"You thought we just brought you up for your looks?"

"I always wanted to be arm candy." Nelson's expression clouded over. "Just put me near the door. I'll spot him."

"We were hoping you'd feel that way. You give us the signal, and we'll grab him up fast." Ron took a deep breath. "But make sure it's him."

"I don't do wrong." Nelson didn't smile.

"OK." Ron nodded.

"Not bad." Chang thought of all the groups moving in and out. "The waitstaff?"

"Don't ask me how, but I actually got that twerp Prager to make a real concession."

"Yeah?"

"All the food will remain in the outer hall. Heavy hors d'oeuvres and such on steam tables, all that equipment and personnel will stay outside the inner perimeter."

"How'd you manage that?"

"The power of positive prejudice, my man."

"Huh?"

"In private I voiced my concerns about how hard it might be to vet all the necessary waitstaff who'd have access to the room." Ron shook his head in disbelief. "I had this whole explanation lined up, and Prager just agreed. Then he says, swear to God,

'You never know where those people are from. The last thing we need is some immigration dustup with ICE agents.'"

Chang laughed. "You have his voice down, but you should show more respect. Glacier gets to be president, that guy might be the next secretary of state."

"God help us," Ron said.

"That leaves all the people with the circus."

"Right. They've provided us with a detailed list of every performer and worker. I'll give them credit, the Solara Circus runs a tight ship. We should be able to verify all the players the day of the performance."

Chang wasn't totally convinced, but he felt like the security picture was beginning to take shape.

Laura spoke up. "What about the unions setting up and running lights and stuff? You need the plumbers' union to flush the toilets in this town."

This case hadn't entirely erased Ron's years of arm's-length hatred for Laura. But Chang saw some grudging respect in his eyes. "Good point. Funny, outside of closed-shop towns like here and LA, those guys do everything themselves and that's their preference. They made that point clear to anyone and everyone."

"They should have expected that," Laura said.

"Expected, yes. Accepted, that's an open question. But again, we were able to use that friction to our advantage. We argued in the name of safety and wrung off-the-record concessions that some of the Theater Guild employees would get credited and paid for the work while they *supervised* the circus guys who will do the actual setup. The upshot of it all is we cut down on extraneous personnel. Most of those guys have done the necessary work already."

"How's the room look now?" Chang felt a gnawing unease.

Ron turned toward him. "Amazing. There are trapeze sets and scaffolds going all the way to the ceiling."

"Do you know the guest list for the night of the event?" Chang asked.

"We'll have it. I'm getting photo IDs as well."

"You mentioned the scaffolds to the ceiling. Who's got the roof?"

"We do. Secret Service pushed back a little, but they have their hands full with the principals. We'll put a couple guys up top, and we'll also have a chopper on station but not close enough to spook the guests."

"So where do they want me?" Chang asked.

Ron grinned. "You should have seen the drama Glacier put up about outsiders. But I think he wants you there, he just won't admit it."

"And?"

"You get to be out of sight but not out of mind. You'll be on the balcony overlooking the ballroom with the circus director. Guy named Henri Larousse."

"Fellow Chinaman?" Chang said.

"Right out of the Quebec dynasty." Ron smiled. "Actually, he speaks Mandarin if you want to shoot the shit with him in Chinese. I met him, and it's something to hear him yelling directions to the cast in different languages. They're from all over the world."

"So why do they want me with him?"

"You get sort of a bird's-eye view of the crowd, and they have a spotlight. Also, Henri choreographed every second of the show, so if our guy interrupts anything, he'll know right away."

Chang wasn't sure where he would have put himself with all the different agencies running around. He might have been most helpful right next to Laura, but with the mayor at her side that was a nonstarter. This wasn't a bad spot.

"Doesn't sound like I'll be able to move in if I do see something."

"You'll have a radio to contact me. And I'll be near Nelson, so if either of you sees anything, I can sound the alarm. As for direct action, you're thinking like a cowboy again. We'll have an army down there, and the last thing we'll need to worry about is you swinging in on your one good hand. Muscle we got; we're loving you for your mind this time."

"When you put it like that…" Chang knew Ron had a point, and if something did go down, he'd probably just be in the way.

But he'd never been comfortable as a spectator.

50

HOUSE LIGHTS

Empire Hall, Three Days Later

The spotlights playing on the entrance reminded Chang more of a Hollywood awards show than a high-level diplomatic breakthrough. There were even velvet rope lines and plainclothes agents in place. He knew there would be plenty of additional agents once the event got rolling. The mayor's edict for discretion would have the men dressed down, but a trained or even observant eye would spot them easily.

Chang and Nelson crossed Broadway. Chang wished he'd taken the time to get his pant waist let out a bit, but he hoped his Armani suit, which he'd kept from his clotheshorse days, still looked OK. Once upon a time, it had fit like it was built around him. His injury, Shu's departure, and then this case had cut into his training, and he felt softer than he had in years.

Still he had a sense that—for better or worse—the case was going to wrap up that night.

"I don't miss wearing these every day." Nelson tugged on his sleeves. He practically rattled inside his clothes, a well-worn blue blazer and gray flannels. Chang noticed that Nelson had punched a hole through the belt to cinch it tighter. He'd combed his wispy hair down flat, which made his head appear more skeletal than ever.

But the eyes in that head sparkled with the same fierce intelligence as always. Chang thought stationing Nelson by the door was the smartest move of the night.

"When this is done, we need to get some calorie shakes into you."

"I'm just small-boned," Nelson countered.

They reached the front door, the only apparent entrance. Chang knew the police had been busy all day screening equipment and service people.

Chang didn't recognize the guard, an athletic-looking man with an earpiece, so he figured he was with one of the agencies. Chang and Nelson showed their IDs, and the man found them on a list. They were cleared to enter the outer hall of the building.

Inside, Chang saw the food tables getting set up and large metal boxes of equipment being wheeled in on carts. Most of the circus gear was already in place, and had been checked already, he hoped. He was pleased to see a uniformed officer with a K-9 checking the incoming equipment.

Ron had told him how the dogs had hit on one of the boxes earlier, and it had turned out to be the pyrotechnic charges for the show. The Solara Circus representative had submitted all the required paperwork and details about the charges to ATF, but somehow NYPD never got the memo. Gaps like that terrified Chang. With so many cooks in the kitchen, it was too easy to exploit the confusion.

Chang heard Ron's voice. He was working with one of the fire marshals and explaining the plan to lock the fire exit doors but avoid blocking them in the event of an emergency.

The fire marshal kept shaking his head, and Chang saw Ron's face flush. Then Ron got on the radio. Soon a couple more men with gray enough hair to imply rank—probably with the Secret Service and the FBI—showed up to gang up on the fire marshal.

"Just like the school yard, huh?" Nelson said.

"Bigger stakes here." Chang knew everyone was just trying to do their jobs, which might explain why he felt so out of place. They'd given him a nice, specific spot for the event, but really he was an extra, and possibly superfluous, set of eyes and ears. He was used to working on his own or as the lead of a special operation. The vagueness of his status felt alien to him.

Ron was the coordinator for the NYPD, whose SWAT teams and other units had their own command structure, and all the other agencies answered to themselves.

That such operations ever worked at all continued to amaze Chang. He hoped they would that night but reminded himself again that these folks weren't all obsessed with Max. They had every conceivable threat to prepare for and had to be wrong about only one to court disaster.

Ron broke away and joined Nelson and Chang by the door. He chatted with the officer on station and pointed to Nelson. The guy scrunched his face for a moment, then regained his composure, nodded, and spoke for a moment into his sleeve.

Ron spoke. "This night can't end soon enough."

Chang couldn't have agreed more.

❋ ❋ ❋

The balcony area had looked spacious when the great room was empty. Now, with a group of live musicians to one side and a makeshift light and sound booth fit for a rock concert on the other, Chang felt hemmed in. It looked like an improvised skybox in a stadium, with plywood walls covered in acoustic foam erected on the sides and one open end for observation of the stage and audience two stories down.

Henri, a frenzied little man with thick black hair and wild eyes, had explained that the musicians' mikes were sensitive enough to pick up his directions to the performers, so whenever they were positioned nearby, they used the walls to block out his voice. Chang didn't complain. He could still see floor to ceiling, at least when he wasn't in the way. More than once already, Henri had barked at him to move and called him "ox" in Mandarin.

Chang didn't bother to take offense. The man had bizarre eyes, one gray and the other blue. The gray one wandered on its own agenda, reminding Chang of a pale, hyperactive chameleon. Henri's attention wandered more than the eye, so one second after his insults, he was on to the next rant, either to his lighting tech or into the microphone. Ron had been right. The guy seemed to know terms of abuse in every language spoken on the planet.

Chang noticed that the crew around Henri matched his frantic energy and seemed to respect their boss. Maybe he was the genius everyone claimed.

At least he'd agreed to tolerate Chang's presence. When the mayor's staff explained what Chang was doing there and asked Henri to let him know if anything looked out of place during the show, Henri replied in a heavy French accent, "Monsieur, *everyone* will hear it if the show is not perfect."

Chang had seen snipers with less focus.

※ ※ ※

Outside the ballroom, Ron ran down a seemingly endless checklist while he helped get Nelson situated near the front door. He knew they were doing everything they could. No. He knew they were doing everything they'd been permitted to do. He didn't know if the distinction would matter.

327

"It'll be OK." Nelson looked at Ron with a calm expression and took his last sip of water from a wide-mouth plastic cup.

Ron wasn't used to seeing Nelson in a jacket and tie, even if he did look like he shopped at Goodwill.

"You think?" Ron led Nelson to a spot near the door and let him sit near the last table. This would give Nelson a chance to look at all the guests when they passed through the metal detector and were either wanded or moved on to the ballroom. Nelson would hand out programs to help him blend in. Chang's idea, and Ron thought it was a good touch.

"I don't know, but you've done your part. I'm ready. He's coming, I know that." Nelson put the empty cup down on the table and picked up a stack of programs.

When he wasn't busy trying to keep track of all the teams and agencies and whatever fires might spring up, Ron wanted to be close to the door to keep an eye on Nelson. He'd given all the men at the door strict orders to respond if Nelson alerted them, but the guy had no formal place in the command structure, and Ron had no idea how forceful Nelson would be. He had faith in the brain inside that goofy exterior, but he'd never worked closely with Nelson and didn't know how he reacted when it hit the fan.

Ron heard in his earpiece that the signal to let the guests into the ballroom was about to sound. Right now they were milling around the exterior, eating and drinking and trying to be seen. They weren't his problem until they passed through security to the interior ballroom. The plan called for the regular invited guests to enter first; the dignitaries would enter only after the crowd had been screened. Their limos would pull up, and the agents would get them inside right away. Ron made a mental note to turn off the audible alarm on the metal detector when they came through, since it would call attention to the armed guards arriving with the VIPs.

A guy in a tux, from the catering company, walked around the outside perimeter ringing a triangle chime where the gathered crowd could hear it. Ron recognized some high-profile socialites from protection details in years past. Many others he knew he should know, but didn't. They all seemed well acquainted with each other and doubtless shared memberships to clubs that cost more to join than he made in a year.

That's OK. They probably can't bowl for shit.

Ron saw the least self-absorbed of the guests begin to queue up. The security screening began smoothly. As Nelson handed out programs, Ron saw a stunning woman in a tight, black dress turn to her much older husband. Ron heard a sharp, "Chester!" and she inclined her head toward the table.

Huh?

Chester reached into his pants pocket and dropped a five-dollar bill into Nelson's empty water cup. They entered the room. Nelson simply nodded and continued to pass out programs. Ron lip-read one of the other guests and could have sworn he'd said something about the guy passing out the programs being "handicapped." Now that the precedent had been set, cash flowed into the cup, and soon it was stuffed with bills.

The wanding of guests dripping with jewels went better than Ron had expected it would. He'd been braced for a flurry of irate "Do you know who I am?" comments, but so far, so good.

And no sign of Max. Ron could see Nelson's eyes sweep the wave of incoming guests, but he hadn't given anyone a second glance.

Ron checked in with the various agencies' commanders and the contact for Homeland Security. Soon the chatter subsided. That meant one thing: the dignitaries would be arriving soon.

Right behind the well-to-do guests, Ron saw the first of the media start to line up. He walked over to Nelson and whispered in his ear.

"Watch the media people. Glacier handed out press passes like candy."

"Will do." Nelson fumbled with several programs that were stuck together.

An older woman in an off-white evening gown gave Nelson a gentle pat on the arm. "You're doing just fine."

Nelson nodded, and Ron turned away to avoid looking like he was laughing at the poor man. He scanned the media lineup. Looked like several portable TV rigs—though he knew the event wasn't being broadcast live—and an assortment of cameras for still shots. The on-camera talent, all coiffed and made up, were a nice contrast to the slobs wielding the heavy units. They probably thought wearing khakis and turtlenecks *was* dressing up. Ron dug a finger under his collar and tried to stretch it out. His rental tux hadn't been made for a lifter's neck, that was for sure.

It was sort of a joke to think that he or any of his security teams blended in, but they were required to make the effort. He admired the way the Secret Service boys did so with practiced ease.

Ron saw some of the K-9 guys check the cameras before they got through the line. The dogs would go a long way toward ensuring a big device wouldn't slip through. They'd hit on every pyrotechnic charge on the stage. Ron still couldn't believe they allowed fireworks in the first place, but Glacier had insisted they stay. Ron made the bomb guys inspect underneath each charge to ensure that it was the only thing the dogs had detected. That little French director, Henri, had had a fit, and Ron wanted to smack him one, but at least the bomb squad knew they'd done their job thoroughly.

"You almost look civilized."

Despite the crowd noise, Ron nearly jumped when he heard the voice near him. He turned to see Laura Stark, looking stunning in a dark blue dress that showed a tasteful hint of cleavage. If he didn't hate her, he'd have to concede that she looked downright attractive. Maybe *hate* was too strong a word, but old habits die hard. "Laura. You too. Ready for the big interview?"

Ron saw the bomb dog, an intense Malinois, sniff the camera gear that Laura's guy, Eddie Tua, was carrying. He too was dressed up in a tux, likely because he would be standing so close to the mayor. Eddie looked even less comfortable than Ron felt.

"I think the interview will be a welcome distraction." She lowered her voice. "I just want to get to it. I feel like bait."

"Well, you smell great," Ron blurted out. *Where the hell did that come from?* Her puzzled expression eliminated any hope that she hadn't heard him.

"Thanks, I guess. Better get inside. The stars are on the way, I hear."

Drew hovered just behind her and seemed at home in a perfectly tailored tux. He looked away as soon as Ron made eye contact. *His idea of going incognito*, Ron supposed.

✳ ✳ ✳

Laura had been to several events there over the years, but Empire Hall never failed to impress. "Eddie, you good?" She watched as he finished getting checked, and he nodded to her. She went ahead. It wasn't like there was any reason for them to enter arm in arm.

Ron had looked like a nervous wreck, and she wasn't sure who would be more relieved when this was over. The thought sent a shiver through her body. She reminded herself of all the security there, with more arriving with the mayor and the VIPs. Max was just one guy. Maybe he'd see the folly. Wouldn't he?

Laura saw Nelson by the door. He was dressed all wrong for a black-tie event, but nobody seemed to notice. He was handing out programs. Clever. She saw his spooky, dark eyes scanning the clusters of people outside the hall. When he spotted her, she saw him light up with recognition. She gave him a smile.

Then she saw a large cup overflowing with small bills. Was he supposed to be selling the programs? She reached him. "I'm sorry, I don't have my purse."

Nelson gave her a program. He spoke in a soft voice. "You'll get our bill later. I seem to have become a charity case."

Laura got it and was about to feel sorry for him, but he didn't appear to care in the least. It wasn't even that he seemed to be above the potential embarrassment, more like outside of it. "Anything?"

"Not yet. Believe me, I won't keep it to myself. I only look special."

She moved into the room. *Wow.*

The first thing she noticed was the mesh net that hung from the ceiling. It ended about twenty feet above the crowd, and through it she saw an array of trapezes and scaffolding rising up to the ceiling. The net's thick ropes made it look like a web, and several cords hung straight down from the ceiling. Pipes ran across the room connecting a variety of platforms and rigs for what she assumed was the show. It made sense, she supposed, since the show was called *Danse des Araignées*, or Dance of the Spiders.

"Beats the hell out of the Saving Face Gala." Drew craned his neck around, and Laura could see everyone else was taking in the unique adaptation of the cavernous space.

"Sure does." She'd taken Drew to that event last year, a posh but straightforward benefit for children with birth defects.

Colored lights, mostly blues and reds, played across the marble walls. On one side a giant video screen showed a view of the stage.

The house lights provided enough illumination for people to find their seats. Laura moved down the center aisle. The rows in front of the stage remained empty, roped off and guarded by several gigantic "ushers."

"See you later. I'll be in good hands." Laura glanced at a member of the security detail and hoped Drew caught the subtext to stay out of trouble if anything happened. His protective streak had a way of dropping his IQ.

"As long as you leave with me, I'm not complaining."

Yes he was, but that was his problem for now.

She looked up at the light rigs and saw the control booth. One short man paced frantically, and another, bigger man looked like he was trying to stay out of the way. And failing. It had to be Paul.

51

THREE WISE MEN

"I don't care what the rules say," Henri shrieked into the headset. "If he gets in your way when the show starts, you throw him out."

Chang admired the man's energy and intensity, but try as he might to avoid it, he felt like he couldn't be more underfoot. "Problem?"

Henri looked at Chang like he'd just appeared. "Eh?" He waved Chang off. "Nothing. Just the union, how do you say... babysitters? They get in the way like you do, but they also think they know things and bother my people for no reason." Henri twisted a knob on the soundboard and tapped a gauge with a manicured fingernail.

Chang disappeared from Henri's awareness again, at least until the next time the man was about to bump into him. For some reason "lummox" didn't sound so bad when spoken with a French accent.

Chang's earpiece crackled. He pushed it deeper into his ear and turned up the volume. He could monitor communications and speak, but he knew better than to say a word unless it was mission critical. There was enough chatter already, and it could get confusing fast.

"Three Wise Men crossing," a mechanical voice intoned. Probably Secret Service. He loved the call signs they gave their protectees. The mayor and his party were arriving.

Chang could picture the outer area and the sterilized corridor the agents would create. If it were up to them, they'd instruct the subjects to sprint into the room to minimize exposure to potential threats. Of course, each dignitary and his entourage had to strut in and preen for the cameras.

"Move!"

Chang let Henri squeeze by. The prima donna act was wearing thin, and Chang had been fixated on the radio chatter.

He leaned over to get a better view of the doorway where they would come in. He scanned the audience. He thought Laura had seen him earlier, but he resisted waving like a parent at the school concert. They hadn't lied. They seated her right next to the mayor's spot. The rest of his entourage would fill the empty seats.

Henri muttered into his headset mike, and a musician began to play a strange instrument. It looked like a rectangular ukulele, and the music sounded like some sort of folk song. While its sad sound filled the hall, Chang watched a trio of guards, dressed in black shirts and pants and traditional wool caps, enter the room. Each of them wore a leather belt with an ornate dagger. Behind them walked Ali Musaev, president of the Chechen Republic. The briefings had pegged Musaev as pro-Moscow, but he'd been given permission to speak on behalf of the Chechen rebel leader of the Sword of Jihad, Ibrahim Gadeyev. It was an odd arrangement, but Chang figured that at least Musaev and the Russian representative wouldn't come to blows in the hall.

Once the Chechen had taken his seat, the music shifted to a traditional Russian tune, part of Tchaikovsky's 1812 Overture. Chang heard Henri muttering curses under his breath.

Chang tapped Henri. "What?" If something was wrong...

Henri frowned and seemed to understand. "No, nothing like that. They make me change the music. Monsieur Prager said nothing 'politically offensive' to the Chechens, so he chose a song to commemorate the defeat of General Bonaparte instead. *Salopard!*" Chang understood the word and knew it wasn't he who was being called a bastard.

Several lean men in suits entered, and Chang made them for Russian security. Likely armed to the teeth. Funny way to run an operation, but this wasn't his show.

Then in walked the Russian foreign minister. He looked young despite his reddish-brown beard and wore a gray business suit. No black tie for him either. Chang recalled from the dossier Ron had shared that his name was Arkady Romanovich, a powerfully connected man with suspected ties to the Russian underworld and—surely by no coincidence—a childhood friend of Russian president Borodin.

Romanovich sat on the opposite end of the aisle from the Chechens and gave a slight nod in their direction. Laura sat in the middle, an awkward buffer between the two sides.

Finally the orchestra struck up an instrumental version of the familiar chords of Lennon's "Give Peace a Chance."

Chang looked over at Henri, who shook his head. "For these, they pay extra. Not my choices."

After all the abuse, Chang thought it was funny that Henri would care about his opinion.

Without a trace of humility, Mayor Malcolm Glacier stood in the doorway, waiting until the spotlight fixed on him. It tracked him and caught part of Prager, who followed behind like a faithful hound. The crowd clapped, and the cameras flashed and popped. Glacier beamed.

When the entourage reached the front row, Glacier turned to Laura and made a show of kissing her hand. Laura's expression told Chang she hadn't been briefed on that little twist.

Glacier waved to the crowd and made his way to the front of the stage. It was clear and set for the performance, but Prager handed him a wireless microphone.

"*Merde.*"

That was all Chang needed to hear to know that this was an unscripted move. He knew the peace accord ceremony was scheduled to begin immediately following the forty-minute performance. They planned to add the podiums and other accessories to the stage right after the show.

Glacier apparently couldn't wait, however. Henri barked some commands to the light tech on the spotlight, then spoke rapid-fire into his headset.

Ron was right, it was fascinating to hear him switch languages in midsentence.

When the spotlight focused on Glacier, Chang noticed from the image on the big screen that the mayor had arrived in full makeup.

"Welcome, friends and honored guests. Especially those who have come so far for such an important mission of peace." Glacier nodded to the two diplomats before him. A translator whispered in President Musaev's ear. He covered his surprise at the impromptu speech with a quick smile. The Russian recovered even more quickly and flashed diplomatic teeth.

Henri made no effort to disguise his contempt. "Like a dog. Can't resist peeing all over the stage to say, 'This is mine.'"

Chang thought that sounded about right.

"Before we enjoy the marvelous performance we've planned for you," Glacier continued, "let us all take a moment to reflect on what has brought us here tonight. A historic peace accord in which I'm fortunate to play a minor role. Yet nothing is more important than settling our differences, however ancient, not just for our own sakes but for all Russian and Chechen children. Their shining example can show all the world that peace is possible, while we never forget that peace is not inevitable." Glacier beamed.

"*Mon Dieu*, I shall need a bucket. I will soon be sick." Chang smiled out of politeness but quickly realized that the longer Glacier spoke, the more exposed he was. Chang's earpiece buzzed with various cops and agents checking in with their respective commanders. Chang scanned the restless crowd.

Henri looked like a storm about to erupt. Chang understood. The man's high-pressure job relied on exquisite timing, and he had an entire cast itching for this windbag to shut up.

"And now we will see what is possible when artists of many nations cooperate. Following that, we will create our own tapestry of peace, thanks to the courage of the two fine men here, who will say with one voice, 'No more.'"

Though the smiles on the men's faces remained fixed, Chang noticed that their jaw muscles bunched.

Glacier, perhaps sensing the restlessness at last, motioned for quiet—an unnecessary gesture as nobody was clapping. "But enough. You didn't come to hear me."

His expression said the opposite.

Chang couldn't read Laura's face but figured she knew the camera was around and that she should remain "on" for the evening.

"Sit back, relax, and enjoy the Dance of the Spiders."

52

DANCE OF THE SPIDERS

Laura toyed with the idea of sneaking in a question to Glacier, who kissed her hand a second time before sitting down. What the hell was that all about? The guy looked so pleased with himself.

Any line of inquiry vanished from her mind because the lights went out the instant Glacier took his seat. The netting was just visible thanks to the red lights, and the sound system began to pump night sounds into the hall. Crickets and distant animal calls gave the hall a jungle atmosphere, and special-effects lighting transformed the hall's dome into a tree canopy, with stars and the moon peeking through. It reminded Laura of a planetarium. Slow New Age music set the mood.

Dancers dressed as elves and woodland nymphs took the stage. Laura knew from attending prior Solara Circus performances not to try to make literal sense out of the show. The key was to just enjoy the spectacle and appreciate how effortless these performers made their movements appear.

Human pyramids, acrobats, and Chinese plate spinners using props that looked like chunks of bark instead of dishes all wove their trademark spell. One clown, dressed like an elf, reminiscent of Puck from Shakespeare's *A Midsummer Night's Dream*, interacted playfully with the audience. He teased the dignitaries from a safe distance and goofed around with the outermost bodyguards. Laura assumed they had been warned ahead of time as they took the ribbing in stride. Although Laura had felt a twinge of fear when the clown first appeared, she quickly saw that he was short and wiry.

✻ ✻ ✻

Chang watched Henri as closely as he watched the show. Henri was like the invisible conductor. Less vocally than earlier, he ran off some internal counter that told him just where the choreography needed to be at any given moment. His body language spoke volumes; he would appear to go limp when a sequence went off without a hitch, only to tense up again with the next act.

Chang couldn't tell the difference—to him, the show looked brilliant—but whenever the timing was off, Henri looked physically pained. No doubt the performers would hear about it later. Chang kept an ear on the radio. So far, it was all still routine check-ins, from the roof to the ground.

He hoped he'd seen enough of Henri's gyrations to be able to tell if something was really wrong. For the time being, all he could do was watch the show, which didn't follow any kind of logical sequence.

Chang jumped right along with the audience when the pyrotechnic charges went off on the stage. Nobody had told him when that would happen, and his hand instinctively drifted to where he normally kept his pistol. It wasn't there, of course, and he saw Henri grin at him. "You like the thunder?" The sound of rain piped in, and silvery bits of confetti fluttered down to simulate a storm in the jungle.

Chang scanned the audience and the stage area. He strained his ears on the radio, but other than the momentary shock from the blast, everything appeared to be going according to plan. When the storm sequence concluded, the stage played out the jungle coming back to life. Actors dressed as animals flitted about.

Then the lighting began to play off reflective strips woven into the thicker portions of the safety net that covered the stage and stretched out over the audience.

"*Araignées,*" Henri whispered into his headset.

❋ ❋ ❋

Laura heard the audience gasp when the lights hit the web suspended over their heads. Then three performers in spider outfits slowly descended from the ceiling on ropes that looked like silk. Costume legs mirrored limbs that moved like those of arachnids. They dropped in time to the music, gradually getting closer and closer. She noticed that they were descending almost directly above the three dignitaries, which meant that the middle one was right over her head. She watched on the screen.

Neat effect. The spiders rose and fell, she guessed by some sort of pulley.

When they reached the web they scampered into a big circle, then returned to hover over the diplomatic group. Each performer grabbed onto what Laura thought were called aerial silks and began to sway in time to the music.

The spiders over the Russians and the Chechens reached through the net and extended their arms toward the dignitaries. The one over Laura and Mayor Glacier did the same, their hands only a yard or so above the spectators' heads.

Too close, Laura thought, but again the guards' lack of reaction suggested this was expected.

The performers to her left and right opened their hands, each releasing a white dove that flew out over the audience.

The performers to the sides then grabbed a thick cord next to them, shot into the air, and grabbed trapezes. They climbed up through holes in the ceiling and disappeared. The spotlight shone on the one over Laura.

She wondered what this guy would do to top that.

The last spider opened his hands and dropped something into the mayor's lap. She looked over as he cried out in revulsion.

It was a dead pigeon.

Or looked like one. Some of the audience laughed, but the people right around her weren't sure how to react. Was it a gag? The guards looked at each other.

The performer ran one limb down the net and the threads parted, and then he lowered himself down by one hand on a strip of aerial silk until he hovered right before them.

"My, my, my, my! So sorry." The performer squeaked in what Laura guessed was supposed to be a spider voice. His face was covered by his costume's mask.

Mayor Glacier looked confused but put on a game face as he picked up the thing to hand back to the spider. The guards edged closer.

"Here." Glacier glanced at Laura. "This feels real. Yuck."

"Gotcha." The spider's voice came out coarsely, and Laura felt all the air being sucked out of her lungs.

In a flash, the performer grabbed the mayor's wrist and pulled him out of his seat. His free arm whipped forward and snaked a cord around the man's waist.

"No!" Laura screamed. And Glacier just yelled, "Hey!"

The guards moved down the row, but too late.

The spider hooked the cord to his own waist and tugged twice on the silk. He faced Laura. "Love that color on you, babe," Max said in his natural voice.

Confusion radiated in waves through the audience, with some of the crowd still laughing and others commenting in panicky voices.

Max and the mayor rose into the air together as the first agent arrived in the center of the aisle, his hand under his jacket. The agent tried to grab Glacier's leg but missed. Now back through the slit in the netting, Max pulled the mayor in close and wrapped himself and his captive in the strip of stretchy silk. Now cocooned together, they looked like one fat spider's meal as they continued to rise above the audience.

When the guns came out, the room erupted.

53

PANDEMONIUM

"Check fire, check fire. Up the service access to the stage." Chang heard the calls in his earpiece and gave thanks for the cool heads of the commanders. Despite his better vantage point, he couldn't distinguish between the shapes. They'd almost reached the ceiling.

It had happened so fast. Henri had seen it first, but even he was still in shock. The three-spider bit was clearly part of the show. Right up until Max dropped that thing into Glacier's lap. When Henri said something in French, Chang realized it meant "dead bird?" And when Max cut through the net and lowered himself down to the mayor, Henri had gone berserk.

Chang knew he didn't have the authority to call out anything, but the moment he saw Henri's reaction, he knew. He'd radioed a warning to Ron, and the guys moved fast, but not fast enough.

Before Max and the mayor reached the ceiling, the Secret Service had swooped in and grabbed the Russian and Chechen leaders. Their own guards were slow to react as the Secret Service men whisked the principals out of the room. The men were hustled to the nearest door, which sprang open for them. The guards followed.

When the audience saw what had happened, they acted as one to the danger. The sight of guns created a wave of panic, and clumps of well-dressed people began to swarm toward the single exit.

Chang heard a jumble of radio calls, all coming in simultaneously, but he managed to pick out several discrete messages. He heard the order go out for the fire doors to be opened, which would allow the crowd to escape via the row of doors around the circular ballroom. Where was Laura?

He checked her seat and spotted her moving toward the edge of the room. Among the tuxedoed men surging to the exits like a herd of startled zebras, he picked out Eddie Tua, bulling his way against the flow of people toward Laura, using his camera like a wedge. Chang knew he'd look out for her for the moment.

The Secret Service whisked their charges to waiting cars. Chang didn't detect any other threats. While one half of the force was occupied with the escape and evacuation, the other half started to chatter about getting to the mayor.

"Is there any other way to the service area over the ceiling?" Chang shouted to Henri, who looked lost as he bellowed into his microphone. Chang had to repeat himself, practically picking the man up to make sure he was heard.

"Just the two stairways. They also lead to the roof."

That was what Chang remembered too. He pictured SWAT teams storming up the stairs that minute and knew he'd get shot or trampled if he tried to join the fray.

Max and the mayor had reached another access hole and were now out of sight. Some of the crowd—and no shortage of news cameras—remained in the room, and the big screen gave rolling footage of what had just happened.

But what had happened? What was Max going to do with the mayor?

Chang heard the distorted howls of frustration over the radio as the SWAT commander hollered for a battering ram. Apparently the access doors to the roof were blocked.

Chang hoped they wouldn't turn to shotguns. The gunfire would stoke the panic into a full-blown stampede. He knew the rams were in the vans parked outside. They might even have had one inside, though he hadn't seen it.

He hated just sitting there. He turned to Henri. "Ask the other performers up there what's happening."

Henri spoke fast into the microphone and shook his head. "*Merde!* Nobody is answering."

Chang didn't get a chance to say another word. A high, wailing scream came from the ceiling. Some of the microphones picked it up and blasted the sound across the room.

Chang saw a body drop from the center hole in the ceiling. Glacier. His arms and legs flailed as he fell straight toward the hole in the netting in what felt to Chang like slow motion.

Then the mayor jerked to a stop and his body snapped back on a tangle of cords.

Chang's mind couldn't process what his eyes saw next. The mayor's pants flew off his body, and papers scattered out of his clothes right through the web netting, showering the room like oversize confetti.

Glacier's ongoing screams assured Chang that the man was very much alive, and he swung in the air, naked from the waist down, on what Chang could now see was bungee cord and rope twisted together. It looked designed to make for a jarring but not lethal stop.

Cameras flashed, and the big screen left nothing to the imagination.

A moment later, the screen went dark. Chang listened in on the radio for the progress of the SWAT teams. It sounded like Romanovich and the Chechen, Musaev, were clear and away in their cars. He heard another call for the battering ram, but then

Chang was certain he heard the SWAT commander's voice call to the two snipers on the rooftop.

"Eagle One and Two, he's coming up the west stairs right to you. Hurry. West stairs doorway."

Chang heard them acknowledge.

How could the commander know that, if they were still trying to break down the access door? Chang almost spoke the question aloud as it popped into his head.

The sniper team came back on the radio. "In position."

Then the commander's voice came on and said, "Wasn't me. I repeat, that wasn't me."

Then Chang heard the sniper reply, "Say that again? Repeat last known location of—target sighted! By the *east* stairs. Running for the roof. He's got a parachute, say again, a parachute..."

He'd heard enough. Chang bolted from the balcony and down the stairs to the ground floor. Crowds of people still clogged all the doorways and the interior hall. Quite a few of them had stopped to gawk at the mayor, who continued to sway back and forth in the air and scream for help. Some crew members were trying to get a ladder, but until they reached the maintenance area above, he wasn't going anywhere.

As Chang shouldered his way through the crowd and made for the front door, he heard screams outside, and the chaos escalated. He couldn't get outside right away, so he pressed the earpiece with his hand and listened to snippets on the police radio.

"Target down. I say target down."

"Shots fired?"

"Negative," Chang heard one of the snipers report. "We're at the roof edge. Target made unsuccessful jump. Looks like the chute malfunctioned. We'll need an ambulance. Get your guys on the ground to cordon off the body."

Now the commander. "We're on it. Looks like he got as far as halfway across Broadway."

Chang squeezed out the door and saw the helicopter's spotlight shining on a red silk shape and scarlet stain. White parachute silk billowed out onto the street, one end flapping where the strings had all broken. Already the police were forming a perimeter around the body.

Chang tried to get closer. Rubberneckers and displaced guests clogged the street. Cops diverted traffic while the first ambulance arrived, its siren whooping. Chang followed the hole it made in the crowd until he was stopped by a member of the NYPD. A young kid he didn't know.

Chang searched for Ron and saw him coming across the street with the SWAT commander. Chang could hear over the radio that the stairway door had finally been breached, and the SWAT team was heading up the stairs.

"Ron!" Chang shouted, repeating himself several times in order to be heard over the crowd. Ron waved him over, indicating to the patrolman that it was OK.

Chang started to approach him. "Everybody OK?"

Ron signaled for Chang to wait. He and the commander were on their radios and trying to get a report on what was happening inside. "Say again?" He covered one ear. "Well, have somebody bring his goddamned pants up."

Chang couldn't hear the other side of the conversation but decided not to fool with the radio to find the frequency Ron was on.

"All right. How many down? Got it. Still breathing? Yes, they're on the way." Ron talked to Commander Jennings, then turned to Chang.

"Several of the performers were found knocked out and tied up. We're sending ambulances now. They hauled the mayor up. I guess he's OK. Well enough to be pissed. You guys hiring? 'Cause my ass is probably grass after this fiasco."

"Let's figure out what happened before you toss out your shield," Chang said, though he thought Ron might be right, unless some other scapegoat could be found.

"Can I take a look?" Chang indicated the body. The paramedics were standing by. They'd checked for vitals just to be able to say they had, but the body was a wreck.

"How the fuck did he get in?" Ron walked with Chang over to the sheet, which had replaced what was left of the parachute to cover the crushed remains.

The spider costume had fared far better than the mush inside. Chang could tell the real limbs from the fake ones by the blood leaking from the sleeves. Ron had some cops hold up another sheet for some privacy and to avoid giving a show to the crowd and the growing number of cameras.

The first thing Chang noticed was that the body appeared to have been compacted. *Did he land feet first?* But the costume was too small, and it had held up fairly well. *Wait a minute.*

He stepped closer, careful to avoid the gore, and gently lifted the mask.

"Chang, wait!" Ron tried to restrain him.

Chang tried not to think about the way the mask felt more like a bag full of wet gravel so he could concentrate on getting a peek at the face.

"Ron, look." Smashed up or not, one glance left no doubt. "We found Marty Potempkin."

54

SEE YOU IN THE PAPERS

Laura stood off to the side near Eddie. She was holding her microphone but wasn't sure she had anything to say. Drew stood out of camera range.

Eddie Tua continued to shoot footage.

The mayor was hauled back up, and she could see the man's face had turned a deep crimson.

Drew waited for Eddie to pan the camera around for more crowd shots. It wasn't really much of a crowd anymore, since most of the civilians were now outside.

"Hon, we should go," Drew said.

Laura felt like she was in a dream, but the camera and the semblance of her work routine helped her keep moving. She saw people on the mayor's team scooping up the papers that had showered down on them after the mayor fell. They'd snatched a stack of papers from another news crew right out of their hands.

Drew was right. "Eddie, have you got enough? We need to cover whatever's going on outside. I'm not sure if our field crew has arrived yet."

Eddie shrugged. Nothing seemed to faze him much. "Yeah. I don't think they'll let us back in, so I wanted to get as much as possible. You think the mayor is ready for a close-up?"

Laura had to smile, and the three of them headed to the nearest fire exit.

"Check her."

Laura turned to see who'd spoken and saw that weasel Prager from Glacier's office. He was talking to a uniformed police officer, who looked uncomfortable. The guy probably knew that Prager wasn't exactly in the chain of command, but he also wasn't anyone he wanted to annoy either.

"Ma'am, I need to check you for any papers. They're evidence."

She thought about arguing, but she didn't have any and hadn't gotten a good look at them. They'd gone everywhere, and she'd seen a bunch of numbers on them, but then things had happened so quickly that she forgot about them until they were being scooped up.

"Sure." She raised her arms, and the guy gave a halfhearted frisk.

"She's OK."

Drew stood to the side. Prager ignored him and looked at Eddie, who towered over him. "What about him?"

The cop hesitated.

"You got probable cause?" Eddie pointed at Prager and turned to the cop. "Who's he anyway to be giving you orders? I was told to evacuate, and I am."

The cop's heart wasn't in it, and he hesitated again. Prager dropped his gaze, but not before he noticed Drew watching and smirking.

"What are you gaping at? Get out of the building." Prager sounded shrill.

Drew held up his hands and backed off, leaving Laura and Eddie.

❋ ❋ ❋

Outside the building, the crowd had grown around the cordoned-off area where the body had hit.

The body. Laura tried to be clinical, but waves of mixed emotions rolled through her. She thought for a moment that she might be sick or pass out, but she stared at the camera in Eddie's hands and by reflex she managed to retain her self-control.

"Eddie, get in there if you can and get some footage. I don't think I'm up for a reaction shot." He nodded and bulled his way into the crowd.

Hey, your crazy ex-husband just created an international incident, then spattered himself all over Broadway. How's that make you feel?

"Hon, you OK?" Drew rejoined her. He looked like he wanted to smile, but she heard concern in his voice. She hugged him and felt some strength return to her legs.

"I will be. Why'd you take off so quick back there?"

Now the grin spread across his face. Drew looked around, but nobody was paying any attention to them. "I got a nice set of those papers. I thought you might want to see what all the fuss was about."

"What are they?"

"Not here. But they're account numbers. There are some notes, but I don't want to read them here. When can you get away?"

Laura thought fast. "I need to stay for a bit. Get those papers to the station, and I'll meet you there. I'll call Sid and let him know you're on the way."

❄ ❄ ❄

"He's gone," Chang said to Ron, who was about to try to round up the crowd.

"Fuck." Ron's arm fell to his side. "Gotta try though." Ron called out to the commanders to let their men know to be on the lookout and to search the interior.

Chang could see by Ron's body language that he knew it was all barn-door closing. Chang looked at the people still streaming out the front door and scanned the faces in the crowd. No luck. More and more folks from the streets were mingling with the guests, and it soon became a swirl of people.

He saw the top of Nelson's head by the door. He was trying to talk to one of the cops. Chang stepped up on the bumper of the ambulance for a better view. It looked like the police knew who Nelson was, but Chang couldn't hear what had Nelson so excited.

"C'mon. I see Nelson."

Chang darted through the crowd, and Nelson spotted him approaching.

"That was Marty." Chang hooked his thumb over his shoulder.

"I saw him." Nelson was out of breath.

"Who?"

"Max. He was one of the union guys. In all the confusion, I looked over at one of the emergency exits and there he was."

"You're sure?" Ron asked.

Nelson didn't even respond. Chang knew he never made mistakes about things like this. "What happened?"

"He looked right at me. Then he blew me a kiss. But he was near the outside door. Everything was bedlam."

"And?" Ron looked like he was going to explode.

"I tried to tell someone, but everyone who knew why I was there was gone. The random cops doing crowd work looked at me like I was nuts, so I just ran after him."

Chang took a moment to picture this but didn't dare laugh. It also occurred to him how dangerous that was.

"Where did he go?"

"Headed toward Korea Town. I lost him fast, but I think he dropped this." Nelson reached into his pocket and pulled out a bumper sticker: GLACIER 4 PREZ.

"We should check it for prints," Ron started.

"Go ahead, but we already know who our guy is. You check the records and IDs for the union workers. He'll be there," Nelson said.

"I'll pull it when the smoke clears," Ron said. He ran his hand through his hair and turned back to Empire Hall.

Chang saw Laura and her big cameraman emerge from the crowd. He waved and they came over.

"You OK?" He saw a flash of irritation.

"Do I look that bad? I'm going to have to go live later."

"After all that?" Chang was surprised.

"You think we're going to let everyone else beat us to the punch? Besides, I wasn't the one hanging in the air. All he did to me was tell me I looked nice."

"He spoke to you?" Nelson said.

"That was it. He was kind of busy, but it was him."

Chang realized she didn't know. "Where are you two going?"

"Back to the station. We have video to edit and voice-overs to do for the package. Plus Drew got ahold of the papers Max dropped. They might give us a clue to why he pulled this stunt." Laura stopped when she noticed Chang and Nelson staring at her. "What?"

"We'll go with you and explain on the way. That's not Max over there."

"But he's dressed like a spider," Eddie said.

Chang shook his head. "Yeah, but it's a guy named Marty. He must have been meant to be a diversion. It worked. I don't know if Max intended for it to be quite so effective."

Laura wavered on her feet. Then she smiled. Chang wasn't sure which was worse.

"I should have known that part was too good to be true. Wait, that's not what I mean...crap. It's never going to end, is it? He's like some sort of ghost."

"A ghost with every cop in the city out to get him now. And the Feds too. If I were him, I'd go deep underground or leave the country," Chang said.

"We can't depend on that." Nelson spoke up.

Chang was pleased. Nelson could get into criminals' heads, but he could have a real blind spot when it came to security.

"We won't. We've just got a lot of help after tonight's attack," Chang said.

Eddie gestured to Laura.

She snapped out of her daze. "All right. Come with us if you're coming. We're in a race with the other channels."

55

BREAKING NEWS

WBAC

When they arrived at the station, Chang noticed there was more security at the door than was normal for that time of night, and he figured it was Sid's response to Laura's telling him that Max was still on the loose. Drew had to be inside already.

They all went into the lobby, and the guard waved them through. Chang didn't recognize him and noted that he was armed. Nelson looked at the guy, and Chang realized he was watching out for Max.

Chang felt naked without his pistol and planned to retrieve his .45 as soon as they were clear of the station.

Sid met them at the door. "Tell me you got it on tape."

Laura and Eddie exchanged a look. "The fall? I doubt anyone did."

"No, the mayor."

Eddie grinned. "I think heights make it shrink."

Sid whooped and said, "The fewer blurred pixels the better."

"I'm fine, Sid, thanks for asking," Laura said.

"You look better than fine. And yes, I'm glad you're OK."

Chang would have guessed the man was high, but realized in a way he was. Sid lived for this kind of thing.

As the group headed down to the editing room, Drew emerged from a side room. He reeled like a boxer during a standing eight count, but without the bruises. "Uh, guys? You're going to want to see this."

✳ ✳ ✳

Eddie took the tape into the editing room while Sid, Laura, Nelson, and Chang all crowded into the small research room with Drew. They huddled around the computer. Drew took a deep breath. "OK, this is early, but these are all account numbers and routing numbers."

"The *Reader's Digest* version, please. I've got mayor porn to clean up." Sid sounded more impatient than he was, Chang could tell.

"The short take is that there's more to come, but I see this kind of movement when we audit a company that's trying to shield lots of cash in a hurry." Drew cracked his knuckles and pointed to the papers. "In this case what we have is someone moving a huge amount of money, we're talking a couple hundred million, out of several accounts here in the US. Let's see here, one chunk went to Switzerland, and the other went to Gazprombank."

Sid cut in. "As in Russia?"

"Yeah, what we in the biz call 'a coinkydink.'"

Now, Chang knew what Drew was like when he was cocky. But he had to give him his due. Even Nelson couldn't have found all this so fast.

"Give me some time and I'll be able to see if the Swiss stuff got moved, but I'll need a stealthier ID. I might be drifting into a gray area, legal-wise."

"How gray?" Chang asked.

"Totally illegal."

Chang looked at Sid. "You protect your sources?"

"I just look like a flake. Ask anybody." Sid grinned. Laura nodded.

"Nelson, can you help Drew find himself? Make it one we never see again." Chang had just told Nelson to burn one of their best false identities. "Li Qi Won" would enjoy a vigorous day of activity and vanish from the face of the earth. Chang hoped any trackers enjoyed the names—and that they would take the hint not to bother investigating further.

Chang left Drew and Nelson alone to take Mr. Li for a cyber drive. Nelson's ability to remember ID numbers made security easy and convenient. They'd have to move fast, though, since other news agencies would be trying to track down the same information.

※ ※ ※

In the editing room, Chang saw Eddie fast-forwarding through the video. He noticed another unit was making high-speed duplicates. Smart.

"OK, Eddie, a little more there. Right when Max—I guess we can say his name now—cuts through the net. Jeez, he really was close, wasn't he? Sorry, Laura." Sid glanced away from the screen.

"Until he dropped the dead bird, I thought it was all part of the show." Laura shuddered.

"Quick hands. Look at how fast he hooked the mayor up." Sid sounded like a sportscaster.

It *was* impressive. Almost as fast as Shu.

They ran through the entire sequence, and when the crowd panicked and the mayor was swinging from the rafters, Chang saw something in the background.

"Can you run that back slow? This was right after I heard that fake radio call that sounded just like the commander."

Eddie backed up the frames.

"There, see it?" In the background, they all spotted a dark-clad figure scampering down the back side of the scaffolding.

"I bet nobody saw it. I didn't. Damn, that dude's slick." Eddie gave a low whistle.

"That's my Max," Laura said. "He used to tell me the biggest secret of a magician is that it's all in the distraction."

"Naked mayor is a hell of a distraction," Sid said.

Chang hung back while the three of them prepared the video package and went over what Laura would do. They would throw out a breaking news report, including the fact that Max was at large, something that Chang wasn't sure anyone else would have. He thought about asking them to hold off in case Ron thought it would help to keep that secret, but he didn't think there'd be any stopping Sid. Besides, all this would be out there by morning.

Laura seemed to be reading Chang's mind. "Let's get this done before the shakes set in, or I get detained for questioning or something. Paul, will they grab me for info on Max?"

"They might, although Ron can give them most of the stuff we had on Max already. The big difference is that now, I bet they'll pay attention. I can't speak for all the agencies though. So yes, I'd get your taping in now and start broadcasting."

Sid nodded. "I like how you think. If they get prissy about content, we fall back on asking forgiveness instead of permission."

Nelson stopped in the doorway. "Where's your copier? We should get a set of these papers hidden quick, in case they want to seize them. It won't help them, but they might try."

"Which they?" Sid asked.

"When you see what we found, the mayor's people, for sure."

* * *

Chang sat in the control room with Sid, Drew, and Nelson. Laura sat at her news anchor's desk, cool and collected despite the evening's madness.

After Drew had explained what all the documents revealed and vouched for the authenticity of the account activity, Sid wanted to get it out there immediately.

They decided Laura would recap the news of the night, then reveal what they had learned.

Eddie signaled from behind the camera.

"Good evening. I'm Laura Stark with breaking news on this evening's incredible story in which this correspondent literally had a front-row seat to the events as they unfolded." She paused. "We have new information to reveal, based in part on the documents scattered by the suspect. In addition, in the spirit of full disclosure, the prime suspect, a man still at large, is none other than my ex-husband, Max Stark. Just prior to the assault on the mayor, the performer we showed you on tape spoke to me and confirmed his identity."

Laura continued to voice-over the video of the mayor (complete with FCC-compliant blurring). "Contrary to earlier reports by some outlets, and conflicting statements by the authorities, WBAC can confirm that the man who died in a failed effort to escape the scene by parachute was *not* the attacker."

The video froze, and the climbing figure appeared enhanced by video highlighting. "We have it on reliable authority that this is the real attacker and that the other man is believed to be a convicted criminal known as Martin Potempkin." The video dissolved, and the shot returned to Laura.

She's doing great, Chang thought.

"In addition, we have spoken to eyewitnesses familiar with Mr. Stark who saw him leaving the scene during the confusion."

Laura stared straight into the camera. "Where tonight's events leave the peace process itself is a matter of conjecture.

However, our initial analysis of the documents Mr. Stark distributed in his own bizarre fashion tells a troubling—but we think accurate—tale of corruption at the highest level of government."

Chang half expected a SWAT team to blast into the room and terminate the transmission. He noted that Sid was making duplicates of everything and making arrangements to get the information hidden and broadcast from different locales. Chang admired his paranoid streak.

"According to the documents, which contain records of account transfers and also e-mail exchanges," Laura continued, "it appears that members of the United States Senate, with access to intelligence and classified budget funds, transferred taxpayer money to the tune of more than a hundred million dollars to offshore accounts belonging to both the Russian government and an as-yet-to-be-identified recipient in Chechnya."

They pulled in graphics of the area and a map showing both Moscow and Grozny.

"E-mail exchanges between the senators and Mayor Glacier's office suggest that the diverted funds could influence the peace process and bring otherwise reluctant parties to the negotiation table." Laura hit her stride. "Further, the notes imply that Mayor Glacier could serve as the go-between and that playing such a prominent role would serve to bolster his foreign policy credentials. We note the open secret that Mayor Glacier plans to seek the nomination for president during the next election cycle."

Sid signaled for Laura to wrap up.

"How would a man like Max Stark gain access to such information? We don't know at this point, nor do we have anything to indicate why he would go to such lengths to disrupt the proceedings in such a dramatic and graphic manner. Stay tuned. The moment we have new information, you'll hear about it on WBAC."

56

MORAL OF THE STORY

WBAC, the Next Morning

Chang's back howled in protest from sleeping on a couch in the station's green room. Laura looked rested enough after spending the night on the pullout in her office. Sid might not have even slept.

Everyone was planning to meet in the station's conference room to strategize how to capitalize on the breaking story and make the most of their insider knowledge.

Chang was primarily interested in nailing Max, but that wouldn't happen until they sorted out what on earth was going on politically. The previous night, they'd agreed to stay at the station in part due to sheer exhaustion, but also because of the threat of Max. Nelson had gone back to his hotel, and Eddie had worked with Sid late into the night. Drew kept chasing down more leads on the computer, and he crashed for a few hours with Laura at some point.

Funny, after all the madness, the first thing Chang had thought of when he woke up was that Colleen had insisted he call her to let her know he was OK. That simple request—and the relief in her voice—had felt like a comfortable set of clothes he hadn't worn in a long time.

✳ ✳ ✳

Sid waved a copy of the *New York Post* at his news team as if nobody had seen it yet. The cover featured a clear shot of the mayor dangling from the rope, and was less blurred-out than WBAC's video. The headline, in huge block letters, read simply BOTTOMS UP.

"All the news outlets are feasting on the tentacles of this story." Sid pointed at the paper. "We won't keep our advantage if we don't hustle. Did you all read the article inside?"

Chang and Nelson had retreated to the back of the room with Drew. They'd get to work once the meeting ended.

"With all due respect to Drew here, the *Post* guys did a nice job with the financials, and I give them points for speed, especially under a print deadline. I doubt they're sorry they pulled the run they had going." Sid laughed. "The mayor's going to have a stroke before this is over."

Sid grew serious. "This is one time I'm kind of glad we're with the pack on this coverage. At least as far as he's concerned. I hear he's not just furious, he's gone psychotic over this. Rumor has it the chief had to talk him down from issuing a bounty on Max Stark."

One of the reporters, Chang forgot her name, chimed in. "Sid, we confirmed the fifty-thousand-buck reward for info leading to his arrest."

Sid waved it away. "I said bounty, as in head on a platter. What you confirmed is the watered-down version. Word on the street is the treaty partners may be getting ready to fly home as early as tomorrow. Nothing signed, which tells me the crap Max dumped is accurate."

Laura spoke. "Every time we dealt with STP, which was Max, the info always panned out. I think it's good here, but how he got hold of something like that is beyond me. Assuming it's true, this not only kills the accord, but Glacier's political career too."

Sid rattled off some leads and assignments to the other reporters, giving them impossible deadlines. But the protests appeared to be pro forma, so Chang figured that must be Sid's modus operandi with a big story.

But never this big.

When the room had cleared and only Drew, Laura, Chang, and Nelson remained, Sid relaxed a little and let some of his game face slip.

"OK. You two don't work for me, but I think we're after the same thing." Sid reminded Chang of a guy on a meth bender: he never stopped moving.

Chang had his doubts, but Sid was his client's boss, so he thought he should listen. He shifted in his seat to keep his Kimber .45 from digging into his side. He'd slipped out the previous night to get it, which may have been the only reason he was able to manage some sleep. Better than a teddy bear.

"We still don't know why Max pulled this stunt, but I think it's safe to say it wasn't just him going renegade," Chang said.

Laura spoke. "Why? If he was working with the Russians, why wreck the accord? We know what they stood to lose financially, not to mention the motives Ron Sieger dug up on them."

"You mean the missing missile truck? The one they were worried had fallen into Chechen hands? Think they got cold feet?"

Drew spoke. "I don't know about cold feet, but from what I saw, the transfer to the Chechens went through, and you said that Ali Musaev was acting as a proxy for the Sword of Jihad."

"What do you mean?" Laura asked.

"I'm just the money detective here. But if those funds made it out of the Swiss accounts and over to the rebel groups, do you think they're the kind of folks who do refunds?"

"A rip-off?" Chang thought about it. "Could be. But we were sure Max was working for the Russians. And since he dealt with their government, the US could reasonably ask for the cash back."

Nelson spoke up. "Or, they counted on the embarrassment being enough that our government would shut up about the money and write it off. It's not like it came out of Glacier's or any senators' pockets."

"Nope, just ours," said Sid. "Lots of possibilities."

"But Max is at the center of it all," Nelson said. "Laura, he told you several times he wanted you to see and cover the event. So we know he knew about it before anyone else."

Laura nodded. "That's true. And I don't remember him being a hacker. Then again, we split so long ago he could be a computer engineer for all I know. The stunts were all him though, I'd bet on that."

"He could be putting his own style on things but still doing contract work, so to speak," Nelson said.

"I suppose so. But he was there with Marty. If Marty hadn't died, where would they have gone?"

Chang jumped in. "I'm sure Ron could shed some light on this, if he can get away long enough to talk."

"He's going to be under the gun and under the microscope. We may have to wait," Laura said.

"Not my strong suit," Sid said. "We need to figure out the next angle on this story and get ahead of the other guys."

Nelson spoke up again. "Let's set aside the why for a moment and look at the outcomes." Nelson was drawing on a piece of paper half full of doodles. "First and foremost, as of now, the treaty is ruptured, maybe irreparably. That means the Russians and Chechens are back at each other's throats. Maybe it even flares back up into active fighting. Second, all the benefits of such a successful treaty are lost. And third, the reputations that stood to gain the most have now lost the most. Especially those senators, and most of all the mayor, who will now lose any chance at the presidency, if not his own seat here."

"OK," said Chang. "Now who gains?"

Nelson pointed to Laura. "She does, for one."

"You don't think…" Laura looked resigned, but not stunned.

"No, but I think part of all this was done for your benefit," Nelson said. "Just like the other STP stories, which, as you pointed out, all turned out to be true."

"OK, but who else? I get that I have a huge story, and Max said he wanted to help me, but Russia resuming a battle with Chechen separatists is hardly helpful. If not for the drama last night, it'd be just another item for our anchors along with any other news of the day."

"Don't forget the mayor. Who'd want to see him fail?" Chang asked.

"All his political opponents. But that seems like a stretch," Laura said.

"Maybe so, but it could be regarded as a bonus to some." Chang hoped they wouldn't have to go near the mayor for a while. The man's fury was seeking a target, and he didn't want to be in its sights.

Sid cut in. "Getting back to the conflict. Who'd benefit from the peace process failing?"

Chang answered. "Anyone who wanted to keep fighting or see those two sides fight."

57

COLLECT CALL

After giving Ron a couple of days to get his bearings, Chang figured it was time to give him a call. The mayor was so angry, in so many directions, that maybe Ron had a breather. Ron beat him to the punch.

"How're you holding up?" Chang asked, testing the waters.

"I might kiss the chief if he asked for my shield." The evident stress of the last few days came through in Ron's raw voice.

"I was worried the strain might be too much for you."

"Whiskey makes an excellent substitute creamer."

"I'll have to try that sometime."

"You guys heard from our friend?"

"Max? Nope." Chang suddenly felt a wave of suspicion. Max may have heard Ron's voice over the radio. *Enough to imitate?* "Hey, what was Nelson's weapon of choice when he was on duty? Do you remember?"

"What are you talking about? Oh right, Max the mimic. It's really me, but so I can get down to business, Nelson liked to pack an air pistol."

Ron was referring to the fact that Nelson used to get in trouble for leaving his weapon at home when he was on duty. It never occurred to him to carry, maybe because Chang had done enough shooting for both of them back in the day. No way Max could have known that.

"Sorry. I think we're all punchy. What's up?"

"We figured out how Max had the inside track on the show without being spotted."

"Yeah?" Chang had a good idea, but it couldn't hurt to get it confirmed.

"The union reps who observed the circus crew work, at full pay of course, seemed to have a mole."

"That's what I thought. Which one did Max impersonate, and where was he while Max was taking his place?"

"Paul, you don't understand. Max *was* the union guy. Passed a background check with his ID and had all the union backing."

"So he watched and supervised the whole setup? He could come and go as he pleased?"

"Right under our noses, yes. We're all very proud here."

"I've seen him at work. Don't beat yourself up."

Ron gave a bitter laugh. "I think I may need to get in line for that, buddy."

"Max had to have had help." Chang could see Max tricking the union for a short time, but this had taken weeks.

"We think so too."

"The union wanted to screw up the treaty? Why?"

"Slow down. We leaned on some of those guys pretty hard. The mayor is dying to blast someone, and he's not too choosy about who's in his sights as long he gets to pull the trigger."

"So what did the union guys say?"

"More than you'd think. They have good instincts, and they got caught by surprise on this. They told us, unofficially, that a rep by the name of Sam Trawler was pushed on them as a favor to a guy tied to the Russian mob." The name lit up in Chang's brain as Ron kept talking.

"Wait, wait. Did you say Sam Trawler?"

"Yeah, why?"

Chang suddenly remembered. "That name is a joke or a hint from Max. It's the name of an unsolved murder victim from way back. Happened in Georgia, but we suspect Max."

"No shit? Like I was saying, it seems favors got called in, and they put our boy on the roster under a sort of mob patronage deal."

"Russians again. And Marty Potempkin worked for Viktor Markov. Too many coincidences."

"Want another?"

"What?" Chang wasn't sure he did.

"You guys see Viktor Markov lately?"

Chang felt his stomach drop. "I was just thinking we probably should look him up."

"So did we. We were ahead of you on that one. Resources haven't been an issue the last few days."

"You went to his place? Did you talk to him?"

"Here's where it gets weird," Ron said.

"Gets?"

"Right. Markov is nowhere to be found."

"Left the country?"

"Possibly. We're on the lookout and working with agencies overseas to let us know. No, what's odd is his bodyguards— the ones you *didn't* beat up—were around, and they looked spooked."

"How so?" Chang didn't remember those goons as the type to scare easily.

"For starters, they'd been in another scrape. I'll assume it wasn't you, but they looked like they'd been running their own fight club. Bruises and slings and nobody claiming to know anything. But I saw it in their eyes."

"What?" Chang wished this information weren't coming to him secondhand, but he trusted Ron's judgment.

"When they said they didn't know where their boss was, I believed it. They didn't say why, but Paul, I think he's missing. Not gone underground, but gone."

"Dead?"

"No idea. I think they're still looking for him, so they believe he's alive. And they're scared."

Something clicked in Chang's mind. "Ron, we've been running in circles trying to figure out why this keeps leading back to the Russians, but it still doesn't make sense why they'd wreck their own negotiation."

"We have some ideas, but finish your thought."

"What if this was a rift or power play within the various Russian contingents?" Chang wasn't sure if that was exactly it, but it felt like the right direction.

"I'll add that theory to the pile." Ron sounded exhausted. "I know the Russians are embarrassed and pissed off at all the information that leaked. The Chechens hightailed it out of here yesterday, and everyone is saying the treaty is toast."

"So is the mayor, at least nationally."

58

SCAVENGER HUNT

Chang sat in the empty conference room at WBAC. He'd seen all the latest news, looped on some of the screens in the building. The tensions between the Russians and the Chechens had ratcheted up. Without the treaty, they appeared ready to resume fighting.

He felt his own tensions were ratcheted up too as he cooled his heels trying to figure out his next move. What could he do that the whole police force of New York and the Feds couldn't do?

But they haven't caught him either, have they?

Laura stared at the pile of stories in her in-box and winced at how high it had grown. She toyed with the idea of going out for lunch but chucked it. No time and too much hassle. She appreciated Chang and all his efforts on her behalf, but at that moment the idea of a salad at her desk and ten minutes with her own thoughts sounded great. Twenty minutes would be even better, but she mustn't be greedy.

Her cell phone rang before she could place an order. Her mouth turned to cotton when she looked at the display and saw it was STP. She took a deep breath and dug her nails into the palm of her left hand.

Take it before it rolls over.

She hit the button. "What?" Thank God she sounded brave.

"Am I interrupting something?"

"You had your show. Haven't you done enough?"

She wanted to run into the newsroom and find Chang, but knew she might lose Max if she did so.

"No. Are you ready for the story of your life?"

"You've already reached that goal. You can stop now."

"Not yet. I'm offering an exclusive interview with me, on camera, no holds barred. I'll explain everything."

"You're not a trustworthy source." What the hell was this new game?

"Laura, that hurts. If I've been anything, it's a fount of truthful information. Or did you throw away your Emmys?"

"You'd come in here? On camera?"

Max laughed. "That's as subtle as asking me to turn myself in for world peace."

"You're not far off. Have you been watching the news?"

"Every night."

Laura shuddered at the leer in his voice.

"Then you know the two sides are talking war."

"They're always talking war, and that fraud of a treaty wasn't going to solve anything. But that's boring. I want to tell you all about it on camera. I pick the place," Max said.

Anger and fear flared in Laura's chest. "And after that?" She pictured her death as the grand finale.

"You have your story and I retire. This town isn't loving me back like it used to."

"You know what? I've had enough of your help. And if you think I'll meet you somewhere, you're nuts."

"I'm sorry to hear you're reluctant, but I won't take no for an answer." Max sounded anything but sorry.

"I'm calling the police as soon as I hang up. You know that."

"I do. And you will tell them this…" Max gave her an address. She jotted it down out of habit.

"What's that?"

"That, my dear, is where I have placed an explosive device in a trash can next to a school."

"You—"

"Just listen. The bomb isn't armed, but it's quite real. You need to understand I'm deadly serious."

"But why…"

"Hush. I'll know when it's recovered. I have others, and they *will* go off if you don't agree to interview me."

"You're joking."

"Once you verify it's legitimate, I'm going to call back on another phone and give you the location for the interview. I have no intention of hurting you. Quite the opposite. Nor do I want to terrorize the city, but you must meet me on my terms. Do that, and I'll give you the location of the other devices. Refuse, and the blood they shed will be on your hands."

"Why should I believe you?"

"You don't have to. Up to you. Bring your bodyguard if you like."

"You mean Chang?"

"Why not? Just not the police. As I said, I intend to retire, and I gather the NYPD and the mayor have hard feelings toward me."

This didn't make sense. "You aren't worried Chang will stop you?"

"He won't want to."

"Why? Are you going to hurt him?" Now she pictured herself as the only person left standing.

"Not if he behaves."

Laura saw the carnage of the bombs like footage running through her mind. She envisioned a children's recess and felt her eyes fill with tears.

"All right."

"That's my girl."

* * *

"You don't have to go." Laura looked pale and trembled as she told Chang about the call.

"You're not forcing me. Even if you're paying me." Chang smiled to try to reassure her and saw he'd failed. "Who else would go? Eddie?" He always went with her for field reports.

She shook her head. "Don't say a word. He's as stubborn as you. He'd insist, and I don't want to put anyone else in harm's way."

"You really think he planted a bomb?" Chang saw the answer in her eyes. "We better call this in."

"Wait."

"What do you mean?"

"If we tell Ron, and the cops find out we know where Max is, they'll insist on taking action. We'll never get close to him with half the force following us. There's no way Max wouldn't know."

"I get your point." He was glad she was thinking this through. He could also see she was terrified.

"Paul, could you take care of a bomb?"

"No. I know more about explosives than a regular civilian, but talking shop with guys from the bomb squad over beers doesn't exactly make me a certified expert. The thing could be booby-trapped. No, you need pros on this." He took out a disposable cell phone.

"What are you doing?"

"Trust me. And get the camera you plan to use. We're rolling as soon as I get off the phone."

Chang thought about the best approach. There was no way to do it and not enrage him. He dialed Ron's cell.

"This is an anonymous call from an untraceable phone. We clear?"

"No, but go ahead," Ron replied. Chang knew he'd recognized his voice.

He recited his old badge number so Ron could be sure it was him, then gave the address.

"I can't tell you why, and please don't ask too many questions. I want you guys to be extra careful. You're dealing with Max."

"Where is he?"

"Listen. The thing is supposed to be inactive and in the trash can."

"You know where he is." Ron sounded furious. "You can't go cowboy on me here."

"Not my choice. And I don't know where he is. I also don't know what the game is, but until I do, lots of lives could be at stake."

"OK. I understand."

"Just text me when you confirm the package is real."

"All right."

Chang knew Ron had given in way too easily. That could only mean one thing. He would try to have them followed.

Laura returned with a portable camera and a tripod. He knew Eddie wasn't around or she'd never have gotten away with touching his stuff without questions.

"Let's go. Max will call you when he sees the cops got his device."

The last thing Chang wanted was to tell Ron that Max would be nearby watching. They'd launch a clumsy manhunt, and he didn't know how Max would respond.

* * *

They left the building by the back door and jumped into one of the several bland white news vans. The small ones didn't carry the array of equipment that turned the big panel trucks into mobile TV studios. They'd never avoid detection that way. The vans were low-key and lacked the TV station graphics. Chang drove. As they pulled away, Chang saw two cruisers speed by, heading toward the station.

The reaction time told Chang how many resources were at Ron's disposal. Short of a major terror attack, they'd keep putting the pressure on until they caught Max. And terror was what Max had just threatened. Chang didn't even care if Ron messaged him or not. He believed Max, and as long as the man was on the loose he could plan and execute just about anything.

Chang drummed his fingers on the steering wheel while they waited for the light to change. Before it turned green, he heard a loud thump on the side of the van. Laura screamed.

"What the..." Chang looked in his side mirror and saw a thin guy pull up on a bicycle alongside the driver-side window.

"Learn how to drive, stupid yellow cur!" The guy wore a bicycle helmet and round wire-rimmed glasses. His face was red and contorted with rage. "You almost hit me back there." He pounded his fist on the hood.

Enough. Chang reached for the door handle.

Laura grabbed his arm. "Paul, let it go. No time for a street fight, huh?"

She almost sounded like Colleen, but she was right. Chang waved at the guy, who flipped him the bird and swooped through the red light, dodging traffic and nearly causing several accidents.

"Friend of yours?" Laura asked. He could see her relief that he'd stayed in his seat.

"Never seen him before. He keeps riding like that, he'll be dead by the end of the day. Those guys are another breed."

"So now what?"

"Now we wait for Max. If we get out of traffic somewhere uptown, we can wait, and Ron shouldn't be able to guess where we are."

"I think I know a place." Laura directed Chang, and he kept his phone in his lap.

* * *

Chang and Laura sat in the van near a public pool in Washington Heights. It had decent sight lines so they could keep an eye out for approaching police.

It wasn't long before Chang's phone chirped. He saw a text message from Ron. "Package real. No tricks. Just like he promised. Now talk to me." Chang turned off the phone and took out the battery. He was sure Ron would call, and if that failed, he might well have the signal tracked.

"Let's move again." Chang fired up the van just as Laura's phone rang.

He heard her breath quicken, and he pulled over a few blocks later.

After she answered, Max did all the talking.

59

PERFECT TOGETHER

Jersey City, Sebby's Scrapyard

"Nice place for a trap," Chang muttered when they pulled up to the dilapidated, oversize, corrugated-tin structure.

"All Manhattan has felt like a trap," Laura said. "Maybe we'll finally get this over with."

"I'll be right there with you. If you need to tell him no to something, go ahead. Whatever he does is on him, not you."

Chang carried the video camera with his left arm. His left hand ached as he gripped the tripod, but most of the weight rested on his shoulder. He wanted to leave his right free to draw his pistol. He expected to be disarmed, but until then he took some comfort in its presence.

They were next to Liberty City State Park and the Morris Canal, which fed into Liberty Harbor, where Chang could see a boatyard. On the other side, he saw the elevated concrete of I-78. The traffic noise sounded like rushing water in the distance. All in all, there was a decent view from this eyesore of a building.

The reek of raw diesel was another matter.

Chang focused on a nondescript blue sedan parked nearby.

"Now what?" Laura asked.

They heard a voice echo from inside the barn-size shack.

"Yo! You get lost or something? Door's open."

Chang reached for the door. "Ready?"

"No."

"Me either. C'mon."

Chang pulled open the door, which creaked and appeared to be on a spring hinge that would close when he released the handle.

Inside was mostly a large storage space. Over in the far corner it looked like there might have once been an office of some kind, but the interior walls were mostly gone. A small television and a couch were set up in the old office space.

Video monitoring. And plenty of open space around them to make sneaking up difficult.

"Holy…" Laura broke the silence.

Seated on the couch was a large man with disheveled hair and a battered face. He was filthy, and Chang got a whiff of stale cigarette smoke and body odor mixed with the stench of urine.

Chang gave his eyes a second to adjust. He didn't see Max anywhere, but the guy looked familiar. He stepped farther into the room and looked up and down, wary of a sudden appearance. He looked back at the guy on the couch.

It couldn't be.

His eyes and mind registered that it was Viktor Markov. He was wearing what looked to be a suicide-bomb vest.

"How do you like my vacation pad?" Max stepped from the shadows, where a small area had been curtained off.

Max wore a full clown outfit complete with orange hair, red nose, white face, and giant black shoes. Under the greasepaint, the dark eyes shone like wet marbles.

"Rustic. The sign outside says Sebby's. The owner? Where is he? And I see you have a guest." Chang nodded toward Markov.

"Sebby is an old friend, and he's out of town. As for Viktor, he's not here by choice, admittedly, but just wait, he'll liven up." Max walked over to the couch and fluffed some cushions. Chang noticed a transmitter device around his neck and saw Markov eyeing it too.

Markov looked at Chang, and behind the fear that the man was trying to hide, Chang saw fury. "He is insane. I'll pay you anything to get me out of here."

Chang looked at the man's unbound wrists and saw deep, red ligature marks.

"Silly. Save it for the camera. Always wasting his best material offstage." Max bowed, approached Laura, and took her hand. "My dear, you look ravishing as always." Max flicked his wrist and presented her with a silk flower. She recoiled, as if from another dead bird.

"Is the face too white? I don't want to wash out on camera."

Chang noticed that Max had even set up his own lights.

"We're here, Max. What's the game?" Laura spoke in a strong voice.

Chang put down the camera. Remembering Max's threat, he fought the urge to draw down on him.

"Business first. Mr. Chang, if you have brought any sort of tracking devices, tell me now. You see, I have the area under observation. If the cavalry arrives, not only will we go up in smoke, but many innocent people will die too."

"The battery is out of my cell phone, and no tricks. I believe you."

"I knew you were smart. Laura?"

"My phone is in the van. Do you want me to get it?"

"Nope. If they're following it, they'll go there first and be too late," Max said.

"Why aren't you searching us?" Chang didn't want the guy any more squirrelly than he already was, and he knew that was a detonator around Max's neck. He'd seen training vids on what a bomb vest could do.

"For what? You won't shoot me. I'm not going to hurt Laura or anyone else if you cooperate. Outside of that, your conscience is my shield." Max turned his back within arm's reach of Chang.

He was tempted. If he could get the controller from Max, he had a good chance of defusing the situation, and the bomb squad could render the vest safe. *As for the other devices Max said he'd planted*...Chang thought he could get Max to talk. The dragon stirred in Chang's chest. Speed was the key. He had to be quick as a snake, a cat, a...

Max's shoulders started shaking, and for a wild moment Chang thought the lunatic was crying. No. Laughing.

"I'm such a tease." Max turned, and the detonator was in his hand. "Never a chance, Detective." He flicked his wrist again, and Chang saw the silver flash of a throwing knife. "You had to think about it. I do understand. Now set up the camera and behave yourself. We have a great deal to do."

The dragon retreated with a silent snarl. He knew Max was right. He held all the cards. *Just play the game and wait for an opportunity.*

"What is all this, and why is he here?" Laura pointed to Markov.

Max gestured to the camera that Chang had just set on the tripod. Laura went to help him.

"Let me get the lights, and you can interview me on the couch. It'll be just like the old Carson show." Max skipped over to a wall switch, flicked it on, and took a seat on the edge of the couch, so that Laura was between him and Markov.

"House rules. Viktor, can I call you Vic?"

"Fuck you."

"You're lucky this is being filmed before a live audience but will be edited for broadcast, Mr. Pottymouth. I wish I'd built a Taser into that thing"—Max looked at Chang—"but sometimes you gotta go with what you have on hand, right?"

"Sometimes," Chang said.

"The rules. The vest Viktor is modeling is from his own custom-built line of involuntary terrorist clothing that he was going to roll out this fall. Brash, but the earth tones keep it from being too much, I think. Anyway, I made some modifications. If he tries to remove the vest it will go off, so no ideas, Detective. I can trigger it as well, and there is a trendy keypad that allows me to disarm it." Max settled into the couch and crossed his legs so that one of the giant shoes waved at the camera.

"If Viktor plays nice, he will receive the number as a parting gift. Not that he deserves it, but I don't want to jump ahead.

"Laura, ask whatever you want. I'm prepared to share with everyone what Paul Harvey would say was the 'rest of the story,' and then"—Max affected a Nixon voice—"you won't have me to kick around anymore."

60

THE REST OF THE STORY

Under the lights Chang saw through the camera lens that the setting looked like a low-budget talk show. Markov resembled a trapped animal, the clay-color blocks sprouting wires serving as his prison bars. Laura looked like her news anchor self, and Chang figured she was using her professional persona to conceal her fear. He stood near the camera and let it run on its own. They weren't going for high production values. Survival was the order of the day.

Max preened for the camera, but his eyes watched every-thing. The getup was just one more distraction. Chang noted that Max had moved the security camera monitor within his line of sight. Chang prayed that Ron hadn't come up with a way to track them. He knew all the NYPD tactics, and while a sniper could take Max out, it did no good to send a bullet through the only person with knowledge of the hidden bombs.

Chang heard a faint vibrating buzz coming from Laura that sounded like her phone. He felt his blood run cold.

Max heard it too and gave her a sad shake of his head. He held out his hand. The buzz-ring continued, and Laura handed the phone to Max. She glanced at Chang, and he braced for what might come next.

Max looked at the phone's display. "Nelson Rogers. Whatever could he want?" Max gestured to Laura. "Stay. You're working. I'll get this." He picked up and put it on speaker.

"Laura Stark's phone, how may I help you?" Max fixed a prissy expression under his painted smile.

After a pause Nelson spoke. "Where is she, Max?"

"For me to know and you to not find out."

"Do you have any idea how many agencies are after you?"

"All of them?" Max eyed the monitor.

Chang could see that for all the bluster, controlling so many people was stressing Max out. The twitching foot and nervous glances were giveaways.

"Too bad you can't see me, Nelson. I've got more makeup than you had on that time near the deli." Max made an exaggerated kissing sound.

"The only time I want to see you in makeup is when the mortician is done and they put you in the ground."

Chang heard the icy fury in Nelson's voice.

Max snarled into the phone. "Hope you like going to funerals. If all your buddies listening in find me, they can thank *you* for a pile of dead kids."

"They're not..." Nelson sounded surprised, and Chang wondered if Ron had tricked him into calling. Whether they had been tracking the call or not, there would be no convincing Max otherwise, he was sure.

"Good-bye, scarecrow." Max ended the call.

Then he smiled for the camera and dropped the phone to the floor. Max stood up and proceeded to dance a fast version of the tarantella, stomping on the phone with his huge feet. By the time he finished, the phone was a scattered mess of plastic and circuit boards.

Max sat down again and took a breath. "We may not have much time. Let's get started. Ms. Stark?"

Laura looked stunned but managed to find her voice. "Max, why are you doing this?"

"Can you be more specific?"

"That was you at the treaty event in Empire Hall. You promised something big; then you pulled off that elaborate stunt. What on earth for?"

"Some questions answer themselves. Partly anyway. How's the treaty looking?"

"From what I hear, it's in shambles."

"Hear that, Vic? Do I deliver or what?" Max grinned at Markov.

"He kidnapped me. I am a businessman."

"Shaddup. How do you say 'rhetorical question' in Russian?" Max turned back to Laura. "Sorry. I was tasked with doing my utmost to disrupt the proceedings, and to do so in a manner that exposed the fraudulent premise of the entire process."

"Tasked by whom?"

"Markov."

Markov shook his head. "You lie."

Max ignored him. "As is our established custom, I have extensive documentation and corroborating evidence to support my position. In the interest of time, please take me at my word, and you will have ample time to verify my claims after I have left the stage."

Markov, who appeared miserable and furious, grew even more uncomfortable.

"But why? Markov, you work for the Russians. Why would you want to sabotage your own interests?"

Markov just shook his head.

"He's camera shy. That's OK. You aren't on trial here. Laura, I shared with you because I wanted to give you the best seat in the house. He had me prove myself before he trusted me with the big score. He never minded that I let you amplify the stories."

Laura spoke. "The STP stories? He arranged the takedown of the Lambs of Strife charity? And Griffon Lewis?"

Max nodded, his orange hair waving like underwater fan coral. "That's right. The charity itself was collateral damage. He had a personal beef against Orrlov, and he really wanted me to snag some rare jewelry he knew Orrlov owned."

Chang watched Markov turn bright red. Max also seemed to notice.

"I knew this was going to be worth it. Look at him squirm. You know it's true."

"Lies," Markov spat out.

"He told me Orrlov was dirty, but I got inquisitive—and lucky. I found both sets of his financial records. Laura, you already know the information was good. The guy was filthy. Maybe someone will set up a clean one with the same mission." Max's painted smile exaggerated his grin.

Laura didn't smile. "I used to know you. Why'd you have to kill Griffon Lewis, and why *that* way?"

In his mind's eye Chang couldn't help but see the explicit shots of the man's final moment, dangling by his neck in the closet.

"I didn't have to, and I didn't kill him. In *that* or any other way." Max stole a peek at the monitor.

Laura looked indignant. Chang admired her ability to focus with a vest of high explosives right next to her. "You're saying he died by accident?"

"Oh no. I'm sure he was killed, but not by me. Not by Vic here either." Max leaned forward to catch Markov's eye. "Got your back on this one, boss."

"Then who?" Laura said.

"Can't prove it, but my best guess is that the Russians did it. I think they wanted to make it look like an accident to the world. But in addition to embarrassing the man and his memory, they were sending a message to some people who would know that Lewis would never have died that way."

"You lost me. You just said Markov didn't…"

Max shook his head. "You guys don't get it yet."

Chang couldn't remain silent. "Wait. Griffon Lewis was close to the mayor *and* the treaty negotiations? Right?"

Max pointed to his red nose like he was playing charades. "Getting warmer."

Chang continued. "After the stolen-art fiasco, he was a risk to the treaty. He knew too much?" Chang thought of all the inside negotiations Lewis must have seen. "Lewis knew about the pay-offs. Facing charges of his own, was he going to cut a deal?"

Max applauded. "Bravo."

"So why do I still feel in the dark?" Chang asked.

Max waggled one of his feet. "Another shoe has to drop."

Laura spoke again. "You still haven't explained why the Russians wanted to ruin their own treaty."

Markov began to sweat. More waves of acrid stench rolled off his body. Chang knew Laura must be able to smell him, but she gave no sign.

"I wasn't supposed to know why I was doing things either, but I'm not just a pretty face. Plus, never trust a rube, even if they are paying the bill. Right, Vic?"

"What do you mean?" Laura pressed.

"The Russians killed Lewis to protect the treaty. But…Viktor Markov's interests are not the same as the Russians'. He counted on everyone making that mistake."

"Shut up," Markov growled.

Chang interrupted. "But why would Markov want the treaty to fail? Even if he wasn't in line to benefit like the Russian government, why would he care?" Chang pictured Mayor Glacier swinging in the air. "Or was that just a way to ruin the mayor?"

Max laughed. "Very good. You did remarkably well considering you didn't have the last piece of the puzzle. I admit the theatrics with the mayor were inspired by what happened to Lewis, but it was a nice touch if I do say so myself. Markov was more than happy to ruin the mayor's career as punishment. He hates when things interfere with his sales, right Vic?"

Markov cursed at him in Russian.

"And he's a poor loser. But he hasn't seen anything yet."

Chang could tell that, under the rage, Markov was listening intently. He was sure that the Russian was hearing not only information he already knew but also new revelations.

Max continued. "The Russians wanted the treaty in place, but Viktor couldn't afford for that to happen. So he used me to ensure that it failed; then the world would blame some crazed clown while he kept his hands clean."

Chang spoke again. "Max, why are you doing this now? You never had any trouble getting your message out before."

"Our working relationship has become...strained. Vic, you really need to sweep your office for bugs. You see, Mr. Markov tried to get out of paying me."

"More lies."

Max held up his hands to concede the point. "OK. Not exactly true. He tried to have me killed, but he messed up. You see, my buddy Marty was supposed to knock me off after we escaped the treaty event. They had the route all planned, and he was going to take me out at our rendezvous. I had to get snippy with him"— Max pulled out a small pair of scissors—"and his chute."

"No," Markov said.

Chang saw by his expression that Markov had revealed more than he'd intended.

"Vic, you're smart but too cocky, and you never could see past my greasepaint. To you, I was just a crooked clown. For a guy who is a professional criminal, you should be a whole lot better organized." Max held up his white-gloved hand and ticked off bullet points on his fingers. After each one Markov grew more agitated.

"Your security is a joke, your guards are unskilled thugs with guns, and…" Max looked at Chang. "You wouldn't believe how easy it was to crack his safe."

Now Markov looked like an old steam boiler on runaway. Chang pictured him blowing up on his own without the vest. He sensed a new danger in the air. Whatever Max was about to say was nothing Markov had heard before, and he was panicked about what Max was going to reveal.

Max hooked a thumb toward a briefcase. "It's all there."

"What is, Max?" Laura was absorbed, and Chang knew her mind must be racing.

"Markov's game. The story of a lifetime. All for you."

"Do not."

"Quiet, Vesty." Max waggled the detonator at Markov. "Our Viktor isn't just a thug over here in the States. He splits his time over in Russia and does dirty work for the Russkies when they need weapons and such slipped to the right people. Apparently he got tired of getting the crumbs and branched out."

"No more," Markov growled.

Chang wondered if a bomb vest could short out if it was soaked with sweat.

"But he didn't just sell to Russian operatives working clandestine activities in Chechnya. He also sold to the other side."

Chang felt a flash in his head that he thought was a real explosion. "The missile truck. *He* stole it, not the Chechens!"

Max crowed with delight. "You *are* so much smarter than you look!"

Laura caught on fast. "The Chechens bought it from him?"

Max beamed. "Atta girl! Close. He was sitting on the truck, when all the peace crap broke out. The Russians freaked and the

Chechens backed off on the sale, leaving Vic with a large, incriminating hot potato."

Chang got it. "So he needed hostilities to resume to unload the truck and preserve his interests?"

Max didn't answer and frowned at the monitor. "What's this?...Too damn fast." Max spun the monitor. "Who're these rubes, Vic?"

"Police?" Markov failed to conceal the relief that washed across his face.

"Bull."

Chang could see a pair of figures emerge from a sedan and move toward the building. Very cautious, like amateurs. They wore sports coats, and the bigger guy had a white bandage across his nose. As the smaller guy got closer, Chang could make out his round, wire-rimmed glasses. It was the courier who'd hit the van. "Max, they're Russians. They followed us. I didn't know."

"Gizmo," Markov blurted out, looking joyous.

"Gonna be deadmo in a minute." Max shook his arm, and two silver throwing knives seemed to jump into his hand.

Laura turned to say something to Max, and Chang felt paralyzed. Things were happening so fast. Markov seized Laura in a bear hug and stood up.

"Drop her!" Max shrieked.

Markov held her body with one burly arm and wrapped the other around her head. "I will break her neck."

Max held the button. "Go ahead. You won't last a second more."

"Then we all die."

Chang reached back and gripped the handle of his .45, but he didn't draw. He was ten feet away from Markov and maybe eight from Max. They were focused on each other and ignored Chang. He didn't want to change that with a sudden move. If Markov remained focused on Max, Chang had a chance if he was fast enough. Had to be a head shot, and Laura was close. He couldn't risk hitting the vest, and Markov could carry out his threat in less than a second.

Chang had to hit the brain or nothing.

This was new. He concentrated. He needed speed, and he needed control. The dragon gave him one, but he had to maintain the other. It thrived on his fury and made him strong. It wanted to take him over, and it had no use for guns.

"What is the code?" Markov squeezed down, and Laura struggled to no effect. From the way he was holding her, Chang knew she'd be unconscious soon.

"The code!"

Chang felt his senses and reflexes sharpen. He glanced at Max and saw weakness. Chang knew there wasn't much time. He concentrated on anticipating the draw, aim, and fire in one fluid motion. He'd aim for Markov's left eye. When the Russian took his next breath to yell…

Time slowed down. Chang felt the dragon inside, fully awake and savage under threat. This side of Chang cared nothing for facts about explosives, collateral damage, or anything but the direct threat and how to dispatch it. With all his will, Chang reined in the adrenaline, deploying it to steady his arm and sharpen his vision.

Markov's eye looked as big as a melon. Chang pulled the short-barreled weapon clear of the holster and, in a silver blur, brought it up amid shouting in the background. The frightened, dark orb of Markov's eye and the top of Laura's head had become his entire universe.

Pure muscle memory sent his thumb down to snap off the safety, and the cocked weapon was ready to fire. He saw Markov's eye turn in his direction, and he put his finger on the trigger. The

Chang part of his brain screamed at the dragon to squeeze gently. He felt the pressure under his finger and heard more shouting.

"No! You'll hit her."

Chang detected an upward motion out of the corner of his eye, and then he felt a burst of pain in his damaged left hand. The gun discharged, but he knew it was a miss, high.

An instant later time returned to normal, and Chang realized that he'd been kicked, hard. Max had used his big shoes, which felt like they had steel toes.

Chang managed to hang on to the gun with his right, and he looked to Markov to set up another shot before it was too late.

This time Max's kick connected with Chang's skull. His knees buckled, and the room dimmed. He shook his head like a prizefighter, and it began to clear.

When he stood up, he was near Markov, who'd thrown Laura to the floor and recovered Chang's gun.

The dragon sent adrenaline flooding through Chang's body. Time slowed again as Chang closed the distance, but Markov raised the pistol and fired two shots. The muzzle flashes looked like yellow flowers suspended in the air.

Max fell back. A dark bloodstain soaked through the white clown suit. Chang saw Max raise his hand with the detonator. It looked like he pressed a button, but the last rational shred inside Chang knew he'd be gone if it had detonated.

Chang cocked his fist and lashed out with every bit of force the dragon could muster. If Markov saw it coming, he appeared frozen. Chang's right fist connected with the man's jaw, and he felt the punch follow through.

Markov collapsed, twitching like he'd been Tasered, then didn't move.

Chang pivoted and saw Max still on the ground, large crimson spots blooming out from his upper abdomen.

Max smiled, still clutching the detonator. "Too slow, Vic."

"Don't press it!" Chang shouted. "He's out. I got him."

"Nice punch. I got him too." Max coughed. The bloodstains spread. "Check the timer."

Timer. Chang pushed aside the dragon, which was content to let him figure things out. His left hand felt like fire, but he knelt beside Markov. The digital timer was counting down from five minutes. He checked and saw that Markov was breathing.

Chang glanced at the monitor and saw the Russians crouched down by the van with guns drawn. They look confused. It must've been the sounds of the shots.

Laura recovered and went over to Max. "What happened, Max?"

"To us?" He chuckled at her confusion.

Chang looked over at Max. Not good. The guy would be out soon and dead not long after. "Max, the code, quick."

Laura, more alert now, seemed to understand the situation. "And where are the bombs, Max? Please, they don't deserve this."

Max ignored Chang and looked at Laura with a gentle expression. He motioned her in close and whispered something to her. She stood and grabbed the camera and the briefcase. "Paul, he won't give the code. Grab Max, and let's get clear."

"Markov..." Chang said.

Laura moved toward the door. "I tried, he won't tell."

"You go." Chang didn't see any point in her staying. With the Russians outside, he thought about giving her his gun, but that would just get her shot. If he could get the bomb switched off, he could deal with those two. If not, then there'd be a giant distraction.

"Max, just give me the code. He'll get justice."

Max pulled his lips back in a faraway smirk. Chang's words were keeping him from another world. "I hope you got my good side…" His eyes began to roll back in his head.

Chang glanced at the timer and saw he had three minutes. He racked his brain for everything he knew about those vests. But there were too many types, too many ways to trick a bomb squad, let alone an amateur. He didn't know where to start.

He pounded the floor in frustration. "I'm sorry," Chang said to the unconscious Markov. He slung Max over his shoulders in a fireman's carry and ran for the door. He hid his gun in his waistband.

They didn't get far. The two Russians were standing right outside the door, and Laura sat on the ground.

"Keep coming," the big guy said. He waved a Glock at them.

Chang did as he was told. "Listen, Markov is inside, and he—"

"We know." The spectacled Gizmo smiled and pointed at Max. "Put him down. Pietr, cover them."

Pietr searched Chang and took his Kimber.

Gizmo was holding a tool kit. Pietr made Chang sit next to Max. The bleeding hadn't stopped, and he'd grunted in pain when Chang set him on the ground.

Gizmo ran inside.

Pietr laughed. "Gizmo builds these vests. He will disarm."

Max chuckled in response. "I built more than five minutes' worth of booby traps, dumb ass."

Apparently Gizmo reached the same conclusion as they heard a torrent of cursing in Russian. He raced back outside.

They had to be under two minutes now.

"You have code? Give me code, clown." Sweat poured down Gizmo's face.

Max tried to shrug but changed his tune when Pietr handed his gun to Gizmo and grabbed Laura by the arm. He seized a pinky and torqued it around until she screamed. "I break them all in front of you."

Max crumbled. "Wait. Nineteen eighty-four. Got it?"

Gizmo tossed the gun to Pietr and sprinted back into the building.

Laura cradled her hand and flexed her finger, not broken after all. "The year we met?"

Pietr stepped closer to the doorway and called in to Gizmo. Max mouthed to Laura and Chang, "Cover your ears."

Before he could, Chang heard Gizmo scream and the pounding of footsteps.

Chang threw himself over Laura and Max, trying not to crush the wounded clown.

He felt the pressure wave first.

The windows in the building burst, and sheets of tin shot off like popped buttons. The van windows shattered, and tin fragments rained down for a few seconds.

Then it was over.

Chang looked over at Pietr. The blast had knocked him down, but he was still alive, and the Glock lay nearby. Chang saw blood pouring out of the man's ears and realized his drums were ruptured. He snatched up the gun and checked the chamber to ensure it was loaded. Pietr had made it to all fours when Chang kicked him in the ribs and rolled him onto his back. He pointed the gun at the stunned man's face and had tightened his finger on the trigger before he regained his senses. He wrapped his finger around the trigger guard and hauled the guy up long enough to pistol-whip Pietr in the back of the head.

He retrieved his Kimber, then raced over to Max and Laura. Laura sat up, looking shaken but alert.

Max's eyes were open. Chang thought for a moment that he was gone, but then he saw him blink. He was barely breathing. Max spoke in a whisper. "That hurt."

Chang turned to Laura. "You're OK?" Chang didn't see any blood on her.

"I...I think so. How is he?"

Chang told her with his eyes, and she knelt next to Max.

Chang saw a look on Max's face like a junkie getting a rush from a fix. "You saved the camera?"

"Max, we'll get an ambulance."

"You saved it?"

"Yes..." It was intact nearby with the case of papers.

He took her hand. "I told you I'd make you a star."

Then his head slumped back, and one last breath rattled out of his lungs.

61

BOMB THREAT

Chang put the battery back in his phone and let it boot up and search for a signal. He figured emergency equipment would arrive soon, but he really needed to reach Ron.

Pietr didn't move, and Chang planned to tie him up in a minute in case he was playing possum.

He left Laura alone with Max. She looked stunned, but there was sadness there as well.

A minute later, a bar appeared on his phone. Good enough for a call.

"Laura, I have a signal. What was the location he gave you?"

She wobbled toward him, pulling herself together as she came. She repeated the address of an intersection in downtown Manhattan.

Ron picked up after a single ring.

"Where are you? I'm in the air. We never got a clear fix, just in Jersey, other side of the river."

"Never mind us, I have a bomb location."

"Go."

Chang gave the address.

"Bomb squad's rolling. I'll monitor from overhead. Just got word, fire and rescue on the way to you. Fill me in."

"How'd you track us? Nelson?"

G

J. GREGORY SMITH

Ron had to shout to be heard over the helicopter. "Yeah, but we had to trace his phone. We thought he'd call you, and he wouldn't give us any other way to reach you. We figured you might have had another phone."

"You could have gotten Laura's cell phone anytime."

"We had it, but it kept turning on and off. We didn't know for sure until Nelson called it and we heard Max's voice. There are a lot of people on standby. We didn't want to chase shadows. Are we now?"

Chang gave him the short version of their time in the "tin studio." "I wish I could have saved Max and Markov. Both those guys knew a lot more." Chang told Ron about the missile truck. "Max didn't seem to know where it was, but he figured out that Markov was involved."

"Hold on. I got the bomb guys on the other line. Call you back. We need to clear the area."

Laura pored through the papers Max had left for her. When she looked up, Chang saw tears tracking down her face. "Don't blame yourself, Paul. How were you supposed to know how to take off one of those vests?"

"I don't know." Yet he still felt like he should have come up with a solution. Chang sat and leaned his back against the van.

"If Markov was some sort of arms dealer, do you think Max got the explosives from him?"

Chang thought about the beat-up guards and the stash of information Max had on his old employer. The guards were lucky Max hadn't just killed them. "Makes sense. If so, then that was Markov's own bomb, and if he or his own expert Gizmo didn't know how to get it off without exploding, why should I?"

Chang found some electrical tape in the van and used it to secure Pietr, who never budged.

A minute later Ron called back. Too fast. "Chang here."

"Paul? We found it. Is Laura there?"

"Yeah."

"Put me on speaker if you can."

Chang did and turned up the volume all the way. Their ears were still ringing from the blast. "Go ahead. She's right here."

Sirens sounded in the distance. About time.

Ron spoke again. "We passed by the trash can with a dog to make sure we had a good reason to clear a large area and start a panic. The K-9 didn't hit. We checked the can anyway, but the only thing we found besides today's newspapers were a dozen dead roses with a locket clasped around the stems."

Chang saw Laura go pale. He remembered the one item missing from her apartment. He knew without asking about the pictures inside.

"You guys get that? A locket?"

"Yeah. We heard you."

"That mean anything to you?" Ron sounded impatient.

"Once." Laura gazed toward Max's body, and fresh tears flowed. "Not anymore."

62

NICE PLACE TO VISIT

Colleen's Apartment, Three Days Later

Colleen folded the last of Chang's shirts and put it into his suitcase. "Don't get used to the service. This is just so you'll rest that hand."

At least Max hadn't broken it.

"I know. You just can't wait to get me out of here and have the place all to yourself again." Chang pulled her in close and kissed her.

"That's it. All that hair in the shower, the socks on the floor..."

Chang laughed. For years she'd joked that they'd be able to put their kid through college with all the money they saved on maid services thanks to Chang's near-compulsive fastidiousness.

That was before they'd learned Colleen was infertile. Then, after Chang's nightmare, it hadn't mattered, because the marriage was over.

"This has been one of the strangest cases I've ever worked, but I can't say I minded getting to see you so often."

"Me either. You're getting less scary in your old age."

Chang wondered. He knew the dragon wasn't gone, but maybe it was maturing and becoming easier to control.

Sure, if that helps you.

"That reminds me. Nelson said there's a postcard from Shu." Chang didn't want to show how worried he'd been. He hadn't known himself until Nelson called him about it.

"Oh, good. Where is he?" Colleen had always gotten along well with Shu while they were married.

Chang smiled. "We're not sure exactly. But we know he made it to China somehow."

"Why somehow?"

Chang didn't want to betray Shu's trust, but thought he could make an exception in this case. "He doesn't have a passport. Not a real one, anyway."

"Do you think he's in trouble?" Colleen looked worried.

"No. I think he's having a blast. The postcard was a picture of those famous terra-cotta soldiers, and all he wrote on it was: "No plans to join.""

Colleen's nose crinkled. "Huh?"

"It's his idea of a joke. I think it means he can move around unafraid, but has plans to return. If he got in, I guess he can get out. Looks like he finally got me to underestimate him." Chang of all people knew Shu was as crafty as he was tough. "I wonder what he would have made of Max."

"Sounds like you'll get a chance to tell him about it sometime." Colleen paused. "How's Laura handling things? Is she going to be OK?"

"I think so. I'll see her later, before I head back." Chang hoped it was true. "She's strong, but I can't tell if she's working so hard she can't drop the newscaster veneer or if she's using it to hide."

"She got the best coverage of the fiasco and had a built-in advantage." Colleen knew all too well how sharp the competition was in the news business. "I watch her, and would even if you weren't working for her."

"Everybody is. They're taking bets on how many Emmys this will get her." Chang wondered how that made her feel, but so far she hadn't cracked. "I guess Max was successful in achieving his final goal after all."

"How's that?"

"Something he said. He wanted to give Laura the story of the decade."

Chang knew they were both stalling for time.

He hugged her again. "Never was good at these."

"Me either. But you won't mind if I find more time to take the Orient Express?" Colleen gave him one of those little smiles that cut through his defenses.

"Come down any time. And I'll be back soon enough. You never know what kind of work this will shake loose. I still have a license in this state."

"If Glacier doesn't find a way to blame you and get it yanked."

"I'm sure I'm down on his crap list. But after this last week, I think he'd rather abolish a free press."

The *New York Post* and *Daily News* had traded bawdy headlines and the now infamous still shot of Mayor Glacier, with minimal essential blurring. BUM RUSH said one, TAIL WIND another. They seemed to be in stiff competition with the late-night comedians. Chang's favorite so far was CRACK OF DOOM.

"Call me when you get back." She kissed him and handed him his suitcase.

✳✳✳

"I thought you were getting a quickie," Ron said, leaning against the hood of his car. Ron would chauffeur Chang to the TV station, and then he'd take the train (aka Orient Express) back to Delaware.

"Sorry I didn't tape it. I know how hard up you are these days." Chang tossed his bag in the backseat.

"I'll be radioactive until all this shit settles down. But if I survive the mayor, I'll be OK. Between you and me, I think he'll step down before they throw his ass—and the rest of him—out of office. Sorry. They're too easy."

"You've earned it."

Ron turned serious. "You really think so? Won't be just the mayor looking for my scalp. I didn't exactly get my man or prevent the whole treaty from going down the tubes."

"We all get a piece of that pie. Me too." Chang thought maybe more than anyone. "But now we know the grounds for the treaty were a lie, and the mayor is at least getting his share of the blame."

"True that. Hey, get the little guy on the line. I want to share some off-the-record stuff, and he deserves to hear it." Ron waited while Chang dialed.

Nelson picked up. "Coming home?"

"Soon. Ron has some news for both of us."

"You got booted off the force, and you're taking my spot in the agency?" Nelson spoke in his usual dry tone.

"Not yet, but it could happen." Ron smiled, then turned serious. "This hasn't hit the news so it stays with us, but the Russians are pretending to be outraged. I mean they really *are* pissed about the money they had to give back."

"But?" Nelson asked.

"Nelson, you were right. Aside from the money, the reason they wanted to come to the table was to buy time to find that damn missile truck." Ron turned up Broadway. "They might have anyway, but once they learned it was Markov—I'm hearing from my contacts—they've been rolling up Markov's operations overseas. Word is, they sent their very best to lean on folks, and it didn't take long before they sang; and lo and behold they hit a warehouse in Grozny. Found, one S-400 missile truck."

"I'm glad I wasn't on the other end of those interrogations." Chang suppressed a shudder.

"You and me both, brother," Ron said. "Want to know the ironic part?"

"Shoot."

"Both the Chechens and the Russians are so *offended* at outside manipulation that they have called a halt to hostilities for an indefinite cooling-off period."

"So the truce survived?" Chang said.

Ron laughed. "Until they decide they're mad enough at each other again. But funny how things work out, eh? The Chechens have no reason to complain. Their share of the money, I hear, is long gone."

They pulled up to the WBAC building. Nelson said good-bye and hung up.

"All passengers out," Ron said. He got out of the car and gave Chang a bear hug. "You're a pain in the ass and an Asian cowboy, but it was good to work with you again."

"Likewise, round eye."

"I wasn't kidding when I said they might send me down the road. I think it all depends on what happens after the mayor leaves. Any chance you'll keep a seat warm for me in Delaware?"

Chang was surprised that the guy seemed serious. "There's nothing at the moment. But I need freelancers sometimes. And decoys in case there might be shooting."

"Have Kevlar, will travel. I'll keep you posted, amigo."

✳ ✳ ✳

When the elevator door opened, Chang saw an explosion of confetti, and horns assaulted his ears from all sides.

Sid and Laura stood with other members of the news team and production crew, who'd evidently been tipped off that Chang was on his way up.

"Chinese New Year isn't for about six months."

They laughed, Chang assumed out of good manners, and Sid and Laura led him into the conference room where they'd spent so much time.

"It's going to be strange not having you here."

"I keep hearing that. If I'm no longer welcome in Delaware, I'll be back full time," Chang said.

Sid handed Chang an envelope. "We have to get back to work soon, but here's a little something for everything you've done for Laura—and frankly, for us. You kept our star safe."

Chang opened it and saw a check with way too much printed on it. He looked up, certain his expression must say what he was thinking.

"I know. I already fought with Laura about this. We decided to pick up your tab for her. She finally backed off when I promised to count it against her next contract."

"I haven't seen the final bill yet, but I know this is way more than she owes." Chang looked at it again. It was easily 50 percent more than his high estimate.

"A bonus. You earned it."

Chang didn't know what to say. Sid clapped him on the shoulder and left.

"Drew wanted to be here, but he'll send you a note later," Laura said. "Thanks, Paul, for everything."

Chang balled his left fist to let the ache mask his discomfort. "I don't think I earned my fee, let alone a bonus."

"You saved my life. And you protected me day and night when it was clear Max was a real threat and not just a kooky ex."

Between his unconventional tactics and his sharp mind, Max had been a unique opponent. Chang had to concede that much. He hoped never to see one like him again.

"Maybe I burned through the last of my luck." Chang smiled. "I'm glad it worked out. Are you going to be all right?"

"Funny. Everyone else sees me and assumes I'm loving the ratings and all. Plus I'm rid of a stalker." She shuddered. "All true, as far as it goes I guess. But you know, right to the end he cared about me. Deeply, passionately..."

"Insanely," Chang added.

"That too. But he could have done so much more damage, and he didn't. I know he killed people, I understand that, but he wasn't just a bloodthirsty lunatic. He spared Markov's guards, and in a weird way, I think, he believed Markov and Marty were acts of self-defense."

"You have a point, but do you want to spend that much time in his head to justify his actions?"

"I don't know. I suppose I just want the record to reflect the facts without piling on."

"Spoken like a true journalist," Chang said.

Sid tapped on the glass in the door and pointed to his watch.

The End

ACKNOWLEDGMENTS

As always I want to thank my wife, Julie, for her endless support and encouragement.

Thanks to Weldon Burge for helping me with research, and a huge thank-you to Cindy Burge for her information on hand injuries and rehabilitation.

Thank you Mark Tobin of the New Castle County Police for answering endless questions, both technical and absurd.

Thanks to Christina Henry de Tessan for the wonderful editing and terrific feedback. Also to Elisabeth Rinaldi for the outstanding and meticulous copyediting, Jessica Fogleman for the proofreading, and to the entire Thomas & Mercer team, especially Andy Bartlett, Terry Goodman, Jacque Ben Zekry, Alison Dasho, Justin Golenbock, and Reema Al-Zaben, along with all the rest of the crew who work so hard behind the scenes to turn an author's dreams into reality.

A huge thank-you to my writer friends who understand the toil and blood that go into creating novels. I also thank my family and friends who are learning what it takes to be a writer, whether they want to hear about it or not.

Finally, I want to thank all the readers, especially those who took the time to review my books (good or bad). Your time and attention inspire this writer to keep going and always to try to improve.

ABOUT THE AUTHOR

A native of Washington, DC, J. Gregory Smith earned a master's degree in business administration from the College of William & Mary in Virginia and built a career in public relations before turning to fiction writing full-time. His debut novel, *Final Price*, made the quarterfinals of Amazon's Breakthrough Novel Award contest in 2009. He is also the author of *Legacy of the Dragon* and the award-winning novel *A Noble Cause*, which was a Kindle best seller. He lives with his wife and son in Wilmington, Delaware.

Made in the USA
Charleston, SC
12 November 2013